# THREADNEEDLE

# THREAD NEEDLE

## CARI THOMAS

HARPER
Voyager

Harper*Voyager*
An imprint of HarperCollins*Publishers* Ltd
1 London Bridge Street
London SE1 9GF

www.harpercollins.co.uk

HarperCollins*Publishers*
1st Floor, Watermarque Building, Ringsend Road
Dublin 4, Ireland

First published by HarperCollins*Publishers* 2021

1

**MIX**
Paper from
responsible sources
**FSC** www.fsc.org **FSC™ C007454**

This book is produced from independently certified FSC™ paper
to ensure responsible forest management.

For more information visit: www.harpercollins.co.uk/green

*To my parents, who showed me there
is magic in this world.*

Goddess of Silence and Secrets:
Seal our mouths, so we can't speak.
Pierce our eyes, so we can't seek.
Knot our hearts, so we can't feel.
Bind our spells; to you we kneel.
What is forgotten, can't be known.
What isn't planted, can't be sown.
Lock the door and turn the key.
We bear our magic silently.

*The Binders' Blessing*

*The bells rang out as they had done for hundreds of years, their sombre music sweeping over London with grace and stillness, bright as the moon which was full and ripe in the sky. Despite the late hour, the city below was restless, tossing and turning in the darkness with lights and buses and cars and people – everywhere people – walking, rushing, working, drinking, dancing, sleeping; none taking any notice of the bells at all.*

*Within the tower, the sound was deafening. Yet the women did not flinch as they stepped closer, forming a circle, their feet bare on the cold stone floor and their hair loose against plain robes. They pulled back their hoods, feeling the vibrations of the bells in their bones; feeling the buzz and blur of the city below; feeling the silence of the moon through the windows; feeling the languages of their own magic rising. The last chime rang out with finality.*

*Midnight. It was time.*

*They raised their arms to the sky.*

*They did not scream when it happened – the Seven were not made for such expressions, but even so they did not have time to scream. They possessed infinite years at their fingertips but not a moment of warning when it came—*

*The glass of the windows shattered. The night bled in. Words were spoken: impermeable and unbreakable. The women were yanked backwards, bare feet dragged along the floor. They were raised into the air, robes flaring, limbs frozen in the moonlight. All they could feel now was futility – the deep knowing that there was nothing they could do as the ropes wound around their necks and they dropped into the empty night.*

*Only then, as their bodies ceased to belong to them, did they do what any bodies would do: squirm and jerk and gargle and choke – slowly die.*

*Below, London carried on as before but the bells of Big Ben had never been so silent.*

# JOY

*Fifteen Years Old*

*The neighbourhood was much like any other in the suburbs of London: straight-backed terraced houses, tall and narrow, abrupt faces, neat gardens, iron gates – closed now. Curtains were drawn and windows glowed against the darkness outside. It was quiet – only the distant jangle of traffic, footsteps carrying someone home, a dog barking, the whisper of trees in the wind – but one house was quieter than all the others.*

*Silent.*

*A silence so deep and still it went unnoticed, just like the house itself. Nobody turned to it as they walked by. The house was but a passing shiver – not a stone out of place on its gravel pathway, its porch primly adorned with hanging baskets, its white front door closed to the world beyond. Nothing stirred. Even the wind seemed to die at the door.*

*Not a sound could be heard from beyond its walls and yet inside, in the living room, a piano was playing of its own accord – the melody so fragile and heart-achingly beautiful it seemed to be made of silence itself. It fluttered against the windows but, not being able to escape, turned in on itself, disappearing into the emptiness between each note.*

*Seated in an armchair, a woman drifted her hands along to the music. Upon the floor, a girl had her eyes closed as if lost in it entirely, but her hand was clenched around a piece of knotted cord. She could not listen to the music. She could hear it, but she could not listen to it. Her knuckles were white.*

*The music slowed and a single note rang out, like a bell, pure and true and full of feeling.*

*The girl could take it no longer. She let a little of the sound through her defences, breathing in the joy of it. She gasped as the music began to fill her lungs. She grabbed at her throat, trying to breathe, but the air was too thick, too heavy with music – drowning her.*

*The woman's hands continued to flutter through the air.*

*The girl pulled one of the knots in her cord tighter. Tighter. She tried to wade against the panic, removing the music from her body, her mind. She pulled the knot so tight her fingers screamed. The joy in her heart silenced itself abruptly. The music washed against her but went no deeper. She took a tentative breath—*

*Relieved only for a second, she quickly tightened her eyes, clenched the cord and hardened herself. The song continued, beautiful no more, just a sound, an interesting arrangement of vibrations in the air. Not music.*

*It grew dark outside. The girl drowned again, and again, and again. Eventually the woman ceased to move her hands. The music stopped.*

*'Magic is the first sin; we must bear it silently,' said the woman, making the disappointment in her voice plainly heard.*

*'Magic is the first sin; we must bear it silently,' the girl responded.*

*'Go to bed, Anna.'*

*The girl was too tired to reply. She stood up, kissed her aunt goodnight on a cold, turned-away cheek and went upstairs.*

*The woman continued to sit in the armchair, thoughts turning slowly and heavy as the wheel of a mill. Soon it would be the girl's birthday. Would she be ready when the time came? She had to be ready. She moved her hands in the air and the piano began again.*

*She was pleased to find nothing but silence in her heart.*

# STITCHES

*Stitch in, stitch back, I sew with fear,*
*The needle's eye watches me clear.*
*Stitch in, stitch back, I sew with blood,*
*A secret trapped in every thread.*
*Stitch in, stitch back, I sew with might,*
*Silence in each knot pulled tight.*
*Stitch in, stitch back, and now I see:*
*The tighter the stitch, the stronger the knot,*
*The sweeter the embroidery.*

Stitch Chant, Pastimes, *The Book of the Binders*

Anna woke with something tugging at her. An ache. An urge. A feeling she couldn't place. She tried to chase it but it was already gone. *A dream?* She did not dream.

She looked up at the dreambinder hanging above her, a few knots caught down its length. The Binders' twisted take on a witch's ladder, Aunt had put it there years ago – a long length of cord – to prevent her from dreaming. *It catches each dream with a knot.* As the knots began to undo themselves, the dreambinder unwinding itself back into a gnarled string, Anna yawned, exhaustion weighing heavy on her. She had not slept well. She never slept well. She did not have to look at the clock to know the time. She waited.

A knock on her door. It came every morning at half past six. The first stitch in their daily routine. *Stitch in, stitch back.*

'Anna!'

'Coming, Aunt.'

'The early bird catches the worm but the earliest worm escapes from the bird.'

*I know because you say it every – single – morning.*

'Coming,' Anna repeated, trying to make herself sound more lively, trying to feel more alive. The book she'd been reading when she eventually fell asleep was still perched on top of her quilt – her only escape in the empty hours of the night. She moved it aside and pulled herself out of bed. She padded to the doors on the other side of her room. She threw them open and walked out onto her small balcony at the back of the house. Suburban London stretched out before her, the same as always: the sky a distant, grey wall, a patchwork of tight-knit roofs and dark brick houses threaded with tired greens. The gardens were motionless – shorn lawns and sculpted flower beds; a water feature tinkled neatly next door.

She breathed in the wind and thought, or perhaps imagined, she could smell a change in the air: a stirring of smoke, of autumn, of Selene. A smile rose to Anna's lips before she could catch it.

*Three more days.*

Three more days until her birthday – until Selene arrived. Several evenings ago they'd been sitting silently in the living room, as usual, sewing embroideries, as usual, and then, as if it was nothing, Aunt had announced: *We're expecting visitors for your birthday.*

Anna's heart had jolted with fear, her thoughts swerving violently to the Binders. *Were they coming? A celebratory interrogation?* But then Aunt had said Selene would be visiting and that she was bringing her daughter with her. Anna had nodded quietly at the news, but it had been so unexpected and she'd been so excited she'd sewed the last part of her embroidery with untidy stitches that looped up and down as big as the beats of her heart. She'd been made to unpick it and redo it all before she'd been excused.

Selene hadn't visited for years and the last time had hardly ended well. She was an old family friend, having gone to boarding school with Aunt and Anna's mother. They'd all been inseparable back then – so Anna had been told – although she'd always struggled to imagine Aunt and Selene ever having been friends. During her brief and explosive visitations they had barely seemed to tolerate one another. But for Anna, Selene had been a wonderful, intoxicating interruption in the tedium of her life; a ribbon of colour amid a length of plain cord; a bright key to another world. She was everything Aunt was not: full of life, full of joy, playful and hedonistic; a temptress, a wonder, a witch. A witch like them and nothing like them at all. Certainly not a Binder.

Anna went back inside. She shook out the sheets, made the bed, put on her slippers and dressing gown and picked up her Knotted Cord from her bedside table, placing it in the pocket. She tied her hair back in the mirror. She'd always felt as if some part of her were missing and she saw it whenever she looked at her reflection – not quite there, not quite whole – the girl staring back at her dreadfully pale, eyes shadowed and faded, red hair tangled; a spot gaining slow but steady ground on her chin. *What will Selene make of me now?*

'ANNA!'

'Coming!'

She hurried down the stairs, tightening one of the knots in her Knotted Cord until she felt her excitement fade. If Aunt caught a whiff of it, she'd no doubt cancel the visit out of spite. They prepared and ate breakfast without speaking. Toast and kippers. The portion was small and Anna was still hungry. She was always hungry. Aunt flicked through the headlines on her tablet, tutting methodically.

'UK economy slumps as PM vows "bounceback".'

'Are migrants robbing young Brits of jobs?'

'Sexual harassment at work causing depression'.

*Tut, tut, tut,* like the tick of a metronome, her long, regal face remaining neutral as she read. Aunt was adept at arranging the lines of it, placid and polite, suitable for addressing the world, but Anna knew how tightly the lines were pulled, how, stretched too far, they could snap at any moment.

'Can you please locate the clock for me?' Aunt said without looking up.

Anna looked towards the clock hung on the kitchen wall.

'Ah! There you go.' Aunt switched the tablet off and locked eyes with her. 'You *are* aware of its location. Why then are you still sitting at the table when it is almost half past seven? Are your chores completing themselves this morning?' Aunt was always difficult, but she'd been particularly irritable the last few days, as restless as Anna herself.

'Sorry, Aunt.' Anna stood up quickly and began clearing away breakfast. 'On it.'

Aunt made a displeased noise. 'I need to go to the super-market to get some things for this weekend's *visit*.' She laced the word with her particular brand of acid. 'I expect every room sparkling by the time I'm back. I won't be long.' She stood up, tucking the stray wisps of her red hair into her bun and pulling her scarf tighter. Aunt always kept her neck covered, like the other Binders. 'And, Anna,' she added sharply, 'don't forget the leaves. They're beginning to fall on the path – we'll be the talk of the square.'

*God forbid!* Anna waited to hear the front door slam shut and then looked around despairingly at the ordered cupboards and white surfaces of their kitchen. Everything was already *sparkling*. Perhaps sparkling was the wrong word. Stale, silent, still. All the rooms of the house were the same: cream walls, floral curtains, antique furniture, sparsely and specifically ornamented. If she'd taken a vase and moved it to another table the house would not have looked right. There was an order here; things had their place. Even the potted roses in the corner of every room: dark leaves shiny as tongues and tightly sealed rose buds that never opened.

*Even me.*

Anna went to the fridge and stole a few strawberries, sweet on her tongue – one, two, three – not enough to notice; then she pulled up her sleeves and got to work. Carpets needed hoovering, surfaces dusting, bathrooms bleaching, leaves sweeping, all signs of life scrubbing away. *If one's house is in disarray one's mind will follow suit, Anna.* Every day of the summer holidays had been the same: chores, studies, piano practice, evenings of sewing, Binders' training, back to chores – on and on in an endless, inescapable loop. *Stitch in, stitch back, three . . . more . . . days.*

During Selene's last visit three years ago, Aunt had caught her trying to teach Anna magic – love magic – a language certainly not tolerated by the Binders. They'd argued and seemingly cleared the air but then Selene had thrown a dinner party . . .

Anna remembered coming down the next morning to find their perfect house in disarray: people passed out on the sofas, glasses everywhere, wine stains on the carpet, what appeared to be whipped cream all over one of Aunt's still-life paintings in the hallway and their barbecue set releasing ten-foot-high purple flames in the garden. Sent to her room, Anna had tried to listen to the ensuing shouting match. She thought she'd heard Selene scream, *We wanted marshmallows!* Aunt hissing, *What if the neighbours had seen!* and repeating the words *abominable behaviour!* over and over, but then their tones had grown hushed, if not harsher. She hadn't been able to make out any more before the front door had slammed shut. Anna had never expected to see her again.

*Why would Aunt allow her to visit now? After all this time?* Then again, Selene had a way of getting exactly what she wanted, and even Aunt wasn't impervious to her persuasions. She'd never brought her daughter before. Anna vaguely recalled seeing a picture once: a skinny girl her age with black hair and a scowl. *Effie.* She remembered feeling only an uncomfortable jealousy for the girl lucky enough to have Selene for a mother. She hadn't wanted to meet her then and she still didn't now. Effie would no doubt be as charming and magical and overflowing with life as Selene: everything Anna was not.

She fetched the broom and went outside, glad to clear the stench of detergent from her nose. The clouds had loosened, the day brightening, etched with a fine wind, a feeble scattering of leaves on the ground – summer was almost over. The houses of Cressey Square stared back at her shrewdly, every one identical, front doors closed like disapproving mouths. Anna gathered the leaves together from the front garden and threw them in the bin but one sprang free, landing back on the path. Reaching down, she picked it up and turned it over in her hands; this one was already dry and brown. *Lifeless.*

Without thinking, she dashed back into the house, discarded the broom and grabbed one of the keys off the key rack. She ran across the road to the garden in the centre of the square: 'Private Garden – Residents Only'. She unlocked the iron gate and swung it open with a shriek of metal. Aunt would be home soon. She wouldn't have long.

The garden was empty, but it was always empty; after all, it was not meant to be enjoyed but merely admired from lounge windows. She ran down the path, past overgrown flower beds and the drying-out water fountain, to where the trees gathered and shadowed her from the eyes of nosy neighbours. Anna sat down, her back against the familiar curve of the old oak tree, breathing in her moment of freedom. She'd dreamt of escape often when she'd been young. It had become a kind of hobby: imagining herself in the books she read, making up stories in her head, playing songs on the piano that made her feel somewhere else, like someone else. She'd given up on most of that by now. But the garden still felt like a kind of escape. Only metres from the dark shadow of the house, but its own world, nothing but the wind and the clean slice of sky above her. No one to see her, judge her, punish her . . .

Anna placed the leaf on her lap and selected two fresh cords from the bundle in her pocket. She quickly tied them together with a loop in the middle, like a heart, three pieces of cord falling away from it like veins: the Ankh Knot, *Life Knot.* She focused on the leaf and let the energy build beneath her fingers. She envisioned it bursting back to life, uncurling, growing strong, the green reclaiming its brightness. The knot in her hand quivered with energy. She pulled it free, feeling a release. The leaf twitched, a pulse of green appearing by the stem, and then . . . nothing.

*Lifeless, still.*

The cords dangled limply in her hands, the veins drained. Anna picked up the leaf and crushed it, trying to ignore the familiar feelings of frustration and shame. It was the hope that hurt the most, thin and fine as a needle into her heart. *A witch who can't cast spells. Am I the world's biggest joke?* The garden might be her last escape but it couldn't help her. She was a failure and – at the end of the year – any last hopes of magic would be extinguished. Escape would no longer be possible. She'd become a Binder herself.

A dog barked in the distance, startling her. She shoved the cords into her pockets and looked around, fear quickly replacing her burst of eagerness. If Aunt caught her casting . . . Anna didn't want to contemplate what she'd do.

*Magic is the first sin; we must bear it silently.*

She hurried back towards the house, glancing nervously at the surrounding windows but the neighbours' houses were still. No one was around. Anna stared up at their house. The top floor was built into the gable roof – a window at the front. It was dark, the curtains drawn as always. The third-floor room. Anna had never been inside it. Aunt claimed it was used for storage and Binders' documents and that she didn't want her poking through it all and Anna had been forced to accept the explanation, accept – as always – what she was told.

She let herself back in and stopped at the key rack hung on the wall. It was heavy with the keys of their life. House keys. Car keys. Work keys. . . Anna put the key for Cressey Square garden back among the others, but her hand hovered in the air – moved towards the key on the final ninth hook. It did not look particularly out of place – a little smaller, a knotted iron head – but it was different from the others. Quieter, stiller. It gave nothing away. Aunt's key. The key to the room on the third floor.

She'd tried to steal it once, when she was little. Aunt had been in the bath and Anna had sneaked downstairs and removed it from the hook. The moment it was in her hands its blade had begun to move, the pattern of it altering continuously, folding and unfolding, shifting and reshaping, as if it was changing gears. Anna had studied it with hypnotic wonder when she'd felt the shadow loom over her. She'd spun round to find Aunt, every line in her face snapped in anger, but when she'd spoken it had been with cold authority: *Only in my hands will the key find its true form.*

Aunt had made a knotting motion in the air with her hands. Anna remembered with a shudder the feeling of the bone in her finger breaking. The key had dropped to the floor. She'd learnt the hard way never to try to take it again.

Anna dropped her hand and reached into her pocket, finding her Knotted Cord. She tightened one of its knots, tying away her curiosity. It was not welcome in this house. She turned from the hook and went upstairs to wash her hands and comb the wind out of her hair.

'Red cord?'

'Strength.'

'Orange cord, two knots?'

'Bind two opposites.'

The last of the day's light receded from the living-room window. The room was cold. The TV off. The piano closed – the buds of the rose bush upon it small and shivery as goose pimples. Aunt was typing up hospital reports from her armchair, testing Anna on her correspondences without looking up, Anna reeling off her answers dutifully while her fingers worked on an embroidery. The whisper sound of thread did not break the silence of the room between Aunt's questions; instead it pulled it tighter.

*Stitch in. Stitch back. Stitch in. Stitch back.*

'Yellow cord, Knit Knot, Monday?'

'To heal an injury.'

'Brown cord, six Mute Knots?'

'To banish unwanted thoughts.'

Aunt had picked out a verse from her Bible for the centre of Anna's embroidery: 'Keep me safe, Lord, from the hands of the wicked; protect me from the violent, who devise ways to trip my feet.' The Bible verses were a good stand-in; Aunt could hardly have verses from the Book of the Binders up on the wall. That's where her embroidery would go once it was finished.

The wall behind them was covered with them, devouring every inch of space, encasing colourful images and fearful verses in dark frames. *Spells of silence and protection,* as Aunt referred to them, *for out there and in here,* touching her heart.

'Black cord, seven Shackle Knots, Wednesday.'

'To restrain another from speaking.'

'Wrong.'

Aunt made a small movement with her hand; the needle slipped into Anna's finger. She didn't cry out. She was careful not to let the small well of blood drop onto her embroidery. It had ruined many before that way.

'To restrain another from spreading secrets,' Anna corrected quickly.

'White cord, Servant Knot?'

The questions continued relentlessly. Anna had never been a gifted seamstress but she'd been forced to sew for so many years the stitches came to her easily. She responded without thinking, longing to go over to the piano and play. Let the confusion of her thoughts free. Instead, she'd become accustomed to making up songs in her head as she sewed – *stitch in, stitch back* – fusing together the notes of the thread, the rhythm of the stitches, the melody of their patterns. To her the embroideries were not spells of protection, they were songs of longing.

But this evening, even her music would not come. She could not stop thinking of the leaf in the garden, berating herself for her magical ineptitude. Why must her Binders' training be so mind-numbing, so torturous? Reeling off correspondences, reciting the Book of the Binders, tying knots, unrelenting emotional tests, stitches, stitches, stitches . . . She rarely got to do any actual magic.

'Grey cord, Lover's Knot, Friday?'

'To protect – protect yourself from sexual desire—'

'Wrong again!'

The needle slipped into Anna's flesh a second time, a drop of blood dissolving into the canvas. *Perhaps I can cover it with a rose . . .*

'Sorry, to suppress sexual desire.'

'Focus, Anna! What has got into you?'

*Nothing! Nothing is inside me, that's the whole problem.* Would Selene be able to tell she was a failure now? A witch without magic? But the leaf had pulsed – *hadn't it?* Perhaps there was hope, somewhere a little hope that had not yet been stifled.

When Aunt finally announced they had finished, Anna put her embroidery down. 'Aunt,' she said tentatively.

'Yes, Anna.' Anna could hear the impatience in her voice already. Aunt always seemed to sense what she was going to say before she had said it.

'We – er – haven't tried casting all summer. I wondered if it was time we did some practice?' Anna said the words quickly, desperately, wanting to get them out before the more sensible part of her brain could hold them back.

Aunt closed her laptop and fell silent. Anna knew her silences well. There was silence of her questions: narrow and pointed, full of dead ends and sheer falls. The silence of her disapproval, tight and unforgiving as pursed lips. The silence of her anger, which was like lightning without thunder – you know it is there but the rumble is too distant, too deep to hear, and hearing it would somehow make it better, less frightening—

'What is the Binders' third tenet, Anna?'

'We shall not cast unless it is our duty.'

'And yet you suddenly believe it is your duty to do so?'

'No, I—'

'What does it mean to become a Binder?'

Anna knew all too well what it meant. One year left until her Knotting. 'My magic will be bound.'

*Stitch in, stitch back, snip the thread and tie the knot.*

Anna gripped the Knotted Cord in her pocket. 'I just thought that—'

Aunt made a knot in the air and Anna's mouth snapped shut. Aunt had been bound once too, but now she was a Senior Binder her magic had been released for her to carry out her duties.

'You don't think, Anna. You just feel. That's your problem. Do you feel magic's pull?'

'No.' Anna's fingers twisted around her Knotted Cord.

Aunt came and sat on the sofa next to her. 'Your mother felt its pull, did she not?' She spoke gently.

'Yes.'

'And where did that lead her?'

'To her death.'

'Magic killed her.' Aunt's voice was hollow with despair. 'You're not a Binder yet, you do not carry the true weight of magic around your neck. It is still all fun and games to you.'

'No.' Anna shook her head, regretting ever having spoken at all.

'No?' Aunt flicked her laptop back open. 'You have requested casting practice and tomorrow we shall do so. I think we shall continue with the correspondences after all.'

Anna nodded and returned to her embroidery.

'Choke Knot?'

*Stitch in, stitch back.*

# MOTHS

*Choke Knot: To bind another's will.*

*Knot Spells, The Book of the Binders*

The next day Aunt heaped extra chores on her. Anna settled into their dull monotony, only slowing in her dusting to pick up a picture from the mantelpiece. She wiped the dust gently from it. It was the only photograph in the house that contained her mother: Aunt and her mother together in their early twenties, her mother at the forefront, eyes playful beneath her black fringe; Aunt standing behind. Anna stared at her mother's face and tried to feel something. She had nothing to give.

She put it down and began to dust the other photographs – she and Aunt at various ages in various staged poses. People said they looked alike, with their green eyes and red hair. Aunt had always told her they were alike too, that they were cut from the same cloth; her mother coming from a different type of fabric altogether: *Weak. Soiled. Corrupted with magic.*

Anna didn't know why Aunt had brought magic into their lives at all if she loathed it so much. After all, they had lived for six normal, magic-free years together – or as close to normality as they had ever come. It was when she turned seven that everything had changed. A few days after her birthday, without warning, Aunt had taken her to the doctor.

Anna remembered her childlike fear. She hadn't felt unwell, which surely meant that an injection, some routine vaccination, was waiting for her, but when Aunt took her into the room, old Dr Webber had leant forwards, eyes bulging, and asked her how she was feeling. Anna had said she was feeling fine, that nothing was hurting, and he'd smiled dispassionately, revealing sharp yellow teeth. 'I'm talking about your feelings inside, little miss. Have you felt particularly happy or sad the last few days?' That had thrown her. She'd been excited about her birthday but she wasn't sure if she was meant to have been excited so she told him no. 'Excellent,' he'd said, wheeling his chair over to an unassuming cabinet at the far side of the room which she'd never noticed before. He'd taken a key from his pocket and opened it, extracting several implements, while she was made to lie down on the bed.

He'd put a stethoscope, which didn't look quite like any stethoscope she'd ever seen, to her chest and she'd felt a strange sensation inside, as if her heart were drawing towards it. He made various concerned noises as he listened and had then produced the dreaded needle. Anna remembered the sharp pain of it in her arm and wishing Aunt would take her hand, but Aunt had not moved as the blood flowed into the glass bottle. He'd poured a few drops of it onto a thin metal disc, and the moment her blood had touched the metal it had begun to sizzle and spit.

'A vigorous iron test – the magic is pure; however, heart readings show considerable emotional charge. Considering everything, we ought to take precautions.'

Anna had been ushered out of the room before she could hear anything more. When Aunt eventually appeared she'd had a small packet in her hand and a frown furrowed into her brow. Anna had felt as if she'd done something wrong but she wasn't sure what. The doctor had spoken of magic . . .

Anna smiled as she recalled her childish reaction. She'd hoped if she was somehow magical that it would be like the magic of fairy tales, that she'd be able to call a fairy godmother to her, or speak to birds, or send whole kingdoms to sleep. She'd soon learnt their magic was not the stuff of fairy tales, it was not to be enjoyed but endured—

'Anna!'

The duster fell from her hand.

'Casting practice. Dining room. Now.' Aunt's voice sharp as a cut lemon.

*Why did I have to open my mouth?* Anna knew why, but even so, her momentary yearning for magic, diminished against the growing dread she felt as she entered the dining room.

It was gloomy and unwelcoming as always, set aside for rare special occasions and dinner parties that never happened. A small window filtered light onto the long table in the centre; a mahogany dresser displayed their best china plates begrudgingly. Another rose bush grew from its pot placed at the far end, dotted with rose heads, tightly sealed. *My Hira is twine and thorn.*

Aunt sat at the table, a moth dancing in the air above her. Her heart began to beat as fast as its movements. She twisted one of the knots in her Knotted Cord.

'If I wanted to tie this moth's wings together, what colour cord would I use?' Aunt's eyes landed on her.

Anna tried to focus. 'Er – black for restriction.'

Aunt nodded, picking up a black cord from the selection on the table.

'Which knot should I use?'

'The Servant Knot could work, or the Shackle Knot perhaps?'

Aunt tied a knot in the cord with such quick precision

Anna was barely aware of it happening. She pulled it tight and the knot snapped shut. With that, the moth fell to the table, wings locked together, legs squirming madly. Aunt held up the cord for Anna to see – a single knot in its centre.

'That is all you need if your Hira is focused and strong.'

It was an easy knot but absolute in its power: the Choke Knot.

When she was young, Anna had quickly learnt that there was nothing fairy tale about the Binders' magic. No magic lamps. No wands or capes. Knots were the only magical language tolerated by the Binders. *A knot is concise. It is secure. Above all, it is discreet,* Aunt had explained. *It can be done out of sight without anyone seeing. It keeps our secrets safe.*

As if that wasn't dull enough the correspondences made it endlessly worse. You couldn't simply tie a knot, you had to consider the material of the cord, its colour, how many cords, the type of knot, the number of knots, the month you cast, the day, the time: they all had certain magical associations or correspondences: *Imagine each spell is a sentence, each cord a word, and each correspondence a letter that helps to form it.*

That was manageable perhaps, but there were innumerable combinations which could alter the meaning of a spell by degrees. Nearly half of the Book of the Binders was dedicated to detailing them, a vast vocabulary with little room for error and no room for joy.

'Your turn.' Aunt untied the knot in the black cord. The moth's wings fluttered back to life and it flew up into the air.

Anna took the cord and prepared the knot. She studied the silent motions of the moth and allowed the intention of the spell to form in her mind: *As I tighten this knot so may the moth's wings be locked.* She could feel Aunt watching her. She let the intention harden. *My Hira is twine and thorn.* Focusing on the strength of the cord beneath her fingers, she pulled the knot tight. The moth fell to the table, but before Anna could celebrate her small moment of magic, its wings flickered and it flew back into the air. *No.*

Aunt closed her eyes, but a small, satisfied smile escaped from her lips. 'Your Hira is weak. This is simple magic. Simple.'

Anna was used to Aunt's disappointment, but when it was about her magic it still stung. The moth landed on a candlestick, its feelers twitching and assessing her. It flew off, as if it had found nothing of interest. Anna glowered at it and then felt stupid for glowering at a moth.

'When you decide to pay attention, we shall continue.'

Anna turned to Aunt, her expression one of solemn dedication. Aunt's hands were a flurry of activity as she tied two cords into a series of Twin Knots, little figures-of-eight looping up and down its length. There must have been ten in total before she finished. Anna looked at the moth in the air but nothing had happened.

Aunt untied the first knot. Anna looked back at the moth and found with surprise there were now two. Aunt untied the second knot and Anna watched as the second moth became two. It happened as quickly as a single beat of their wings, like an origami trick where the paper seems to grow as it's folded. Aunt's hands traced down the remaining knots, untying and producing further moths above the table until there was a shivering, shadowy cloud of wings above them. Anna felt the strong urge to scratch her head all over.

Aunt tied a Choke Knot in her cord and one of the moths fell to the table.

'How do you do it so quickly?'

'It looks like chaos, doesn't it?' Aunt watched the thrumming cluster of moths. 'It is chaos, but contained, under my control. Everything is connected by threads, Anna, and if you know the true nature of a thing you may pull the strings of its life – forwards, backwards, up and down. The moth may feel itself free – but it is not. I own it.'

'You believe—'

'I believe nothing. I know, I know with a certainty beyond all else. My Hira is twine and thorn.'

'My Hira is twine and thorn,' Anna repeated. It was the way of the Binders.

'Now make one fall,' Aunt commanded.

If she'd failed with only one moth, Anna couldn't see how contending with multiple would make her task any easier. It wasn't meant to. Aunt worked in illogical ways like that – if Anna had found it difficult the first time then it would be all the more so the second, by way of punishment. Anna focused on one of the moths, following its movements. She drummed up the same intention as before, adding force to it. *Twine and thorn. Twine and thorn. I own you, little thing!* She pulled the knot tight.

Nothing happened. She groaned loudly and in frustration tied another before Aunt could stop her. Still nothing.

'Bloody stupid moths!' Anna cried, throwing the cord onto the table.

'Anna.' Aunt did not raise her voice, but it had tightened like a screw. 'How dare you speak like that.' She made a small movement with her cord.

Anna felt a flickering inside her mouth. With a deep and nauseous revulsion she knew what Aunt had done. She opened her mouth, releasing a silent scream – a moth flew out, its thick, furry body rising into the air. Anna retched, wiping frantically at her tongue, trying to rid herself of the feel of its legs twitching against the side of her mouth.

'That will teach you to watch your tongue.' Aunt smiled at her own joke.

Anna felt for a moment angry enough to bring a whole cloud of moths down on Aunt's head but she reached for the Knotted Cord in her pocket and lowered her eyes, afraid to say or do anything again.

'At least we don't have to worry about binding your magic.' Aunt turned to her and smiled faintly. 'There's hardly any there at all.'

Anna knew Aunt was right, but still, her words stung. Aunt picked up the black cord and tied Choke Knots across it with rhythmic purpose. The moths fell one by one from the air, until the dark wood was covered with a sad pool of spasming legs and broken wings. As unnatural as they were, Anna felt sorry for them – brought into existence only to be cut down.

'Clean them up,' said Aunt, pushing her chair away from the table and heading for the door.

'But they're still alive.'

'That's your fault.'

Anna tried – different cords, different knots; tying and untying – trying to set their wings free so she could open the window and let them out, but she could not. The moths lay on the table twitching desperately. *I'm sorry. I can't save myself and I can't save you.*

Aunt sharply pulled the brush through her hair while Anna sipped on the glass of milk Aunt had brought for her (*calcium for growing bones*). It was how all their evenings ended. Their little ritual. The knot that tied the threads of their days together.

Anna had little left in her but weariness and she submitted to the hard brush. Aunt pulled out the waves of her hair into a soft, unflattering fuzz. When she'd been young, people had made a fuss of its colour, caught somewhere between red and blonde, *like the sunset on a field of straw,* a woman in a shop had once exclaimed admiringly. As she'd grown older the comments had dried up along with her hair. It was no longer ablaze. Its spark had turned to ash.

'Did you enjoy your little spell practice earlier?' said Aunt with a yank of the brush.

Anna sensed the question was a trap. 'I shouldn't have asked.'

'No. You shouldn't have. I decide when and how you are allowed to practise magic. You should not be craving it.'

'I'm not, I promise.'

'You think I don't know where this is coming from? Selene's arrival.' The lines of Aunt's neck pulled taut, like a ship's sail under harsh winds.

'No, it's not that—'

'What have I always told you? Magic is a terrible curse, Anna. It makes us weak. It makes us vulnerable. It makes us prey. It is a threat to us, to all witches. And people like them, *her*, are everything that is wrong with the magical world: casting flagrantly, openly, attracting attention, endangering us all. You must be in control. You must be ready for your Knotting.'

Anna was unnerved by the new urgency in Aunt's eyes; she could not escape from it. A thread of blood ran silently from Anna's nose. She got nosebleeds all the time. Dr Webber had said they were a result of her anxiety. Aunt handed her a tissue with irritation.

Anna dabbed at it and tried to find the right words. 'I just thought that . . . I still need to learn, don't I? That, maybe someday, when I've proved myself a responsible Binder, when my bindings are released—'

'*If* your bindings are released.'

'If my bindings are released, there may come a time when I will need to carry out magic in the name of duty, like you, to serve the Binders. That is why we train and practise—'

Aunt laughed silently. 'You think that's why we let you practise magic? No. We let you taste it so that you know exactly what it is you're giving up, so that you understand the true meaning of sacrifice.'

*Sacrifice*. Yes. Anna knew that much about her Knotting

initiation ceremony. The Book of the Binders explained that her magic would be bound inside of her, but how? The details were fearfully sparse: 'With control you will be ready to make the sacrifice required.' Anna had never liked the sharp, slicing sounds of the word. What sacrifice? Her magic? Or something more? She'd tried to extricate further detail from Aunt on many occasions before, to no avail. The ceremony was a tightly kept secret and she knew she'd have no true idea of what she'd be facing until she was facing it. Anna looked up at herself in the mirror – through herself. *Will I be ready? Does it really matter?* She had so little magic in her, she might as well give it up.

'You think now I am a Senior Binder that magic is easy for me?' Aunt's long fingers fluttered to her neck. 'No one understands sacrifice more than I do, Anna.'

Anna's stomach tightened. 'I know.' She wished she did not know.

'If only your mother had been bound, she would still be with us now.'

'No.' Anna shook her head weakly. 'My father killed her.'

'Your father's hands might have done the killing but it was magic that made your mother weak to it. Magic and love. Love and magic. They destroy everything in the end.'

Aunt did not believe in love. They had never had a man in their lives; Aunt insisted they did not need one, that she was quite capable of doing everything a man could. Anna did not believe in love either.

Aunt sighed, putting the brush back in its set place within the antique silver-plated vanity set: brush, comb and mirror. 'I know you think me hard on you, but I'm just trying to protect you. You've only got one year left until your Knotting. School will be busy, boys will be joining your classes now you're in sixth form, emotions will be running high. You have to keep them in check. You know where they belong. Weakness in feeling; strength in control.'

'Weakness in feeling; strength in control.' Anna nodded, touching her Knotted Cord, doing her best not to think about the year ahead at St Olave's School for Girls. It was no escape.

'If we don't have trust . . .'

'We don't have anything,' Anna replied.

Aunt lowered her face until it was beside Anna's in the mirror, their eyes side by side in a unison of green. 'How alike we are, my child.' She smiled, resting a hand on Anna's shoulder. It always pleased her to compare them. Their features seemed as if they should match, but did not. Aunt's were cut from marble, arguing with their own beauty: high brow, angular cheekbones, glassy skin, deep eyes set in a bony scaffolding. Anna's followed the same outlines but were softer, more easily lost. She wished she was less peculiar looking, so pale and strange and haunting. Aunt continued to watch her, an uncomfortable silence growing between them.

Of all her silences, the silence of her love was the hardest to bear.

'Sixteen tomorrow. I can't keep you a child forever.'

Anna noticed a little of the defences that held Aunt's face together crack. Anna lightly placed her hand on top of Aunt's and breathed in the familiar magnolia scent of her perfume. Aunt was many things, none of them easy, but she was also the only mother Anna had ever known. The person to whom she owed everything. Aunt gripped her hand back and then let it go. She made a gesture and Anna's hair responded, knotting itself gently into a plait. Aunt was so adept at knot magic she didn't need a cord at all; she could make knots of the air.

She picked up the empty glass and made for the door. 'They'll be here at three. I want you up early. That silver isn't going to polish itself.'

Anna smiled. 'It'll be polished before dawn!'

Aunt allowed her a small smile in return. 'Goodnight, Anna.'
'Goodnight, Aunt.'

Anna never slept well, but tonight, she knew it would be impossible. Her emotions flapped about her like moths: agitation, fear, excitement. She looked at her Knotted Cord, knowing she could use it to bring them back under control. She resented every knot along its length: the years of training, the cruel tests, the parts of herself she could no longer feel.

She threw off her covers, crept to her bookshelf and selected the Book of the Binders. She remembered Aunt presenting it to her matter of factly after she'd turned seven as if it were a perfectly normal birthday present and not a large and heavy book full of the Binders' tangled, suffocating words. Its black cover was engraved with the image of a circle studded with nine knots; in the centre of the circle was a rose, its petals closed. The Nine-Knotted Cord and the Closed Rose: the symbol of the Binders.

Anna knew it off by heart: the rules, the blessings, the knots, the spells, the correspondences – every damn, dull word, but one chapter she returned to in secret over and over . . .

She sat down in the light which poured through the balcony windows – moonlight and street light and the general, incessant light of London; the only sound the rustle of pages as she opened it to 'Banned Magical Languages'. She lay on her front, white nightie pooling, and began to read them quietly, so that she alone could hear the words: *Planetary. Botanical. Runic. Ogham. Imagic. Divination. Necromancy. Elemental. Symbolic.* She would never get to practise them, but still, she could taste them, couldn't she? Each one a droplet of syrup on her tongue. *Potions. Wands. Words. Mirrors. Image Magic. Hexes. Sex Magic. Blood. Emotional.*

She tasted each word and found herself desperately, feverishly hungry.

# SHARDS

*Magic is the first sin; we must bear it silently.*

Tenet One, *The Book of the Binders.*

The light was already beginning to fade when the doorbell finally rang.

The day had unfolded as always, preparations and chores and tense silence, but this time it had been edged with something, as if the strict contours of their routine had been pulled out of shape in anticipation – frenzied – drawing towards whatever was coming. Aunt had been intolerable. Anna was halfway down the stairs when she appeared below. 'Six hours late! *We'll come for a Sunday lunch, darling! We'll see you at three!*' She performed a whining mockery of Selene's voice. Selene always had a way of disturbing her careful silence. 'I might cancel the whole thing. Dinner is ruined. Your birthday is ruined!'

The doorbell rang impatiently.

Aunt made a get-down-here-now-or-else gesture at Anna. 'Have you even bothered to brush your hair?' It was the fourth time she'd snapped at Anna about her hair. *If I'd shaved it off this morning it would have saved everyone a lot of grief.* Aunt pulled her hands through it roughly, pinning it back with two slides, while Anna tried not to scream *OPEN THE DOOR!* before her heart burst.

*Knock! Knock! Knock!*

Aunt started towards the door again but stopped abruptly and turned back to Anna with sudden intensity, digging fingers into her shoulders. 'What is the Binders' first tenet?'

'Magic is the first sin; we must bear it silently,' Anna replied.

'Do not forget that tonight.'

Aunt finally turned and clicked open the latch.

Golden hair, blazing yellow coat, red lips: Selene arriving like a comet to their house, radiant against the darkness around her. Her face serene and breaking into a wide smile that hadn't changed since the very first moment Anna had seen her. Anna dropped her Knotted Cord and let Selene's light wash over her.

'Look at you! My little matchstick! Aren't you a beauty!' Selene exclaimed, but Anna noticed the momentary concern that clouded her bright eyes. She smiled and it was gone. She ran her hands through Anna's hair and enclosed her into a hug. She was wearing an expensive perfume. Anna breathed deeper and found the familiar scents she knew beneath. Summer flowers and rich, warm smells: honey and cloves and the amber candles Selene loved to burn. She buried herself in them and was surprised to feel tears threaten. She forced them back. She did not cry.

Selene turned to Aunt. There were a few seconds of silence where it seemed neither woman quite knew what to say, then Selene moved forward and gave Aunt a kiss on each cheek. 'Vivienne! So good to see you too, darling. You look fantastic. A little tired though – hope we haven't kept you up. We only flew in from New York yesterday, it's been chaos.'

Aunt shuddered just a little. 'You're six hours later than you said you would be, but I expected nothing less.' Her face stiffened into something that might, from a distance, resemble a smile.

'I've brought gifts!' Selene clapped her hands together. 'Anna, be a doll and take my coat. It's new and fabulous, don't you think?' She shrugged it off. Underneath she was wearing a grey, figure-hugging dress that fell just below her knee. Her shoes were black stilettos with criss-crossed straps and a heel that made a pleasing dent in Aunt's carpet. She didn't take them off.

'Going to bother to introduce me?' A girl's voice drifted in from the doorway, even colder than Aunt's. Anna hadn't yet noticed her behind. She was a direct contrast to Selene: pale skin, long black hair, a face full of shadows where the other seemed to dispel them. Her expression was impassive, and yet somehow – although Anna couldn't work out how – she seemed to be frowning. She was wearing an oversized grey jumper, black jeans and leather boots. Aunt's gaze lingered on the dirt encrusting their soles. Silver hoops crept their way up her earlobes. Anna felt absurdly dull in her skirt and baby-blue cardigan.

'Effie, you're not a child, you can introduce yourself. Come in and stop being dramatic.' Selene rolled her eyes at Anna.

'It's nice to meet you,' said Aunt stiffly.

'A pleasure, I'm sure,' Effie responded flatly, stepping inside without wiping her shoes. Aunt's eyes widened.

Anna moved forward, extending a hand. 'I'm Anna, nice to meet you.' Effie looked at her outstretched hand as if Anna were offering her cyanide and then dropped her hat into it and brushed past.

'Ignore her, she's in an awful mood, got in a fight with the taxi driver.' Selene threw her hands up in exasperation. Anna laughed quietly, unsure if this was the right thing to do. Silence followed, as everyone stared at everyone else with disapproval.

'So . . . it feels awkward in here,' a deep voice boomed. 'Everyone making friends?'

A young man appeared in the doorway, two bags at his

feet. He had dark, unruly brown hair and a smile that promised many things, none of them good. *Is he the taxi driver? Or one of Selene's lovers again?* He was her type: tall, tanned, roguish, but he didn't look old enough. It was hard to tell, his face had an ageless quality to it, as if he'd always have a boyish countenance, even when old and grey-haired.

'OK. I'm going to hug it out,' he announced, pulling Aunt into an overpowering embrace. She disappeared somewhere into the jacket he was wearing. She looked in shock when he let her go. He put out his hand formally as if the previous exchange had not occurred. 'I'm Attis. You must be Vivienne. I've heard so much about you.' His accent was strangely nomadic as if it had collected the interesting parts of other accents on its travels: English, hints of American and something lilting and Celtic.

He turned to Anna and crossed the corridor in one stride. She backed away into the banister, concerned he was going to do the same to her. The teeth beneath his knowing smile were a little uneven; his eyes were grey and yet somehow startling. 'You must be Anna.' He held out a hand, obviously sensing her disinclination to be held. She shook his, finding it hot around her cold fingers. She found herself looking anywhere but directly at him.

'I am Anna,' she replied idiotically. Effie snorted behind her.

'There's just one last bag in the boot, Attis, if you would be a gentleman, which you always are,' said Selene with a sardonic, dismissive edge. *Probably not a lover then.*

'Ever at your service.' He bowed with equal sarcasm, heading back out into the evening.

Aunt released a forceful breath and snapped her head round to Selene. 'Who is he and why is he here? I planned lunch for four! I can't feed a boy, especially not a large oaf like that one.'

'Oh, he's a son of old friends of mine. He's been living with us in New York, did I not mention?'

'That hardly explains why he is on my doorstep and why you didn't tell me he was coming.'

'Well, he's moving back to London too and it's impossible to pin down the plans of teenagers; he was going to go meet someone on the way but then they couldn't make it . . . Oh, these things happen. Come on, Viv, play the gracious host.' She rubbed Aunt's stiff arm gently, smiling. 'He can have my food. You know I only graze. You wouldn't want to ruin the evening now, would you?'

Anna half expected Aunt to cancel the whole evening then and there. Of her many intolerances, there were two at the top of the list: surprises and men. Selene had managed to bring both to her doorstep.

Instead she released an irritable exhale and beckoned Selene impatiently down the corridor. 'Just come through.'

Selene followed, winking at Anna. She knew how to get around Aunt more effectively than Anna had ever managed. Effie had disappeared. Anna spotted her through the doorway to the living room, peering with distaste at the embroideries covering the walls, moving to the pictures on the mantelpiece. Anna watched her with interest.

'Am I allowed in or am I too much of an oaf?' Attis appeared again, making Anna jump. He was balancing a bag on his finger. Anna reddened at the realization he'd heard Aunt's words, even though she'd only said them quietly.

'Er, come in. I'll take these through.' She fumbled with the bag, realizing that she was just getting more in his way. He watched her with amusement. 'Effie's in there.' She pointed to the living room and carried on down the hallway to the relief of the kitchen. She was just as out of kilter as Aunt. She didn't know what to make of either Effie or Attis, but knew with crushing certainty what they would make of her: *strange, dull, forgettable*.

Aunt was serving food into bowls and huffing over what

she obviously considered a spoilt meal. 'Anna, take this through and get everyone seated. You'll have to add an extra place setting.'

Selene followed Anna into the dining room. The table had been laid to within an inch of its life: the plates were stacked, the silver shone brightly, candles stood to attention. Selene made fearful eyes at Anna as if the table were an instrument of torture with which they were about to become acquainted, making Anna laugh. She realized she hadn't laughed in a long while. Selene trailed a finger up one of the candles and it sparked into life with a clear, bright flame. She touched each of the others in turn, uttering *bibbity-bobbity-boo* until they were all lit. Anna marvelled for just a moment but then she shook her head at Selene. *Not now.*

The door swung open. Aunt came in carrying a bowl of potatoes; Selene pulled an exaggerated alarmed face at Anna behind her back. Anna hid her smile as she helped set the food out, her heart swelling with feeling. At least Selene saw her as something more – someone worth seeing.

Once they were all settled around the table, Aunt served the food in tense silence. 'There's gravy there.' She jabbed at the jug in such a threatening way that even Effie, who was still in a foul mood, picked it up immediately.

Anna studied her through a series of quick, sideways glances as she helped pass the food around. Effie was striking; not classically beautiful, but beautiful nonetheless, in a way that was hard to pin down. Perhaps it was exactly that – the wildness of her gamine features, the distracted hunt of her deep eyes beneath dark arched eyebrows, the mocking twist to her full lips. There was the hint of dimples on her cheeks, although as she hadn't smiled Anna couldn't be sure.

'Anna, tell me about your life. Who are you dating? School starts in a couple of days. What are your plans this year? Anything exciting?' Selene turned her twinkling cat-like eyes onto Anna; they were mostly blue but shot through with flecks of violet so that the overall effect was something purple and galactic.

'Um,' said Anna, uncomfortably aware of the sudden attention. What could she say? *My plans are to survive another year in the hell that is otherwise known as school. Dating is entirely irrelevant. Then I'm due to become a Binder, my magic bound forever, to be followed by a life under Aunt's control, on and on until I die alone, in a house full of embroideries.* She forced a smile. 'I'm more interested in what you've been doing. How was New York?'

'Oh, New York was New York.' Selene waved her hands. 'This is such a treat. I don't think we've had a home-cooked meal in about a year, have we? There's just so much great food on your doorstep and so many people to see. Remember that Korean place?' She turned to Effie and Attis, her questions to Anna forgotten. Relief flooded through her. 'That pork belly dish with those little pickled greens, it was beyond melt in your mouth, it melted your entire being, I swear. What was the owner's name again?'

'Choi Minho,' said Attis.

'Oh yes, Minho. I wish I could have brought him to London so you could have tried it. I think he may have eloped with me if I'd tried.'

'Where were you living?' New York was on Anna's list of places to travel if she ever managed to escape the life Aunt had planned for her.

'We had an apartment in the East Village for a while, and then we moved into a house outside, on the coast. I met this wonderful gentleman who let us stay with him. He owns MacElson & Faber Holdings?' she said, as if Anna might somehow know it. Anna gave her a blank look. 'We bonded over our love of baroque art.'

'A very sudden love of baroque art that coincided with

finding out he lived in a massive fuck-off mansion,' said Effie.
Aunt choked on a carrot.

'Effie, don't swear during dinner, darling,' said Selene.

'We don't allow swearing in this house full stop.' Aunt's
voice had taken on a tone that could strip bark from a tree.

Effie just laughed, helping herself to more potatoes.

Selene intervened. 'What have you two been up to this
summer then?'

'We've been busy,' Aunt replied tersely. 'We make the most
of every day, don't we, Anna?'

Anna nodded, acutely embarrassed by the dullness of
their lives.

'Lots of studying and Anna just finished sewing the most
charming embroidery, didn't you?'

Anna nodded again, feeling worse.

'Gosh, that sounds fascinating,' replied Effie, her dimples
finally popping, punctuating her smile with deep-seated
sarcasm. 'Tell us more.'

Anna didn't know how to respond, feeling as small and
pathetic as it was possible to feel. Apparently no one else
knew how to respond either, the table descending into
awkward silence. Attis made a slight whistling sound. Anna
shot the smallest of looks at him and saw that he appeared
to be enjoying himself. It seemed he found her humiliation
entertaining. She looked away but his face stayed in her
mind, elusive as the candle smoke.

'These potatoes are incredible. Tell me, what did you cook
them in?' he said, quite cheerfully.

'Olive oil,' Aunt replied sharply.

He leant back into the chair. 'You see, people always say for
good roast potatoes goose fat, but I think with a good quality
olive oil you can get a better result. These are impeccable.'

Aunt smiled briefly in his direction, softening to his none-
too-subtle flattery.

'And what do you do, Vivienne?' He turned all his attention to her, eyes dancing. They were grey and distant, like an autumn sky, retreating under a cloud of heavy brow.

'I'm a nurse,' she said, in the self-effacing way she always replied to that question. 'Senior nursing officer at King's College London.'

'Wow. You must make a difference to so many lives.' His reply was so obviously constructed to please that Anna found herself rolling her eyes. She happened to catch Effie's and found she was doing the exact same thing.

'You do what has to be done,' she replied nobly. 'It can be a thankless job.'

'Well, if I ever have any medical needs, I know where to go. You know what they always say. Those who make a mean roast potato save lives.'

Aunt looked at him quizzically; she didn't do humour and she obviously didn't know what to make of this boy. Neither did Anna.

Aunt's eyes narrowed. 'Are you back from New York for good?'

'I go where she goes.' He pointed at Effie, who wrinkled her nose at him, but showed the first hint of a genuine smile Anna had seen from her. They were a couple then. *Of course they were a couple. Anna could imagine them now – young, wild and beautiful – New York falling at their feet.*

'Besides, it was best you left New York . . .' Effie gave Attis a knowing look.

'And why is that?' asked Aunt, placing her knife and fork delicately together.

'Oh, Attis put an iron hex on an ex of mine. He got mad.'

Aunt dropped the fork with a clatter.

*We shall not cast unless it is our duty.*

'Effie,' Selene chided.

'What?' Effie shrugged. 'I didn't do it.'

'He deserved it,' said Attis.

Any growing warmth Aunt had had towards him withered and turned to dust. She had been proven right. He was the immoral reprobate she'd suspected. Aunt seemed reassured by this, becoming dignified in her anger, back on steady ground. She turned on Attis. 'Magic is a duty, not a toy to be played with.'

Anna shrank at her words – words she knew all too well – but Effie and Attis seemed only to find them amusing. Anna couldn't imagine being them, living without fear, worlds of magic at their fingertips . . .

'What hex?' Anna said quietly. Aunt's head snapped around to her instead. She knew she'd be in trouble for asking but her curiosity was too great.

Effie showed a hint of a smile at her disobedience. 'Let's put it this way: the guy suddenly had a penchant for taking his clothes off in public spaces.' She laughed and Anna saw how it transformed her face, the black of her eyes illuminated suddenly like a storm. Attis chuckled silently into his plate. Anna found herself smiling with them but stopped abruptly when she saw Aunt's face.

'Anna, take the plates out,' she snapped. 'It's time for dessert.' Anna didn't know it was possible to imbue the word dessert with such violence.

Anna followed Aunt out into the kitchen. They did not speak. Aunt pointed at the dessert plates. Anna took them and went back into the hallway. She almost dropped the plates on the floor – Effie was there, leaning casually against the wall, face to the light, her black hair part of the shadows. 'We're going out in a bit. To a club. A magical club. You coming?'

Anna struggled for words. Aunt was in the kitchen. Effie was ahead of her. She was trapped between them.

'I can see you're desperate to get out of this prison.' Effie rolled her head towards her.

'It's not a prison.'

'Fine, a prison with wall tapestries. Now come. It'll really piss off your aunt.'

Anna hesitated. She couldn't believe she'd hesitated. It wasn't that she was going to go out with them, the idea of *that* was beyond comprehension. It was just that she'd never been asked to go out before, even if Effie seemed more focused on irritating her aunt than actually spending time with her. And then, where they were going . . . *a magical club. Are there really such places?* Surely Effie was only mocking her.

'I can't.'

'Why not?'

'I just can't.'

Effie gave her a look that made her feel even smaller than she had all evening. 'I would say suit yourself, but you obviously don't.' She laughed and turned back towards the dining room, just as Aunt bustled through from the kitchen carrying a lit birthday cake.

'Anna, the plates! Go!'

Anna scurried into the dining room with Aunt following. Attis began belting out Happy Birthday at the top of his lungs. Selene joined in, clapping cheerfully, while Effie remained as silent as Aunt. Anna took her seat in front of the cake and at the end Attis cheered as if they'd been old friends for years. Anna had the strong feeling he was ridiculing her.

'Cast a wish.' Selene squeezed her hand.

Aunt narrowed her eyes as if the last thing Anna deserved was wishes, but Anna formed one in her head nonetheless, hoping the magic of the room might somehow seep into it. She wished only that she would be able to spend more time with Selene this year. She was sure she wouldn't see Effie or Attis again, but Selene, if she would just come back – just one more visit. She doubted Aunt would allow it after this evening.

'Mmm,' said Selene as Aunt distributed the cake. 'You know cake is my weakness, Viv.'

'Where was my cake then, Mother dearest?' Effie looked over at Selene, unimpressed. 'If I recall for my birthday last month I was given a glass of champagne and a takeaway . . .'

'Well, champagne is my other weakness.' Selene laughed and turned to Aunt. 'I forgot to thank you for putting me in touch with the headmaster.'

Aunt skewered a strawberry with her fork. 'Did you manage to get Effie a place? I wasn't sure it would be possible with term about to start but I know how persuasive you can be.'

'Oh yes, she's in.'

'Me too,' said Attis with gusto.

'Him?' cried Aunt.

'I'm afraid so. Lock up your daughters.' He winked at Aunt.

Anna was trying to understand why they were talking about terms and headmasters. 'What school?' she asked with a growing feeling of dread.

'Yours,' Effie answered with a satisfied bite of cake.

'What?' Anna turned to Aunt.

Aunt was still focused on Selene. 'I wasn't aware you were looking at two places.'

'Well, Attis needs to go somewhere and that Headmaster informed me there was a spare place at the nearby Boys' School. He was very obliging.' Selene smiled. It was a smile that Anna doubted had ever been denied. It was the first time it had not made Anna happy. Her face felt hot; her stomach had fallen to her feet. She could hardly believe what was being said. *Her school?*

Anna had spent years hardening herself to the cruelties of St Olave's, turning herself into a nobody. If they turned up, with their wild eyes and threat of magic, she felt as if it would rip open that pain all over again. She'd be reminded every day that she wasn't just a nobody, but barely a witch.

*And Selene.* Selene would find out just how tragic her life really was.

'It's an exceptional institution,' Aunt continued. 'I hardly think he will fit in.'

'Why thank you.' Attis put his hand on his heart.

'Attis, you're just not exceptional enough,' Effie sniggered. 'Whereas I'm going to study hard, make friends with all the teachers and sew an embroidery so perfect they will hang it upon the school walls forever.' Her eyes flashed at Anna. Anna turned away, knowing this is how it would be: they'd be at her school and they would taunt her.

'You see, Vivienne, you need me there to keep her under control,' said Attis.

Aunt glared at Selene. Selene glared at Effie. Effie glared at them all. Anna pulled at her Knotted Cord. The cake lay half-eaten on plates; the candles down the centre flickered, as if in response to the invisible battle lines being drawn across the table.

'Wine!' Selene exclaimed. 'I think it's time we opened a bottle, don't you?' She disappeared through the door. Silence followed in her wake. Effie whispered something to Attis, who laughed.

Selene returned with a small, dark bottle, distracting Anna from her shock. 'A dessert wine, from a little shop in New York, French owner. He makes it with grapes that aren't grown any more. These ones are from 1345, from a small French village just outside Saumur. It's divine.'

Her words didn't make sense. *How can the wine have come from grapes that no longer existed?* Aunt looked disapprovingly at the bottle's magical content.

'Oh come on, Viv, I know dessert wine is your favourite,' Selene coaxed.

*Is it?* To Anna's surprise, Aunt conceded but shook her head at Anna.

'Oh, Vivienne, don't be such an old purse,' said Selene. 'It's her sixteenth birthday – give the girl a drink. I recall you getting completely rat-arsed on your sixteenth birthday.'

'One small glass,' Aunt relented, blushing.

Attis poured Anna a large one.

'To Anna!' Selene cheered, raising hers.

Anna took a long gulp. She'd secretly tried a few sips of wine here and there before, left over in Aunt's glass, and had found it tolerable, if not a little sour. This was something else. It was sweet and deep and luxurious. She could taste the grapes bursting in her mouth in piquant, fruity explosions. She took another sip and experienced a sudden awareness of sunshine, flower-strewn meadows, somewhere laughter and the buzz of honey bees. She had the distinct feeling of being in France, although she'd never been.

Aunt inspected her glass with beady eyes. Her face was flushed and the veins in her neck had gone slack. She took another suspicious sip and then looked at Anna disapprovingly as if she'd somehow orchestrated the whole thing.

As the wine flowed there was a change in the air. The light seemed softer, the room warmer; chocolates were passed around. Selene told them stories of New York and of her outlandish younger days in London – she was spot on at impressions. Anna even caught Aunt laughing once, albeit briefly, when Selene reminded her of the time her university supervisor had been found by security with his leg stuck in a fence after attempting to creep out of Selene's room.

When the clock struck midnight, Aunt sat up with a start. 'I didn't realize the time.'

'Shit. Got to go. Got a thing,' said Effie, looking at her phone. Anna tensed, remembering Effie's offer.

Aunt looked at Selene in horror and then back to Effie. 'You are not going out at this hour!'

'I wasn't aware you were in charge of my schedule,' said Effie, full lips curling with amusement and revealing vampiric incisors.

Aunt turned to Selene. 'You can't let her go now. It's gone midnight – she could be out anywhere, up to anything.'

'Up to anything?' Effie laughed without amusement.

'It's a deduction,' Aunt replied, looking at Effie as if she were a piece of food that had been trodden into the carpet.

Selene breathed out a slow sigh. 'Vivienne, you can't tell my daughter what she can and can't do. Effie, you have two hours and he has to go with you.' She nodded at Attis.

'He was always coming with me. I wouldn't want him to miss out on the drug-fuelled orgy I have planned.'

Aunt looked at Effie as if she might strangle her. 'Anna would never be let out at this time of night.'

Anna sank lower in her seat, her cheeks burning.

'Your precious Anna, she couldn't possibly!' Effie mocked.

'Mark my words.' Aunt had gone very still. 'It's girls like you who amount to nothing in the end.'

Effie's smile didn't drop but her eyes moved to the wine bottle on the table.

It exploded.

It happened so quickly Anna didn't know what was going on, aside from registering a loud bang. She looked up to find hundreds of shards of glass balanced in the air; red wine, dark as blood, spiralled across the white table cloth. Selene cried out. Attis jumped up, as if ready to pounce. Effie laughed, her eyes on Aunt.

Aunt's were focused on the glass in the air and Anna realized that Aunt had halted the bottle mid-explosion with impeccable magical reflexes. The shards turned slowly and threateningly in front of Effie's face, glistening at the edges. They dropped to the table suddenly.

'For the love of the Goddess!' cried Selene. 'What's with

all this drama?' She turned to Anna with a high, unnatural laugh. 'You've probably never seen anything like it.'

Anna attempted to smile back, but found her face was too tense. Her nose began to bleed. She pressed her napkin against it. Attis frowned at her curiously and then began to gather the pieces of glass from the table into his hands.

'Leave that.' Aunt snapped. 'And get out.'

'With pleasure.' Effie was already making her way to the door.

'I'll see you both later,' said Selene brightly, as if it had been a perfectly lovely evening.

They left. The next moment Attis's head appeared around the door. 'See you at school, Anna.' He winked and was gone.

'Anna.' Anna could tell by Aunt's tone she was meant to leave.

She was all too happy to escape to the kitchen. Her head felt as if it had exploded too. Her body was trembling with fear and shock and excitement. She thought of the red wine pouring across Aunt's ironed tablecloth; the glass filling the air with sharpness; the crackle of magic. Despite everything, it had been the best birthday she'd ever had.

She heard the latch of the front door and could hear Aunt and Selene talking. She crept through the dining room and cracked open the door to the hallway.

'Don't you dare threaten her ever again.' The softness of Selene's voice had disappeared. Anna had never seen her looking so angry.

'I was not the one who exploded a bottle of wine,' seethed Aunt. 'What have you been teaching her? What have you been allowing her to do? I saw no casting, I heard no words. That came straight from her.'

'She's powerful, Vivienne, she was always going to be. We're not all as desperately afraid of magic as the Binders.

They're delusional; everyone is practising, freely, openly. We don't live in the Dark Ages any more.'

'Until the dark finds us.'

They held each other's eyes.

'And letting her go out all hours of the night!' Aunt hissed. 'You obviously have no regard for her safety.'

'At least I don't keep her locked up like Anna. At least she knows what's out there.'

'The only thing out there for them is pain and death. You know that.'

'I know you haven't changed one bloody bit—'

Anna heard the front door open and closed the door, creeping back through into the kitchen. Selene was right. She was hidden away, like a nasty secret. Locked in Aunt's world of delusion where magic was a thing of terror not wonder.

Part of her longed to go out with Effie and Attis, off into the London night, not a care in the world but being young and having fun. *Not that they really want me going with them.* Despite her mocking offer, Effie obviously hated her and Anna wasn't sure if she liked her much either, but it didn't seem to matter. *Effie had stood up to Aunt!* She began to stack the glasses into the dishwasher, feeling their weight and strength in her hands. She couldn't imagine mustering up enough magic to explode glass. Effie had simply looked at it.

*She's powerful, Vivienne.* Of course Selene's daughter was powerful.

*Effie is everything I am not.*

# FAIRY TALES

*The Great Goddess or the Great Spinner, as they call her, is no more
than the Great Sinner. Do not believe their weak venerations. The
Great Sinner spun our secrets into the world and in doing so we were
all undone. She brought magic into light and in doing so invited the
shadows forth.*

*The Goddess, The Book of the Binders*

Aunt's hair-brushing that night was not gentle and neither
was the look in her eyes. She was seething. *Well, I'm angry
too*, Anna thought bitterly. Angry that Aunt had ruined things
with Selene. Again. Angry that her life had to be so different
from theirs. Angry at herself for being herself. She found it
quietly satisfying to recall the look on Aunt's face as Effie
had exploded the bottle.

'What did I tell you?' Aunt's brushing yanked her head to
one side. 'Witches like them ought to be bound on the spot.
That girl should not be allowed to practise magic, so untethered and impulsive, she has no idea of the consequences.
She'll end up like your mother, mark my words.'

Anna had spent her life marking Aunt's words and it didn't
seem to have got her anywhere. Aunt put the brush down
and made a knotting gesture; Anna's hair wound into a tight

plait. 'And you. Don't think I couldn't see how you were looking at them, that look you've still got in your eyes now – all dazzled and desperate. Pathetic. Magic is the first sin.' Aunt twisted her hand in the air and Anna's plait yanked tighter again, pulling her eyes wide in her skull.

*Why let her go to my school then?* Anna wanted to scream but she was too afraid to move, the plait was holding her tightly, straining painfully, threatening to rip the hair from the roots.

'You know the consequences, why the Binders do what we do, why magic must be kept concealed, why we must never forget. You know of the threats we face. The Ones Who Know Our Secrets. The fire never dies; beware smoke on the wind.'

The Binders' final tenet. 'The fire never dies; beware smoke on the wind,' Anna repeated. She knew the words, she knew of the *threats*, and they'd never seemed to have got her anywhere either.

Aunt pulled the plait a fraction tighter – Anna resisted crying out – and then let her grip go. 'Drink your milk,' she said irritably. Anna finished the glass in one gulp. Aunt picked it up. 'You'll be cleaning up that broken glass tomorrow,' she threatened ominously, giving Anna one last cold look before leaving.

Anna sagged in the chair, undoing the plait and running her hands through her hair. Selene was gone and she hadn't even had the chance to talk properly – the chance to say goodbye. A small part of her lamented the fact Selene had not given her a gift. Selene's infrequent visits had always been timed around Anna's birthday and she always brought a gift. An extraordinary gift.

Anna reached into the back of one of her drawers and pulled out a small black drawstring velvet bag, soft and supple. Selene had given it to her just after she turned seven. Anna remembered exclaiming how pretty it was.

'Oh, its prettiness is just a distraction,' Selene had said. 'It's a nanta bag. It's not meant for looking at but for storing secrets.'

'Oh! How?'

'You whisper them into it and it'll keep them for you. You must have lots of secrets; any respectable woman should.' She'd winked.

Anna had not understood. She'd opened the neck of the bag – finding its insides darker than its outsides – and whispered hello into it. She'd felt the words pull from her lips as if a breeze had carried them away. The bag had felt heavier.

'It heard that?' she'd said in wonder.

'Of course. I know how hard secrets can be to bear alone and I think you spend a lot of time alone, my little matchstick . . .'

On her ninth birthday Selene brought her a pair of golden shoes. 'They'll grow with your feet so you'll have them forever!' On her third and last visit, when Anna turned thirteen, Selene had given her a golden comb. 'It'll bring back all those natural curls that Vivienne has tried to strangle.' Selene had drawn the comb through Anna's hair and her over-brushed frizz had bounced back smooth and shining, like straw spun to gold.

Those presents had kept Anna going over the years. After a tough day she'd go upstairs and admire the golden shoes or run her fingers over the comb. She did not use them; but kept them there waiting like a promise. She used the nanta bag though, whispering secrets into it that she ought not to have had – how she hated her life, how she missed Selene, how she longed for magic. The bag had grown as heavy as her heart . . . *nothing but silly, childish secrets.*

Anna put the bag away and looked up into the mirror. The eyes that stared back at her were empty.

She imagined exploding the mirror to pieces. How it would feel. She thought of Effie's eyes, the way they'd seemed to express everything while giving nothing away, the way they'd looked at the world, as if it consumed her and bored her all at once, no match for the storms inside of her. Her disdainful scowl that so quickly became a smile when she looked at *him*, and that way he'd looked at Anna herself – *as if I were no more than a child . . .*

They might be everything wrong with the magical world but they were still part of the magical world and that was more than she would ever have. She crept back to bed and took out a book, determined not to think about Effie or Attis any longer. They made her feel as if she was lacking and now she'd have to face them every day. She was already worried about returning as a member of the sixth form – the top years of the school. They'd be having joint classes with boys from the nearby St Olave's Boys' School for the first time. Things would be changing and she'd had very specific plans to stay out of it all: keep her head down, focus on her studies, pass her exams and get into medical school, just as she or, more accurately, Aunt had planned. And now this.

*What if they speak to me? What if they taunt me? What if they don't notice me at all?* No scenario was comforting. Anna had been lectured her whole life about never exposing magic to humans – sending Effie into the ordinary, humdrum corridors of St Olave's was surely like throwing a live firework at a haystack? It made no sense. To have convinced Aunt, Selene must have greater persuasive abilities than Anna had known she possessed. Anna drummed her fingers on the book and attempted to read while devising strategic plans on how to avoid them at school as much as humanly possible.

A tap on the French windows broke the silence.

Anna dropped the book on the floor. It came again. Someone was on the balcony. She went to get up but the doors burst open of their own volition. A yellow coat with golden hair stepped through. Selene. Anna's tangle of thoughts fell away. Selene smiled and stretched out her arms. Anna ran to her. They hugged, the rain on Selene's coat soaking into Anna's pyjamas. It didn't matter.

'I can't believe you came back.'

'Of course,' said Selene, throwing her coat off and dropping it on the floor. She kicked off her shoes; there were deep red marks where the straps had dug in. Mascara was smeared under her eyes from the rain. 'No one kicks me out of a party.'

'I'm just glad you're here. Do you want a cardigan or a dressing gown? You look cold.'

'I'm marvellous. Come sit down, my little matchstick.'

Anna brought over a towel and a small heap of clothing just in case and sat down next to her on the bed.

'Did you have a good birthday?'

'Well, it was . . . it was . . .' Anna smiled. 'Fun.'

'I'm sorry Effie was so unforgivably rude to you. She gets like that. I've spoken about you in the past and she knows how close I was to your mother. She gets jealous easily.'

It took a moment for her words to sink in.

'Jealous? Of me? No.' Anna refused to believe it.

Selene waved a hand. 'Well, you can get to know her when you go to school, can't you?'

Anna made a face that implied this was highly unlikely.

'Oh, she'll come round.'

'I'm not sure we're going to be sharing lunches and making friendship bracelets for one another, let's put it that way.'

Selene smiled at her. 'I wasn't sure I liked your mother when I first met her.'

'Really?'

'It was the first day of school and I had to sit by her on account of our surnames being next to one another in the alphabet. She had this official-looking pencil case and thick black hair, so straight and shiny, and mine was a frizz of yellow curls.' Selene ran her hands through her now glossy hair. 'We had to practise speaking French and she pronounced each word perfectly and I felt so clumsy trying to reply. She wrote notes while I doodled all over the textbook. I decided she was perfectly boring and a goody two shoes. Then she spent ten minutes trying to fit a new cartridge in one of her pens and ended up spilling ink all over herself. I laughed so hard.'

Selene smiled at the memory. 'She turned to me and I thought she was going to tell me off but she started laughing too, then I laughed harder and she flicked ink all over me. We couldn't stop then – we'd set each other off. The teacher came over and Marie blamed herself and smiled and apologized in such perfect French that we didn't get in any trouble. I think I learnt that from her, my propensity for getting out of difficult situations with nothing more than a smile.'

'Did you always sit together after that?' Anna asked, eager for more.

'Always, and she taught me too, until I could keep up with her. She was like that, your mother, always helping people. It was her strength and her weakness . . . Anyway, enough of this blabber.'

'I want you to keep telling stories.' Anna liked it when Selene spoke of her mother's magic: how easily it had come to her; how powerful it had been.

'Well, tough. It's gift time.'

'A gift?' said Anna with growing excitement. 'I didn't think—'

'You didn't think I'd forgotten? It's your birthday and I shall spoil you.'

'If you have to.' Anna nudged her playfully, as Selene handed her a badly wrapped gift, sealed with plasters.

'I couldn't find any sellotape.' Selene laughed. 'Open it! Open it!'

Anna peeled them away to reveal a book. Its cover was a rough cream cloth, stained with age, cloud-like patches blooming across the front, collecting the rains of passing time. She turned it over and written in gilded gold script was the title: *East of the Sun and West of the Moon*. Beneath was an engraving of two trees: one upright and one upside-down, their roots locked together, their leafy branches hung with apples. They were perfect mirror images. Seven apples on each.

'It's lovely.' Anna ran her hand over the engraving and wondered what strange magic it did, what tricks it would soon reveal.

'It's a book of fairy tales. Your mother's favourites. I found this copy in an old magical antique shop. Your mother knew them off by heart; most witches do . . . Oh, there are hundreds of versions of them and a thousand other stories out there besides, but these are the classics. You ought to know them.'

'Fairy tales?' Anna repeated, waiting for Selene to announce they read themselves out or would grant wishes, but Selene continued to smile at her. Anna smiled back, not wanting to reveal her disappointment. Selene's gifts were always so magical but she was turning sixteen – what did she want with a book of children's fairy tales? What good would they do her? She opened it, feigning interest. The paper was whisper thin. The first tale was called 'The Eyeless Maiden'.

Anna knew it. She remembered Aunt telling it to her when she was younger. At the end, the curious maiden, having survived her quest through the woods, gets her eyes pecked out. Aunt relished that bit. Her stories had always been laced with such lessons and warnings, but Anna had still loved it when she told them – had still found herself lost in the words, the possibilities they offered, the spaces they opened up, like paths through a forest. She'd liked how Aunt looked when she recalled them too. Softer. Not quite herself. Transferred to some other place. Perhaps she'd read them with her mother when they were young?

Aunt had stopped telling her the stories years ago; she'd decided they excited her emotions too much. Anna closed the book. 'This one doesn't have a happy ending,' she said.

'Well, true fairy tales are not always kind or pleasant but neither is life and we must live it anyway. Stories must be lived too; only then can they be understood.'

Anna's eye was drawn again to the mirrored trees on the front cover.

'Hide it,' Selene urged. 'Hide it from the kraken. I have another too . . .' Selene seemed unsure, her red lips twisted. 'It's not a gift as such, just something I thought you should have.'

She handed Anna what appeared to be a photograph. Anna turned it over and there was a woman and a man sitting together, turned towards each other, a baby folded in the woman's arms. They were somewhere outside; there was a tree in the background. He had short dark hair, slightly curly. He'd crinkled his nose up and was looking at the woman teasingly. Their smiles were a mirror of one another. The baby was asleep, a little round, contented face.

Anna looked at the photo for several long moments.

'Is that—?'

'Your father.'

Anna had never seen a photo of him before.

'They loved each other,' Selene said gently.

*Love.* Aunt had said that too. Aunt had told her the full story when she was ten and the horror of it still didn't feel real. Her father, an ordinary human, had met her mother and they'd fallen in love. A couple of years later, when Anna was just three months old, he'd strangled her mother in a fit of rage after she'd accused him of having an affair and then stabbed himself in the heart in the same bed. *Do you see? Love destroys everything, Anna.*

'He killed her,' Anna muttered, but it was hard to imagine

now she was staring him in the face. He looked so ordinary; the lines around his eyes seemed kind. He was hardly the monster she'd always imagined – or tried not to imagine. She turned the picture over.

'You don't have to keep it if you don't want to, but I felt like it belonged to you.'

Anna opened the drawer of her bedside table and placed it at the back between a pile of books. She didn't know if she ever wanted to see it again.

'Oh, but you do look like her,' said Selene, touching Anna's cheek, 'and I loved her too.' She took Anna's hand. 'How are things, my little matchstick? You've said so little about yourself.'

'I am—' Anna started and then realized she couldn't finish. She wanted to tell Selene everything. About her life. Her pain. Becoming a Binder. Did Selene know it was her future? Selene had always been the one who'd tried to teach her magic, with some success at first, but later – she'd given up. *She couldn't find any in me.* The shame cut through Anna like a glass shard. 'I'm glad you're here.' She smiled, gripping Selene's hand. 'Please don't leave.'

'Never. I want to know everything you get up to this year. What rules you break. What magic you create. Who steals your sixteen-year-old heart. Got your eye on anybody?'

There was one boy. Peter Nowell. He went to Olave's Boys' and Anna had seen him during shared school socials and events over the years, but he didn't know her. She knew him though. She knew exactly how blue his eyes were. *Will he be joining my classes this year?* Anna shook her head at Selene. There was little point in indulging feelings of that sort at all.

'Well, if you need any help I have a repertoire of spells, some more appropriate than others.'

Anna laughed. 'I shall try my very hardest to be as utterly fabulous as you.'

Selene cackled. 'They'll be dropping like flies.'

'Shhh, you'll wake the kraken.' Anna swatted at her playfully.

'Oh, sod her.' Selene glared up to the floor above. 'By the hour of the moon, it's time for cake. Proper cake.'

She rummaged around in her bag and pulled out an impossibly large box. Anna peeped inside and sitting in the middle was a cake, plump as a goose, covered in creamy icing and dusted with a red powder.

'Red velvet with cream cheese. Die right now if you please.'

Anna collapsed onto the bed. 'Best. Birthday. Ever.'

Selene handed her a fork and they delved into the cake, its centre oozing red as blood.

# CURIOSITY

*Ten Years Old*

Aunt snipped a thorny stem from the rose bush. She held it steady in her hands and it began to change, its waxy green hardening, its thorns turning inwards, twisting, smoothing, becoming a thick thread of cord, plain-coloured and rough.

Anna watched in wonder.

'Do you wish to know the secrets of magic, Anna?' said Aunt, weaving the cord between her fingers, which were so pale and bony they always looked as if they would snap in half, although Anna knew them to be strong. 'You may ask me now. Go on. Don't be shy.'

Anna's mind sped into overdrive. Aunt had never let her ask about magic before. 'How do you—'

Aunt made a knot in the cord and the question locked in Anna's mouth. A deeply unpleasant sensation. She felt herself able to speak; her tongue could move, and yet the question would not come, as if someone had stapled it to her tongue.

'Ask again.'

Anna was more tentative this time. 'Is there—'

Aunt made a second knot and the question stopped at Anna's lips. It felt as if she was trying to force a large cushion through a keyhole. Aunt smiled frustratingly.

'How are you—' Anna's mouth snapped up and this time the question forced its way back down her throat. She threw herself back onto the sofa, exhausted, deciding not to speak any more.

'Are you curious, Anna?'

Anna nodded, defeated.

'A cat has nine lives and curiosity still managed to kill it.' Aunt undid the knots in the cord and offered it to Anna. 'Go on, take it. It's yours. Your Knotted Cord.'

Anna's eagerness had long fled. She took it hesitantly, finding it coarse beneath her fingers, as if its thorns were still there.

'Now, make a knot of your own.'

Anna fumbled with the cord; it did not flow as easily in her hands. She made a tentative knot in its centre.

'Now. I want you to focus on that curiosity, that feeling, let it fill up your whole body.' Aunt brought her face close. 'Then I want you to tighten that knot and as you do so imagine that curiosity being tied up inside of it. Strangle it. Weakness in feeling; strength in control. Unrestrained emotions will only make your magic more dangerous. Tie them tight. Lock them up. That knot is your world now.'

# THE BINDERS

*The Path of the Binders is the hardest path to take, but the only path to salvation, for ourselves and for all. All other paths lead only to destruction, lead only to death.*

*Introduction, The Book of the Binders*

Anna woke early with a gasp.

The dreambinder above her was tangled and misshapen with knots. Too many to count. *What on earth have I been dreaming?* The scene of her and Selene's crime still on the floor: the book of fairy tales and the open cake box, cake half-decimated, forks discarded, crumbs and cream cheese debris.

The clock read 6.29 a.m.

Anna launched herself out of bed, scrabbling to put everything back in the box. She shoved it in her wardrobe and hid the book of fairy tales on her bookshelf, beneath the cover of another book. She jumped back into bed, waiting for the knock on her door with a hammering heart.

It didn't come.

She waited a few more moments; then she sat up and listened to the house. It was quiet. *Too quiet.* There were none of the usual early-morning sounds: creaking floorboards, Aunt banging doors, clattering dishes. Instead, she was met with pin-drop silence, as if the whole house were holding its breath. Where was Aunt? Had she known Selene was here? Was she angry? Maybe she'd just slept in? *No.* That had never happened in all their sixteen years of life together.

She picked up her Knotted Cord, trying to ease her growing alarm, and crept barefoot into the hallway. It was shadowy and heavy with silence, a grey, sluggish light seeping through the windows from the dull morning beyond. Anna walked upstairs to Aunt's room but it was empty, the bed unmade. She hesitated at the bottom of the third-floor staircase. It was silent above, but the third-floor room was always silent. She knew better than to go up there.

Downstairs the rooms were dark, their curtains still drawn. Anna approached the kitchen slowly, the back of her neck prickling, the low hum of the fridge washing against the quiet like breaking waves. The blinds of the window were still closed, casting bars of light over the table where a silhouette of Aunt sat with her head in her hands, perfectly still. A full cup of tea beside her released a spiral of steam.

'Aunt?'

She did not move. Anna crept closer, remembering a fairy tale she'd once read where the witch had been turned to stone . . .

'Aunt . . .'

Aunt stirred slowly. 'Anna.' Her voice was a tight, vibrating string. A few strands of hair had come loose from her bun as if she'd been running her hands through it. Her dressing gown had opened slightly revealing the Binders' necklace beneath.

Anna reached out a hand to touch her shoulder but left it there in mid-air. She was unsure how to react to this sharp swerve away from the aunt she knew, the woman who was loath to waste a single drop of the day, whose hair was never loose, who would normally be berating her for not wearing her slippers or not brushing her hair before breakfast, who drank her tea in three large swallows. She didn't sit and do nothing. Ever.

That was when Anna saw the headline on the tablet in front of her: 'Six women found hanging from the windows of Big Ben'. Aunt turned it over.

'What was that?' Anna asked, too confused to feel as horrified as she should.

'Nothing.'

'It's weird.' She itched to turn it back over. 'What happened?'

'What do we say of questions?'

'Ask no questions; seek no answers.'

'Then why are you asking them?' Aunt stood up and opened the fridge so forcefully the glass bottles in the door clattered together.

Anna bit her tongue. 'I was just worried, that's all, you seemed . . . agitated.'

'I'm fine.' Aunt slammed the door shut, holding a bottle of milk. She looked surprised to find it there as if she wasn't sure what she had intended to do with it.

'Is that story something to do with magic?' Anna waited for the rebuke but Aunt didn't snap back at her; instead she put a hand to the counter as if to hold herself up.

'What's happened is certainly unprecedented. Unexpected. Probably nothing, of course, but there's no telling – we must remain vigilant for threats at any cost . . .' She trailed off. Aunt always directed her words with clarity; they were a means to an end. Anna wasn't used to such half-formed thoughts. This wasn't Aunt's agitation of the last few days, this was something different. She realized with shock that Aunt was afraid. Aunt's life was full of fear but she was rarely afraid.

'Shall I make you some breakfast?' Anna suggested gently.

'Breakfast! We have no time for breakfast. The Binders are coming.'

Anna couldn't breathe for a moment. 'But they're not due till next month—'

'Change of plan.' The Binders did not just change their plans.

'But—'

Aunt seemed to come to her senses, smoothing her hair and looking at Anna as if for the first time that morning. 'But nothing. Why are you still in your pyjamas? Go and get yourself ready and find your slippers; your feet are going to freeze. I have calls to make.' She made an urgent shooing motion and finished the remainder of her tea in one large gulp, her delicate neck expanding to an impossible volume.

Anna ran upstairs and paced up and down her room, full of frustration. *Why were the Binders coming out of the blue?* It was that news story, whatever it was; she was desperate to read it but had no means without a phone or computer.

She would have to wait.

The morning was hectic with preparations. Cushions were plumped black and blue, cakes baked, china cups polished, all signs of magic from the night before purged – not a single shard of glass left. Thankfully, Aunt had not had time for her promised punishments. Just after lunch, Aunt went out to buy a few supplies and Anna took her opportunity.

She watched Aunt disappear down the street and then ran to the living room and took out Aunt's laptop. She was only allowed to use it with permission. She knew with a fearful, terrible certainty she shouldn't but she had to know. She quickly searched 'Big Ben Hangings' and was met with a barrage of results from all the major news outlets. She clicked on the first link – the *Mail Today*:

## Ding dong dead! Six women hanged in Big Ben

This morning, Londoners woke to a horrifying scene: six women hanging from the windows of Big Ben, one of the capital's most iconic landmarks.

The victims, who are being widely called 'the Six Faceless Women', were discovered hanging in six of the windows above the clock face of the Elizabeth Tower just before dawn yesterday. The seventh window also contained a noose but no victim was found.

Police have confirmed death by asphyxia in what is suspected to be a mass suicide, although homicide has not been ruled out. The identities of the women are as yet unknown, but the bodies have been removed for investigation.

Reports began flooding in from concerned commuters and tourists in the early hours of the morning with shocking images and videos emerging on social media. The most mystifying aspect of the event is the faces of the women which appear to have an unsettling similarity. Caretaker Ron Howard, who discovered the bodies, posted an up-close picture of the deceased women which captures this disturbing likeness. The image was quickly removed but not before it was picked up and widely recirculated, fuelling the nickname the Six Faceless Women.

Big Ben's world-famous clock has been damaged during the action with the hands frozen at midnight. Its windows have now been covered over but the scenes will not be forgotten, leaving the capital shaken to its core.

Anna studied the picture: the bodies of the women, taken down, lying on the floor as if not really dead, but only sleeping. Their hair pooled beneath them – a spectrum of colour and lengths, but it was true, their faces were eerily similar. She looked closer. *So similar. Identical, perhaps?* It was hard to say; the features were so ordinary and bland they were almost featureless, doll-like. She shivered involuntarily. The more she stared at them the less she felt as though she was seeing anything at all.

At the bottom was a video. Anna clicked play; the footage was shaky but the image was clear enough: bodies hanging, swaying in the breeze.

Anna closed the browser. The whole thing was so terrible, so strange . . . had magic been involved? She rarely considered the magical world beyond what Aunt wanted her to know, but nothing else could explain Aunt's sudden terror. The Binders did all they could to prevent magic being exposed to the ordinary world, to keep it locked away behind doors; brushed under carpets; tied in necklaces and tucked beneath blouses. And now here was a national news story: bizarre, unsolved, whispering at magic.

*Whispers divide; in secrets we thrive.*

She promptly deleted the internet history and put the laptop back in its place. She tightened her Knotted Cord and tried to put her curiosity back where it belonged too.

At two o'clock the doorbell rang.

Aunt pulled herself tall, the tension in her face dissipating into an artful smile, assertive and airy all at once. Anna marvelled at the performance as she disappeared into the hallway. 'Mrs Withering, do come in . . .'

It took ten minutes for them all to arrive, prompt as ever. Anna prepared the teas, listening out for any talk of *Big Ben* or *hangings* but heard nothing of the sort, only the usual strained greetings.

When she went through she was met by the familiar row of bob haircuts and cable-knit cardigans and pearls, necks artfully covered, wafts of flowery perfumes so heavy you could taste them, like a paste on the tongue. Anna had come into contact with various Binders over the years, but these nine were the most senior: a narrow spectrum of the middle class and middle-aged perched stiffly upon the sofas and armchairs of their living room. They all had the same pinched look about them, as if they'd smelt something that wasn't to their liking several years ago and had never quite got over it.

Anna held the tray of tea at the entrance, shifting from foot to foot, wishing she could be anywhere but here. 'Earl Grey for anyone?' She smiled like a deer caught in nine pairs of surrounding headlights.

'Yes please,' said Mrs Dumphreys, a rounded woman with an unfortunate attachment to silk blouses. She was wearing a purple one today, done up to the top. 'How's school, Anna?'

'It's the summer holidays.'

'Oh yes. Well, keep at it.'

'English breakfast for me.' Mrs Bradshaw's high treble voice rose on the other side of her. She pincered a biscuit from the tray. 'What subjects are you taking?'

Anna began to answer but Mrs Bradshaw cut through her. 'Well, my Charlie is due to take Maths and Further Maths this year, quite the brain for numbers.'

'Did I say Bella has just been accepted into the Royal Academy of Dance? That's what you get for paying for three extra hours of training every day . . .'

Anna poured out the tea and handed out treats while the tittle-tattle continued, their conversations moving in gentle rallies to the tinkle of china, attempting to outdo each other using all the politeness they could muster. Perhaps they would get sidetracked talking about whose new curtain fabric was the most expensive and she could escape unnoticed.

'Aren't we being spoilt.' Mrs Withering perused the offerings and smiled – if the spasm of her face could be called a smile: lips pursing, nose squirming. It was a smile that put you in your place and did not reach her eyes. She was a little older than Aunt: attractive, slim, malicious. 'Are they home-made?'

'The cake is, not the biscuits,' Aunt replied tersely. 'There was hardly time today, under the circumstances . . .'

The Binders were always competing with one another and none so more than Aunt and Mrs Withering. They appeared to be the leaders of the group, but Anna had never quite been able to tell who was truly in control.

'Of course. Although I would be happy to send you a wonderful biscuit recipe; it's awfully quick. You can use it for next time.'

'Thank you,' Aunt replied, through a grating smile.

Anna began to back out of the room but Mrs Withering turned her smile back on her, a gesture which rarely ended well.

'Don't leave, Anna. We're not done with you yet.'

Anna fought the urge to drop the tray and run.

'How's your training coming along?' A mole on Mrs Withering's lip twitched as she spoke, sniffing ahead for her answer.

'Very well.'

'Binders' tenet number two?'

They turned their eyes on her. The rose bush in the corner seemed to shift towards her too.

'Weakness in feeling; strength in control.'

Sweat began to collect along her forehead. She rubbed her hands nervously against her dress.

'Tenet three?'

'We shall not cast unless it is our duty.'

'How *is* your casting coming along?' Mrs Withering stirred a spoon slowly around her cup.

'With due diligence and control.' It was an Aunt-approved answer.

'Perhaps we ought to see some . . .'

Anna's mouth opened and closed like a fish on land. They liked to question her, to put her on the spot, but they had never asked to see her magic before. She looked to Aunt but she was nodding in agreement.

'Pass me that frame.' Mrs Withering tilted her head towards the mantelpiece. Anna walked over and reached for a picture of Aunt and herself when she was younger. 'No. The one to the right.' Anna realized she meant the picture of Aunt and her mother. She picked it up, hesitantly, and handed it over.

'Very sweet.' Mrs Withering studied it and then, to Anna's consternation, turned it over and began unpinning the frame. She removed the photograph and promptly tore it into four pieces, splitting her mother's face into quarters and scattering the pieces on the table.

Anna didn't cry out. She clenched her fists and found that her heart felt as if it had been torn along with the picture. The women watched with eagerness in their faces. Anna didn't dare look at Aunt. If she was enjoying this it would be too much to bear.

'Now make it whole again.' Mrs Withering sat back in her chair and stirred her tea. There were other clinks of china as the rest of the room followed suit, enjoying their refreshments during the show.

Anna didn't know what to do. Was she meant to try to bind the picture back together? Was she meant to fail or manage the feat? Perhaps she was meant to resist the task altogether to prove she was against the very idea of magic.

'Go on. We're all waiting.'

Anna pulled out a bundle of fresh cords, hands shaking, and selected four lengths of blue cord – blue for calm. Slowly she began to tie them together with Stitch Knots, trying to focus as the circle of eyes closed in on her. *My Hira is twine and thorn.* She could hear Mrs Withering's teaspoon grating against the edge of the cup; her loud, hot-tea breath.

She pulled the knots tight. Nothing happened. She wiped a sweaty palm against her dress, refocused and tried again.

'I can't tell if she's started yet or not?' said Mrs Aldershot. The others tittered with laughter.

'Anna, your poor mother!' Mrs Withering exclaimed. 'One of the only pictures left of her and you don't have the heart to put her back together again.'

Her words stung and brought with them feelings Anna had long tried to hide from. She looked at the torn pieces of her mother's face and felt a sudden, immense sadness. *I have always failed you.* She looked towards Aunt and there was something in her eyes that suggested she understood, that this charade, this mockery was hurting her too – but she did not move.

Anna tied another knot but the photograph remained ripped on the table.

'That's enough,' said Aunt.

Mrs Withering smiled with supercilious satisfaction, dropping the spoon into the cup with a final, violent tinkle. 'You were right, Vivienne. There is nothing to worry about. She is weak. That must be hard, Anna; your mother had no problem with magic, but then again, she was weak too, in her own shameful way.' Her mole was practically vibrating with pleasure.

Anna clenched her fists and shot her a look. *You don't get to talk about my mother!* Aunt always spoke about her mother's deficiencies, but she was allowed to – they were sisters. This woman had no claim on her. No right.

'But wait! There it is! The true Anna hiding behind the pale hair, I saw a glimpse of her then. Didn't I?'

Anna attempted to control the anger that had followed in the wake of the grief. She shook her head.

'That's right, girl, control yourself or we will be forced to bring your Knotting forwards. Considering this morning's events, the sooner you are knotted the better. Our old enemies may be stirring. Beware smoke on the wind.'

Anna looked up.

'Anna's Knotting will proceed as planned,' said Aunt. 'When she is ready. You know it can't be rushed.'

Mrs Withering screwed her lips into a tight-as-a-button smile. 'When she is ready, of course, Vivienne. You'd just better make sure she is ready soon.' She turned back to Anna. 'You do wish to join us, don't you?'

Anna surveyed the room – the circle of women with their preened hair and lipstick-stained smiles, goading and questioning – and felt them all to be hideous. They were most certainly mad.

'There would be no greater honour.'

'It is not an honour, Anna. It is a duty,' Aunt corrected sharply.

'Yes,' Anna agreed. 'I'm sorry. Shall I leave now?'

'Clear this mess up first.' Mrs Withering pointed at the torn pieces of the photo. Anna began to gather them up but Mrs Withering turned to the grate and with a flourish of her hands the stale logs sat within it began to burn, a small, concentrated fire. 'You can throw them in there.'

*Please, no.* 'Could I not just—'

'Throw them in the fire. When you become a Binder you will have to understand what sacrifice means.'

Anna walked to the fire and threw the pieces into the flames. The face of her mother curled and blackened. She turned back to Mrs Withering with the hardest smile she'd ever had to form.

Mrs Withering smiled back. It reached her eyes this time. 'Silence and secrets.'

'Silence and secrets.' Anna joined the others in their answering chorus.

'You may go now. We have serious matters to discuss,' said Aunt.

Anna turned to her and nodded. *How could you just watch?*

She made for the door as quickly as she could without actually running. It slammed shut behind her and she nearly collapsed against the wall. She had escaped. For now. But why would they move her Knotting? What did she have to do with six women hanging from Big Ben? Her ceremony had always felt like a distant threat, but Anna could feel it now, coming closer, hanging over her like a noose.

She would have given anything to hear what they were saying, what was really going on, why they were so disturbed by the news story, but she knew there was no point. When she was younger she'd often looked through the keyhole during their meetings, but it never revealed anything, only darkness. With her ear glued to the door, she'd never heard a sound. Just like the room on the third floor, whatever went on was enveloped in silence and secrets. It was not for her to know, not until she became a Binder herself. The thought made her feel cold and sick, but what choice did she have?

*There is no choice,* said Aunt, *it is either that or let magic destroy you.*

# NOBODY

*Weakness in feeling; strength in control.*

*Tenet Two, The Book of the Binders*

'Behave, work hard and stay away from Effie! And that boy! The risks are greater than ever. Remember, Anna, fine pearls make no noise.' Aunt assessed her for any last flaws she hadn't yet spotted and then gave her a perfunctory hug. 'Now go, you'll miss your train.'

Anna left the house, her new uniform uncomfortable, ironed into stiff lines. Black, white and maroon: the sixth-form colours. It would give her standing, make her conspicuous. She couldn't be conspicuous. *I'm a nobody.* She touched each of the six knots along her Knotted Cord, every one tight with emotion.

The last few days of the holidays had settled themselves back into their usual shape. Everything appeared the same as always and yet nothing was quite the same. Aunt was tense, not her usual, irritable kind of tense, but an erratic kind – energised and frenzied one minute, jumpy and snappy the next.

Anna hadn't been able to get the hanging women and the leering faces of the Binders out of her mind. The burnt-fear smell of their words. Aunt and the Binders had spoken of old enemies and threats and worse her whole life, so much and so often that it had become like background noise, like embroidery stitches forming a pattern she could not see and did not understand. But now it was different: a shock of real fear, like the prick of a needle.

There was only one threat the Binders truly feared. *The ones who know our secrets.*

She hadn't been able to stop thinking about Attis and Effie either, unsettled to find that she wanted to see them again. She just didn't want them to see her. They knew her secret – that she was a witch – and the thought made her feel dreadfully exposed. Anna was sure not even they were crazy enough to reveal their magic to ordinary people, but she didn't think they were going to be particularly careful either and she couldn't take those kinds of risks. She had Aunt to deal with, and the Binders ready to knot her at a minute's notice. There were reasons of her own too – she had to remain a nobody.

She walked through the quiet of their neighbourhood, past the uniform houses, the church in its expanse of graveyard, the tidy parks. Just before the station, she stopped outside the newsagents and picked up a newspaper from the rack:

### All gone cuckoo? Faceless Women mystery deepens

Despite the story's national coverage and more than 500 witnesses speaking to police, the identities of the women remain unknown. Police are calling on anyone who might have any information . . .

Anna scanned the article quickly. It contained several new grisly photographs but nothing of use. *How does no one know who these women were?* She put it back down and checked her watch. She needed to go.

Running the rest of the way to the station, she took the train to Dulwich. She briefly fantasized about not getting off at her stop, staying on the train until she found herself somewhere else, someone else, but before she knew it she was traversing the long driveway to the school entrance, cars roaring past and the cut-grass lawns sparkling green. The school reared up before her: a sprawling, red-stoned beast, grand and prowling as an old lion, all high windows and turrets and spires rising above the trees, looking as if it had been transplanted to London from the pages of a Gothic novel. It had in fact once served as a Victorian workhouse, a place where the poor were housed to work and die quietly. Behind its grand entrance doors lay a labyrinth of corridors, narrow and claustrophobic as a hive.

Fellow pupils stepped out of their four-by-fours, kissing mothers and fathers goodbye, but Anna didn't stop to greet anyone. She hurried to the entrance, finding her stomach in knots, just as it had been the first time she'd walked through the doors; after a childhood of homeschooling, she'd been so excited, so full of hope to be experiencing the real world, to be getting away from Aunt. *Now all she felt was dread.*

It wasn't that she hated school. She enjoyed her lessons, she was top of the class in several subjects, she loved escaping to the music room to play the piano – it was just all the rest of it. She had to stay focused, as Aunt had said. Get the grades, get into medical school. Even if she lived with Aunt forever, at least if she was a doctor she'd have something of her own life, her own independence, skills that could help people. It wasn't magic but perhaps it could be something like freedom.

The smell of polished wood greeted her, familiar as the navy carpets beneath her feet. Groups collected around her, friends seeking friends, constellations forming, drawn together by the pull of summer gossip. Whispers stirring. Phones beeping. Anna listened to it as she passed:

'Yeah, broke up but then he posted those pics of her—'

'I missed you! Where have you been all my life?'

'Not a virgin any more – the beach club toilets apparently.'

'Lost so much weight—'

'She's not coming back, not since Darcey shunned her.'

'Did you see the new girl?'

The air was feverish with excitement, a bubbling anxiety beneath the surface. The gossip mill had begun turning and everyone was required to make their offering.

No one batted an eyelid as she passed. Anna breathed out with relief.

*A nobody, still.*

She made her way to the Athenaeum – the main school hall – for assembly. It was an exceptionally grand room, with mahogany-panelled walls, stained-glass windows and a raised stage at the end; stiff-backed chairs creaked and groaned as the pupils took their seats below it. Anna quietly took a seat at the end of a row and looked out for Effie, but couldn't spot her among the crowds.

All grew quiet as Headmaster Connaughty took up his position on the stage, only just tall enough for the wooden lectern behind which he stood. 'Welcome back to St Olave's School for Girls. This year is the start of the rest of your lives . . .' He was as wide as he was short with a florid, shiny face, an inelegant combover and a bulbous nose. His speech – like all his speeches – was merely an excuse for him to discuss his own exceptional feats in life in getting to where he was today: head of one of the most prestigious schools in London: 'You must mould your ambitions! Just as I moulded mine and achieved greatness,' pounding his fists on the lectern, dabbing frequently at his melting forehead with a handkerchief.

Anna looked behind him to the prefects seated on the stage. Darcey Dulacey front and centre, scanning the rows of pupils before her regally, bone structure pure-bred pedigree, hair bronzed, make-up impeccable, a proprietorial smile and cruel eyes, judging and assessing. Anna felt her stomach churn with acid.

'Look at Darcey's tan,' a girl in the row behind started to whisper. 'Did you see her summer pictures from the Amalfi coast? Sickening . . .'

'All those couple selfies with Peter. Life's not fair.'

'Are they back together then?'

'Oh yeah, big time . . .'

Anna tried to block them out. So Darcey and Peter were back together – *what does it matter to me?* Peter wouldn't look in her direction, whether Darcey existed or not. Unfortunately Darcey did exist and there was no escaping her; everyone would be talking about her all day. She was smart, rich, exceptionally dressed, a talented ballerina, spoke Mandarin and ran the school student council, but all of that was merely an accessory to her main skill. Darcey was popular because she knew how to control the conversation, how to place herself at the centre of the gossip web – and how to ingest anyone who stood in her way.

'And now to introduce the new joiners this year. I hope you will make them all feel welcome and show them what it means to be an Olave's lady.' Headmaster Connaughty's chins wobbled. Anna hated how he always used the word *lady* as a weapon against them.

*Sarah Egerton.*

*Tiana Oakley-Smith.*

The new girls came up on stage one by one, receiving their school badge and shaking hands with Connaughty. Most looked uncomfortable and self-conscious; others rose with their head held high, fuelled by an air of self-entitlement. Darcey watched them shrewdly.

*Charlotte Robinson.*

*Effie Fawkes.*

Anna sat up at the sound of her name. Effie made her way onto the stage slowly, casually. She did not fit into either category. She wore the uniform as if it was a mere suggestion and her hair was loose, against regulations. Headmaster Connaughty looked at her with mild irritation. She held his hand for a few seconds longer than the others had, looked at him – right at him – until he almost seemed to recoil, and then she turned away and scanned the row of prefects as if they were faintly amusing to her.

As she left the stage it felt like she ought to carry on walking, out of the hall and to somewhere she belonged, for she did not belong here, not at St Olave's. Everyone else seemed to feel it too; whispers spread in quiet ripples. Anna saw Darcey strain to get another look. *She's got you worried.* Anna smiled and then hid it, lowering her head once more.

Afterwards, the lower years were led out, leaving only the sixth form. Headmaster Connaughty gave them all a knowing look. 'Now, as you are all aware, the final two years at St Olave's ceases to remain distinctly girls only and we welcome gentlemen from St Olave's Boys for mixed classes.'

Charged whispers sparked among the remaining pupils. Connaughty put up his hand. 'Control yourself, ladies. I know, it is overwhelming to be joined by the godsend that is the male sex.' His words writhed with sarcasm, but he straightened himself up taller, as if he clearly considered himself at the forefront of the male species. 'St Olave's Boys are also permitted to use your sixth form common room and dining area, just as you will be able to use theirs. However, canoodling or other inappropriate forms of relations on school premises will not be tolerated. Neither will any pregnancies.' Headmaster Connaughty laughed loudly at his own unsavoury joke before dismissing them, the whispers breaking free in an overbearing torrent of noise.

\* \* \*

The morning's lessons were full of introductions. New text-books, new teachers, new syllabuses and new scandal and slander to overhear. Anna listened, knowing that, without a phone, she was only hearing the surface of it. She was perturbed to find that Effie was already caught up in it, despite being a member of the school for a matter of hours.

'Transferred from NYC—'

'I heard she got expelled for drugs?'

'I heard she set the place on fire.'

'I heard she had an affair with a teacher . . .'

No one knew anything really but the gossip mill fed off lies; it could turn pure water to tar. *A shut mouth catches no flies.* That's what Aunt said about idle chatter.

Anna was doing her best to keep her distance from Effie but before lunch their whole year would be gathered together for the annual torture of the uniform inspection. Anna made her way to the allotted classroom, fiddling with her Knotted Cord, her dread increasing because as the head prefect of their year, Darcey, would be in charge – but Anna couldn't deny she was curious too, interested to see how Effie might fit into the hierarchy.

She slotted in at the back of the queue. Effie didn't appear to have arrived but Darcey was already in full swing – she and her usual accomplices, Olivia and Corinne, sitting on high stools at the front of the classroom, slurping on green juices as they picked over their victims. Darcey had the juices delivered every morning and you always knew who was in her inner circle or current favour by whom she gave one to. They were known as the Juicers.

'Necklaces aren't allowed,' Darcey declared. 'I'll have to confiscate it.'

'But it was a gift from my boyfriend,' the girl cowering in front of them attempted to protest.

'Sorry, do I look like a therapist?' said Darcey. 'We don't

have time for this. Hand it over.' Darcey put out her hand while the girl struggled to unclip the necklace.

She gave it to Darcey. 'Just – when will I get it back—'

'Next!' Darcey called over her.

'Lucie Brown,' Olivia read off the register in her mono-tone voice, before returning her attention to her phone. She rarely looked up from it. Olivia hadn't always been popular, but she'd worked and bought her way into the Juicers' circle with the ruthlessness she was renowned for on the lacrosse pitch. Deemed neither as attractive nor as charismatic as Darcey, she'd tirelessly transformed herself. Now she ran a fashion blog and had amassed a following who pored over endless pictures of her affecting various vacuous poses: short dark hair cutting into her cheekbones, lips pouting, designer outfits dripping off her tall, muscular frame. Once a girl had emulated one of her photographs and Olivia had sued her, successfully.

'Lucie, hi! You've changed – what is it?' Darcey smiled at her next victim. 'You've had your nose done.'

Lucie's cheeks reddened to beetroot.

'No need to be embarrassed, we all need a little help some-times. Your noise certainly did.'

'Suits you, gorgeous,' Corinne agreed, twizzling her dyed red hair, wearing her usual dreamy expression on her owl-like, blinking face. Corinne did her hardest to cultivate an aura of being a free spirit and friend to all. She ran the school Yoga Club, which had a members' only policy, and was always preaching vaguely in her breathy voice about the importance of the natural world, global warming and animal welfare, while seemingly doing very little about it.

Darcey flashed her phone in Lucie's face, taking a picture before she knew what was happening. 'I'll spread the word.'

'Rowan Greenfinch.'

A girl with a head of wild brown hair stepped forwards.

Anna knew her vaguely. They'd had classes together over the years; she was lively and talkative and liked to voice her opinions, but Anna normally agreed with what she said so it didn't tend to bother her. Standing before the Juicers there was no sign of her usual cheerfulness, just a defeated look on her face as though she knew her fate and had already accepted it.

'Skirt length?' Darcey nodded.

A lower prefect stepped forwards with a ruler and measured the skirt. 'It's fine.'

'Really? Check again.'

The prefect did as she was told. 'Yes, it's within the regulations.'

'Oh. Weird. It just looks shorter on her. Maybe it's like a proportion thing, because of the size of her thighs.' Darcey surveyed Rowan's legs. Olivia snorted over her phone.

'I get it. I'm fat. Ha ha.' Rowan attempted to smile along with their snide jokes as if they were of no concern to her.

'No, I won't hear it,' Darcey said sympathetically. 'Not fat, just unmotivated. I'm all for body positivity. Corinne, can't you give her a free pass to one of your yoga classes?'

Corinne smiled down at Rowan. 'I'm not sure there's space,' she said sweetly.

'You could order in bigger mats?' Darcey suggested.

'Extra air freshener, perhaps?' Olivia muttered audibly.

Some in the room began to laugh. Rowan's lip wobbled. Anna felt a surge of anger so intense she grabbed onto her Knotted Cord in her pocket to steady herself.

'On second thoughts, I don't think it's worth it,' said Darcey. 'Go on. Go. Keep down those portion sizes!' She gave Rowan a gesture of encouragement, then dispensed her empty juice cup to the minion prefect.

Corinne handed hers over too. 'Make sure you recycle that now!'

'OK, next!'

When Anna's name was called out she gripped her cord tighter and walked to the front, head trained to the floor. *I'm a nobody. A nobody.*

Darcey's eyes passed over her without interest. 'Do you still go here? Skirt length, fine. Heel height, fine. No jewellery. No personality . . .' she muttered. 'Next!'

Anna was so relieved she could have cried – if she'd had any tears left for Darcey. As she walked away she glanced up to find Effie watching her. She dropped her head again, feeling a wave of shame. *I did nothing but cower. But Effie doesn't know what this school can be like.* She'd had to learn the hard way.

In the beginning Anna hadn't understood the rules, hadn't known how to disappear. She'd attracted attention: the new girl with the insipid hair and the weird shoes, living alone with her aunt. Dead parents. Not a winning combination. She'd hoped to pass under the radar, make a few friends, work quietly, but the rumours had started quickly. Darcey, Olivia and Corinne had enjoyed the game, stirring, spreading them, calling her names, making sure any friends she'd made, she'd quickly lost.

*Such a freak – doesn't even own a phone.*

*Probably in a cult—*

*I reckon she killed her parents—*

*No, they took one look at her and killed themselves—*

Aunt had warned her, had said people like them would get noticed if they weren't careful, and she'd been right. Anna had used the only technique available to her: tucking herself away in her Knotted Cord, disappearing, becoming the nobody they all thought she was. The trick was, she gave herself nothing either: no anger, no self-pity, no tears. It had to work both ways; they had to see it in her eyes – that she wasn't there any more. Eventually they'd lost interest. There'd been no fun left in it.

'Effie Fawkes.'

Darcey called out Effie's name nonchalantly, but Anna knew better, that Darcey was waiting to laud her power over the girl who'd stolen all the attention on their first day back. A murmur travelled through the room as Effie walked to the front.

Darcey tapped her straw against her lips, looking her up and down. 'Your heels are too big. If they're not replaced by tomorrow I'll have to write you a detention slip.' Effie cocked her head and smiled. Darcey's eyes narrowed. 'And your skirt is too short.'

'Slut,' Olivia coughed.

'Me? Why, thank you.' Effie waved a hand, unabashed.

Darcey appeared unfazed by Effie's insubordination but Anna knew she would be furious. She walked up to Effie slowly, testing the waters. She flicked her finger at the collection of studs and hoops in Effie's ear. 'Really? We're not allowed to wear earrings.'

'You're wearing earrings.'

'I'm sorry, let me be clear, *you* are not allowed. What's more I know you have a tattoo. I saw it on your arm this morning.'

'Wow, was someone taking a close look at me? I'm flattered, I didn't know you like me that way, Darcey. I'm open to it.'

The sniggers came again but this time at Darcey's expense. She jerked her head around and was met by silent, guilty faces.

'Tattoos aren't allowed.' Darcey's voice sharpened. 'You'll have to get it removed or face expulsion, I'm afraid.'

'I don't have a tattoo.'

'I saw it. It was of a spider. Gross, if you ask me. It was at the top of your forearm.'

Effie pulled a face of innocent confusion.

'Pull up your sleeve.'

'No.'

'Hold her arm,' Darcey barked at one of the prefects. They gave Effie a look as if to say, *Please make this easier.* Effie rolled her eyes and put her arm out. Darcey pulled up her sleeve. Everyone had grown tense and quiet, leaning forward to get a closer look.

There was nothing there.

'It must be on the other one.'

Effie rolled up her other sleeve, revealing nothing on that arm either. A few people laughed. Anna found herself stifling back a laugh of her own.

'Probably some scabby temporary thing then,' Darcey snapped irritably, looking unconvinced.

'Sure, why not.' Effie smiled at her curiously. She made to leave.

'Wait there.' Darcey regained her composure. 'Your hair.'

Effie turned back with a look that suggested the entertainment value of this little game was growing thin. In that moment, Anna wasn't sure who was the more unsettling of the two.

'It's too long.'

'I'll tie it up.'

'No, it needs to be cut – it's matted and dirty. When did you last wash it? I'm sorry but that's a health hazard. If it isn't gone by tomorrow then I'll have to give you a week's detention.'

Effie took a long hard look at Darcey and then walked over to the teacher's desk and lifted a pair of scissors from the pot. She turned to the crowd and began slicing through her hair. It fell away in thick, black shards. Darcey's mouth dropped open. Shocked whispers ran through the onlookers.

When Effie was finished the remaining hair fell to her shoulders. It didn't even look bad – the length and sharp angles suited her. Holding a mound of hair, she walked over and offered it to Darcey, who, still in shock, took it.

'You can wash it yourself.' Effie smirked and walked off.

Darcey stood frozen. No one else moved either.

Her hand opened and the hair dusted onto the floor. She turned to the rest of them vehemently. 'If any of you thought that was amusing, rest assured, she's going to spend the rest of term in detention and if I see you laugh again, Jane, your boyfriend will be finding out exactly what you got up to this summer. NEXT.'

Anna made her way to the sixth-form common room at lunch. It was the first time she'd ever been in it. The space had been designed to feel informal, with sofa areas and tables to sit and eat at or work at. There was a canteen at the far end serving food. It was busy and loud. Anna collected her lunch and walked through the crowded room as quickly as possible, taking harbour at a distant table. She took out a book and listened to the discussions around her – everybody was talking about the uniform incident. Anna shook with sudden laughter as she recalled the look on Darcey's face. Some girls from the next table glanced over and she shrank further behind her book. She shouldn't be laughing. Effie was getting herself noticed and people like them couldn't be noticed.

When Darcey, Olivia and Corinne arrived they were surrounded by a small army of the year's most popular boys, booted and blazered. Anna spotted Peter among them and her stomach exploded with small butterflies. *Ridiculous.* She ought to knot their wings.

Still, he looked better than ever: tall and lean, that clean, healthy, fresh-air look, his blond hair lightened by the sun. There was an intelligence to his face, something in the set of his jaw, the knot that gathered between his eyebrows and his blue, quizzical eyes that kept a careful distance, as if he didn't accept the world as it appeared to him until he had reflected on it himself. He was unbeatable on the school debating team and competed internationally in swimming. He was on track for a place at Oxbridge but was going to take a year out to travel and carry out volunteering work first. Anna had gleaned all this despite having never exchanged a single word with him.

They took up residences at a table, Olivia returning to her phone and Corinne settling on one of the boy's laps. Darcey made it clear that Peter was hers; she sat with one hand on his knee and an arm over his chair, throwing her head back with laughter and flicking her caramel hair side to side. Anna couldn't understand how he liked her – how he couldn't see through her. Then again, Darcey was beautiful and accomplished, their parents moved in the same circles, and he didn't know her like Anna did. As she'd grown older Darcey had learnt how to hide herself too; her true nature buried beneath artful, tooth-whitened smiles, her sharp words coated in sugar.

Effie and Attis entered. A dark-haired, dark-eyed alliance.

The room hushed. Heads turned. Effie answered the stares with a challenge of her own. Darcey carried on talking but glanced over several times, her eyes travelling up and down Attis's tall form.

He appeared to be entirely unfazed by the attention, jovially slapping some new friend on the back as he passed. They turned towards the food and he said something that made the serving man laugh. Effie collected her meal and turned around. Her eyes met Anna's. For one horrified moment Anna thought she was heading for her table but she veered off and sat at one in the centre. Attis followed her path, also catching Anna's eye. He waved at her – the sort of wave a mum would give her child on their first day of school. Startled, Anna waved back.

She glanced at Darcey, who looked right at her and blinked, clearly wondering what on earth the Nobody had to do with them. *Nothing! Nothing at all.* Anna shrank further into the corner. *Why did he have to wave? To humiliate me!*

'Excuse me.' A voice sounded to the side of her. 'Is this seat taken?'

It was Rowan and she was already pulling out a seat beside her with loud and attention-attracting noise. 'So.' She pinned Anna down with intense eyes hooded by thick pipe-cleaner eyebrows. 'Do you know him?' She nodded unsubtly towards Attis. 'The one with the come-hither-and-have-sex-with-me-now face. My, he's . . .' She made a biting motion with her mouth. 'I mean, we need to talk about this. What's his name? How do you know him?' Her hair was somewhere between curly and frizzy, as manic as her general demeanour.

Anna began shutting her books. She needed to go. She thought about running out without replying, muttering some apology, but Rowan seemed back to her normal, chirpy self after the cruelties of the uniform inspection, and Anna didn't want to make her feel bad again. 'Attis. I don't know him. I just met him once, and her, Effie.'

'Oh, so they're a thing then – her and him, him and her?'

'I don't know. I have got to go, though—'

'Well, how did you meet them? What was he like? He has a kind smile. Ugh, look at Darcey, she's eyeing him up for sure. She'll have her claws into him in no time, claws, talons, beak, the whole works, but then, after what happened this morning – *can you believe what happened!* – Effie can obviously handle herself, with or without scissors. Either way, it's going to be an interesting watch. We should get the popcorn ready.' She elbowed Anna playfully. 'I'm sorry, I'm harassing you, aren't I? I do that. Mum says I have no boundaries. You're Anna, right? I think we have a class together. I'm Rowan.'

Anna was surprised she knew her name. 'Yeah, Anna, nice to meet you.'

'All right, Miss Formal, shall we shake hands? I'm joking,

don't actually put your hand out.' She batted Anna's away. 'Now, shall we go over there and say hello to him? Bad idea. That's a bad idea right? It's not as if people like us' – she pointed back and forth between them – 'can just mosey on over to people like them. I hate the rules. Where are you going?'

Anna had started shuffling out from behind the table. 'Class, sorry, but if I ever talk to him again, I'll put in a good word for you.'

'Don't you dare say *Oh, she has a bubbly personality*. That's what they always say about the fat girl. Tell him I'm super flexible.'

'Sure.'

'And super chilled.'

'OK.'

Anna waved an uncomfortable goodbye and made a beeline for the exit, not looking back. It had been far too dangerous in there. The whole day had been far too dangerous.

*Whispers divide; in secrets we thrive.*

She went to her locker, deciding to head to class early where she could sit alone, unaccosted. When she opened it there was an apple perched on the shelf inside.

It stared back at her, round as an eye, red as a kiss.

Anna couldn't remember putting an apple in her locker; in fact, she definitely hadn't put an apple in her locker. She looked up and down the corridor but no one was around. Panic blossomed. *How did it get there?* It had been locked. Only she had the key. *Some new school healthy-eating policy? A prank? Or – something worse?*

She reached in tentatively, plucking the apple out. It looked to all intents and purposes like a normal apple. She turned it around and there, carved into the flesh, was a message, small but direct: 'Who are you?'

Anna stared at the words for a moment and then went directly to the bin. She threw the apple in and fled to the music room. She leant her head against the cold wall, thinking with unease of Effie's smile, Attis's wave. *Was it them? What does it mean? Who are you?*

*I'm a nobody. A nobody!*

# APPLES

*The Goddess of Silence and Secrets knows all. Lie to yourself and you lie to her.*

The Goddess, The Book of the Binders

Anna sipped at her glass of milk and surrendered to Aunt's hair-brushing.

'I tried to get hold of Selene but she's disappeared again. Probably off with some man. You could never leave her alone with a member of the opposite sex and expect her not to go chasing. The worst kind of woman.' Aunt caught a knot in Anna's hair and wrenched the brush through it. Anna hid her disappointment. She was surprised Selene had left so soon, but then it was Selene. Effie and Attis were still here so presumably she'd be back. 'Does she feel no sense of responsibility? She's left that girl on her own, free to do as she likes. How *is* Effie getting on?' Aunt's eyes landed on Anna's in the mirror.

'Fine. I barely see her,' Anna lied.

It had been over a month since the start of term – since Effie's explosive introduction – and nothing significant had happened. Everything had changed. Anna had been careful not to interact with Effie in any way but she'd found herself becoming attuned to her movements: what classes she had, when she ate lunch, the points in the day when their paths might cross. They did not speak but sometimes caught each other's eye, regarding the other with a mutual, guarded curiosity. Although what Effie could ever find interesting about her, Anna didn't know.

'I hope she and that boy are not drawing attention to themselves.'

Anna almost laughed out loud. Attention was the only thing that Effie and Attis had drawn to themselves. For reasons Anna couldn't fathom, Rowan had taken her on as an ally, delivering her a daily dose of gossip. Only that morning she'd come up behind Anna and whispered: 'Cold showers,' in her ear.

Startled, Anna spun round to find Rowan, hair flying in contradictory directions. 'What?'

'The number of cold showers I've had to take thinking about him.' Her gaze was fixed down the corridor where Attis had appeared, chatting to a group of girls. 'I know I'll never even get close enough to smell his aftershave but still I can dream, right?'

'Sure.'

'Ergh, everybody loves him. Did you hear he got into the rugby first team? Strolled right into trials and impressed them so much he got a position.'

'I'd heard something along those lines.'

'I'd hoped he was going to be so much more than another dim-witted rugby shirt but he doesn't seem to amount to much in class, does he?'

Anna had English with Attis. They hadn't spoken but sometimes he acknowledged her with a smile or a wave or, worse, a wink. He generally turned up late, leisurely and unkempt – shirt untucked, clad in a pair of grey jogging bottoms that were just about the same grey as the official school trousers – and then simply sat back and listened. He didn't appear to take any notes or own any books. A couple of times she'd caught him sleeping.

'Did you hear about the initiation? Apparently he drank the team under the table and he was tasked with stealing the rugby mascot from their rivals at Dallington without any clothes on.' She raised her eyebrows. 'Dallington's mascot is a goat. A live goat! And, get this, apparently it's disappeared. *Can you imagine?* I mean, I've imagined that boy naked but never with a goat. *If* he did it. Not even our team knows if he did it because Attis isn't claiming anything. And did you hear about him and Marina? Caught in the storage cupboard . . .'

So much for no canoodling on school grounds. Anna had never found someone so infuriating. He barely tried and yet almost everyone seemed besotted with him. Anna could see through his so-called charm – but to what she wasn't sure. Not that her feelings were relevant; he didn't appear to want to get to know her and he already had plenty of women occupying him. *What does he want with them anyway, when he's got Effie?*

'I'd get in a cupboard with him any day, although, as Mum says, he's the type to leave you thirstier than a willow tree.'

'What?' said Anna.

'You know, onto the next one. Apparently, he's out with Chelsea tonight – she's been all over him for weeks, but I heard she's terrified of Effie. Isn't everyone? She "accidentally" hit Olivia in the nose yesterday with the netball. It was kind of funny, actually. I really thought Attis and her were a thing, but obviously not – she's got plenty of her own interests anyway. I just wish she hadn't gone out with Tom cocky Kellman. He's claiming all sorts – ugh – that guy, obviously he wanted to be the first to mark the Effie territory. Darcey's playing it all up, of course. Anyone would think

Effie had slept with half the school from the things they've been calling her, not that she seems to care . . .'

Anna had heard as much. No one quite seemed to know what to make of Effie and the rumours swirling around her had taken the unimaginative turn into the realms of *what a whore* and *slut much*, the only category they seemed to have for a girl who scared them. Anna didn't find it particularly fair considering Attis seemed to have hooked up with far more people and no one was calling him anything. Still, Effie didn't seem to care; in fact, she appeared to enjoy playing up to all their insinuations.

'You know a lot of things,' said Anna.

Rowan had barely taken breath and her cheeks seemed to be already filling up ready to unleash another instalment. 'I have an incredible memory for crap. Now, as I was saying—'

'I have to go to class.' Anna began moving away from her.

'Don't pretend like you don't love it!'

'You scare me,' Anna had shouted back with a hint of a smile, picking up her pace. She had got on perfectly well without any friends – she didn't need one now.

'There has been no magic?' said Aunt, bringing her attention back to the mirror.

Anna kept her gaze steady. 'Of course not.'

It wasn't entirely a lie. There had been no outright magic, but there'd been another apple. It had appeared a week after the first. A juicy, red apple with the words 'Take a bite?' carved into its delectable skin. Anna was sure it was them – Effie or Attis; no one else would have a way into her locker and they were the only witches in the school, at least as far as she knew. Aunt talked little of other witches or how many there truly were; there was just the general sense of division: of witches who were like them and witches who were not – those who would drag them all to their doom if left free rein. *Could there be others?*

Anna had held the apple at arm's length, as if it was more likely to bite her, and had thrown it in the bin before fleeing down the corridor, unable to get the mouth-watering summer scent of it from her nose. She could almost smell it now in the cold dark of her room.

Aunt yanked her hair sharply. 'Anna, are you even listening to me?'

'Sorry, what?'

'I said: There can be no magic! We can't risk any kind of exposure at this time.' She elucidated no further. Anna's initial horror of the hanging news story had faded but her curiosity had not. It wasn't front-page news any more but people were still asking questions, though there were, as yet, no answers.

'I thought things had settled down?'

'Settled? You think something that has been building for centuries has simply settled down?' Aunt replied ominously. 'The fire has only just been lit. The Hunters may yet be rising.'

Aunt made a knot in the air and Anna's hair tied together as a shiver crept down her spine. *The Ones Who Know Our Secrets, the Hunters* . . . Aunt had spoken of them before but never so vividly, never so urgently.

'Just stay away from Effie. I know who she is and what she's capable of. I gave up everything to raise you – don't make it all for nothing.'

'I won't,' said Anna, feeling the lies on her tongue – they were only small, but still, the guilt of them was heavy. *If we don't have trust, we don't have anything.*

'And what of boys? Any who have taken your interest?'

Anna wasn't expecting that. 'No.' It was hardly a lie; she had no intention of involving herself with any boys.

'You must tell me if you develop feelings for anyone. Lust is an animal response,' said Aunt, but she wasn't looking at her. She was looking at herself in the mirror. 'Heart beating fast, sweaty palms, tongue tied. It's nothing more than the desire for sexual gratification. A chemical reaction. Testosterone and oestrogen coursing through your body.'

Anna had never wanted to hear the words *sexual gratification* come out of Aunt's mouth. She felt her face burning.

'The pupils dilate when a person sees someone they are sexually attracted to. Lust lives inside the eyes, Anna, and so do lies. Don't lie to me.' Aunt looked back at her. 'They called your parents' death a crime of passion. Did you know that? Passion was their poison.'

After Aunt had gone, Anna lay in bed trying to get the scent of apples from her mind. Some time in the early hours of the morning she heard a door opening: Aunt leaving her room. Anna stilled, listening. The footsteps were moving further away. Up. To the room on the third floor. The room that Anna was not allowed inside.

*Where are you off to tonight, dearest Aunt?*

Over the years her desperate curiosity had drained away, but it still bothered her that she wasn't allowed in the room, that Aunt claimed it was for nothing – a room full of Binders' documents, and yet she only ever visited it at night. *Who does admin at two in the morning? So much for lies.* Anna listened harder but the sounds died away. She was met with nothing but silence. *Silence and secrets.*

The next morning Anna opened her locker with a surge of dread, thinking of Aunt's threats and warnings. There was nothing out of the ordinary inside. *I'm getting paranoid . . .*

A voice she knew distracted her. She peeked past her locker door and there he was: Peter Nowell, several feet away, talking to a group of people. He looked briefly in her direction and Anna hid back behind the door, feeling her heart rate rise, her palms turn clammy. *Testosterone and oestrogen coursing through your body.*

'He's just so dreamy.' A lilting voice, so close it tickled her ear. Anna spun round to find Attis behind her, eyes amused. One was darker than the other, like two puddles, one caught in light and one hidden in shadow. It was the first time he'd spoken to her.

She slammed her locker door shut. 'I was just putting my stuff away,' she retorted.

'Oh right. I thought you were drooling over Mr Goldilocks.' Attis nodded unsubtly in Peter's direction. His accent lent a music to his words that made his sarcasm sing all the more. Anna could feel herself turning red. She went to reach for her Knotted Cord but found that it was more gratifying to be angry at him. 'Want me to set the sprinklers off above him? Get his shirt all wet? Could be sexy?' Attis continued, producing a paperclip between his fingers. Anna noticed that the tips of his fingers and the skin around his nails were black.

She remembered Effie's words from the dinner party with sudden dread. *Attis put an iron hex on an ex of mine.*

He began to shape the paperclip into some sort of symbol, eyes on the sprinkler. Anna batted it from his hand and jumped into a side corridor. 'What are you doing? You can't talk about magic – you certainly can't do magic!'

'If you've got it, flaunt it. Quickly, act natural,' he said with sudden urgency, putting his arm on the wall behind her. Peter and his friends passed by, not noticing them. 'Phew.' He wiped imaginary sweat from his brow. There was the faint scent of warm smoke about him.

She pushed him away, more irate than before.

'What? I was thinking on my feet. If they saw us together – two casters – what would they have suspected? We could be doing magic right now. Magic might be doing us. Danger is everywhere.' He scanned the corridor with narrowed eyes.

'My life was fine two minutes ago and now you're in it.

Please piss off.' Anna had never told anyone to piss off. It felt good, especially directed at him. The bell rang.

'Can I offer you an arm to assembly?'

Anna gave him a threatening look. 'You don't go to our assembly.'

'A pity.' He smirked and turned down the corridor, gaggles of girls looking at him as they passed. Anna rolled her eyes at the world.

She'd heard so many girls talk about him but he seemed to be a different version of a man to every adoring fan: from prince charming to sensitive free spirit to dangerous bad boy. It seemed to Anna that in all cases Attis was merely a mirror of their own desires and she had no doubt he had manipulated it to be so. His boyish good looks, his imposing presence, his playful smile had made him an instant favourite. It was a convincing performance but it was all distraction. His eyes gave him away. They were mirrors: grey, smiling back at the world, but ultimately empty. No one knew who he was at all. Especially not her.

She walked back to her locker, having not yet dropped off her bag. She opened it and choked back a scream.

There was a third apple inside.

She closed it shut. *Attis?* But it had been shut the whole time and he hadn't gone near it. She thought of his smirk with unease. It had to be them. Effie. Attis. Attis. Effie. *What the hell were they up to?* A flare of anger quickly followed her fear. *This is ridiculous.* She wouldn't let them intimidate her!

She yanked her locker open again, stuffed her bag inside and took out the apple. There was no message on it this time. Nothing but the apple itself, its skin freckled and gleaming red. She marched to the bin, intending to dispose of it immediately. It was warm to the touch; she could smell the juices beneath it, sweet and crisp, as if it had rolled off a tree in some dewy orchard that morning. She wondered how it might taste.

*No! What am I thinking?* She dropped it into the bin. Only when she looked down, she found it still in her hand. She tried again, but her hand would not let go. *Just a little taste . . . it won't hurt . . .* She raised the apple to her mouth. Something inside her tried to fight it but as soon as her lips touched it, she knew it was too late. She took a deep and satisfying bite.

It was as delectable as she had imagined, toffeed by the sun, cut through with sharp shards of sunlight. She almost went to take another bite but then realized with throat-clenching horror what she'd just done.

She leant over the bin and spat the half-eaten flesh out of her mouth, dropping the apple in after it. The juice was sticky on her hands, but she had no time to wash them – assembly was starting in two minutes. She fled down the corridor, still tasting the sweetness in her mouth, and something else . . . *Magic?*

The hall was full by the time she arrived. Headmaster Connaughty was already on stage but he didn't notice her creep onto the end of the front row. Anna glanced around, spotting Effie several rows back. Effie caught her looking and smiled. Anna turned away, disturbed by that smile.

When they'd finished singing their morning hymn, Headmaster Connaughty told them a story about a lesser-known pioneer from the civil rights movement who was arrested after refusing to leave a restaurant, somehow managing to relate the victim's struggles to his own battles in becoming a headmaster: 'You have to stick to your principles and even when everyone else is telling you no – say yes! When they say that you are only deputy-head material, you don't have it in you to run a school . . . well, look at me now!'

Once finished, he locked his hands in front of himself and affected a solemn look, chins descending into one another. 'And now the part of assembly that I don't look forward to. The Detention Roll Call.'

He secretly loved his little discipline method: calling all those due a detention onto the stage so the rest of the school could be made aware of their transgression. Effie was becoming a common fixture:

*For skipping class . . .*

*For attempting to bribe a teacher with chocolate pretzels . . .*

*For skipping detention . . .*

*For aggravated behaviour during the school uniform check . . .*

He began reeling off names, girls scurrying up on stage red-faced. 'And finally,' he huffed, 'Effie Fawkes, for stamping on an item of teacher's property. Two weeks of evening detention.'

The crowd broke into murmurs. Effie walked onto the stage, but before she took the slip she turned towards the audience and shook her head penitently.

'I'm sorry, Mr Connaughty, and I'm terribly sorry to Mr Tomlinson too for stamping on his wig.' The crowd giggled in response. 'As I explained, it had fallen off his head and I only stamped on it because I thought it was a rat. If he requires a new hairpiece I told him I'm happy to buy him a new, more tightly fitting variety, one matching the colour of his hair this time perhaps?' She smiled benevolently. The laughter grew louder and Anna realized she was laughing along with everyone else.

'That's enough, everyone! If you don't remove yourself off this stage right now, Miss Fawkes, it'll be two months of detention.'

'I'm sorry, Mr Connaughty. You are welcome to come with us if you want? To the wig shop . . .' Effie took a look at his thinning hair, which had been formed into an indelicate combover. Connaughty's whole face vibrated with jelly-like rage. The laughter swelled and Anna found herself caught up in it. It was strangely freeing. She threw her head back and let it rise from within her.

'Everyone be quiet!' Connaughty yelled. 'Whoever makes the next sound will be joining Miss Fawkes in detention.'

The laughter faded then, but Anna found she had so much left in her it was impossible to stop, as if she'd kicked the lid off a deep well and there was no way of putting it back on. It was erupting out of her in great waves, rolling belly laughs and gurgling giggles.

She wasn't the only one. There was laughter coming from elsewhere . . . Anna looked around through watery eyes and saw that Rowan was at it as well. She was chortling away to herself, touching her head as if to mimic putting a wig on, every time releasing a loud snort.

There was a high, piercing noise too: Miranda Richards, who was quivering with quiet intensity, doing her best to hold back the laughter, but high-pitched reverberations escaped from her like steam from a kettle. Anna couldn't have picked out anyone less likely to be openly laughing during assembly.

Miranda was a law-abiding student, so much of a goody two shoes that she got on the nerves of most teachers. She ran several lunchtime clubs, including Craft Club, Bake-a-cake Club, Pen-a-poem Club and Bible Study. Anna couldn't believe it – *Bible Study Miranda!* – but then she couldn't really believe that she was still laughing.

*Why am I still laughing?*

'GIRLS, IF YOU DO NOT STOP YOU WILL EACH BE VISITING MY OFFICE AFTER ASSEMBLY.'

But Headmaster Connaughty's anger was hilarious. Anna tried. She tried desperately to halt the eruptions. She put her head down but her shoulders jumped up and down and it escaped through pursed lips. She couldn't even remember what she'd originally been laughing at. It was the whole world, the whole world seemed utterly ridiculous, and the very fact that she was alive and walking amongst it was the biggest joke she'd ever known. Rowan let out a monumental snort.

'YOU, YOU AND MIRANDA RICHARDS, ARE ALL DUE IN MY OFFICE RIGHT NOW. ASSEMBLY IS DISMISSED!'

Anna's stomach hurt, her jaw felt as if it was going to fall off, she could barely breathe – *please stop*. She fought with as much strength as she had, clenching her stomach, trying to take in deep breaths and, although the giggles still bubbled, the overall feeling began to pass. It was only then that she could begin to comprehend what had just happened. Sixteen years of repression under Aunt's rule and she'd finally flipped. That had to be it. But she hadn't been the only one . . .

Effie appeared in front of her. 'That was quite a display for someone normally so quiet. You obviously needed a release.'

'You!' said Anna, eyes growing wide. 'The apple—'

'I don't know what you're talking about. You better get going, Connaughty's waiting for you.' She smiled, the flash of cunning in her eyes telling Anna all she needed to know. *It was her. She did this! Why is she trying to ruin my life?* Anna wanted to shout and scream at her. Effie hadn't only brought magic into the school, she'd turned it into a big, public spectacle: the kind that raised suspicions, the kind that would make the Binders threaten murder. Everything Aunt had warned her against. A sudden, hysterical laugh burst from Anna's lips. She clamped her mouth shut, tasting apple.

Rowan grabbed Anna's arm. 'What just happened? We're dead! Connaughty's going to string us up, I know it. Seriously though, what just happened?'

'I – I – don't know.'

'We'd better go,' she said, her voice hoarse and miserable. 'You coming, Miranda?'

Miranda was still frozen in her seat, the little chin dimple in her heart-shaped face wobbling, tears running down her cheeks. She had the kind of face that might have been easy to like, but there was something haughty about it – the way her nose turned up and the way she held her head too high as if everyone around her was privately distasteful to her. She raised it higher. 'Not with the likes of you. I'll go on my own.'

'Suit yourself.'

'Have fun.' Effie waved as Anna and Rowan made their way out.

'People are staring, aren't they?' Rowan asked.

Anna looked around at the emptying hall and nodded.

Rowan groaned. 'Can't blame them. We just lost our shit in front of the whole school. It was like – like I couldn't control it, like this thing had taken over me, like – well – something unnatural . . .' She gave Anna a strange look. 'I mean, hell, the whole wig thing wasn't even that funny. Actually, don't let me think about that, I don't want to start again.' A stray giggle ran free from Rowan's lips and she slapped a hand over her mouth, eyes panicked.

They reached the secretary's desk. 'We're here to see Headmaster Connaughty,' said Anna, afraid to open her mouth for more than a moment.

The secretary pursed her lips. 'Wait there a moment. I'll call you in, one at a time.'

They sat down and Rowan turned to her again. 'Did you – er – have anything in your locker this morning? Anything weird? Anything that wasn't supposed to be there?'

Anna widened her eyes momentarily, unsure what to say – what to give away. She shook her head. 'I didn't notice anything.'

Rowan gave her a searching look that made her feel exposed. 'OK. If you say so.'

'Miss Greenfinch, you can go in now.'

'Pray for me.' Rowan smiled. Anna put her hands together in consolation, feeling awful for Rowan as she disappeared into the room. She stared at the closed door, wondering at Rowan's questions – the way she had said *unnatural*. *How could she know anything?*

'Excuse me.' Anna heard Miranda say behind her. 'I'm here to see the headmaster. Miranda Richards.' Her voice wavered.

'Wait there.' The secretary pointed at the seat next to Anna. Miranda looked at her with open disdain and sat down, tying her black hair back into a neat ponytail. After a few moments she put her head in her hands and started to whimper.

'Are you OK?' Anna whispered, but Miranda fastidiously ignored her, then proceeded to cry harder.

After what seemed like hours Rowan was released, looking utterly deflated.

'You next.' The secretary pointed at Anna. Her heart began to hammer against her ribs, the taste of apple turning bitter. How could she possibly explain herself? She could hardly blame it on a piece of fruit. If Aunt found out . . . She didn't want to imagine it. Her life would be over. No, not over: *bound*.

Connaughty was sitting at his desk, his chair not pulled all the way in, to allow for his expanse of stomach, on which his fingers lay, looking as plump and shiny as slugs after the rain. His face was slug-like too, features drooping into one another. His eyes, though, were sharp against the formless-ness; they followed Anna to her seat. She sat down and gave him a smile, hoping that would help.

'Anna Everdell, is it?'

'Yes, Headmaster Connaughty.'

'I haven't had you in my office before, have I? I suspect it's because you are normally a very well-behaved girl. Which is why this out-of-character outburst concerns me all the more. Do you wish to explain yourself?'

Anna looked down. 'I don't know what happened. I can't explain it.'

He tapped his stubby fingers together. '*I don't know* isn't really good enough.'

'I'm sorry, Headmaster Connaughty. I promise it will never happen again.'

'Was this some sort of prank? Was it something to do with that Effie girl? Did she make you do it?'

Anna shook her head, despite her strong inclination that Effie had everything to do with it.

'I see. So you're telling me three students who have never put a foot wrong before are suddenly all visiting my office and it comes after Effie's little performance on stage? Wish I'd never let her in. It's not as easy to expel a pupil as they make out, all sorts of red tape these days, forms and bureaucracy, otherwise that girl would have been gone from day one.'

Anna held his gaze. 'It wasn't Effie.'

He walked around and sat on the edge of his desk, leaning towards her. Uncomfortably close. 'I can tell you're a good girl, Miss Everdell.' His breath smelt like wet slugs too. 'I suggest you don't end up with the wrong crowd. So many promising students lose their way at this age. Do you think I would have made it to where I am today if I had gone off the rails? The headmaster of one of the most prestigious schools in London?' Anna shook her head. 'But if you get caught up in anything else like this, I'll be finding a way to expel you instead, are we clear?'

If she got expelled Aunt would find out what she'd done. She'd be locked away at home forever. She would die doing correspondence practice with Aunt and no one would ever have known she existed. She'd never get the chance to live her own life.

'Nothing like this will happen again,' she promised.

'Good. However, I can't let it go without punishment.'

Anna clasped her hands together. *Please don't tell Aunt.*

'I want you to write me a five-thousand-word essay entitled "The Meaning of Respect" and attend a week of evening detentions starting Monday.' He took a long look at her. 'On account of this being your first misdemeanour, I won't send a formal letter to your parents, but I will trust you to tell them why you're going to be late every night next week.' He returned to his seat.

'I'll let them know,' said Anna, deciding not to tell him her parents were dead. It's not as though he cared. He wasn't going to tell Aunt. Nothing else mattered. Now she just had to find some convincing reason for why she would be late every night next week, which would be easier said than done. *Aunt always knows.*

'I suggest you go now before I change my mind.' Connaughty raised his short arms above his head and sat back, rearranging his sparse hair into an ineffectual combover. Anna felt a small bubble of laughter rise in her throat, she coughed loudly and ran out of the room.

'Miss Everdell.' He stopped her at the door. 'I expect to never see you in my office again.'

She nodded and left. Miranda was still weeping quietly to herself, face spotted with bits of tissue. Anna took a fresh tissue out of a packet in her blazer and offered it to her.

'I don't need anything from you, thank you very much.' Miranda swatted it away. 'You and your friends can stay away from me.'

'They're not my friends,' said Anna, but Miranda hadn't heard, she was already being called through for her reckoning.

# IRON

Our vision is a world purged of the sin of magic – the Great Spinner unspun; the Eye closed back up. Until this is achieved, we must carry out our duties: prevent magic from being discovered, protect our hearts from sin, and bind the Unbound. The greater our number, the greater our silence.

*A Binders' Duties, The Book of the Binders*

Anna remembered the sound of the stem snapping.

She had felt the sound in her body back then, when it had happened. Selene had broken one of Aunt's closed rose heads off the rose bush. Anna's heart had begun to pound with childlike confusion and fear, knowing that Selene had done something very wrong.

'Don't look so worried, matchstick.' Selene's voice had twinkled with her eyes. 'I'll cover our tracks. It's just a little game. Your aunt won't be back for hours – she'll never know. Here, take it.' Selene had held out the rose to her. Anna had been reluctant but Selene had insisted. In her hands the rose didn't feel so scary and Selene's smile was so encouraging . . .

The memory had been looping around Anna's head all day – one of Selene's games during her first visit, when Anna had first experienced magic.

'Now,' Selene had said. 'What does that look like to you?'

'A rose,' Anna had replied, not knowing if she was teasing.
'Describe it to me.'

'Um. . . it's red. Dark red. And pretty even though it's all closed up.'

'What does it feel like?'

Anna touched her finger along the petal. 'It's soft, like cotton wool, no, like Aunt's velvet cardigan, but different, more alive . . .'

'What does it smell like?'

Anna breathed it in. It was hard to know what it smelt like other than like a rose. 'It smells sweet, like the garden in summer.' She took another sniff. 'But – it smells dark too, like the night, like a secret . . .'

'How does it sound?'

Anna looked up at Selene, puzzled. 'It doesn't have a sound.'

'Are you sure?'

Anna held the rose to her ear and – though now looking back she had no idea how she'd done it – she remembered replying: 'It whispers, doesn't it? Like lots of whispers all at once, like questions, like, I don't know . . .'

'How does it taste?'

Anna frowned.

Selene pulled away an outer petal and took a nibble. 'See, perfectly fine. Go on, try some.'

Anna giggled and tried the edge of it. 'It tastes nice actually . . . like strawberries and marshmallows, like. . .' Anna had no words for the things she could taste. 'Like perfume, like midnight, like love . . .' She did not entirely understand what she was saying.

'Marvellous. Now. What did the taste feel like? What did the sound look like? What did the smell feel like? What did the look feel like? What did the feel of it sound like?'

Anna's seven-year-old mind had boggled.

'Don't answer out loud. Just focus on the questions. Hold

them in your mind all at once, let them become one.'

Anna remembered staring at the rose, trying to hold all of its . . . rose-ness inside her. After a while she'd called out. 'I can feel it! I can feel it! What *is* that?'

But that was where the memory began to fade. *What did I feel?*

'Magic.' Selene had clapped delightedly. 'You found the world of the rose. You see, everything has a world inside of it.'

Had the rose begun to open in her hands? Anna had a faint recollection of petals fanning open . . . The memory pulled at her, but she couldn't bring it back and she couldn't feel what she had felt then no matter how hard she tried. There was no magic left in it.

*No magic left in me.*

She couldn't remember ever being told off for the incident, which meant Aunt had not found out, and yet Anna felt that on some deeply buried level Aunt had known – that she always knew – every lie, every deception.

It was not a comforting thought as she trudged her way to her first evening of detention. The day had been hard enough – she'd had to ignore everybody commenting on her outburst in assembly, but it was the lie she'd spun Aunt that was really unsettling her. Over the weekend she'd told Aunt she wanted to attend extra study sessions after school. Aunt had only relented after Anna had insisted just how much they could put her ahead. She had a week to try them out – *so long as you're home before seven and not a moment later!* Anna still couldn't believe she'd got away with it but as she left the house that morning, she'd looked at the rose bush in the hallway, unable to shrug off the feeling that the roses were watching her. Sealed up, closed tight – but watching.

It was all Effie's fault. *That bloody magical apple! What does she want? Why did she do this?* Anna didn't want to contemplate the answers as she knocked on the door to the detention room.

'Come in.' A young, blonde-haired female teacher was sitting at the desk.

'Is this detention?'

'Yes, take a seat. Do your school work, no talking, no eating, no laughing . . .' She gave Anna a pointed look. 'You'll be released in an hour.'

Miranda was already working in the front row, a squadron of highlighter pens laid out on the desk. She studiously ignored Anna as she passed, raising her snub nose in the other direction.

Rowan swung the door open with a bang. 'Sorry, Miss Pinson.' She was out of breath. 'My last class overran and I didn't want to be late but then I needed the loo so I had to find a toilet – detention is not exactly a common occurrence for me. I mean I've had a few lunch ones over the years but not for anything serious. Once was for trying to take the school hamster home, but I wasn't stealing it, it just looked lonely and—'

Miss Pinson put a finger to her temple. 'Please take a seat.'

'Yes. I brought books. Wow, I am sweating.'

'No talking.'

'No talking.' Rowan dropped into the desk next to Anna.

Effie arrived late. Her black hair had grown quickly since she chopped it off, almost past her shoulders again.

'The starting time of detention is not a suggestion.' Miss Pinson glared. 'If you're late tomorrow we will extend your detention by another week.'

Effie turned around and smiled at them. Anna felt her anger subside a little, but then she saw what was in Effie's hand: an apple. She took a bite out of it with a crunch and sat down.

'No eating, Miss Fawkes.'

Effie placed the bitten apple at the end of her desk. Rowan and Anna looked at each other. *This is all just a game to her.*

The first few minutes passed in slow, seething silence, the only sounds the ticking of the clock and the scratch of Miranda's pens. Then, without warning, there was a loud thump. Anna looked up to find Miss Pinson's head slumped on the desk.

'Oh my God.' Anna jumped out of her seat and ran forwards. Effie started to laugh. Miranda started to scream.

Rowan took out her phone. 'I'll call an ambulance.'

Anna studied her. 'I think she's asleep.' The teacher was definitely breathing. Her eyes were shut and she murmured under her breath as if dreaming. Anna shook her shoulder lightly but she didn't wake up.

'She's going to be that way for at least the next hour,' said Effie, taking another bite of the apple.

'You . . .' Anna spun round to Effie. *She did this! In front of others – non-witches!* It would have been one thing if it had just been them in the room together, but this was unthinkable! Every Binders' tenet she'd ever been taught began screaming at her in her head.

She tried to keep calm. 'Look, we can just carry on with detention until she wakes up—'

'Oh, good idea,' said Effie. 'The teacher is sleeping, but let's just carry on like good little girls. Wait. I have another idea. We could do magic.'

Anna froze. Effie had said *magic.* Out loud. The word hung awkwardly in the air, at odds with the dull, institutional surroundings of the classroom. She made desperate eyes at her – *What the hell are you doing?* Even Selene would be mad. There were rules – you couldn't just go around talking openly about magic. Rowan shifted uncomfortably. Miranda, still holding a highlighter in her hand, looked terrified.

'Ice-breaker.' Effie laughed. 'You're all witches here. No

secrets, nothing spoilt. I've gone to a lot of trouble to get us all in detention together. Can't say it wasn't fun though.'

Silence followed. Anna's heart hammering in her chest. They surveyed one another. *Can it be true? Perhaps Rowan, but Miranda? A witch?* She'd once branded someone a follower of the Antichrist for swearing in class.

'Come on,' Effie rallied. 'You all want it; I know you do. You bit the apples after all . . .'

'We didn't choose that. You enchanted them!' Rowan folded her arms.

'Oh, but you did choose. You bit deep into the fruit of hidden knowledge. It seemed fitting.'

'You could have got us expelled!'

'It was just a little cantrip.' Effie sat herself atop one of the desks.

'Those apples – magic—' Miranda's voice shook. 'What's going on?'

Effie exhaled loudly. 'I've been watching you all closely. Rowan, you're a witch, from a family of witches, am I not right? Miranda, you've been upping all those desperate prayers in church because you suspect you have the Devil in you. Congratulations, you don't! You're just a witch. Anna, you might be one of the most subdued witches I've ever met but you are one. You know I know so you have nowhere to hide.' Effie twisted a finger at her. 'Now we've cleared all that up, shall we discuss the details of starting a coven?'

They were silent again. The teacher murmured under her breath. Eventually Rowan shrugged. 'Fine, I'm a witch, big whoop.' She looked at Anna apologetically.

That was when Miranda began to panic. She grabbed at the pens on her desk and started stuffing them into her bag. 'You're freaks! Freaks, the lot of you! What is this? Some kind of sick joke?' Her voice oscillated like the leg of a mouse in a trap, her mouth trembling. She looked over at the teacher fearfully, obviously torn between her desperation to leave and an inbuilt reservation about leaving without permission. 'If anyone has the Devil in them, IT'S YOU!' Miranda pointed at Effie, storming towards the door. The handle turned but it didn't open. She twisted at it frantically.

Effie made eyes at Anna and Rowan.

'What have you done?' Miranda cried, banging against the door. 'We're locked in here, it's locked! HELP! HELP!'

'Let her out, Effie, you've had your fun,' said Anna.

'But I really haven't. Let's give her a moment until she calms down.'

'WE'RE TRAPPED! THEY'RE TRYING TO KILL ME! HEEEEEELP!' Miranda ran over to the windows and started banging on them, but they were three floors up.

'Come on, Effie, this is ridiculous.' Rowan had obviously never tried to sound angry before – it didn't suit her.

'All I'm asking is that you hear me out,' said Effie, sounding entirely reasonable even though she'd just locked them in a room with an unconscious teacher.

'Miranda, Miranda.' Rowan went over to her. 'Stop freaking out. Let's just listen, then we can all go home.'

Miranda slumped against the wall and started to cry. 'Not if she kills us first.'

'No one is going to die,' said Anna, joining them. 'Let's not blow this out of proportion.'

'But she's doing it, she's locked us all in here with her satanic arts. She's going to force us to sell our souls to her!'

'I don't want your souls.' Effie stood up. 'I just want your attention.'

'I could think of a hundred more civilized ways you could have achieved that,' Rowan muttered.

'Isn't this fun though? Our first adventure as a coven.'

'We're not in a coven! I'm not a witch!' Miranda cried.

'Look.' Effie attempted to speak softly. 'Based on my observations I believe each of you is a witch. I could be wrong but it's unlikely. However, it's not the only reason I've brought us together. You aren't just witches – you're outcasts. The friendless. The forgotten. The ones who don't fit.'

'Why thanks, Effie, I'll make that my online bio,' said Rowan.

'Rowan, you're bullied for your weight and your . . .' Effie made an inarticulate gesture. '. . . general oddness.' She turned to Miranda. 'You're the Bible freak of the school, plus no one likes you.' She looked at Anna. 'You're just nobody at all.'

Anna knew it was true, that she'd purposefully made it so, but still, it wasn't easy to hear coming out of Effie's mouth. The others all had a reason for being the odd ones out, strong personalities that didn't fit into the school's popularity hierarchy, but hers was an absence. A space in the air.

'And I'm' – Effie put a hand to her chest – 'the one everyone's afraid of.'

'I'm not afraid of you!' Miranda shouted.

'Oh really?' Effie clicked her fingers and the lights went out.

Miranda screamed and started praying. Effie laughed.

'Effie, you're really not helping your case here,' said Rowan through the darkness.

The lights clicked back on. 'So as I explained: we don't fit. Maybe because we're witches or maybe because we're all just a bit messed up. Either way we've got nowhere else to go. But together – we could be part of something. We could help each other.' Effie was on a roll, as impassioned as Aunt speaking about the Binders. They both had a way of commanding attention while hardly moving at all, simply increasing the intensity in their voice, the depth of emotion in their eyes.

She moved towards them. 'Miranda, I know you're scared. You're scared of the things you've done, the times things have happened around you that you can't explain, but I can help you. I'm not asking you to turn away from your religion,

I'm just asking you to take a moment to look at the other parts of who you are. If you decide you don't like it, you can just leave. I know we're all frightened but we're curious too and there's nothing like the curiosity of a witch . . .'

'I'm not a witch,' said Miranda quietly.

'I know that you like how it feels when magic courses through your body.'

'I'm not a witch.' Miranda pulled her head up. Her face was contorted with anger, her hair coming loose from its ponytail.

'Prove it and you're free to go.'

'I don't have to prove anything to you!'

Effie sighed. 'Then it's going to be a long night.'

'How do we prove it?' said Anna.

'Iron.' Effie pulled at one of the many necklaces around her neck, selecting one with a star pendant on the end. 'It's iron. Attis made it for me.'

> 'Iron is the seeing eye.
> It sizzles when the witches cry.
> Red as blood, black as hell.
> What secrets shall the iron tell . . .'

Rowan recited the verse, then said, 'It's one of the old songs.'

'Indeed.' Effie nodded. 'Iron was used as a method of detecting witches back when they were hunted. Any bodily fluid will work – blood, saliva, tears, urine. If you're a witch it will make the iron spit and sizzle—'

'I told you she'd kill us! We're going to burn!'

'Get a grip, girl.' Rowan put a hand on Miranda's shoulder. She flinched away. 'You just have to spit on the iron. If you're a normal human nothing is going to happen.'

Miranda looked at the necklace as if it had been mined and forged in the depths of hell itself. Anna remembered her visit to the doctor's all those years ago, when Dr Webber had dropped her blood onto that metal disk – *was it iron?* It had sizzled.

'If you're not a witch, you're free to go,' Effie confirmed.

'I'll go first,' Rowan volunteered. Effie nodded and placed the pendant on the desk. 'I'd love to make this all dramatic and draw a knife down my palm, but . . .' Rowan leant forwards and spat on it. The moment her spit touched the iron it began to sizzle, rising up as steam. 'Yes.' She fist-pumped. 'Still got it.'

'Anna.' Effie nodded at the necklace.

Anna stood frozen. She couldn't just go over there and spit on the necklace. It was against the rules. It was dangerous. It was terrifying, but for the wrong reason . . .

What if she spat on it and nothing happened? *There's no magic left in me any more, remember?*

'Anna . . .'

It was impossible to think straight under Effie's unrelenting stare. Anna walked over to the desk, trying to reason sensibly with herself – if nothing happened that was a good thing, *wasn't it?* Effie would leave her alone and magic could forever be kept at a safe distance – an Aunt-approved distance.

'Come on,' Effie prompted. 'What have you got to lose?'

*Everything,* Anna thought as she leant over the necklace and spat.

It sizzled. Loud and clear and definitive. *Magic. It was* buried somewhere inside of her, still. Relief washed over her before she felt the shame, the stupidity, of her actions – revealing herself to a group of witches she didn't know and certainly couldn't trust. Aunt would kill her.

'Good, good.' Effie smiled a smile that Anna was not sure was for her benefit. She turned to Miranda.

'Just get it over and done with.' Rowan gave Miranda a gentle nudge on the back.

'You're all going to be sorry.' Miranda went over to the

desk, tearing up again. Anna felt bad for her. 'You'll all see.' She bent her head over the pendant, went to spit but stopped herself, shook her head, then bent over again and released a small sliver of saliva onto it. The pendant sizzled. Miranda jumped back, more shocked than anyone else. 'A trick!' she cried. 'It probably does that no matter whose spit touches it!'

Effie picked up the necklace and walked over to the sleeping teacher who was snoring peacefully. She stuck her finger in her mouth and wiped it on the necklace. Nothing happened. Miranda's mouth gaped.

'Also I saw you do a spell two days ago,' said Effie. 'Corinne made fun of you for doing an extra homework assignment. You wrote her name on a piece of paper and stabbed your pencil through it and she got a terrible migraine during class and had to go and see the nurse.'

'I did not!' Miranda yelled and then looked ashamed. 'I just wrote her stupid name on a piece of paper. Anyway, I can't be a witch, no one in my family is magical.'

'You sure about that?' said Effie.

'Yes,' Miranda snapped. 'My dad's family are from a small town in Shropshire and find anything beyond the realms of a magazine horoscope a bit too out there; my mum's from Richmond and basically runs the local Evangelical church. Her parents came here from Nigeria, but they brought over Bibles and crosses, not broomsticks and voodoo dolls! There's never even been the faintest suggestion—'

'Magical abilities are not necessarily inherited,' Effie interrupted. 'It does run in families, but not always. Sometimes it just finds you. Aren't you lucky?'

Anna wasn't sure if Miranda was going to start crying again. Rowan flung an arm around her. 'Come on, Manda.'

She sniffed. 'It's Miranda.'

'We're not so bad. My whole family practises magic and they're honestly a nice bunch of people, except my grandma

on my dad's side, she's meaner than a bramble in winter but
she can barely string a spell together any more.'

'I'm not going to force anyone to join this coven, but I
invite you to consider it,' said Effie.

'Why would you even want to hang out with us?' Miranda
scowled. 'As you said, we're the outcasts of the school.'

Effie shrugged. 'Witches are always outcasts, still better
than being a cowan.'

'What's a cowan?' asked Miranda.

'An ordinary person,' Rowan explained as if it was obvious.

'Plus, four witches are better than one.' Effie smiled.
'Together we can discover new languages, hone our skills.
It'll be like a support group for the magically inclined. Weekly
therapy. Holistic life-coaching with the odd ritual thrown in.'

Rowan laughed and Anna smiled. It felt good after the
intensity of the past forty minutes.

'Friday's detention can be our first proper coven-meet.
We won't cast any spells, just get to know one another.
Who's in?'

'What the Mother Holle,' said Rowan. 'It's not like my
social calendar is brimming.'

Effie looked at Anna. All she had to do was say no. *Just
say no. Why can't I say no?*

'I'll see how Friday goes,' she said, realizing she'd been
holding her breath. She was in detention anyway and had
already lied to Aunt – *what does one more lie matter?* She could
indulge Effie for now and then, once the week was up, find
a way to stay away from her forever.

Effie smiled briefly and then looked to Miranda.

'Of course not! You really think after all this and THAT'
– Miranda gestured towards the unconscious teacher – 'AND
THAT' – the locked door – 'that I'm going to join you freaks?
I'm not a witch.'

'OK, Miss In-Denial, you're free to go.' Miranda rushed

towards the door. 'But one last thing – I've recorded this little meeting of ours.' Effie pointed at a phone which was balanced against the apple on her desk. 'Out of genuine concern, I might have to send the video to your parents. My, my, they're going to be quite shocked. Did someone say exorcism?'

Miranda's hand quivered over the handle. She turned around, eyes aflame with hatred, chin dimple wobbling. 'You wouldn't . . .'

'Come to our next meeting and you'll never have to find out.'

A bang on the door made Miranda jump. A face appeared in the glass: Attis.

'Let me out,' she cried hysterically. 'Help! Oh help!'

Attis opened the door, assessing the screaming girl with interest. He held it open for her. Miranda stayed where she was.

'So how was the first coven-meet?' He smiled.

Miranda's eyes widened as she realized he was in on it too. 'You're the Devil come to lead us into hell!'

'I just brought snacks.' He held up a tub of chocolate rolls. Rowan started to giggle. The rest of them joined in. Anna thought she saw the hint of a smile appear at the side of Miranda's mouth, but if it had been there it quickly disappeared.

'Feed me.' Effie slouched back into her seat. 'This has not been easy.'

He strode over and began to massage her shoulders.

'I suggest you sit down,' Effie advised. 'The teacher is going to be waking up any minute.'

Miranda scurried back to her desk. Attis took a seat next to Effie, cramming several chocolate rolls into his mouth at once. 'Want one?' he asked through a full mouth, thrusting the tub in Anna's direction. She shook her head although she was starving.

Miss Pinson made a murmuring noise, then jolted upright,

a thin line of drool running down her chin. 'Whaoaap,' she said incoherently. Everyone was working quietly. 'Must have nodded off for a moment . . .' She registered the time on the clock with surprise. Her eyes fell on Attis. 'What are you doing in here?'

'I'm giving Effie a ride home.'

'Well, wait outside.'

He stood up, offering her some chocolate. 'Um, no thanks.' Miss Pinson wiped the drool off her chin self-consciously. 'Right. It's six, you can all go.'

Effie jumped up. 'See you all tomorrow.' She smiled and waved her phone at Miranda before leaving with Attis. Miranda dashed off to meet her mum, and Rowan and Anna made their way back down the corridor together.

'Well, that was interesting,' said Rowan. The school was eerily quiet after hours, the classrooms dark beyond their doors. 'A coven could be fun though and if he pops in and out every week in his training kit – well, I'm all in.'

Anna laughed, barely able to wrap her head around the fact they were openly discussing magic.

'I had sort of begun to suspect about you,' said Rowan.

'Really?' Anna replied, taken aback.

'I just kind of had a feeling. Did you not have an inkling about me?'

'Maybe. I don't know. My witch skills are not very honed,' Anna admitted.

'Well, now you have a full-on support group to help you.'

'I'm not so sure it's going to be the quiet support group Effie has sold us.' Anna gave Rowan a sceptical look.

Rowan nodded. 'I do suspect we have sold our souls.'

# SEWING MACHINE

*The power of Hira must not be given room to expand. It should be turned inwards, bound with twine and pierced with thorn; used only for duty and even then intolerable to bear.*

*Binders' Magic, The Book of the Binders*

On Friday morning the dreambinder above Anna's bed was unusually full of knots. She took it down and began untying them. It had been such a fixture of her life for so many years that she rarely wondered what secrets her dreams might hide – if they were as riddled with fears as her waking thoughts. She hadn't agreed to join the coven but even admitting she was a witch, the iron test, agreeing to tonight – *it's all so wrong.* Even if she did join the coven that brought with it a fresh crop of worries. *Will school change? Will I be able to remain anonymous?* The iron might have sizzled but *will my magic even work?* Exposing herself as a witch was one thing, but exposing herself as an impotent witch was another. *Better to be bound than a magical failure . . .*

She spent the day in a jittery state of agitation, her nose bleeding all over her notes in Biology. When detention finally came around, she stood outside the door thinking of all the ways she might be able to get out of it—

'Anna.' Effie appeared behind her, full lips, shadowy red, threatening a smile. Anna had noticed that Effie did not smile often, not truly. These half-smiles she wore were instruments she used to unsettle and cajole.

Anna held the door open and followed her in. Miranda was already there, working diligently, but the shadows beneath her eyes told Anna she wasn't sleeping either.

'Sit down, girls. Let's get this over and done with.' Miss Pinson looked as if she'd rather be anywhere else on a Friday night than here.

Rowan swung the door open with a bang. 'Sorry I'm late! I had to run across from the science building and it's dark out now. I ran into a tree. Got any weekend plans, Miss Pinson?'

'Take a seat, Rowan.'

They began to work and the minutes that passed were the slowest of Anna's life. She kept glancing up, expecting the teacher's head to drop at any moment. The teacher caught her looking again and frowned. Anna went back to writing nonsense on her notepad – and then the thud came. She looked up to find Miss Pinson's head on the desk as before.

Miranda screamed on cue.

'Please, no loud noises, I'm not in the mood,' said Effie, standing up. 'Are we ready then?'

Anna didn't know what they were meant to be ready for.

'What's taking you guys so long?' Attis appeared in the doorway, making them jump. Miranda sidled from her seat and made her way over to the door, looking as if she were en route to her own funeral.

'Where are we going?' Anna asked.

'Somewhere more private.' Effie gave her a devilish smile.

They wound their way back through the dark, empty corridors and then down several sets of stairs until they reached the lowest floor of the school – below ground. Few classes were held down there any more; it was cold and damp, the mildewed corridors even more claustrophobic than the rest of the school. Anna knew where Effie was leading them: to the old sewing rooms, where it was said the corpses had been stored back when the school was a Victorian workhouse.

'Miranda's not with us by the way.' Rowan nodded her head back down the corridor. Miranda had stopped in her tracks. Effie made eyes at Attis, who turned back. The rest of them carried on walking. Anna couldn't hear what he was saying to Miranda, only the soft, coaxing tone of his voice, a slight giggle from Miranda, and then the sound of their footsteps walking together after them. *Unbelievable! Is no one immune to him?*

Effie stopped at room 13B. Attis arrived and took out a strange key from the inside pocket of his blazer. It was small and white – frail as ivory. He inserted it into the lock. The door creaked open.

'And the award for the most terrifying classroom of all time goes too . . .' said Rowan as Effie flicked the lights on. A dull gloom filled the room, most of the lights had blown and the ones that hadn't lit up funnels of dust swirling over rows of wooden desks. The walls were bare and windowless. An old-fashioned blackboard stared blankly back at them.

Anna walked in and screamed. Someone was standing beside her.

'What is it?' Attis appeared by her side.

Anna realized with embarrassment that it wasn't a person – it was a mannequin.

'Nothing.' She breathed out. 'Just these.' There were five old sewing mannequins lined up against the wall – armless, with neat, hourglass figures and wooden knobs for heads. Attis picked out a dressmaker's pin threaded through one; another still wore drapings of material. It was as if they had been waiting all this time for their pupils to return, their dresses to be finished.

Rowan stared at the mannequins. 'You have to be kidding me.'

Effie laughed unapologetically. 'Coming in?' she said to Miranda in the doorway. 'Either that or you can wait out there by yourself.'

Miranda made a whimpering noise and stepped inside, eyeing the mannequins apprehensively. 'They're terrifying.' Her voice was full of disbelief, obviously wondering how she'd wound up here, among broken desks and old sewing dummies, with these people. Anna was wondering the same thing. She could feel the mannequins behind her, each one of them wearing Aunt's murderous face.

Effie swirled into the centre, laughing. 'Attis, clear a space.' He leapt into action, dragging desks to the sides. Effie placed a series of candles in a circle and, as she muttered under her breath, a flame burst from each of them. Anna wished she could perform a spell so simple. It changed the room, dissipating the gloom, bringing the walls to life with flickering light and turning the mannequins to silhouettes as if they were an audience watching on.

'Come on, sit down,' Effie urged.

Anna took a seat around the edge of the circle of light.

'I thought we weren't going to do any spells,' said Miranda warily.

'We're not really,' Effie replied. 'This is just a little magic compatibility test to see if we can work together as a group.'

'That sounds like magic to me.'

'Look, if magic was sex, think of this as foreplay. We're not going the whole way. Not tonight.' Effie raised a salacious eyebrow. Miranda looked more disgusted than ever.

Effie surveyed the room. 'Attis, bring that sewing machine into the centre.'

The machine was old and cumbersome but he carried it effortlessly to the centre. There was a power lead trailing from it which tapered into frayed wires and its needle mechanism was brown-red with rust.

'Does everyone know the basics of spell casting?' Effie asked.

Rowan nodded. Anna wasn't sure what to say. She only knew what Aunt had allowed her to know.

'No,' snapped Miranda. 'How would I?'

'Why don't you *spell* it out for us?' Rowan grinned. 'Get it?'

Effie groaned. 'Right. To cast you need three things. Magic, a language and Hira. Magic lives over here.' She held up one hand. 'And the physical world lives over here.' She held up the other. 'They don't speak the same language. Witches are the translators in the middle. We have to give magic a language to speak so it can transfer its energy to the physical world. We can't just provide a language though, we have to give it meaning, *belief*. That's where Hira comes in. It's the force within yourself that imbues the language with power.'

'What do you mean by language?' Miranda asked.

Effie bit her lip hungrily. 'There are many types of magical language – candle magic, for example.' She pointed to the candles. 'Or words, or song, or herbs and potions, or dancing, or the light of the moon, or the click of your fingers, or wands, or brooms, metal, crystals, trees, runes, circles and seals, blowing the seeds of a dandelion head or spirits from the land of the dead, or rituals which combine many languages into one. You choose.'

Miranda's cherub mouth formed an O shape.

'My family use living plants to cast our spells. It's been my language since I can remember,' said Rowan. 'What about you, Anna?'

Anna floundered. 'My aunt, she – um – uses mostly cords, knots . . .'

'Knot magic. That's hard.' Rowan nodded.

'How can I know what language I'm meant to be if no one in my family is a witch?' said Miranda.

'You don't necessarily follow your family,' said Rowan. 'Like, my cousin Tansy's family all work with shrub magic but then Tansy decided she wanted to focus on hedges. Big things can happen.'

'You don't *choose* a language either,' said Effie, foot tapping up and down. 'A language chooses you. Some witches know from seven – when their magic first comes in – but mostly it's around sixteen when our powers come to fruition; you'll start to feel drawn to a particular language. It's not like you can't use all the other languages out there, just that you'll excel at one.'

'I'd say connect,' said Rowan. 'You'll connect to one. I'm unlikely to *excel* at anything.'

Anna couldn't imagine any kind of choice. The Binders and their knots was the only path that had ever been open to her – all other doors were tightly locked. 'Do you know what your language is?' she asked Effie.

'Not yet.' She appeared irritated by the question. 'I'm not limiting myself right now. I'm tasting it all.'

'And what's Hira?' said Miranda.

'It's a force. Your force,' Effie replied. 'It sharpens the language of a spell like a whetstone sharpens a knife.'

'It's like fire,' said Attis, his voice undulant. 'If your casting language is wood then your Hira is the fire that makes it burn, that turns its fuel to sparks, to spells.'

'I always think it's like earth,' said Rowan, spreading her hands along the floor. 'Your Hira is the soil within you, helping the roots and stems and flowers of your magic to grow.'

*My Hira is twine and thorn.*

'Sounds stupid,' said Miranda.

'Just roll with it.' Effie smiled without warmth. 'Let's see if we can get this sewing machine to run.'

'What do you propose?' Rowan asked.

'We hold hands, focus on the machine and chant. Keep it simple – see if the magic flows.'

She put her hand out. Anna took it and then Attis's. She'd never held a man's hand before. His was warm – burning, in fact. She was sure her own hands were clammy. She could feel her blood pulsing through them as her heart pounded in anticipation of the spell. *What if I can't? What if I ruin it?*
But Effie had begun:

> 'Path of needles or path of pins.
> Thread our magic, let us in.
> Sew us a spell, so may it spin.'

Her voice sank lower as she chanted, every word distinct as if each one might contain the power they needed. Rowan joined in, Anna followed and Miranda began to whisper along. They repeated it over and over, voices out of sync, different rhythms, different pitches. Anna couldn't imagine the needle pulling itself free from the rust and breaking the stale silence of the room. She tried to focus, to strengthen her own voice – but she couldn't feel anything.

> 'Path of needles or path of pins.
> Thread our magic, let us in.
> Sew us a spell, so may it spin.'

Slowly their voices found alignment and joined in quiet unison. They repeated the words until they seemed to lose meaning, or take on a different kind of significance, deepening. The darkness pressed in around them. The candles flickered. Something began to change though Anna could not pinpoint what. A shift in the air – in the feeling of the air. She began to feel something within herself, like an ache or an urge, like sinking into something half remembered . . .
*Ticker. Ticker. Ticker.*
The machine began to jump with a high electronic hum;

the needle stabbing up and down, up and down, shrieking with rust, piercing the silence.

*Ticker. Ticker. Ticker.*

Anna looked again at the frayed wire. There was no electricity.

'This is so creepy!' cried Miranda, pulling her hand away and breaking the circle.

*Ticker. Ticker. Ticker.*

Effie smiled, satisfied as a cat with a bowl of cream. She let go of the circle. The machine began to slow down and the silence took hold again.

'I guess we've got the mojo,' said Rowan.

Anna let go of Attis's hand, but could still feel the heat of it. He smiled at her and then handed her a tissue. 'Your nose is bleeding,' he said. Anna took it, trying her best to look indifferent about the magic they had just performed, but inside she was jumping up and down as fast as the needle. *I didn't ruin the spell! There's hope for me yet!* And she'd felt something. Something like *magic*. She couldn't explain what that feeling had been, only that there had been one.

'I knew we would.' Effie looked to Attis triumphantly. She turned to the rest of them. 'Do you see now? Magic is in our souls. Do you hear them? Longing to be free?'

Miranda had drawn her legs up and crossed her arms over them. Her face shone hot with the energy of the spell. 'I don't want to be a witch,' she said quietly.

'Why not?' said Effie, jumping to her feet. 'Why would you want to be like other people? I hate other people. We belong to legend, to fairy tale and storybook, to the blood-red paintings on cave walls. Witches, sorceresses and enchantresses, the strega, the vala, the banshee women, fairy godmothers or wizened hags in the dark of the woods. Sacred. Sinners. Wonders. Wicked. Virgins. Whores. Call us what you will. It's our duty to bring magic into this world.'

Anna was used to hearing the word duty, only when Aunt said it the word had the lash of a whip about it, a way to control and restrain. Effie's version was an unlocking, filled with a feverish freedom.

'Together, with our magic intertwined, our spells can become more powerful than anything we could have imagined. Think of the possibilities . . .' She looked up at the swirls of dust in the air. 'We can change the status quo of this dead-end school. We can right the injustices of this world. We can transform our lives. Nothing will ever be the same. Do you want to change your lives?'

She looked down at them and currents of magic seemed to flow from her eyes. Anna didn't know what to say. *Yes! Yes I want to change my life!*

Miranda looked lost for words. 'But – but – how do I know I'm not committing evil? It goes against everything I've been taught.'

Effie snorted. 'Everything you've been taught was stolen from us in the first place.'

'I think what Effie means to say' – Attis spoke gently – 'is that perhaps magic and religion have the same roots. Can they not at least coexist? Are prayers not a kind of spell?'

'To be fair, Jesus turned water into wine. Hello? Wizard for sure,' Rowan joked and then realized she wasn't helping. 'Manda, magic isn't evil.' She reached out and put a hand on her knee. 'It's only as good or as bad as the witch who casts it.'

Miranda breathed out as if the weight of the world were on her shoulders. 'But – but – if I start being seen around with you, what will people say?'

'That's what's really worrying you, isn't it?' Effie smirked. 'Your reputation.'

'It's a clean reputation.'

'Clean or boring?'

'I'm a library monitor. I run clubs. Teachers like me.'

Effie pretended to fall asleep.

'People will talk. Darcey will make my life hell.'

'But you're already set for hell, Manda, remember?' Effie winked. 'You're a witch now; may as well enjoy the fall.'

'My name is Miranda, people! And you really think *that's* going to convince me?' she cried.

'How about this? You join me and we'll take down Darcey for good? It's about time someone did.'

Miranda shook her head as if the idea was beneath her, but Anna was surprised to hear her relent. 'Fine! I'll join your coven, for now. If anything it will be a true test of my faith. However, if you try to steal my soul – I'm out.'

'Darling, I have my own soul.' Effie laughed, sounding exactly like Selene.

'I'm in,' said Rowan. 'I have no reputation to maintain. Maybe if I'm seen around with you, people will forget how unpopular I am – and that story about the time I forgot to wear a bra on sports day.'

They all turned to look at Anna.

She shrank from their gaze. 'I can't.'

'What?' said Effie.

Anna had decided after the spell, with the sensation of magic fading from her body. It had felt too good. If she gave into it – Aunt would know. There was no way of hiding it. In less than a year she was due to become a Binder; she couldn't join a coven now – it was unthinkable.

'Scared of Darcey too?' Effie spat. Anna noticed that her eyes went very still when she was annoyed.

'I don't care about school rumours,' Anna replied. 'It's bigger rumours I'm concerned about. Like you said – we're different. We don't belong. People will notice. We can't risk our magic becoming exposed.'

'I'm not suggesting we go around firing spells in cowans'

faces,' said Effie. 'But we can't not be witches. It's what we are.'

'But what about . . .' Anna felt her heart beat faster. The others leant towards her expectantly.

'What?'

'The Ones Who Know Our Secrets,' she whispered.

'The ones who what?'

The Binders rarely referred directly to them. Anna swallowed her fear and said it. 'The Hunters.'

Effie, Attis and Rowan stared at her for a moment then burst into laughter.

'The Hunters!' Effie guffawed. 'If you mean *the* Hunters, they don't exist. And besides, witches haven't been hunted for centuries. That's like worrying someone with a cold has the plague.'

'Effie's right,' said Rowan more sympathetically. 'The Dark Times have long gone. We don't live in that world any more. I mean, back then people believed in magic and feared the Devil. Now no one believes in anything and the only thing people fear is, you know, terrorism, or global warming, or a picture of their face becoming a meme.'

Anna could hear nothing but their laughter. She knew the Binders were mad, but still, she'd always presumed there was some basis to their insanity. She thought about bringing up the news story – the Faceless Women – but she didn't want to be laughed at again.

'Even so, my aunt would kill me.'

'Are you not sixteen?' Effie rebuked. 'Should you not be in charge of your own life by now?'

'Easy for you to say. Selene's your mother, she's the best—'

'You don't know anything,' said Effie sharply, her breath making the candle flame flicker in Anna's direction. She composed her features and laughed. 'I've met your aunt – she was positively psychopathic – but are you going to let her control you? It's ridiculous. I've been doing magic since my seventh year and no cowan has ever batted an eyelid. They don't see it. If I hovered in front of the whole school and unleashed bats from every orifice I doubt they'd look up from their phones long enough to notice.'

'Why would you do that?' said Miranda, aghast.

'Anyway, no one will find out,' said Effie. 'We'll meet here where we can't be found. I'll leave an apple in your locker in the morning if we're going to meet that night so you all have time to call your parents, aunts, whatever, and come up with some excuse.'

Anna had wondered if Selene had told Effie about her aunt, about the Binders, but Effie's casual disregard suggested not.

'Come on, Anna.' Effie smiled. 'What are the chances of there being so many witches in the same year? It's extremely rare. We're meant to be – we're fated.'

Fate, an enchanted apple and a lot of careful manipulation, Anna reflected sceptically.

'What's your choice going to be?'

That word again. Choice. It was strange how easily other people used it. Anna had never really considered if she had a choice; choice was simply not a consideration. If she continued to play the part of the diligent niece, she'd have to become a Binder. If she joined the coven and was caught, she'd still have to become a Binder; there'd just be more pain and punishment involved. She was doomed either way. *Why not just do it then? One year of fun before it's all over.*

'I'll think about it, OK?'

Effie looked as if she was about to argue when Rowan interrupted. 'And what's his part in all this then?' She made eyes at Attis, who was inspecting the needle mechanism on the sewing machine. He took a screwdriver out from inside his blazer. Anna wondered what else he had in his pockets.

'I'm here to make sure you don't get into too much trouble.' He began to unscrew the side of the machine. 'Or to get you into trouble. I forget.' He shot them all a sideways grin.

'Attis, will you stop taking that apart. He does this.' Effie rolled her eyes. 'Put it back. We've got five minutes before the teacher wakes up.'

He jumped to his feet and picked up the sewing machine as if it weighed no more than the needle itself.

They locked the door behind them, leaving the mannequins alone once more. Anna shivered as she thought of the sewing machine coming to life on its own again in the dark silence, feeding off the tendrils of magic left in the room. They made their way back into the normality of upper school. Where they had just been, what they had just done, quickly felt like a dream.

Miss Pinson was coming round as they hurried to their seats. Thoroughly disturbed by her second unexpected nap, she fled from the room.

'Shall we get some food?' Attis suggested.

'Finally, someone talking sense.' Rowan grabbed her bag. 'There's a noodle place on the way back to the train. Amazing veggie dumplings.'

'I like you,' said Attis, coming over and throwing an arm over her shoulder. 'Take me to the dumplings.'

'I love being in a coven.'

Effie turned to face them. 'Next Friday is Halloween. Let's meet then. Work it out. Coming?'

Miranda shook her head. 'My mum is picking me up. She thinks I'm in an after-school study club.'

Anna smiled at that and then shook her head at Effie. *I have to resist.*

'It's awkward,' said Rowan, heading to the door, 'but I have a date with Attis. You can come if you want, Effie, but you'll kind of be a third wheel.'

Effie laughed. 'It's fine, I ruin all Attis's dates.'

'That's true, she does do that.' He put his arms around them both and they left.

'This won't work without you, you know,' said Miranda, packing up her bag. 'We need your sanity.'

'How do you know I'm sane?' asked Anna.

'Because you're the only one who hasn't agreed to it.'

# BRUISES

*The more beautiful the rose, the sharper the thorns.*

*Binders' Training, The Book of the Binders*

Aunt had set the metronome ticking.

Anna tried to concentrate on the rhythm of the melody as she played, but couldn't stop thinking about the *ticker, ticker, ticker* of the sewing machine, the feeling of magic in her body. The rose bush eyed her from the top of the piano.

'You're going too fast,' Aunt chided. She was irritable – had been for several days. Anna was trying to convince herself it was just because she was busy at work but the more paranoid part of her worried that Aunt had sensed the lies. *The study session was helpful . . . Yes, we practised French vocab . . . I'd really like to try it again next week . . .*

'Will you concentrate! You're all over the place.' Aunt raised her hand and the ticking of the metronome grew louder – so loud it sounded as if it was inside Anna's own head. *TICK, TICK, TICK.* Anna's fingers stumbled. She took her hands off the keys, exasperated, but the song did not stop.

Anna looked up. Aunt was moving her hands through the air, the keys responding, the melody moving in perfect time, not a note out of place. *TICK. TICK. TICK.* 'Do you see how focus works? Purity of thought and purpose.'

Aunt's satisfied sneer filled Anna's vision. 'You're using magic, it's hardly fair!' she cried bitterly and then stopped herself. 'Sorry, let me try again.'

The music stopped. The piano lid shut on her fingers, painfully.

'Fair?' said Aunt. 'You think magic is easy for me? The sacrifice never ends, Anna.'

'I didn't mean that—'

But Aunt was not finished. She began to undo the buttons of her blouse. Anna's stomach tightened. She knew what was coming. Aunt pulled her blouse open to reveal a thick cord necklace knotted nine times, and beneath – around her neck – blooms of bruises, some old and some new, some just beginning to blossom: a dark rainbow of green, black and violet.

Anna looked away. She had seen it before many times, but it never got easier.

Aunt tenderly ran her fingers over the bruises. 'The melody might have been sweet but every time I use magic, my Binders' necklace restricts and hurts me. It is a reminder, Anna, that magic is sinful, a heavy responsibility to bear. There can be no love in it – only pain, only fear. In sacrifice, may our hearts be pure.'

Anna nodded, wanting it to be over, feeling the weight of Aunt's pain around her own neck. Aunt closed her blouse back up. 'We're done. I need to be up early. I have a Binders' meeting.'

*Tick, tick, boom.*

'What?' Anna gasped. *Another unplanned Binders' meeting. Does she know about the coven?* If the Binders knew they wouldn't wait until summer for her Knotting. Anna's hands trembled on the keys. Had Aunt uncovered her lies? Or was it something else? 'Why?'

'What is tenet five?'

'Ask no questions; seek no answers.'

'Then why are you asking them?'

But the questions kept Anna up all night. The next morning she rose exhausted and early to catch Aunt before the meeting and asked if she could borrow her laptop for an English essay. Aunt relented begrudgingly and left. Anna would have stolen it anyway but this way she didn't feel too guilty. She took it upstairs and opened up a new browser page. She typed 'Faceless Women' into it. Several new stories popped up.

## Mysterious mark revealed on Big Ben's Six Faceless Women

Autopsy findings show no evidence of struggle or attack, although police have now revealed a new detail about the women in question. An unusual mark was uncovered on the back of each of their necks: seven concentric circles. While the deaths have now been classified as suicides, police are hoping this mark might open up new lines of inquiry in determining the identities of the women.

Anna stared at the picture of the mark. It was blacker and more concise than any tattoo she'd ever seen: seven small, tight circles, encasing one another, descending to a dark circle in the centre like a pupil – an abyss – a deep emptiness around which the other circles revolved. There was something about it that pulled at her, disturbed her. She had the strangest feeling she'd seen it before. She tore her eyes away, feeling as though, if she stared at it too long, she might fall into its centre herself. Another version of the story on the ever-sensationalist *Mail Today* had a fresh quote from a source that Anna didn't recognize:

Although police remain tight-lipped, Halden Kramer, Head of Communications for the Institute for Research into Organized and Ritual Violence, has spoken out to highlight the suspicious aspects of the deaths: 'The grey robes, the significance of the location, the potential familial ties of the women, lead us to believe this has ritualistic links. The discovery of this mark, an ancient, occult symbol known as "The Eye", only adds more weight to this theory and opens up dark and unsettling questions about what the women were doing there before they died.'

The Institute for Research into Organized and Ritual Violence – *who the hell were they?* Anna quickly deleted the history and continued with her essay, but the words – *ritualistic . . . occult . . . dark and unsettling questions* – spun round in her head. No wonder the Binders were shaken; those words were a hair's breadth, a single tick, away from magic. Surely it was the reason behind their meeting rather than anything to do with herself. The thought was reassuring. And yet Anna couldn't get the image of the seven circles from her mind, as if it had always been there, waiting.

By Monday morning Anna had made her decision. She would not, *could not* join the coven. She had to stay away from them. Whether or not the Binders were entirely insane, something was happening in the magical world that had them rattled and Aunt had returned from the meeting in a foul and dangerous mood. Though it appeared Anna wasn't due for her Knotting – *yet* – it was still too risky.

'Hungry?'

She turned around in the lunch queue to find Attis.

'Starving. Always.' She spun back to the counter, heart beating.

'I like a woman with an appetite.'

'I think you like any woman with a pulse,' she pointed out.

'A pulse certainly helps.'

She moved her tray along. 'Could I get the pasta please?'

'Dennis, how's Mary?' said Attis.

The man serving lunch broke into a wide smile. 'She's a lot better, the infection has passed, thanks for asking, mate.'

'Glad to hear it, my man.'

'Now what can I get you?'

'The pasta too.'

'Extra helpings of pudding?'

'I won't complain.' Attis smiled and moved along.

Anna looked up at him, incredulous. He had everyone in his pocket.

'His daughter had a tooth infection last week,' he explained.

'What?'

'I've been in this school for six years and I don't know that man's name. You've been here for less than two months and you're days away from being invited around for dinner.'

Attis laughed. 'Well, that's because I speak to people.'

'I speak to people,' said Anna defensively, making her way towards a table in the corner. Attis followed and sat down opposite. 'Oh – you're going to sit here.'

'No, you're right, you are a paradigm of friendliness.'

'OK,' she conceded. 'I don't speak to people, but you swan into this school with your – your tallness and your smile and you get in the rugby team and everyone likes you. It's not the same place for those of us who aren't . . .'

'Tall and smiley?'

Anna made a face at him.

'Anyway, I got kicked out of the rugby team. Apparently you aren't allowed to jump on the referee's back, even if it's a friendly gesture.'

Anna couldn't help smiling.

'So why is it you don't have any friends?' he asked through a mouthful of pasta. 'You seem an occasionally nice person.'

Anna shrugged.

'Don't want to be noticed?'

'I can't be noticed.'

'Seems lonely.'

'I'm not lonely,' she said, indignant. 'It's just easier that way.'

'You don't strike me as the kind of girl who chooses the easy option.'

'Well, no offence, but you don't know me at all.'

'We're not going to be friends, are we?' His smile was not limited to his mouth, it seemed to hide all around the features of his face, lighting up the rippling puddles of his eyes.

'You've got Dennis.'

'I love Dennis. He gives me pudding. I give him undying devotion.'

'What are you guys talking about?' Effie appeared, making Anna jump. 'Yum.' Effie sat down, taking a spoonful of chocolate pudding from Attis's plate and then tapping his nose with it, leaving a mark. He shook his head at her. Anna felt uncomfortable, realizing she was wedged on a table in the common room next to Attis and Effie – the two people she was trying to avoid. She glanced around and saw that her presence had already been noted, heads were turning their way. *This is why I can't join the coven . . .*

'We were talking about Attis's friend, the lunch man,' she said, pushing her tray away.

'The lunch man; the sexy young art teacher; Darcey. Flirting is his only talent.' Effie ruffled his hair. 'I'm sure he's flirted with you already.'

'No,' said Anna, flustered. 'Anyway – why would you flirt with Darcey? She's horrendous to Effie.'

'Because,' Attis said with a smile, 'you keep your friends close and your enemies close enough to sleep with.'

Effie cackled, licking the chocolate from her lips.

Anna didn't understand them and she couldn't be seen with them. 'I've got to go,' she stood up, her lunch half-eaten, 'library calls . . .'

Effie's chocolatey smile deepened. 'What if I told you there were magical libraries all around London? Libraries of the like you've never seen. A library made out of books, a library hidden in a forest, a library containing all the books that were ever lost. I'll take you to them if you join the coven.'

'A cat has nine lives and curiosity still managed to kill it,' Anna replied, but she couldn't hide the interest from her eyes. *Magical libraries.* Even Selene had never mentioned anything so wonderful.

Effie jumped up. 'Let's go out.'

'I can't.'

'You can, we're sixth formers, it's lunchtime, we're allowed. Come on.'

Anna wanted to resist it, she wanted to, but she found herself throwing her bag over her shoulder, waving goodbye to Attis and following Effie. Within minutes they were in the fresh air, cold and brisk against her face. It shook the trees with vigour.

'Feels good to get out of that place,' said Effie. 'I need coffee. Let's swing by the café next to the Boys' School.'

The café was where everyone hung out – *everyone popular.* 'Maybe somewhere quieter?' Anna suggested.

'Why would we want somewhere quiet?'

The Boys' School appeared ahead, rising above high walls in the same red brick as their school. The small, fittingly named Red Brick Café was nestled into a corner near one of the entrances. Anna followed Effie inside. It was more spacious than it had appeared, with lots of tables and hidden nooks, a scattering of mismatched armchairs and the re-assuring smell of roasting coffee.

Effie walked up to the counter. 'I'll have a coffee – black – and we'll get two of those.' She pointed at a basket of croissants. Anna ordered a tea and they waited at the counter. A group of nearby boys had turned in their direction. Effie waved her fingers at them, stroking the air.

'Why are they looking over here?' said Anna, alarmed.

'Because we're girls.'

'That's never had any effect for me before.'

'That's because your head is permanently attached to the floor – or a book. If you just looked up, put some make-up on, wheeled yourself out in the sun once in a while, it might make a difference.'

'Thanks,' said Anna dryly, unsure if she was being insulted or complimented.

'I like that one,' said Effie, perusing the group.

Anna glanced over. 'Which one?'

'Dark curly hair.'

'The large one?'

'Yes. I like bear men, but I like the lean ones too. Sometimes I like girls. Depends on my mood.' She took the coffee off the barista and inhaled it deeply. 'Saying that, I like coffee more than all lovers put together.' When it became apparent she wasn't going to pay, Anna handed the barista money to cover the both of them.

Effie's attention shifted to the door of the café. Peter had just come through it, followed by a string of the school's most admired men: Hutton, Digby, Andrew and Tom – who last year had been given the title of *the school's most perfect hair* – possibly by himself.

The others sat down while Peter and Tom made their way to the counter. Anna took a sip of tea, trying to hide behind the cup, but managed to spill some down herself. *Way to play it cool.*

'Hi, boys,' said Effie.

Tom looked her up and down with relish. 'Need some sugar with that coffee?' He was shorter and stockier than Peter. With his black, sculpted hair, square jaw and row of even white teeth, he was considered good-looking by many of the girls in the school but Anna disliked his bullish air of entitlement, the arrogance of his expression.

'Apparently you've already given me some of your sweet sugar or so the rumour around school has been,' Effie replied.

Tom tensed slightly and then shrugged. 'I'm not responsible for rumours.'

'Oh, you're not?' Effie took a vicious bite of croissant. 'I don't mind a good rumour, I just wish you hadn't been the man in it. You, however . . .' She turned and inspected Peter, who had just finished ordering. 'We could have hooked up by now, couldn't we?'

Peter frowned, taking Effie in. 'I'm sorry, have we met?'

'Not yet, but you can get to know me.'

Peter looked momentarily lost for words.

'Peter and every other boy at this school . . .' Tom muttered.

'Except you.' She smiled and it was so cold Anna swore it could have frozen the tea in her cup.

'Come on, Tom,' said Peter, handing him his drink and scowling at Effie. 'I think we're better off away from here.' Neither of them appeared to have registered Anna at all.

'It does smell like trash round here.' Tom gave Effie's breasts a peek and followed Peter.

Effie picked up the spoon on her plate and dipped it into her coffee. She pulled it out, held it balanced, and then tipped the liquid onto the floor.

'Oh shit!' Tom yelled. His cup had fallen to the floor, hot milk spilling everywhere. The boys started roaring with laughter. The liquid had spilt down the front of his trousers, looking distinctly like he'd wet himself. Anna turned to Effie in shock.

'What? Just a little cantrip. A girl's got to have her fun.

Come on, let's go.' She grabbed Anna's arm and pulled her towards the door, giving Tom a wave goodbye.

Anna couldn't help laughing as they burst through the door. 'You're so bad.'

'You think that was bad? We have so much work to do on you.' Effie hooked her arm.

'I don't think the men in this school know what to do with you.'

'Men can't handle me because I play by the same rules as them.' Effie stopped to look in one of the shop windows.

'So, you – er – like the blond guy then?' Anna pretended to look as well.

'Yeah, he's hot if you like that fresh-faced, strait-laced sort of thing. I just wanted to shake him up a bit.'

'He's not strait-laced, he's just not like the other guys in this school. He's decent.'

'How long have you been in loooove with him?'

Anna gasped. 'What are you talking about?'

'I saw how you looked at him – or how you looked at anything except him, I should say.'

'I'm not in love with him! I think he's—'

'An honourable man? No men are honourable.'

'Not Attis?'

Effie laughed. 'He's the most honourable man I know and that's not saying much.'

'Are you two . . .?' Anna asked slowly, unsure if she was overstepping the mark.

'He's like a brother to me,' Effie replied with an unreadable smile. 'You know I can help you with Peter, if you let me.'

'I don't want to be with Peter and I certainly don't want to use magic to get him to like me.'

'Why not? Magic and love go hand in hand. A spoonful of sugar helps the medicine go down. Come on.' Effie pulled at her.

'Where are we going?'

'There's only one magical shop I know of in Dulwich.'

Anna stopped. 'There's a magical shop in Dulwich?' She couldn't imagine it, not on the streets she'd walked so many times before, among the ordinary people who filled them. 'You know, I think I'm just going to head back to school.'

Effie rolled her eyes and continued to pull her along. 'I've managed to get you this far, don't back down now. We'll just pop our heads in, I promise.'

Anna was quickly learning that Effie's promises were extremely flexible and yet she could feel the temptation of it beckon her. *What on earth would a magic shop in Dulwich look like?* 'I have to be back in half an hour for class. Really.'

Effie made a bored noise. 'Fiiiiine.'

They made their way towards the high street, feasting on the croissants.

'So,' Effie said, swallowing a mouthful. 'What's the deal with your parents then? Do you ever think about them?'

Anna was not expecting the question – most people tiptoed around the subject – but Effie spoke with startling directness. Anna looked away, wondering what she could possibly say – how much she should give to this girl she hardly knew. 'I wonder about my mother sometimes. Selene probably told you, she was murdered by my father.' She said it matter-of-factly, as if it was nothing, taking a quick sip of tea to clear her throat.

'I know. So messed up that he killed her. Selene said they had a fight – must have been one hell of an argument.'

Anna nodded.

'You don't wonder about him? Why he freaked out?'

Anna shrugged, glad she was outside. The subject was so claustrophobic, like a room that grew smaller the more you thought about it. She pulled at her Knotted Cord. 'I guess love can be messed up sometimes,' she said, knowing it sounded like a vast understatement. *In what world does love*

*end up in strangling someone and then stabbing yourself in the heart?*
In Aunt's world, where love was deranged and destructive.

'I'm guessing they weren't arguing over who'd taken out
the rubbish last. You must want to know more.'

Anna stiffened. It was easy for Effie to say; she hadn't had
to grow up under the dark gloom of it, the buried pain of it.
'I don't.'

'I would.'

'Well, your parents aren't the dead ones,' Anna replied
curtly. 'You grew up with a mum.'

Effie laughed scathingly. 'Did I? Where is she then? Russia
supposedly, but who knows with my darling mother.' The
word *mother* was tinged with contempt. 'Claims she's on
magical business but she's probably off with some man.'

Selene had regaled Anna with tales of various lovers,
making her laugh with the salacious details, but it had never
occurred to her to ask who was responsible for the creation
of Effie or if there'd ever been someone special. 'Did you –
do you – er – know your father?'

'No,' said Effie, as if it was of no consequence. 'So I guess
he could be dead too.' Anna turned to her but Effie's look
was teasing. 'Unlikely. Probably just a fling who doesn't even
know I exist. Who knows, maybe that's him.' Effie pointed
at a man hurrying up the street opposite. 'Or him.' She
nodded towards an elderly man bent over a Zimmer frame,
making Anna laugh. 'Anyway. We're here!'

It was a street Anna had walked down before but she'd
never noticed the small shop with the green front and wooden
door and the sign in the window advertising 'Vintage Finds
and Memories'. From the outside it didn't look particularly
magical at all. Inside it was tiny and very full – a jumble of
paraphernalia lining the shelves, covering the tables, hanging
from the ceiling, spilling out of chests and onto the floor; the
clothing rails were stuffed to bursting. Anna searched for

anything strange, but could only see the typical objects you'd expect to find in a vintage shop: clothes, hats, boots, bags, pottery, old cameras, mirrors, clocks, odds and ends.

The only thing that jarred was the smell – it didn't have the usual antique-shop scent of mildew and old perfumes and wood polish, of human memories collected and piled up. Instead, it smelt . . . delightful, wonderful. *What's that smell?* Anna tried to place it. She knew it so well, right at the centre of her heart . . .

It was the garden.

Cressey Square garden at the start of spring when the gardener has just been and the grass is freshly cut, the jasmine bush has opened and it's recently rained – the soil and trees waxy with new life.

Anna breathed deeper and could even make out the earthy tang of moss on the stone fountain and the warm complexity of the bark of the oak tree she leant against. It was those exact scents, as if she was there – right there – breathing it in as she had so many times before.

'Can you smell that?' she whispered to Effie.

'I can smell New York at night.' Effie grinned. 'Hot-dog fat and pretzels, sweat and smoke, marijuana, exhaust fumes and exhaustion and the cloying whiff of garbage. Heaven.'

'You'll find it's this candle,' a voice said. Anna spun around. A woman appeared from a back room wearing an outfit that was impossible to take in all at once: what appeared to be a vintage army uniform covered by an Aztec print shawl, delicate lace gloves, several layers of necklaces and auburn hair tucked under an orange top hat. She looked to be in her sixties with a face that reminded Anna of a bird – a beaky nose and small, perceptive lips; an outfit like a nest she'd constructed from the parts of other outfits. She pointed to a white candle burning on the counter. 'The aromas in here can be rather overwhelming, so many old things, clashing memories, so I tend to keep this burning – it turns the scents of the room into the scents of your favourite memory.'

'I see,' said Anna, unable to hide the marvel from her face.

'It only works if you're witches, of course.'

*Witches*. They were witches and she was a witch – and it seemed perfectly natural that they might be talking in a magical emporium. In Dulwich. Anna resisted the strong urge to run from the shop and hide.

*We shall not cast unless it is our duty.*

'That's what you'll find here,' the woman continued, waving a shawled arm. 'Antiques and memories. You like vintage clothes?' Anna nodded and the woman ran her hand along a rail of clothing of all different shapes, colours and sizes. 'Wear any of these items and you'll experience the memory of the one who owned it before – the most powerful memory they had while wearing it.' She pointed to a row of clocks on the wall. 'All of them are frozen at the moment something life changing happened to their owners. I love the mystery of that, don't you? Never knowing what it was that made them stop in their tracks. Those telephones' – she pointed to a table of brightly coloured vintage phones – 'have old conversations trapped in them. That typewriter only writes the ideas of the person who used to own it – I've created some very existential poetry on it. Do you see how it works now?' She nodded, her exposition appearing complete. 'Please, explore.'

Anna and Effie exchanged smiles and wandered around the shop. Anna picked up some photographs from a suitcase. She stared at one of what looked like a family standing in a higgledy line on a beach. The longer she looked at it the more she could feel the excitement of their day out, the silly laughter passing between them, the mischief of the youngest of the tribe who was kicking sand into the air, the mother's love as she looked on her children fondly.

'Can you feel it? They're charged with the emotions at the moment they were taken,' the woman elucidated again. 'Fifty pence a picture or three for a pound.'

Anna nodded, feeling strangely wistful. She put the photograph down and moved to a row of hats. She tried on a rather ostentatious pink one and remembered exactly how beautiful a woman named Joanne had looked on her wedding day as she came through the doors of the church. She had no idea who Joanne was but at the moment she could have described her in intricate detail. She walked past several magic mirrors and saw not her own face but other faces staring back at her. In a daze of wonder, she wandered over to Effie, who was peering at a stuffed taxidermy of a cat. Anna briefly wondered what memories that could possibly hold when she spotted the snow globe next to it.

She picked it out from the pile. It was beautiful. All of London seemed to be inside it, an impossible complexity of dark stone streets and buildings: Big Ben rising above, alongside the London Eye, a miniature of St Paul's, the Thames snaking through its centre – she could have studied it forever and still found more. She hadn't shaken it but the snow was flurrying around inside. She looked more closely; it was hard to make out, but the snow did not look like the white glittery flecks of an ordinary snow globe, each one was of incomprehensible intricacy – a minuscule snowflake – a world in itself. *The memory of a real snow storm?*

'Wow,' said Effie. Anna had never heard her voice sound so soft. 'I think they're real. Actual snowflakes. I love snow.'

'It's amazing.'

'I want it,' said Effie, taking the snow globe from Anna's hands and moving over to the counter.

The owner looked down at it. 'Expensive tastes, I see. This is a rare object.'

'You know my mother, no? Selene?'

'I know Selene Fawkes, yes, and you, Effie Fawkes. I never forget a face or a name.'

'She'll sort out the payment, whatever it is.'

'Will she now?' The woman looked at Effie knowingly from beneath her hat. 'All right, seeing as you were both drawn to it, I shall give it to both of you. Tell Selene I'll be in touch.' She began to wrap up the snow globe.

Anna looked again at the row of frozen clocks on the wall, feeling as if she was lost in time herself. *The time!* She looked at her watch – which was very much unfrozen and ticking – and saw she had eight minutes until her class started. She didn't want to go. She had to go. 'Er – Effie, we better get back.'

Effie took the bag from the shop owner. 'Sorry, my friend here thrives on stress.'

'And what's your name?' said the woman.

'Anna, but I've got to go, sorry, but thank you, thanks, your shop is lovely,' Anna called, heading towards the door.

The woman nodded, disappearing again into the back room. As soon as Anna was outside on the street, among normal smells and normal people, she was barely sure the woman had even existed. She looked back – the shop was still there, definitely still there.

'I thought you were late?' said Effie.

Anna shook her head. 'I am! Come on!'

'Come on? I give you a taste of the magical world and that's all you have to say?'

'Well.' Anna smiled, slowing her pace a little. 'It was sort of incredible. So small and yet . . .' She thought how if you put all the memories held within the shop's walls together, you'd have entire centuries, whole worlds to play with. To her, memories had always been something best left be, sewn shut and forgotten.

'You see, didn't I promise you fun?'

Anna laughed and Effie kicked at a patch of leaves beneath them. They scattered up into the air, swirling around them – around and around like the snow in the snow globe. Effie was doing it. Anna could feel the tendrils of it – *magic*. It tugged at her like nostalgia; made her whole body ache.

'You can feel it, can't you?'

'No.'

'You know why I like you?'

'Honestly, no.'

'Other than the fact I find your constant self-castigation hilarious, I like you because I can see the desire in your eyes, your lust for magic. I can see you want it more than anything in the world.'

Anna considered her words, watching the leaves blow higher. A crow had settled in the tree above. It cried, the sound high and grating, like a violin being played backwards.

'Selene always said your mother was exceptional at magic. What are you so afraid of?'

Where could she begin? Her whole life was built on a foundation of fear. Anna reached for the Knotted Cord, trying to control her fears, to put them in order. Aunt. The Binders. Sacrifice. *The Ones Who Know Our Secrets.* 'It's complicated. My aunt is on edge at the moment—'

'Forget your aunt! She's filling your head with fairy tales! Wolves in the woods! I didn't ask what she's afraid of, I asked what are *you* afraid of?'

Anna let go of the Knotted Cord. She felt as if she feared everything and nothing all at once. 'I don't know.' She watched the crow fly away, shrieking trouble into the air. Her fears were not her own and neither were her memories.

That night, Anna took out the photograph of her parents. She hadn't looked at it since Selene had given it to her. Something about it troubled her. She glanced at her father's face for only a moment and then returned her gaze to her mother. Her eyes traced her features and she felt nothing. She had been trained to feel nothing, to tie the sadness up in knots – blunt knots could not bruise. She wanted to tuck the photograph away and forget it existed, but Effie's words came back to her – *You must want to know more* – like loose threads waiting to be pulled at.

Anna had always liked the fact that she had no memories of them at all. It had kept them at a safe distance. Kept the horror of it all at bay. But for just a moment, she longed for a connection.

'Were you lonely?' she asked her mother quietly, but her mother did not look lonely with Anna's father wrapped around her and a baby in her arms. Aunt had always told her that friendship and love were just an illusion to help you sleep at night. *You and I, we have each other, we don't need anybody else.* Anna had never thought she had, until now.

She put the picture back and imagined her mother holding her, feeling the heavy emptiness that came at night. Perhaps it was loneliness, after all.

# ELEMENTS

*We shall not cast unless it is our duty.*

Tenet Three, The Book of the Binders

The Binders did not approve of Halloween. It was a holiday that encouraged irresponsible superstitions and spread dangerous beliefs. People spoke of witches and devils and spirits and they were far too close to the truth for the Binders' liking. Anna had somehow managed to keep up her study-session cover story with Aunt, buying herself an extra hour after school, *just in case*. 'Home before seven,' Aunt had instructed as she left. 'I don't want you out and about on such a night.'

If Aunt had seen the apple in Anna's locker that morning, she'd have had far more to worry about than Halloween. *Tonight*. Just as Effie had promised. Anna had been waiting all week for Effie to come again and find her, to whisk her off on some adventure, but she hadn't appeared. Anna took the apple out – *trick or treat?* She wasn't sure.

After lunch, Anna went to the music room. For years it had been her sanctuary, somewhere she could go where no one would find her, where she could play the way she wanted to, without Aunt breathing over her shoulder. She loved its dark quiet, the soft light that filtered over instruments waiting to be played, the rich, warm scent of aged wood that drew her to the piano. She sat down at it and placed the apple on top, watching it as it watched her. Then she let go.

A new song unravelled from her fingertips.

When the end of the day finally came, Anna waited for the corridors to empty and then she made her way down the stairs to the murky depths of the old school. *What if Aunt finds out? What if I can't do magic? What if I can?* She silenced the fears in her head. Fear wasn't going anywhere. In a year's time she'd be Knotted and even if one day she became a Senior Binder and was given her magic back she'd still have to wear her own necklace, her own bruises. *Just for a year, I can imagine, can't I? Imagine what it would be like to really live.*

She stopped outside room 13B. She could hear voices from within. She took a deep breath and went in.

> 'Besom, besom, sweep out ill,
> Birch twigs, birch twigs, do your will.'

Rowan was sweeping the room with a broomstick, singing a song. Miranda was watching her in bewilderment, sitting at one of the desks as if class were about to start.

'Maiden, mother and bony crone, it's Anna!' Rowan bounded over. 'You came! Happy All Hallows' Eve! Samhain blessings! What you doing later? I'm taking my sisters trick or treating. I don't care if I'm too old. Society be damned! Then my family and I are going to do a ritual to honour our dead family members and pets; it'll be nice. You should join us. If my mum spoke to your aunt I'm sure—'

'My aunt thinks trick or treating is akin to breaking into people's houses and attacking them with an axe.'

'Oh, right.'

'She sounds like a sensible woman,' said Miranda.

The door banged open.

'Thirteen moons!' Rowan put a hand on her heart.

Effie stepped through with Attis. Her eyes landed on Anna.

'Excellent, you're all here. What's that for?' Effie pointed at Rowan's broomstick.

'Cleansing our new covenstead. Great workout too.' Rowan began brushing outwards from the centre of the room in wide circles.

'Good. I want us to make this room our own.'

Miranda looked around at the gloom and the row of beheaded sewing mannequins with distaste. 'And how do you propose we do that?'

'We make an altar for starters.' Effie walked over to the blackboard. She clicked a hand at Attis, who sprang into action, carrying a long table from the side of the room over to her, his movements free of the awkwardness and self-doubt of those their age, instilled with a kind of leonine energy, flowing with purpose. His body was lean and his shoulders broad, the muscles in his arms flexed – Rowan had stopped sweeping and was staring at him, the broom continuing to move in small circles of its own volition.

'The altar is to be our sacred space: an expression of who we are; the theatre of our power.' Effie tipped up her handbag and a pile of objects, far too big for the bag that they had come from, fell out: misshapen candles, hanging crystals, strange figurines, a pine cone, stones with hollows in them, a diamond skull. Effie picked up an animal skull from the pile and began to mount it on the wall, throwing the clock that had been up there on the floor with a clatter.

'What's that?' Miranda cried.

'A goat's skull. See these?' Effie pointed to some protrusions coming from the top. 'They're the beginnings of its horns. The cool part is they grow as our magic grows.'

'But it's dead.'

'That's why I said it was the cool part. Now put this over

the table.' She handed a black lace cloth to Miranda. 'We need a goddess and a god.' Effie perused the pile and selected a gold statue of a bird-headed Egyptian god, placing it on the right. She selected a Russian doll figurine for the left. 'Attis, put the sewing machine here. In homage to our first spell.'

The snow globe was among the pile. Anna picked it up and, again, she didn't need to shake it; the snowflakes were already whirling.

'I'm glad you came,' said Effie.

'Well, it'll probably kill me, but I decided I'll die of boredom anyway if I don't.'

'What? You mean sitting at home sewing embroideries with your aunt isn't fulfilling you?'

'All right, I get the picture.'

'Time to make some new memories.' Effie cackled hungrily and took the snow globe from Anna, setting it back down. 'Right! We have spell work to get on with.' She waved a hand at the half-finished altar that had minutes ago been so important. 'Attis, stop that.'

He was rearranging the sewing mannequins into a conga line, placing several at a jaunty angle. Effie walked into the middle of the room – the centre of her stage. 'Today we're going to work with the elemental language.'

Aunt didn't trust the elements, she didn't like the rain or wind and she said that fire was full of lies; she wore garden gloves so as never to get soil under her nails.

'It's one of the oldest and most powerful. It will imbue our magic with the Goddess's earthly gifts and help our future rituals. Traditionally there are actually seven elements – earth, air, fire, water, wood, metal, and the spirit, but we tend to work with the core four: earth, air, fire, and water. Their tools – pentacle, wand, athame, and chalice.' She picked up each one from the altar.

Rowan began to sing:

'Needle is the dagger, commanding smoke and fire.
Twig is the wand, stirring wind and air.
Coin is the pentacle, in tune with soil and earth.
Thimble is the chalice, containing water's breath!'

'What's that?' Anna asked.

'Oh, just one of the old nursery rhymes. Mum used to sing it to me. Effie, I already know my element, it's earth.'

'On your own, perhaps, but we need to know what our individual elements are as a coven. It's not necessarily the same thing; it depends on our collective energy and what each of us contributes to it. The elements are all about finding balance – and we need to find ours. Did you all bring your apples from earlier? Put them in the centre.'

Anna and Miranda did as directed. 'I ate mine,' Rowan admitted.

'Good job I brought spare.' Effie rolled several more apples into the centre. 'Now sit.'

They formed a circle, which Effie surrounded with candles. It was unnerving, not knowing what was coming. Attis placed himself out of the way, on a table in the shadows. *He's going to watch us,* Anna reflected uncomfortably.

Effie placed a candle, leaf, a glass of water and bowl of earth into the centre and began to walk around the outside of their circle muttering:

'As above so below, as within so without.
Weave our circle without doubt.'

Her voice was low and soothing, melting into the darkness of the room, her footsteps as quiet as the sound of a book closing. As she passed the candles became living flames, casting a tangle of shadows into the circle. She repeated it three times and then joined the circle and raised her arms.

'I call to the watchtowers of the North, the element of earth, symbolized by the pentacle of old. To the moss on the trees and the humus beneath our feet, to the goddess of worm and root and the rot of our flesh, may you bring us stability and strength. I take you into me through the soil of the crossroads. Through the flesh of the apple – reveal who we are.'

Effie took a pinch of soil from the bowl and placed it in her mouth. She passed the bowl to Rowan.

'Am I meant to—'

'We must each take the elements into us.'

'Gross. OK, OK, I take you into me through the soil of the crossroads.' Rowan took a pinch and put it in her mouth. Miranda took the bowl with obvious disgust and held her nose while she placed the smallest pinch possible into her mouth. Anna followed suit, the soil sour and gritty on her tongue.

Effie continued. 'I call to the watchtowers of the East, the element of air, symbolized by the wand of old. To the leaves in the sky and feathers of birds, to the goddess of dawn and wind and the scents it carries, may you bring us wisdom and intellect. I take you into me through the breath of this leaf. Through the flesh of the apple – reveal who we are.'

Effie picked up the leaf and breathed in deeply. They each followed in turn.

'I call to the watchtowers of the South, the element of fire, symbolized by the athame of old. To the smoke of the flame and the bite of the bale, to the goddess of sun and summer light and snow-white ash, may you bring us energy and desire. I take you into me through the burn of this flame. Through the flesh of the apple – reveal who we are.'

Effie held her finger over the candle until she winced and passed it on. Even if Anna had wanted to refuse, she couldn't now; there was a crackle in the air, a feeling of pressure, a tightening they could not escape from.

'I call to the watchtowers of the West, the element of water as symbolized by the chalice of old. To the seas of life and the rivers of the dead, to the goddess of the moon and the waves and ocean tides, may you bring us intuition and love. I take you into me through this water. Through the flesh of the apple – reveal who we are.'

Effie drank from the glass. The elements in the centre had begun to respond – the flame growing and flickering; water swirling; earth in the bowl shifting as if something were buried beneath it; leaf twitching.

'By pentacle, wand, blade and chalice, through the flesh of the apple pure, reveal who we are. Through the flesh of the apple pure, reveal who we are . . .'

Anna observed the theatrics with growing concern. Suddenly Effie ceased chanting and announced: 'I'll go first.'

Without hesitation she reached into the centre and grabbed one of the apples. She bit deep into its flesh with relish. She cried and dropped the apple to the floor. It split in half. The flesh inside was black and charred, smoke uncoiling from its innards. 'Fire.' Effie smiled with satisfaction, smoke tangling in her hair. 'I knew it. Your turn, Rowan. Choose one.'

Rowan dithered over one of the apples but then selected another. She went to bite it but the apple rose out of her hand and floated several inches above it. Rowan tried to grab it again but it rose higher still. 'Whoa. Air? Me? Air? I don't bring wisdom or intellect to anything.'

'Keep focus,' Effie scolded. 'Miranda.'

Miranda tentatively selected an apple and held it at arm's length, as if it might suddenly explode.

'Bite it!'

Miranda brought the apple to her lips, eyes tightly closed. She nibbled gingerly at it and then immediately began sputtering and spitting. She dropped the apple and it rolled back into the centre, earth spilling from inside. A worm crept from a hole in its flesh – its small, pink head flickering and tasting the air like a tiny tongue.

Miranda tried to scream but couldn't. She gulped at the air. 'I – I can't—' She scrabbled at her throat.

'I don't think she can breathe!' Anna was panicking. Attis stood up in the distance.

'Keep focus!' Effie shouted. 'Don't fight it.'

She locked eyes with Miranda, who let out an almighty cough and then inhaled deeply. Miranda uncoiled the hand she'd coughed into, revealing a small pile of earth within it. She shrieked and grabbed at the bottle of water, drinking it in large gulps and wiping frantically at her mouth. 'What's wrong with me? Why is the apple rotten? That's disgusting! So help me God!'

'It's not rotten, it's just earth,' said Rowan, unable to withhold a giggle as a second worm wriggled out of the apple and onto the floor.

Miranda began to retch.

'Quiet! Anna!'

Anna reviewed the apples before her. One seemed to attract all her attention. She tried to resist it but the apple was insistent, its waxy skin shining and winking at her in the candlelight. She took it and held it to her lips, but just as she was to take a bite its stalk began to sprout and grow small green leaves. It grew longer, curling around itself, erupting with new shoots.

'What is it?' Anna smiled, the leaves tickling at her hand.

'Water.' Rowan smiled too. 'Giver of life.'

Anna took a bite and the apple's juices poured down her chin. Inside it was more water than flesh; a golden lake, sweet as summer. She admired the magic in her palm. She knew it was the result of the group, rather than hers alone, but still – it felt good.

Attis jumped off the table, producing what appeared to

be a magnet from his pocket. He held it out along the ground. One of the apples began to roll towards him and it hit the magnet with a metal-on-metal thud. 'Guess I'm metal,' he said.

'You weren't part of the spell,' Effie chided.

'Well, the spell obviously wanted me to be a part of it.' He walked over to them, surveying the apples and plucking Rowan's from the air where it still hovered.

'Why do I get worms?' Miranda cried. 'Why am I worm girl?'

'Hey, you stole my element,' said Rowan. 'I thought I had an affinity with earth. Now apparently I'm air – all wind and no substance. I guess that makes sense, actually . . .'

'The apples have spoken,' said Effie. 'We are what we are. Now, how about finishing with a game? Have you guys ever played light as a feather, stiff as a board?'

'Only like a thousand times,' said Rowan.

'Well, this is a twist on it. We all feeling OK? Magic can take its toll when you're not used to it.'

Anna was still on a high from the spell – the feeling of magic running through her. A kind of pressure. A buzzing. Something she couldn't put her finger on. At Effie's words she realized she was also very tired.

Miranda grimaced. 'Am I going to have to eat anything disgusting?'

Effie shook her head.

'I suppose I could do one more spell then.'

Anna nodded along.

'Attis, you have to sit this one out again,' Effie told him. 'Your magic is too powerful; there won't be any challenge.'

'I know when I'm not wanted,' he said, hopping back onto the table.

'Right, so normally we'd try to levitate someone off the floor by chanting "light as a feather, stiff as a board," but in this version you have to stand up and then fall backwards. We'll try to hold you up. A magical trust game – of sorts.'

'Sounds dangerous,' said Miranda.

'It's easy. Come on.' Effie raised her hand. Anna found herself rising to her feet and wondered how Effie always got her way. *Is it the authority in her voice? The intensity of her eyes? The threat of her smile?* She was the Pied Piper, playing a dark tune and luring all the rats to the river. Still, it was the rats who chose to jump. 'It's better that I begin the chant. Anna, you go first.'

Anna walked to the centre of the room, unsure of what was coming.

'Turn around and cross your arms over your chest. Yes, like that. Wait to feel the energy build and I'll say fall. Trust us, OK?'

'OK.' Anna didn't trust them, or magic.

They began to repeat the words: 'Light as a feather, stiff as a board. Light as a feather, stiff as a board.' Anna wasn't sure if she was meant to feel anything – she couldn't detect any magic. The idea of simply letting go and dropping to the floor with nothing to stop her felt absurd. *Light as a feather, stiff as a board . . .*

'Fall.' Anna felt Effie's words pull at her and fell back, her arms clasped, her body stiff. The air seemed to thicken around her, like custard, slowing her descent, a warm current pushing her back up. They held her still in the air for a few moments and then brought her gently to the ground.

'That was cool,' said Anna, more loudly than intended, spinning round. Her heart was racing.

'Look at you, all flushed with magic,' said Effie indulgently. 'Miranda, it's your turn.'

Miranda was easy to hold up. She barely fell at all. The force of their magic slowed her and held her thin frame in the air. 'Put me down!' she protested.

'Anyone else tempted to see how long we can keep her there?' said Effie.

Miranda began to whimper and they lowered her to the floor. Anna was still buzzing, but the feeling was a strained one now, as if she'd had been stretched out too far. She felt a crashing wave of exhaustion.

'My go!' said Rowan, taking up her position.

Anna shook her head, trying to clear the blurriness from it. She only had a moment before they began chanting again. It was hard to focus and when Effie cried 'Fall!' Anna was taken by surprise. There was a loud crack.

'Fuck,' said Effie.

Rowan was lying on the floor, not moving. Attis appeared beside her in an instant. A thin trail of blood began to trickle from her head. Anna ran to kneel on the other side of her. Rowan's eyelids fluttered.

'I knew I was too fat for this game.' The corner of her mouth turned up slightly. 'Ouch, that hurt. Shit, am I bleeding?' She sat up and Attis inspected her head.

Anna noticed Rowan's blood on the floor had formed a small but curious pattern – spiralling circles.

Anna saw Attis looking and quickly began to mop up the blood with some tissue she had on her.

'Don't worry.' He turned back to Rowan, reaching into his blazer pocket. 'Head wounds always appear worse than they are. I'll fix you up. I have a magically inclined needle that can sew it shut in seconds. Painlessly, I assure you.'

'Only if you dress up as a nurse.'

'Damn it, I forgot to bring my outfit to school,' he chuckled while inspecting the wound.

'Why didn't the spell work?' Effie's voice was flecked with irritation. 'You two weren't focusing hard enough; it was all on me, I could feel that.'

'Well then, you shouldn't have said *fall*, should you?'

Attis barked. Anna hadn't ever heard him speak back to her.

Anna looked away. She knew it was her fault. She was too weak for the spell. She should've said something, told them she was tired, told them the truth.

'I knew this was going to happen.' Miranda's chin dimple quivered. 'Magic isn't safe, it isn't right. It's always going to end in blood!'

'Isn't Attis healing Rowan with magic right now?' Effie turned on her, her glowing mood entirely dissipated.

Miranda shrank back. 'Well, yes.'

'Then magic isn't all wrong, is it? We just fucked up the spell, it's not magic's fault – it's ours. We need to try harder.'

'It's only our first time. We'll get better,' said Rowan cheerfully. 'Besides, we should've taken my weight into account.'

'Hey, stop it with the fat thing,' said Attis, needle in mouth. 'You're curvy and gorgeous, so deal with it.'

'Did someone just call me gorgeous or did I just fall and hit myself on the head?'

'You haven't said much, Anna.' Effie had turned to her, accusation in her eyes.

'I'm . . .' *I should say something. I should tell them.* 'I'm honestly pretty tired. I didn't realize how tired I was before—'

'You should have told us if you felt that way,' Effie snapped, the accusation drilling deeper. 'We must tell each other everything. We must have no secrets. They will only hold back our magic. At our next session all secrets will be out.'

Anna had an overwhelming urge to step into the shadows, out of sight.

'Right, start clearing up, unless any of you want to stay down here for All Hallows' Eve, night of the dead. We have parties to attend.'

Anna had no parties. She walked back home, the autumn mists shaking themselves loose from the cold ground. When she arrived back, the house was dark and quiet – Aunt was still at work. She sat at the kitchen table and reached into her bag, pulling out her elemental apple. She took a bite of it, trying to remember the taste of magic. Inside, its seeds had begun to sprout with little green shoots and flowers. So hopeful, but so useless. *My magic failed before it had begun.* She thought of Rowan guiltily. Her fall. The blood. Its pattern on the floor – those circles . . .

Anna gripped the apple as she remembered the mark on the necks of the Faceless Women. *Seven circles.*

A deeper memory arose suddenly.

She'd been young, eight or nine. She'd fallen outside and scraped her knee. She'd gone to find Aunt, holding back tears, hoping for some comfort: a plaster, a kiss on the head. Aunt hadn't been in the kitchen – no, nor in the living room. She'd climbed the stairs, stifling a sob. Aunt's bedroom door had been ajar. She'd pushed it open: 'Aunt, I—'

Aunt had been sitting on the bed, her head crumpled into her hands, dressing gown around her waist. The skin on her back had been raw and red with stitch-marks – a pattern sewn into her flesh.

Anna dropped the apple as she remembered: *circles.* The pattern had been circles. She tried to recall more. Aunt had stood up, thrown her dressing gown back on and started shouting. Anna had never got that plaster or that kiss.

Had there been seven circles on Aunt's back? It was so hard to remember clearly. She'd seen Aunt's back since then and there had been no trace of anything. Maybe she was overreacting. It was probably nothing. Just another Binders' punishment, some sort of sick training. There was no good reason to make any more of it except – *Rowan's blood . . .*

The doorbell rang, making Anna jump. She hid the apple away and went to answer it. A handful of children were gathered outside, a miniature collection of ghouls and devils and witches. They screamed: 'TRICK OR TREAT?'

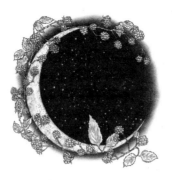

# SECRETS

*Never forget the Ones Who Know Our Secrets for they will never forget our secrets.*

*The Return, The Book of the Binders*

Anna hadn't been able to concentrate on school all week. She was still thinking about Rowan and her fall. She'd hoped that with the magic of the group her own might somehow begin to grow stronger but the accusatory line of blood that had circled from Rowan's head had made itself clear. She was out of her depth.

She trudged her way to English, knowing that it would not help her mood. Mr Ramsden boasted the exceptional skill of turning great works of literature into dried-out husks. *Like me – a dried-out husk of nothing.* At least Peter was in the class and would provide some distraction. The room was empty. She took a seat in the corner and waited, hoping he'd arrive early. The door swung open—

'Hey, witchy.'

She fell forwards onto her desk with a moan.

Attis smiled. 'I love the effect I have on you. I'm not sure if it's pleasure or pain.'

'It's the latter, I assure you.'

'It's a fine line, I assure you.'

He walked over, stretching as he did so, his arms almost touching the low ceiling, making the classroom seem suddenly small. He was wearing the same jogging bottoms as always.

'Do you ever change your clothes?'

'Of course.' He looked offended. 'Except my underwear. Is this desk free?' He sat down beside her before she could answer.

'Why are you early? You're never early.'

'Oh, I just love reading,' he replied and Anna noted that he hadn't actually brought any books with him or even a bag.

'I can imagine. Is that something you do in between hooking up with girls and picking your toenails?'

He laughed. 'Are those the only activities you imagine I engage in during my spare time?'

'I'm trying to think of other ideas but I'm drawing a blank.'

'You forgot all the wanking.'

Anna threw her pen at him, grimacing with disgust.

'Thanks, I needed a pen.'

She was about to swear loudly when the door swung open and Peter, Tom and Andrew came in.

'I'll give you the pen back after class, yeah, Anna? Behind the science building?' Attis said loudly, breaking into a laugh at the look on Anna's face. At that moment, she could have stabbed him through the eye with the pen in question.

'Are there any girls in this school you haven't yet harassed, Attis?' said Peter. *Great, he's finally noticed me and now he thinks I'm one of Attis's conquests.*

'He's living proof that evolution can go in reverse,' sneered Andrew, his mousy nose twitching. Anna was not a fan of Andrew – he followed the popular boys around wherever they went, hiding behind them while making snide comments and statements designed to provoke. They seemed to tolerate him, likely because his family were rich and influential. He turned to Anna with his oily stare. 'I wouldn't get your knickers in a twist over him if I were you.'

Tom banged Anna's desk as he passed. 'You'll only be disappointed. Three humps and it's over.'

'Three very tender humps in my defence,' Attis replied. 'And, Andrew, don't talk about a girl's pants. It's disturbing for everyone.'

Andrew looked as if he was going to retaliate but Peter and Tom had started to chat and he retreated in their direction. The room slowly filled. Mr Ramsden arrived with a frown that anchored the rest of his face downwards, pulling deep marionette lines through it. He always wore the same one-size-too-big grey suit, today with an orange tie with elephants on it. Anna thought of one of those sad old clowns and found the image entirely fitting.

He announced they would continue reading *Macbeth* when Felicity Gibson rushed into the room. 'It's seven minutes past the hour, Miss Gibson, what do you have to say for yourself?'

'Sorry, Mr Ramsden. Cheerleading practice ran on.'

'Waving pom poms around in the air ran on? How much can there possibly be to learn?' he sneered. He was in a foul mood.

'We were working on a new routine.'

'Oh, a new routine! I didn't realize. Why don't you show us?'

Felicity laughed nervously.

'Show us,' Ramsden repeated, the lines of his face hardening. Headmaster Connaughty had made Mr Ramsden deputy head and he liked to take full advantage of his small handful of power.

'Mr Ramsden, I—'

'Show us. Now.'

Felicity began to dance, looking as self-conscious as it was possible to be. The class sniggered. Anna turned away, feeling awful for her.

'Wooo, shake that booty,' Tom hooted.

'Kellman,' warned Ramsden but he let Felicity continue for a few more moments. 'Please stop. After that performance I can see why you need more practice.' He grunted a laugh. Felicity ran to a spare desk looking as if she was on the edge of tears. 'Right. Peter, can you begin reading?'

The class quietened down and Anna sat back, wondering how Mr Ramsden got away with his little power trips. She let Peter's soothing voice wash over her, each word level and smooth as a pebble.

'Would you like to give your thoughts on this scene?' Mr Ramsden said when he had finished.

Peter cleared his throat. 'It's clear that Lady Macbeth is manipulating Macbeth into committing murder. She knows he is a man of war and valour and she provokes him, calling his manliness into question—'

'Is your own manliness so delicate that a few words would call it into question?' Attis spoke up behind him.

'Lockerby, no harassing someone's interpretation,' Ramsden barked.

'I'm not. I'm debating. Isn't that what we're meant to do?'

'Mr Ramsden, if Attis wants to debate my answer I'd be happy for him to lend his thoughts. I'm sure they would be enlightening.' Peter turned to Attis with a faint smile.

'A kind offer, Mr Nowell, but Lockerby is not interested in genuine debate, only disruption.'

'Can I have both?'

Ramsden seethed. 'You can read the next scene is what you can do.'

'I would but I don't appear to have a copy of the book.'

'Where is your copy?'

'To be fair, sir, he probably can't read,' said Andrew.

Ramsden assessed Attis's desk, his lips snarling. 'Lockerby! How dare you come into my class without the book we're studying. It was explicitly stated at the start of the year that everyone had to buy a copy of Shakespeare's complete works.'

'It's fine, Mr Ramsden, I know it all already.'

'Oh!' Ramsden's bulldog face flushed. 'You know the entire play already.'

'Well, roughly.'

'If you know Shakespeare so well why don't we play a little game?'

'Sure.'

'Come up here.'

Attis jumped up from his desk and walked to the front.

'You can recite Macbeth's "Tomorrow" speech to the rest of the class and for every line you get wrong, you get an evening of detention.'

'What happens if I get it right?'

Mr Ramsden looked at Attis like a bug he was about to squash beneath his shoe. 'Oh, you can decide.'

'OK, if I get them all right then you have to perform a cheerleader routine in front of everyone.'

Anna, like the rest of the class, couldn't help laughing at the image. Mr Ramsden slammed his hand onto the desk to quiet them. 'Absolutely, Mr Lockerby. I'll dance around the room with bloody pom poms.'

'And you can apologize to Felicity,' Attis added.

Mr Ramsden's fists balled up, but then he smiled graciously. 'Of course.'

Andrew looked back and forth with glee between Tom and Peter, who broke into a smile. Anna didn't blame them for wanting to see Attis humiliated, but she took no pleasure in watching it herself. Attis, however, looked entirely unperturbed. He straightened his shoulders, held his head up and in a booming voice began to speak.

'Tomorrow, and tomorrow, and tomorrow . . .' His face morphed into a diminished and tortured soul, each tomorrow seeming more desolate than the last.

> 'Creeps in this petty pace from day to day,
> To the last syllable of recorded time;
> And all our yesterdays have lighted fools
> The way to dusty death. Out, out, brief candle!
> Life's but a walking shadow, a poor player
> That struts and frets his hour upon the stage
> And then is heard no more. It is a tale
> Told by an idiot, full of sound and fury,
> Signifying nothing.'

His last word rang out across the silent and stunned class-room. Andrew shrank down in his chair. Mr Ramsden remained motionless at the back of the class. His silence was the loudest.

'Now personally,' Attis continued. 'I don't think Lady Macbeth is responsible for Macbeth's downfall. She has her part to play but Macbeth wants her to play it. It's fear that truly drives him on. He fears events unravelling beyond his control; he fears he is unable to fear and feel human suffering; above all he fears his own disintegration. He's having a bloody existential breakdown. "Life . . . is a tale told by an idiot . . . signifying nothing. . ." It's this nothing that drives him on. He seeks transgression, damnation, to destroy himself and – feel something.'

The class burst into applause. The sound startled Anna; she'd been lost in his words.

'Of course, the witches are also to blame, but witches normally are.' He winked at her. Anna shrank down in her chair. 'Now, Peter, I'd be fascinated to hear your thoughts on the subject? I'm sure they'll be most enlightening.'

Peter gave him a cold smile and went to speak but Mr Ramsden regained the power of speech. 'Lockerby! You obviously planned this whole charade!' His face had begun to resemble the colour and turgidity of an aubergine.

'I thought we had a deal, Mr Ramsden? I can perform another if you like.' Attis flung his head back dramatically:

> 'It is the cause, it is the cause, my soul.
> Let me not name it to you, you chaste stars—'

'Get out!' Ramsden yelled.

'You want me to fetch some pom poms?'

'OUT!'

Attis took a deep bow and made his way out, the door swinging behind him.

By lunchtime, everybody was buzzing about what had happened, all accounts blown completely out of proportion. As Anna entered the canteen she caught herself smiling, recalling the look on Ramsden's purpled face. She'd suspected Attis was smarter than he let on, but even so, had he studied the speech before or did he really know the entire works of Shakespeare? She was reminded of the fact that she barely knew who he was at all.

'Yo.' She heard Effie call out and looked up to find Effie, Rowan and Miranda – who looked as though she'd been taken hostage – sitting together. Effie beckoned her. Anna had spent every lunchtime for as long as she could remember alone, *a nobody*. It felt entirely unnatural and unnerving as she walked towards their table and took a seat.

They surveyed each other. It was the first time they'd all been together in public.

'I normally have Bible Study on Wednesday but the room is in use today so I've moved it,' said Miranda defensively.

'It's OK, Manda, we won't tell anyone you're coming over to the dark side,' said Effie.

'It's Miranda! And I'm not! It's simply an exploration into the darkness and back out again.'

'You make it sound dirty.'

'I do not!'

'Manda, you're going to have to learn to deal with Effie's humour if you want to survive,' Rowan advised. She turned to Effie eagerly. 'So what happened in English with Attis? Everyone's talking about it. Wish I'd been there. Apparently he's being suspended from Ramsden's classes.' Anna was not surprised to hear that but couldn't help being a little disappointed; class would not be as entertaining without him. 'I saw this.' Rowan sniggered, holding up her phone. It was a clip of a cheerleader waving pom poms around; Ramsden's head had been edited onto the body.

Effie laughed. 'Attis did something stupid and brilliant as usual, I presume.'

'I was there,' said Anna and then found herself recounting the story in full.

'So he just recited it on the spot?' Rowan repeated. 'Had he just memorized all of *Macbeth* in case one day this situation arose?!'

'Oh, he has a photographic memory. He's the smartest person I know, a voracious reader,' said Effie with a begrudging kind of pride. Anna tried to piece together this new side of Attis with the boy she had begun to know. 'His dad, an old friend of Selene's, was a professor of English, and a history buff too, so Attis grew up around it all. They lived on campus and by the time he was fifteen he was making money writing essays for stressed-out students. He's resourceful.'

'Where?' Anna asked, wanting to know more.

'The University of – I can never pronounce it – Aber . . . ystwyth in Wales. Beautiful place. Right on the beach.

Selene used to drop me off for whole summers there.' She smiled distantly.

'Maybe we can all go there in the summer?' said Rowan excitedly. 'Coven road-trip?'

'His dad's not there any more,' said Effie, distractedly – she was waving at a boy who had just come into the room. He waved back and promptly walked into a chair, looking terribly embarrassed. Anna recognized him as the large one Effie had taken a liking to during their trip to the café.

Rowan elbowed Effie vigorously. 'I heard you two were a thing now.'

Effie smiled. 'Just trying him out.'

'Can I try Attis out in the meantime?' Rowan asked with an eyebrow waggle.

'Speak of the Devil, or should I say devils . . .' said Effie.

Darcey entered the room arm in arm with Attis. She was laughing with flirtatious exaggeration at something he'd just said. Attis broke away to get food and Darcey trailed past their table, Olivia and Corinne behind her. Miranda froze. Rowan pretended to read something on her phone. Anna reached for her Knotted Cord.

'Wow. Are these the best you could do, Effie?' Darcey made a face. 'You must be desperate, but we knew that already, didn't we? I guess that's how you end up going down on Tom Kellman in the back of his car . . .'

'Well, he said I was better than you,' Effie replied.

Corinne giggled and Darcey gave her an acid look.

'Miranda Richards.' Darcey tutted. 'You ought to know better than to hang out with whores, or have you finally decided to drop the Virgin Mary act?'

'If you'd like to attend my Bible Study class,' Miranda replied with a nervous gulping, 'I'd be happy to explain more about—'

'Uh oh, I think I'm about to be saved!' Darcey put a hand

to her mouth, making Olivia and Corinne laugh. 'The day I go to your Bible Study Club, will be the day you get laid. You really should get laid, you know. It'll help with that uptight grimace you call a face.'

Corinne started massaging Miranda's shoulders. 'I highly recommend it. Twice a day keeps the doctor away.'

'She'll probably manage it before you, hey, Beast?' Darcey nudged Rowan. 'No one's going to want to touch your large . . .'

'Thighs? Ass? Cankles?' Olivia suggested.

'Hey. There's no need—' said Anna, quietly.

'Hold. The. Phone. Did the Nobody just speak?' Darcey turned to her, eyes narrowing. Anna kept her head down, instantly regretting her moment of protest. 'Look at you, defending your new friends. Afraid they're going to tire of you just like everybody else did? Realize you're just a nobody with nothing to offer? Even your own parents couldn't bear to stick around—'

'Hey, Peter! Over here!' Effie shouted. Peter had just entered the room and was trying to determine the source of his name. 'I wonder when he's going to tire of you, Darcey? I'm sure I can help that along.'

Darcey's eye twitched slightly. She smiled sweetly and walked over to Peter; Corinne and Olivia followed. Darcey said something to him and he looked over at Effie with a frown.

'Well, there we go, we just got Juiced,' Rowan groaned. 'Our lives are officially about to become hell. Super glad my year eight nickname is back though. Thought we'd moved on but no.' Rowan nudged her dessert away.

Attis banged his tray down. 'Ah, Darcey's gone, what a shame.'

'I knew this would happen,' Miranda cried, distraught. 'They're going to ruin us.'

'Why are you all so afraid?' said Effie impatiently. 'This school is backward. They wouldn't have got away with this shit in New York. Darcey's just an old-fashioned bully; she tears at people, divides them. Now we have each other, she can't win.'

'She can win,' said Anna. 'She always wins.'

'Depends what you think of as winning.'

'Expulsion? Social extermination? Online harassment for the rest of our lives?' said Rowan.

'Expulsion is a possibility,' Effie conceded. Miranda turned pale. 'But social extermination – no. There's a new social order in town and only we know the rules. You all just need to open your minds. We have a whole magical world at our fingertips, do we not?'

Anna wasn't sure she could claim to have any sort of magic at her fingertips.

'And what does Darcey have?' Effie continued.

'Excellent contouring skills?' Rowan suggested.

'The ability to make our lives hell,' Miranda groaned.

'Miranda's right. Provoking her isn't a good idea,' said Anna. 'She controls the gossip in this school. The last thing we want is people talking about us.'

'Too late, sorry.' Effie smiled, looking around the room. With a sinking heart, Anna noticed the glances in their direction. 'I'm news and if you hang out with me – so are you. It's not my fault the people here have nothing better to do with their lives.'

Anna shook her head, giving in to Effie's smile. 'So long as we don't wind up *on* the news.' She thought of the Faceless Women, the Binders' fears swirling around the story. Anna knew she might get laughed at again, but she was tired of avoiding the questions that had been driving her mad since the summer: searching for scraps of information when Aunt wasn't in the house. 'Hey, does anyone know anything about that story from a couple of months back, those women hanging in Big Ben? This might seem silly but – was magic involved?'

Rowan lowered her eyes. Effie turned to Anna with a dry smile. 'You mean the hanging witches?'

'What?' Miranda gasped. 'Were those women *witches*?'

'I forget you two know so little about the magical world,' said Effie. 'Yes. They were witches.' Her eyes shone hungrily. 'The Seven. The most powerful witches of all.'

Anna was too shocked to reply. She'd suspected they might be witches, but the most powerful . . . No wonder the Binders were losing their minds.

'I thought only six women were found,' said Miranda.

'Well, the seventh noose was empty so we're hoping one escaped,' said Rowan.

'Escaped? I thought they committed suicide?'

'Goddess, no!' Rowan cried and then lowered her voice. 'Mum says they would never. No. Something killed them. She's been kind of jittery since it all happened.'

'What?' said Anna. 'What killed them?'

Effie leant in. 'No one knows, but it had to have been something even more powerful.' She looked delighted by the thought. 'Selene won't tell me anything either. She doesn't seem worried, says the Seven will be back.'

'They'll return?' Anna asked, feeling marginally reassured.

'Yeah, they can't technically be killed. Too powerful for death. I'd kill to meet them, to cast with them. Imagine what they could teach us of the magical world!'

'What about that mark on their necks – the seven circles?'

'That's a curse mark.' Rowan shuddered. 'The Seven protect all witches from harm so they bear the mark as a symbol of protection, to deflect the evil back at itself. Curses are the darkest form of magic, after all.'

'A curse mark,' Anna repeated. *Is that the symbol Aunt had sewn into her back? Why? To protect against curses too?* She could hardly ask Aunt without raising her suspicions.

'I wouldn't worry about it all,' said Attis to Anna quickly. 'Shit happens in the magical world. It gets cleared up.'

But she wasn't listening. 'They referred to it as the Eye?'

Rowan nodded. 'That's one of the old names for it. Looks like one, doesn't it? I remember coming across the symbol in a book when I was young and couldn't sleep for a week. There's something about it that gets under the skin . . .'

Miranda groaned. 'This all sounds dangerous. I miss being a cowan.'

Effie threw an arm around her with a laugh. 'Didn't I just tell you? The only dangerous thing around here – is us.'

After years of grudging acceptance, Anna realized with surprise that she had started not to dread school. It had been several weeks since they had started hanging out as a coven and things hadn't been easy – she was still lying to Aunt, exams were around the corner, and people had started to talk. Little of it was pleasant.

*The Whore. The Virgin. The Beast. The Nobody.*

They were the names going around, in snide whispers, no doubt given life by Darcey. But for the first time Anna had other people to be excluded with. She'd walk to class with Rowan, getting daily updates, hearing about her latest crush from band practice (referred to in code as *trumpet-boy*), or she'd study with Manda (who'd finally submitted to her nickname), or they'd all meet for lunch and swap stories and make fun of Olivia's latest fashion post or Darcey's pathetic attempts to seduce Attis, talk about the things they'd do once they were free of this school. They were slowly and tentatively unfolding themselves to one another.

Aside from Effie's occasional cantrips there hadn't been any magic so Anna was somewhere between excited and terrified when she opened her locker that morning and discovered an apple. When the afternoon's lessons were over she crept through the quiet corridors down to the sewing room.

Rowan rounded on Anna as she entered. 'The Unfathomable Five or Coven of the Daughters of Avalon or Bitches Gon' Be Witches?'

'What?'

'We need a coven name. Which do you think?'

'You said them so fast they all sort of melded into one.'

'We don't need a name,' Manda interrupted. 'It's not a thing.'

'The Wayward Sisters?' Rowan added. 'We need to keep snowballing, Anna?'

'Er – snow – sewing . . . the sisters of . . . order of the long . . . I like bitches being witches.'

Effie threw the door open, making them all jump.

'You have to stop doing that,' Rowan cried.

Effie had changed into a tight black top, tucked into black belted jeans. She'd cut a fringe into her hair and dotted gold make-up beneath the shadows of her eyes. Anna reflected how she never quite looked the same; it was like watching rippling water.

'We're leaving,' she said. 'We need to be outside. We need to connect with something greater.'

'The Great Connectors?' suggested Rowan.

'What's she on about?'

'A coven name,' Anna explained.

'We need one, but not that.'

They met Attis en route, following Effie up through the twisting corridors of the school. The higher they went the smaller the corridors seemed to become, like the bronchioles of a vast and worn-out lung.

'Where are we going?' asked Manda apprehensively.

'Up,' said Effie.

They wound up a narrow circular staircase, darkness closing around them until Anna could barely see anything at all. Ahead was a dead end. Attis took out his white key and fiddled with something on the ceiling – a hatch. It sprang open.

'Useful key that one, isn't it?' Rowan whispered to Anna.

Attis disappeared through the hole. Anna climbed up and was met with cold, biting air and a strong hand to lift her through. She came face to face with Attis and a dome of sky. After the cramped corridors the summit of the school was a different world, its roofs and turrets rising and falling, like a mountainous landscape punctuated by miniature fairy-tale castles. They were enclosed in a small area, surrounded by iron railings. Anna went to the edge, the school grounds unfolding below.

'"Moonless night . . . starless and bible-black,"' said Attis, appearing beside her.

Anna looked up and saw it was true – there was no moon in the sky, nothing to soften the landscape beneath them. The darkness was complete, turning the sweeping lawns below opaque, gathering shadows in the trees, slicing the floodlit paths and lacquering the roads black.

Rowan laughed delightedly, holding out her arms, hair half mad with wind. 'I could fly right about now.'

'Get flying over the castle walls, then,' said Effie, nodding towards the spiked railings surrounding them, beyond which lay a larger expanse of roof. The railings weren't particularly high or sharp, but looked as if they'd still have a go at impaling you if you were inconsiderate enough to fall on one.

'I can't climb over them!' Manda protested. 'I have very poor upper-arm strength. I can't pull myself out of a swimming pool or hold shopping bags for long periods of time.'

Effie rolled her eyes. 'You can hold yourself up on the corner of the roof there and here's a strapping young lad to help you.' She presented Attis.

'I weigh like two stone more than everyone here.' Rowan stared at the railings sceptically.

'Maybe we should be called the Coven of the Cowardly Chickenshits?' said Effie as Attis swung himself over the railings with an impossible ease.

'I like the alliteration, but I'm not quite sure it has the right tone . . .' said Rowan.

'Come on! Anna, give me a hand.'

Anna laced her hands into Effie's, providing foot support for Rowan to pull herself up. Feet hovering on the top, she launched herself at Attis. It took him some time to extricate himself from her grip.

Manda approached the railings with a deep reluctance. She managed to get herself onto the fence and then stood there, clinging onto the wall. 'So I just jump?'

'You just jump. I've got you,' Attis replied.

'Just jump?'

'Jump.'

'I'm going to push her in a moment,' Effie muttered.

With a squeak Manda dropped into his arms, legs twitching in all directions. As soon as she found her feet she bolted off into the wider expanse of the roof – a skittish deer disappearing into the darkness.

'You go,' said Effie. 'I've done it before.' She criss-crossed her fingers and Anna manoeuvred herself onto the fence.

Attis put his arms up and Anna let go. They met her with solidity: a warm, firm grip around her waist. 'You OK?' he said, dipping his head to catch her eyes.

'Fine, thank you,' she replied, aware of his hands on her.

'Hey!' Effie shouted, already on the fence. Attis let Anna go and lent Effie his back; she jumped onto it and they were away, piggybacking across the roof. The others had gone wild on the freedom, galloping and whooping and screaming, weaving in and out of the darkness.

'Over here!' Effie shouted.

'Where?'

'In the middle!'

Anna waded through the darkness to the centre of the roof where they had gathered. They sat quietly for a moment, catching their breaths.

'A witch's magic is more powerful at night and you won't find a darker night than this,' Effie announced, pausing for effect. 'For three nights it shall be so. Yet the moon is still above: the Dark Moon. Its invisible face looks down on us now. Can you feel it?'

They turned heads up to the sky, letting the silence and mystery of the night descend on them.

'I can feel . . . a stone under my arse,' said Rowan. Anna snorted loudly.

Effie gave them a charged look and continued. 'The moon is the ruler of the planetary languages. The sun knows our truths, but the moon knows our lies, or is it the other way round?' She smiled. Their eyes shifted uneasily between each other. 'When the world is denuded of the moon's light, secrets must out. For all of us have a dark moon within.'

Her make-up glimmered; the eyes above were pools of darkness and delight. She loved her games. Anna caught Attis's eye. She couldn't read his expression in the dark – curiosity or concern?

'So, are we all prepared to share our deepest, darkest secrets?'

Anna certainly wasn't interesting enough to harbour any deep, dark secrets, but she'd spent her whole life keeping her thoughts hidden away, pocketing them in her nanta bag, huddling the shreds of who she was to herself. Now she was expected to reveal all in front of a group of people she barely knew. The thought made her desperately afraid. Perhaps if she exposed herself they would discover there was no one there at all. She'd disappear into the darkness of the night forever.

Effie extracted a small silver tin from her bag. 'Thanks for these, Rowan. I introduce the rest of you to the gwiri berry.' She held up something that Anna couldn't distinguish from the darkness.

'No problem,' Rowan replied. 'They also go by the name of moon's tears or mother's mirror. They're rare, very hard to grow, but of course Mum managed it. She spent five years researching them and another five trying to grow the bloody things. She got there though. It's been flowering for the last few years and has grown to a good four feet high, only a few feet off the maximum height the shrub can reach—'

'Rowan,' said Effie.

'Sorry. This is not relevant.'

'What is it?' asked Manda.

'A strange little plant,' Rowan continued. 'It grows on good soil, frequent watering and – secrets. You have to feed it to them.'

'Incredible,' said Attis, sounding genuinely fascinated.

'Oh yes. Mum's been whispering secrets to it over the years; big or small, they all help. The rest of the family have been at it too and when guests come over she asks them to contribute their secrets. Poor Uncle Archie swore blind he didn't have any to tell but she still forced him into the garden, even though his wheelchair doesn't work well on uneven ground.'

'Secrets must have a magical energy of their own, a transference which the plant can feed off.' Attis was talking to himself more than anyone.

'Once you've fed it enough, the berries start to grow. Amazing things. They're invisible in the light, but by night, if you look closely, you can see them. Especially on moonless nights like this.'

Anna looked again at Effie's hand. She could make them

out now: a collection of small, white berries, like delicate glass beads. They were barely there at all, becoming more apparent as Effie moved her hands – revealed in motion like the surface of a dark lake.

'They're edible but most people don't eat them because—'

'When the juice melts twixt your lips, a secret from your mouth shall slip.' Effie smiled. 'So they say. It's powerful magic. Apparently if you try to resist the berry and lie, it will stain your mouth.'

'So? Blackberries stain your mouth,' said Manda.

'They don't stain it temporarily. They stain it forever – all over, black tongue, black gums, black teeth. They say it isn't the berry but the secret itself that does the staining.'

'A secret stained by the Dark Moon, in fact,' said Rowan.

'What?' said Effie, intrigued.

'It's the story behind the gwiri plant; all plants have their stories.'

'I haven't heard this one,' said Attis. 'Do tell.'

'Well, as the tale goes – at least how my Granny Pop used to tell it – after the Great Spinner had spun the sun and moon into the sky, they lived like that, side by side both day and night. Of course, being just about the most glorious things in existence, they soon fell in love. The sun shone lovingly upon the moon and the moon glowed with his love in return. However, as the centuries rolled by, the sun came to demand too much of the moon; he shone too brightly upon her, and wanted to know all of her. He got angry, and demanded to know her secrets. As the moon, she knew it could not be, but he was being such a pain in the arse – I don't think that was how Pop put it – that she ran away into the darkness of night and hid from him.

'In desperation, the sun eventually located her with his light, but she was so far away now, lost in darkness. He called out to her to return but it was too late, she knew she couldn't come back. All he could do now was shine on her from afar and while she allowed him to see her face she kept much of herself hidden and for three days of the month she hid away altogether. The Dark Moon. On those nights she wept bitterly and still does. So they say, where her tears fall to earth, the gwiri berries grow – beautiful and bright as the moon but their secrets dark as the Dark Moon itself.'

The story settled gently into the silence, adding to the magic of the air.

'A good story,' said Attis after a moment.

'I think it's sad,' said Manda.

Anna thought it had been beautiful.

'It's not sad,' Effie replied. 'It gave us the berries and now it's time to feast and face their consequences.' She cackled, opening her hand to the centre. With trepidation and nervous giggles they leant forward and each took a berry. 'Who's going first? Entry, mentry, cutrie, corn, apple seed and apple thorn. Crossroads dirt and casket lock, seven geese flying in a flock . . .' Effie pointed around the circle with each beat of the rhyme. Her finger landed on Manda.

'I think that was a fix,' Manda protested. 'I don't want to.'

'The worst thing you've probably ever done is return a library book late,' Effie scoffed. 'Now eat the berry.'

Manda squeezed her eyes shut and placed the berry in her mouth. A few staccato chews and then the words flew out: 'I don't believe in God.' She clamped her hands around her mouth, eyes wide, as if trying to force the statement back inside. It was too late. 'That's not even true! It can't be a secret if it's not true!'

'Some secrets are so secret we don't even know them ourselves,' said Rowan gently.

'But I do believe in God – maybe just not my parents' version of him. The version I've been taught. But I do believe . . . in Him . . . in something.' Her mouth gaped, searching for the words that could give her secret the shape and form she thought it ought to have. 'Someone else please go so I'm not the only one whose life is now ruined.'

'Go on then.' Rowan popped a berry in her mouth. 'I shoplift,' she announced. 'The ridiculous thing is I don't even steal stuff I can wear. I steal clothes that don't fit me – little summer dresses, hot pants, crop tops I wouldn't be seen dead in.' She exhaled loudly with relief. 'Wow, it feels good to get that out there. I've been feeling guilty about that designer jacket I stole last month. Totally too small, if anyone wants it? Also, wow, that was delicious.'

'Shoplifting.' Effie raised an eyebrow. 'Didn't see that coming.'

'Oh, come on,' replied Rowan. 'Classic teenage cry for attention. I wish I had better secrets, but what you see is what you get with me.'

'I'll go,' said Anna, wanting to get it over with.

She looked at the berry in her hand – its own little dark moon in the universe of her palm. Her whole life was a secret, a hundred tiny, shattered glass secrets.

She turned her mind blank and ate it.

It wasn't so much a taste as a sensation; as though the berry was drawing all of her into its depths. The juices flowed over her tongue, like water suddenly rushing from a geyser, tasting of riddles and doorways and something sweet and endless.

'I can't do magic,' she said, although she wasn't aware of her mouth moving at all. Her heart stopped. *Did I just say that aloud?*

Of all the things, that admission hadn't even occurred to her. She had expected to say something about her parents or her life with Aunt – they were her dark secrets. This wasn't even a secret, it was an anti-secret, a lack, an empty hole in her life. She felt more exposed than ever. She lowered her head, thankful for the darkness.

'Anna,' said Rowan with care, 'you're a witch, you can do magic, you're just learning.'

Her kindness made it worse.

'What do you mean, you can't do magic?' Effie's voice was probing, a little sharp.

'I struggle,' said Anna, voice tight. 'When I was younger, maybe . . . but then it seemed to fade. Aunt doesn't let me cast often so I might just be out of practice, but when I try . . . nothing comes.'

'Magic doesn't just go away,' said Rowan. 'It's probably just a psychological block.'

'Maybe.' *Would I rather face Darcey's persecuting gaze or the four pairs of eyes looking at me now? Darcey. I'd take Darcey every time.*

'My turn,' said Attis. He threw a berry into his mouth before any of them had time to look. He chewed, a satisfied look settling on his face. 'I'm not a witch.'

Silence followed.

'Do you want to tell us what you are then?' said Rowan eventually.

'A gentleman never tells.'

'I thought we were airing all our secrets?'

'Where would be the fun in airing *all* of them?'

His words hung in the middle of the circle, like the trails of sparklers in the darkness; a brief moment of illumination that had now passed. *What is he?* He certainly had magical powers and he looked to all intents and purposes like a normal human, albeit a beautiful one. Anna glanced at him and he smiled at her playfully. *This is all just a game to him.*

'You're not some kind of demon, are you?' asked Manda, looking at him darkly.

Attis pondered the question. 'No,' he said firmly. 'I'm eighty five per cent sure I'm not a demon.'

Manda looked a little afraid of him. 'I'll say nightly prayers for your soul anyway.'

'If you want to think about me in bed that's fine by me.'
Manda made an embarrassed spluttering sound.

Effie cackled. 'Isn't this fun? Now Attis has thoroughly
freaked everyone out, my turn.'

She waited until all eyes were on her, then produced the
berry between her fingers and placed it into her mouth, the
juice collecting on her full lips.

'I'm not capable of love,' she said abruptly. Her expression
of triumph faltered and then she laughed. 'Well, that's silly,
it's not even a secret.' Anna could see in her eyes that Effie
felt just as exposed as she had done. Rowan and Manda
laughed nervously. Attis looked at Effie with an expression
of indulgent amusement.

'So what? It's true.' Effie shrugged. 'I don't do love. What
a disappointing secret. I wish we had more berries, I'd take
another three. Dish some real dirt.'

'I could only swipe five or my mum would notice,' Rowan
apologized. 'She knows everything in her garden down to
the very last weed.'

It began to drizzle, the rain breaking the darkness into
pieces. 'All I can say', said Effie, 'is that as a group we really
need to get some better secrets. Let's make a vow now – to
the Dark Moon and darker secrets.'

'To the Dark Moon and darker secrets,' they repeated.

'In fact, that could be our coven name.' Effie grew excited
again. 'Coven of the Dark Moon.'

'It's got a nice ring to it,' said Rowan.

'Coven of the Dark Moon it is. We deal in that which
cannot be known by the light of day and exact our punishments by dark.'

Effie stood up and opened her mouth to the rain. Attis
caught her from behind and wrapped his arms around her,
as if it was the most natural thing to do in the world.

They clambered their way back into the school. It was

jarring, going from the freedom of the rooftops to the inbuilt claustrophobia of the corridors. They gathered their belongings from the sewing room, making small talk, trying to ignore the awkwardness in the air. The dark-mooned secrets that were meant to have brought them closer seemed only to have built a silence between them instead.

Before Anna left, Effie pulled her to the side and whispered, 'We need to talk about the magic. Soon.'

Anna nodded, unable to meet her eye. She walked to the station and began her journey home, left with little but her thoughts. It would all be over soon, she knew that much. She'd been kidding herself. *How can I be a member of a magical coven if I can't do magic?*

She was already on the second leg of her journey when a shadow appeared, too close. She spun round and found Attis leaning down at her.

'What the hell are you doing here?'

'Did anyone ever tell you you have terrible train etiquette?'

'Did anyone ever tell you not to creep up on girls in quiet carriages?'

'Ah, that's where I've been going wrong.' He clicked his fingers.

'I repeat. What are you doing here? Have you been following me?'

'I've been thinking about what you said.' He sat down. 'Conquer new heights. Visit Peru.'

'I didn't say that.'

'Oh no, I was just reading the advert.' He pointed to a row of adverts above them.

Anna couldn't help smiling. She sat down beside him.

'I was thinking about how you think you can't do magic.'

'I don't think it – I can't. The thing that happened with Rowan . . .'

'You're holding yourself accountable for that, are you?'

'I am accountable. Why are you asking me about this anyway? I could just as easily ask you about your little secret. What are you if you're not a witch?'

'I'm not important; we're talking about you.'

'How convenient,' Anna retorted. She took a deep breath. 'Look, I don't think you can help me.'

The train shrieked to a halt and she made her way off. He followed. 'Can you remember when you could do magic?'

Anna sighed. 'I don't know. I think just after I turned seven but then it stopped.'

'Is that when the nosebleeds started?'

Anna was surprised he'd noticed them. 'I think so.'

'Any other symptoms around that time?'

'This was a long time ago. My hair maybe, it used to be golden red, but now it's – this.' She held up a chunk of it. It looked even more wan under the harsh station lighting. She stepped out into the fresh air.

'You told me you're always starving, is that true? Any other issues?'

'Yes, I'm always hungry. I guess I don't sleep well either. I used to get terrible headaches too, back when I was being homeschooled, but they seem to have gone away.'

Attis stopped her and held her by the shoulders. He studied her face until she grew uncomfortable. She knew what she looked like: translucent skin, dull eyes, underwhelming in every way. His own honey skin was vivid in comparison, a smattering of pinpoint freckles across the bridge of his straight nose. Without warning he put two fingers on her neck, they were hot, as if he were burning a brand into her skin. Anna pulled away.

'Your pulse is weak.' His eyebrows knotted.

'Thanks. Any more symptoms you want to uncover? My hair is falling out? I smell? I have partial leprosy?'

'Do you?'

'No! What is this about, Attis? Do you ask everyone you're becoming friends with for their medical history?'

'So we're becoming friends?'

Anna did not appreciate his teasing tone. 'I'm not sure.' She shrugged nonchalantly. 'I have criteria of my own.'

He laughed.

'Right. We're at the end of my street. You'd better not come any closer. My aunt will have your head.'

'I thought we had got along swimmingly.'

'You left our house alive, so that was something.' That evening, when she'd first met Effie and Attis, felt a long time ago.

'I really ought to walk you to your door. Moonless night and all that.'

'You're probably the most dangerous thing around for miles,' Anna pointed out.

He went to defend himself and then he formed a wide smile. 'You're probably right. I'll watch you to the door, how about that?'

'Still creepy.'

'My forte. Goodnight, Anna.'

Anna walked towards the house. She turned around and waved but he was no more than a silhouette in the lamplight, already disappearing into the darkness.

*Who are you, Attis Lockerby?*

# BINDWEED

*May our Hira be twine and thorn.*

*Tenet Four, The Book of the Binders*

Anna hurried towards the library. She'd spent the last few days avoiding Effie and the inevitable conversation. She had to leave the coven. *I ought to be thankful it's all going to be over. No more lies. No more fear . . . No more friends.*

'Hey.' Manda startled her. 'You going to the library?'

'Yeah.'

'Can I join? I've got so much to do.'

'Sure.'

Manda smiled and Anna appreciated just how sweet her face was when she wasn't hiding behind all of its defences.

'How are you feeling about last Friday? Your secret . . .'

'Not great.' Anna shrugged. 'I think my time in the coven is limited.'

'Effie wouldn't . . .'

'Have you met her?'

'She certainly isn't like anyone else, is she? Maybe it won't come to that. Although leaving would be a relief in some ways, right? You said your aunt is strict.'

'Strict is one word. Your parents the same?'

Manda blew out through her cheeks. 'Oh yeah. They're strict, but it's not even that. It's like they just expect me to have the exact same outlook as them and if they ever found out I didn't, they wouldn't know what to do with me. I certainly wouldn't be a member of the family any more. My perfect older siblings would be even more perfect in comparison.' Manda's voice was bitter. 'If they knew I was in a coven they'd probably kill me.'

Anna was quiet for a moment. She tried to find the words. 'Do they . . . hurt you sometimes?'

'Lord in heaven, no! I don't mean literally.'

'Right.' Anna looked away, feeling the shame of her life with Aunt wash over her.

'Oh.' Manda bit a nail – they were all bitten down to the quick. 'Why are we putting ourselves through this? We're straight A students, we have career plans, we have good, loving families . . .'

'I think it's what sixteen-year-olds do.'

'Screw it all up?'

'Exactly.'

Manda pushed the door of the library open with a sigh. They settled themselves at a table, Manda hissing 'Shhhh' at a group of girls nearby. They rolled their eyes at her.

'That girl is rumoured to be dating Karim Hussain. Do you know him? He's really smart,' Manda whispered. Anna shook her head. 'She only comes in here to catch a glimpse of him. He comes here a lot. Not that I notice. They probably make out behind the shelves. Disgusting. Libraries are for reading not for sin and fornication.' Anna stifled a laugh as Manda looked back at the girl with a scowl.

Anna enjoyed working with Manda. She talked to herself as she worked and stressed out so much about all her homework and revision that it made Anna feel calmer by comparison. Anna learnt that Manda's favourite subjects were

English and Languages and she intended to become a lawyer, although hadn't quite made her mind up on the speciality yet. 'If I don't have a mental breakdown by the time I'm twenty, which, at this rate, is likely.'

Anna left her to panic over her upcoming French exam. She stopped off at her locker and was surprised to see an apple in it. Her heart sank. She'd hoped Effie would dismiss her privately but it seemed they would all be there to witness her humiliation.

When she entered the sewing room later, Anna sensed from the shifty looks that they had been talking about her.

'Ah good, you're here,' said Effie. 'We need to discuss your magic.'

*Straight to the point then.* Anna kept her head held high. She would leave in the same way she'd joined the coven, quietly and with a heavy heart.

Attis stepped forward. 'Anna, I think you're being poisoned.'

Anna felt her mouth fall open. The others looked back and forth between her and Attis. 'I'm not being poisoned,' she said eventually. 'That's crazy.'

'Did I mention I'm never wrong?' Attis replied. 'Your magic is being poisoned. I think specifically by bindweed.'

Rowan sucked air between her teeth.

'What's bindweed? How have you deduced this?' Anna asked, backing away from him.

Attis stepped closer. 'Bindweed is a plant that's used to repress a witch's magic. It binds it from the inside; it's very potent and extremely effective. However, it does produce side effects – a ravening appetite but weakness, insomnia, nosebleeds, head-aches – although, as you've presumably been poisoned over such a long period of time, your body must have learnt to cope with them. It would explain your pale skin—'

'I'm a redhead.'

'I'm not talking about the colour but the quality of it. Your eyes too: they're dull. Your hair.' He lifted a strand of it, studying it. 'Well, that could be the bindweed directly or a side effect of your magic being bound. It's hard to tell. Rowan was right, witches don't develop abilities and then lose them, especially not at such a young age. If you're correct and you were once able to cast magic and then it faded away, the deduction is, when coupled with your range of symptoms: you're being poisoned.'

Anna pulled her hair back and turned her face away. She'd intended to leave the coven with her dignity intact. Now apparently she was poisoned, her skin lifeless, her hair drab? *He thinks I'm ugly* . . . Perhaps she just wasn't genetically blessed; perhaps she'd never been able to cast in the first place.

'Describe to me your typical daily intake. Anything you have every day would be useful.'

He had backed her into the corner of the room. Anna shook her head, still not able to look at him. 'I don't know. Orange juice with breakfast. Porridge, or eggs and kippers, or fruit and yoghurt. Lunch – I have here. Dinner varies – I cook it normally. Then in the evenings Aunt brings me a glass of milk—' Anna stopped. It was the only thing in her life that she consumed consistently, without fail. *Good for the bones.*

'The milk. Every day?'

'Since I can remember . . .'

'I'm going to need a sample of it, to test it for bindweed.'

*Bindweed.* Anna tasted the word in her mouth. *Surely not.* Aunt was protective and strict and cruel but even she wouldn't do this – take away her magic from her, put her through years of side effects, force her to do spells she knew she wouldn't be capable of. The Binders didn't even approve of botanical magic, although the Book of the Binders did allow some room for manoeuvre, Anna recalled the words: 'Botanical magic is banned excepting a small number of botanical plants that have been approved for Binders' use.' The plants were not named.

'Anna.' Attis locked eyes with her. *His should be a duller colour than mine*, Anna thought, *grey as they are, but they're not, they're the pattern of rain, the wind just before a storm.* 'Did you ever see anything in your house? It's probably in tincture form. A green-tinged liquid. It would smell alcoholic.'

'I've never seen anything like that.' Anna thought of the room on the third floor but Aunt didn't go there every evening before bed. It must be somewhere more accessible, in the kitchen perhaps. *It doesn't exist, that's why you haven't ever seen it!*

'Get a sample tonight,' Effie urged. 'This can't wait.'

'OK, but if this is all a big nothing, then I'm out and you all have to leave me alone.'

'You'll be long gone,' said Effie. 'Now for some candle magic. Anna, you might want to sit this out.'

The session was frustrating. Even if Anna had had any drops of magic in her she wouldn't have been able to focus; thoughts of bindweed were coiling around her brain. She had no idea how it would be possible to get a sample. It would certainly be dangerous. Aunt brought the milk to her room and combed her hair while she drank it. She didn't leave the entire time.

Aunt wasn't home when Anna got in, so she began to prepare dinner, spilling tomato sauce down her white shirt. She scrubbed it and left it in the laundry basket upstairs. Aunt arrived back and they ate in near silence. Anna found it hard to swallow. She was hungry but that only made it worse – *am I hungry because I'm being poisoned?* She had so many questions she could barely look at Aunt lest they fall from her eyes as she blinked.

When Aunt knocked on her door before bed Anna took a deep breath. She had to do this to prove them all wrong, even if it meant she'd lose them all.

Aunt began to brush Anna's hair, speaking about her day at the hospital, how *you just can't find good British nurses these days*. It was the usual vitriol but she brushed Anna's hair gently enough. Their little ritual. *If we don't have trust, we don't have anything*. Anna took a sip of milk. It tasted like milk.

'Oh, Aunt.'

'What?'

'I spilt tomato sauce on my blouse earlier. I scrubbed it with baking soda, but I'm not sure the stain is entirely gone. I put it in the laundry—'

'Anna.' Aunt pulled the brush sharply through her hair. 'Baking soda alone won't work, you need salt as well. Wait there. I need to see the damage.'

Anna had counted on it. Aunt swung the door open and left. Anna would only have moments. She opened her drawer and took out the bottle she'd placed there earlier. Hands shaking, she poured a little of the milk into it, spilling a few drops in the process. She screwed the lid back on and threw it into the drawer as Aunt stormed back into the room. Anna put her arm over the spilt milk and let it absorb into her sleeve.

Aunt held up the blouse. 'This is not what removing a stain looks like. How could you be so careless? After I finish with your hair you can go and soak this properly.'

'Yes, Aunt. I'm sorry, I'm really sorry,' said Anna, and she meant it.

Anna woke and counted five knots on the dreambinder above her bed. She hadn't slept well; the sheet beneath her was twisted and veined, forming a map of her nighttime restlessness. She walked over to her dressing table, opened up the drawer and surveyed the small bottle of milk with cynicism. She made her way quickly to school, trying to take her mind off it. Aunt would not poison her: she'd lock her in a cupboard, she'd pierce her fingers, she'd turn her tears to flames; but those were tests and teachings; poison had no lessons to give.

Attis was waiting at the top of the main steps, smiling at her cordially. She tried to smooth her wind-blown hair behind her ears, annoyed he was ready for her before she was ready for him. 'Morning, Anna,' he said. 'Got the goods?'

'Shhh,' she hissed. 'Half the school's here. Let's go somewhere more private.'

'I thought you'd never ask.' He grinned and followed her.

They found an empty classroom, the sound of the hallway fading to a distant murmur as the door closed. Anna unzipped her bag and handed him the bottle. He took it and looked into her eyes for a moment, searching.

She turned away. 'Just to be clear, this is ridiculous.'

'Good. I only deal in the ridiculous.'

'We agree there.' She closed her bag and paused. 'Why are you doing this – trying to help me?'

He shrugged. 'You're Effie's friend. She wants a coven; she needs you. I also believe you are being poisoned and I like proving myself right.'

'Fine. So long as it is not on my account.'

'I would never dream of trying to help you, I know how unhappy it would make you. Of course, I still look forward to you thanking me. Dark chocolate truffles are my favourite.'

Anna shook her head with exasperation. 'I hope you're not right,' she said and realized that her words felt hollow; she hadn't truly asked herself what outcome she hoped for: one severed her from Aunt and the other from magic – her hopes, her newfound dreams.

She hadn't expected to see Attis again that day so when he strode towards them in the common room, a sharp resolve in his eye, her heart stopped and then began to beat in double time. 'Poison,' he announced, towering over their table. He turned the seat next to Anna between his fingers and sat down. 'Bindweed.' He looked at her. 'I'm sure of it,' he said, more gently.

All eyes turned to Anna. She didn't know what to say.

'It can't be.' Her voice was strangled.

'It is. This is a good thing. If we know what we're dealing with, we can fix it.'

'Fix it?' Anna replied. *Everything's broken now.*

Effie released a dark laugh. 'Your aunt really has outdone herself.'

'How? How do you know?' said Anna, eyes still fixed on Attis.

'Three tests. Bindweed contains alkaloids. The dragendorff's reagent is a simple test to detect them. They had all I needed in the chem lab: bismuth nitrate, tartaric acid, potassium iodide. The test was positive. I'll show you again tomorrow if you need proof.'

'What was the other way?'

Attis rubbed his jaw. 'Magic. I devised my own system of testing for it. I carved a symbol to detect the presence of bindweed onto a silver spoon and . . .' He pulled a spoon out of his pocket; it was tarnished a tealy black. 'As you can see, the silver reacted.' Attis offered the spoon to Anna but she didn't take it.

'The third test?'

'I drank it.'

Effie looked at him crossly.

'What? Anna's been drinking it for years. I knew it would be difficult to detect a reaction with such a small dose, but I figured it was worth a shot.'

'And?' said Rowan.

Attis shrugged. 'I have a mild headache.'

Anna reviewed the evidence in her mind. *Magic is the first sin. Would Aunt do it? Take away my magic. Make me believe I'm weak and inept for years. Years!* Anna considered the question honestly for the first time and knew that it was possible – that Aunt's cruelty might run that deep. She felt the realization like a wrenching crack through the foundations of her life. She'd always accepted Aunt's twisted methods because Anna trusted Aunt's intentions, twisted as they were too – but how could poison ever be OK? It was too much, too far, too sick. Aunt had taken everything from her.

'So what do we do?' said Effie, banging the table and attracting attention. She leant in, enraged. 'Anna is being fucking poisoned and we're still sitting around talking about it.'

'Slow down, cowboy,' said Attis. 'Our best option is to devise an antidote. Bindweed is an alkaloid so it might be possible to neutralize it. I just need to think of a plant that could work.'

'Mum will know,' said Rowan. 'She knows everything there is to know about plants and everything that isn't known too.'

'Well, that's that then,' said Effie. 'We'll go to Rowan's house this afternoon. You live in Forest Hill, don't you? Not far away.'

'I'm not going to ask how you know that,' said Rowan.

'We have this little thing called school this afternoon,' Manda pointed out.

'Do you not care that Anna is being poisoned?' said Effie and Anna felt she took far too much delight in saying the word. 'I know your last class today is a free period and so is Anna's. Rowan you have PE so you can get out of that.'

Manda pouted. Rowan looked up from her phone. 'I've messaged my mum; she is around this afternoon. She's replied saying she's excited to meet my "depends". I think she means friends.'

'That's settled then,' said Effie. Anna nodded but she felt hollow, imagining her insides blackened and tarred as the spoon. She remembered Aunt taking the package from the doctor when she was seven – had that been bindweed? *Everything I do is to protect you, Anna. Protect and poison. Poison and protect. Punish.*

Anna reached for the Knotted Cord and found the knot containing her anger. She pulled it tighter but did not feel better.

Rowan's house did not belong in a city. It stood alone, a mismatched building lost in a garden, nobbly stone walls bulging against a heavy corset of vines. A green porch ran around the outside, lined with hanging baskets, overflowing pots and tinkling wind chimes.

The door burst open and a woman who had to be Rowan's mother started running towards them. Her nose was similarly long and her hair just as wild, only hers sported a divergent grey streak down the front. 'My baby,' she said, crumpling Rowan into a hug. *Hadn't they seen each other this morning?* She planted a series of kisses on Rowan's cheeks and then turned to the others. 'I'm Gilberta, but just call me Bertie.'

Manda and Effie were folded against their wills into similar exuberant hugs. She offered Attis a hearty handshake. 'Well, hello! You must be Attis. Strapping lad, aren't you?'

'Mum!'

'I see what you meant.' Bertie elbowed Rowan and cackled.

'MUM!'

'And Anna.' Before Anna could say hello, she was tugged into an all-encompassing embrace, Bertie's voluptuous bosom making it hard to breathe at all. Her jumper was soft and her scarf smelt of perfume and cake batter. For a moment, Anna didn't want to let go; the hug was so what a mother's hug should be, a cure for all poisons. 'Rowan has told me all about you.' Her fleeting look of concern turned to a smile.

She had round cheekbones that shone like autumn apples. 'You must all be half-frozen, come inside right away.' Bertie bundled them towards the front door. 'I've got the fire on.'

Inside it was hard to know quite where the garden ended and the house began – there were plants everywhere in pots of all shapes and sizes, interspersed among the shoes and wellies, coats, umbrellas, bags and broomsticks in the hallway. Family pictures dotted the walls. It smelt like the depths of a warm, fragrant oven.

'I've baked lavender cookies, a crescent moon cake and verbena brownies. I'd watch them though, last time I ate one I slept for twelve hours. Oh, don't bother taking your shoes off. Come on through – kitchen's a state – who's hungry? Don't mind the yapping; the dogs are locked away.'

'I told you she was mad,' Rowan whispered as they headed down the corridor.

Anna smiled. 'I think she's brilliant.'

'Wait till you try her cakes.'

Anna's stomach rumbled in reply.

Herbs trailed from the kitchen ceiling and the surfaces were covered with pots and spilt flour and the kind of homely knick-knacks Aunt never indulged in. A huge Aga gurgled in the midst of it all, hung with tea towels and clothes, a large silver pot of porridge bubbling on the top.

'What are these?' asked Manda, looking with concern at a glass ball hanging from the window. It was one of many, each filled with strange substances: a green mist swirled in one; dark sludge had collected at the bottom of another; a third had moss growing along its surface.

'Witch balls,' Bertie replied. 'They capture negative energies: pollution, family arguments, evil spirits and so forth. Useful things. Anyone for tea?'

'Yes, please,' said Anna, inspecting a ball with a sticky-looking yellow substance moving slowly inside it.

'You're going to have to be more specific than that,' Bertie replied, opening a large cupboard stacked with colourful teapots out of which plants appeared to be growing – green leaves and flower heads poking out of lids and peeking through the spouts, vines spiralling around fat middles and dripping down the shelves. Some were more plant than pot. 'Living teas – a lot more potent,' she explained. 'You all look like you need a pick-me-up. Thyme, ginger and rosehip will work wonders.' She picked out an orange teapot with a tuft of thyme leaves escaping from its spout.

Anna wandered through into the dining room, looking at Rowan's many family pictures, all of them happy and vivid, trying to imagine what it would be like to have an older brother and younger sisters. Bertie bustled out of the kitchen with the steaming teapot, followed by Attis holding a large tray of mismatched teacups and slices of freshly cut cake. 'This way!' she shouted.

The lounge was all sofas and rugs and blankets, a fire snapping in the grate. It smelt divine, sharp as a pine forest, with other herby scents running through it in little rivers.

'I throw in bundles of rosemary and sweet grass.' Bertie sat down on the sofa next to Anna. 'Help yourself to cake and then you can tell me why you're all here instead of at school. Have a bigger piece than that, dear, you're skin and bone,' she said to Manda. 'You two, don't sit over there, there's enough space on the sofa. Come on, trust me.'

There was clearly no space for Effie and Attis, but they did as Bertie instructed and somehow, although Anna couldn't exactly describe how, the sofa appeared to expand as they took their seats. Once they were all on, there was plenty of room. Anna had never liked a house as much as this one. She sipped the tea, its gingery warmth filling some of the emptiness inside her.

'So,' Bertie prompted.

'Anna has been consuming bindweed for nine years. We need a cure.' Effie gave her a challenging look.

Bertie frowned. 'Don't beat around the bush, do you? Sorbus has told me that much already.'

'I'm sorry, *who* is Sorbus?' said Effie.

'MUM!' cried Rowan.

'Oh. I'm not meant to "out" her real name.'

Effie sniggered. 'Sorbus Greenfinch is your name?'

'My parents weren't content with naming us after plant life, we had to be named after their official botanical names. My life was a tragedy from birth.'

'Sorbus – I mean Rowan, you're lucky to have such a beautiful, magical name,' said Bertie. 'It's said the first rowan ash appeared when a fork of lightning struck the earth.'

Rowan rolled her eyes. 'Can we get back to Anna?'

'Well, of course, but I'm waiting on you for that. I've gathered the facts but how or why this poor girl is being harmed in such a way I have yet to ascertain, if anyone would be so kind . . .'

Silence followed. Effie went to say something but stopped.

'I see. Well, I don't feel comfortable devising an antidote for something I don't have any context to.'

Anna thought about telling her the truth, but then Bertie might feel obliged to ring Aunt to discuss the matter – she couldn't risk it. She turned to Bertie. 'Can you imagine any context where feeding me bindweed is OK?' She studied the formation of wrinkles under Bertie's eyes, like the veins of a leaf.

Bertie smiled kindly and they deepened. 'No, my dear. To prescribe something like that against your will is, to my mind, abominable.'

'If that's the case then there's no harm in giving me the antidote. If I'm not truly being poisoned then it presumably won't hurt me and, if I am, then I get my free will back. No harm done.' Anna surprised herself how calmly she could talk about her apparent poisoning.

Bertie gave her a sad look that almost broke through her defences. 'OK, my dear. I can't argue with your logic, but, Anna, if someone is doing this to you it's wrong – perhaps I can help.'

Anna felt the tear within her beginning to open. She took a deep breath. 'You can't. I just need you to help me. Please.'

Bertie sighed. 'Of course.'

'Do you do this often?' said Attis, eyeing another piece of cake. 'Cure people?'

'Oh yes,' replied Bertie, putting a slice on his plate. 'As a member of the Wort-Cunnings I've been practising botanical magic all my life.'

'Who are the Wort-Cunnings?' Anna asked.

'The largest and oldest grove dealing in the language of plants.'

'What's a grove?'

'Rowan, are you not teaching these girls anything of the magical world? A grove is a collection of like-minded witches who practise the same magical language. Multiple covens might belong to one grove or it might have only a few members. The Wort-Cunnings are a friendly, all-are-welcome sort of rabble. We used to have a huge membership, but now it's falling year on year. Witches these days aren't so interested in plant magic – too slow for them, too much to learn. There are lots of other groves out there which also deal in plants, many offshoots – pun intended – that are more focused on a particular aspect of botanical magic, but we do it all. No, I'll pour the tea!' Bertie startled Manda, who had picked up the teapot and released a few drops. 'Only one person should ever pour from the same pot or there'll be a falling out within the year.'

'How many groves are there in Britain?' said Anna, fascinated by the magical world unfurling around her. *Are the Binders a grove?*

'Oh, hundreds, I should imagine. Nobody particularly keeps count, except maybe the Seven,' said Bertie cheerfully and then her smile dropped. 'I still can't quite believe what happened . . .'

Effie perked up at the mention of the Seven. 'Do you know who killed them?' she said.

Bertie put down her mug. It shook a little against the table. 'No. Another grove perhaps.'

'What grove could be powerful enough to kill the Seven?'

Bertie couldn't answer. 'I don't know. There are many mysteries in the magical world.'

'But I thought they were here to protect us all?' said Manda.

Bertie smiled. 'They are. The Seven. Descendants of the Great Spinner. Keeper of the Moonsongs. The spinsters. The virgins. Whatever you choose to call them, they are the witch grove above all witch groves and protectors of the first languages. You have to understand, girls, in the magical world we don't have leaders, or courts, or any kind of judicial system – there are only the Seven. It is they who keep the balance. It is what they were doing that night. I don't know much about the Seven's movements or their magic but I know they perform an annual ritual of protection to keep the magical world safe. It's why they were there, in the centre of the capital, in Big Ben—'

'But they were killed while doing it!' Manda cried. 'Surely that's not a good sign.'

'No, indeed. But what we must remember, my chickens, is that they can't truly be killed. They will return and protect us once more from . . . everything we need protecting from. More cake?'

'From what? When will they come back? How can we meet them?' Effie's eyes had gone wide as dark moons.

Bertie looked at her watch. 'Are we talking about the Seven or are we helping Anna? The girls will be home from school soon.'

'Fine,' said Effie irritably.

'To the garden then! We've got a tisane to make,' said Bertie, springing off the sofa with surprising energy.

They bundled out of the back door through an obstacle course of wellies. The light was almost gone outside, the sky a dusky pink, dusted with clouds. A small toad hopped across the path in front of them. 'Pink sky on all sides and a yellow toad, it'll be a fine day tomorrow again.' Bertie breathed in the air briskly. 'Let's get some light on out here.'

She clicked her fingers and the garden was suddenly transformed, lit by lanterns and strings of fairy lights, and Anna realized with a gasp that several tree trunks were also aglow with a faint, silvery light travelling up their trunks, down their branches and into the veins of every leaf.

Bertie smiled. 'A special breed of silver birch.'

Anna had never seen a garden like it – no flower beds, no paths, no lines, nothing was restricted and yet there seemed to be a kind of order to it all, an agreement among the living things of where they ought to be and how much they ought to grow. The lights brought the swirling, shadowy textures to life. A small stream ran down through the centre, whispering to itself.

'Your garden is so beautiful,' Manda exclaimed.

'It is? How disappointing. It was not my intention,' Bertie replied.

Anna was still marvelling. 'But it's so open,' she said. 'What if someone saw?'

Bertie smiled. 'No one is looking for magic any more, my dear. No one sees beyond their own nose – or their phone for that matter.' Bertie made it all sound so simple – there was magic and it was as natural as any living thing. It didn't have to be hidden away like some sort of sickness. She hooked arms with Anna in the same way Rowan so often did. 'So tell me how you feel, chicken, day to day?'

'Fine,' Anna replied. Bertie gave her a penetrating look. 'I guess – I don't sleep well. I'm tired a lot and I sometimes feel, I don't know, like I'm fading away.'

Bertie frowned then nodded with brisk concern 'Let's wander and see what the plants say.'

Attis coughed and stepped in sync alongside them. 'You don't already have an antidote in mind then?'

'Oh, I have several in mind but there's no point going any further before seeing what the plants think.' Bertie bent down and dug her hands into the soil, rubbing it through her fingers.

Attis smiled courteously. 'The plants have a say in this?'

'It would be impolite to imply otherwise when you're standing in their space.'

Attis looked around the garden and then back at Bertie as if she were mad. 'But surely you already know which plants can combat bindweed, on a chemical level.'

'Do I look like a chemist?' said Bertie, standing squarely in her odd slippers, hands covered in mud.

'Well, no.'

'I don't deal in chemicals, boy. I work with the doctrine of signatures.'

'The belief that a plant looks like what it can cure? Like a walnut looks like a brain so it's good for the brain?'

'Walnuts are good for the brain, even the scientists have proved that now. But don't fall asleep beneath a walnut tree or you might get a headache. They also look like intestines and are excellent at restoring bowel health.'

'Seems all a bit medieval to me.'

Bertie laughed heartily. 'Men are always so quick to slap a label on things. I attribute most of the problems of the world to that. They think they're being clever, carving everything up, but all true wisdom is lost that way.'

Attis formed a propitiatory smile. 'How does it work then, this doctrine of signatures?'

Bertie stopped and ran her hands through a tall plant, its leaves a soft green-blue, the colour just beneath the ocean's surface. 'The doctrine of signatures is not just a plant's shape or colour, it's how it smells, how it feels, its environment, its soil. It's unearthing its story. It's using all your senses at once and then going deeper, saying hello to the very essence of the plant itself.'

Attis stared at the plant, unconvinced.

'Think of when you interpret a poem at school. You have to take into account its context, intonation, punctuation, rhyme scheme, the words and lines and the blank space around it. They all contribute to its meaning, which is not one meaning at all but a world of different meanings. It's poetry. Like the leaves of a book, you have to read a plant between the lines.'

*The correspondences – but alive and beautiful.* Anna thought Attis might laugh at the ambiguity of Bertie's words, but he simply said: 'Show me.'

'This is mugwort. The mother herb, Una, unlocker of dreams and the wayfinder. Feel her. She's comforting but firm, like a mother's hands. She belongs to the moon and will guide Anna back and let her remember.' Bertie laughed suddenly. 'She's telling me to be less wafty, that she packs a punch too.' She moved on.

'Aren't you going to pick some then?' said Attis.

'I can't just go and pick it.'

'I can see I have a lot to learn . . .'

'Plants liked to be picked at the right time and in the right way – if they let you pick them at all. For mugwort that's under the waxing moon, just before sunrise, and only with silver scissors. Now, we need something with a little more bite.' She led them deeper into the garden, to where the trees were thicker, forming canopies of tangled light overhead.

'There's the badger.' Bertie pointed at a patch of stinging nettles. 'The thunderstorm plant. Nature's needle. A wild hag and a man of fire and iron both. I think you need some of that.' Bertie gave Anna a wink. 'As he drives away the evil, she will help you grow resilient, for there's no plant more resilient than this one.'

'Aren't they just weeds? Good for nothing except stinging bare knees?' said Manda.

'And who decided weeds were weeds?' Bertie retorted, sharp as a nettle sting. 'As for being good for nothing, nothing could be further from the truth. There's nothing a nettle can't do.'

'Formic acid, histamine and acetylcholine – the chemicals that form the sting, right?' said Attis.

'Sharp as a spindle this one, isn't he?' Bertie's eyes sparkled with gentle amusement. 'The acid will certainly help to negate the effects of the bindweed, but the nettle will go far beyond that. It'll weave a shroud for the bindweed and suffocate it, fiercely and softly. You'll need courage, mind.' She reached her hand into a clump of nettles and pulled out several strands. 'And courage requires a little pain.'

If the nettles had stung Bertie she didn't show it.

'Hang on, don't you have to pick it, you know, during the full moon, while barefoot, standing on your right leg and chanting Latin at it?' Attis lifted himself onto one foot.

'Well, that would be ridiculous,' said Bertie. 'Although by earth and fallow, thistle and thicket, I will say thank you to the Green-Fingered Goddess for letting me take from her loins.'

'Mum! Please don't say *loins*.'

'Sorry, Sorbus. Right, the next plant can only be picked by a virgin. I'm going to presume you don't qualify.' Bertie made eyes at Attis. 'I guess I'll have to borrow you again then, Rowan.'

'MUM!'

They went on that way, Bertie introducing them to the plants that would go into Anna's antidote. Anna had never heard plants being talked about in such a way – their meanings unfolded, their chemistry invaded by legend and lore. The garden, stirred by the wind, seemed to inhale and exhale around them, releasing their stories into the air.

Attis seemed to have overcome his initial reservations too and had been growing more animated as Bertie took them around – asking questions, studying the plants, somehow getting soil on his nose. Anna was so used to seeing him in school, bored or half-asleep during lessons, but here he was so different: interested, attentive, alive – a childlike shine in his eyes that was curiously contagious. Anna found herself watching him as much as the plants. Who was he? This boy who appeared to care about nothing – and yet could be so absolutely absorbed by the world, who seduced and mocked and made a game of everything – and yet remained utterly dedicated to Effie. *I'm not a witch,* he'd said after taking the berry, and it had been playing on her mind more than she wanted it too. *What did it even mean?* He was clearly magical, so what else could he be? Some other magical entity? A devil? An angel? Someone exceptionally talented at hiding who he really was . . .

They had that in common, at least.

Her concentration was broken by the hollers of two girls who came running out to greet them. 'What's for dinner?' 'Who are these people?' 'Are you doing magic?'

'My sisters, aka spawn of Satan one and spawn of Satan two. They never stop talking,' said Rowan.

'It's getting late. Let's go back inside. Who's staying for dinner?' said Bertie.

Anna looked at her watch and felt her stomach plummet. It was almost seven. Aunt would kill her. 'I'm going to have to go,' she said, the urgency in her voice impossible to hide.

'I'm happy to ring your – aunt, is it? And explain?'

'No, no, it's fine. Thank you so much. Your house is lovely.' Anna headed towards the back door. 'I'll see you guys tomorrow!'

'Escape the madhouse!' Rowan yelled after her.

Anna started to run and, even in the midst of her panic, knew she would give anything to live in a house just like that one. Anna had thought nothing could be more wonderful than the vintage shop, but Rowan's house had been so much more, completely magical but in a way that felt completely, comfortingly ordinary.

When she got home Aunt was waiting for her. 'Where have you been?' The hallway was as dark and cold as her voice.

'Got caught up at the study session.' Anna noticed the soil under her fingernails; she curled her hands into balls.

'Your dinner's cold.'

'I'm sorry, Aunt, I just—' Aunt made a motion in the air with her fingers and Anna's mouth snapped shut; she bit her tongue and tasted blood.

'I don't want to hear it.' Anna tried to open her jaw, but couldn't; it was only when Aunt turned away and walked into the kitchen that it loosened. Anna took a deep breath and followed. The table was bare. 'I had to throw away your dinner. How was the study session?'

Anna tried to scrape the dirt from her nails behind her back. She had to keep calm. Aunt could always detect any tremors of agitation.

'Good.'

'What did you study?'

'Genetic engineering. Biology.'

'What did you learn?'

Anna racked her brain. 'About plasmids, the vectors that carry the DNA molecule into the gene.'

'Which teacher was there?'

'Dr Pinkett.'

'Hmmm,' Aunt replied, smiling at Anna curiously. Anna realized just how much she loathed Aunt's measured smile. It never gave without taking. *How could you do it to me? How could you?* Her anger came welling up fast and hard through the fissure of her Aunt's betrayal and yet Anna showed not a flicker of it on her face.

'I hope you're not lying. If we don't have trust, we don't have anything.'

*I guess we don't have anything then.*

# ANGER

*Aunt positioned her hand over the candle flame.*

*'Your mother was stupid.'*

*The flame quivered.*

*'She trusted love. Who do we trust, Anna?'*

*'Only each other.'*

*'She was a whore. Do you know what a whore is?'*

*'No. Maybe.' She'd heard the girls at school say it. She wished Aunt would stop. She hated the Knotted Cord and yet she found she was holding on to it like a lifeline.*

*'A whore is a woman who gives herself up to a man, gives her body to him to do with it as he likes. It was that stupidity which got her killed.'*

*The anger flared inside Anna and the flame leapt up from the candle towards Aunt's hand. Aunt cried out.*

*'Anna, you must control your anger. You're hurting me.' Aunt's eyes seized tight with pain.*

*Anna tried to put her anger into the knot beneath her fingers, but it would not fit.*

*'If you make yourself vulnerable, you'll become vulnerable. She deserved to die.'*

*The flame shot up into Aunt's hand again. She roared in pain. 'Please stop!'*

*But Aunt continued to berate her mother and Anna grew angrier – at Aunt, at her mother, at herself. She tried to tie it away but to try and control it was only a kind of flapping which seemed to fan its flames.*

*'I'm glad he strangled her. I'm glad and you should be too,' Aunt continued.*

*The flame seared into Aunt's skin until she had to move the candle away. She showed Anna the burn mark on her hand, already blistering. 'This is what anger does. It hurts others more than it hurts you.'*

*Anna lowered her eyes. 'Why must these tests be so painful?'*

*Aunt opened her blouse and showed Anna the bruises beneath her Binders' necklace. 'You know nothing of pain. Not yet.'*

# FEATHER

*In preparation for their Knotting, the Unbound should bathe, dress and ensure their mind and heart are cleansed. The circle must be entered in silence and with control – all thoughts bent upon salvation.*

*The Knotting, Binders' Rituals, The Book of the Binders*

Anna sat down at the piano in the school music room. Her fingers sat upright on the keys like two little roofs, instantly at home.

She began to play. An old tune she'd learnt for her grade four exam. She'd hated it when she'd first been given it – she'd wrestled with its thrumming minor key and tricky timing for weeks but it had grown on her slowly, note by note, until one day she realized she was in love. The irregularities of its rhythm were now flaws her fingers loved to find.

As her mind let go the song metamorphosed into a tune of her own making, fingers roaming, images running through her mind: Aunt searching her eyes for lies; a silver spoon blackened with bindweed; Effie's implacable smile; Attis's eyes studying her own; her mother's burning face in the fire; the symbol of the Eye descending to its dark centre – unravelling her emotions until she could not separate the images from the sounds, the sounds from the feelings, each note a different shadow of emotion: anger, fear, despair . . .

She'd been taking her tisane from Bertie for a couple of weeks. 'A teaspoon steeped in boiling water, twice a day. You can keep drinking your aunt's milk, this will counteract its effects,' Rowan had instructed, handing her the paper bag full of dried leaves and the potent, wild scents of Bertie's garden. Nothing had happened yet. So much fuss had gone into proving the existence of bindweed, creating an antidote – what if she ended up being more of a disappointment than she already was? *What if there's still no magic inside me?* The thought was quietly devastating. She'd come so close. She'd given herself space to hope. What else did she have now? The only person she loved in her life had betrayed her.

From the outside, life with Aunt continued as normal – Aunt had taught her well to hide her emotions – but Anna could feel her anger and resentment simmering just beneath the surface, churning more than ever before. Aunt's control had formed the threads that had kept the embroidery of their life together, but since the bindweed the pattern no longer made sense; every thread had been severed through. Now it was full of loose ends that Anna couldn't stop thinking about – like her parents' death. *Was it really as simple as Aunt made out? Why does Aunt hate magic so much? Where does her fear come from?* The room on the third floor – *is it as innocuous as Aunt claims or another lie waiting to be uncovered?*

Anna could not show even a hint of her curiosity – Aunt had been watching her more closely since her trip to Rowan's house and now Effie was on at her about going to a house party at the weekend. Anna had tried to explain it was impossible but Effie had not been understanding and Anna couldn't help feeling guilty. Effie had gone to the trouble of bringing them together, starting a coven, and all she ever did was say no.

She didn't want to say no any more.

Anna took out her frustration on the keys until there was none left. The melody that followed was caught between hope and despair, the notes full of pain – bruised, tender, alone and afraid; soft as falling feathers . . .

She heard the voice behind her. Her fingers froze over the keys, the song dying instantly. Attis was in the doorway.

'What the—' said Anna and, finding her voice too quiet, upped the volume to a more appropriate level: '—HELL ARE YOU DOING HERE?' The words reverberated around the small room. She turned back to the piano, burning with embarrassment at what he might have seen, what he might have heard.

'Sorry.' He put his hands up in a conciliatory gesture. It wasn't enough. It had been a painfully personal moment, so much of herself exposed, raw to the touch. Anna found herself automatically reaching for her Knotted Cord in her pocket, tucking away what she'd released.

'I was passing and I heard the playing.'

*Of all the people!* He had a little piece of her soul now and she would see it in every single smirk of his. She turned back to face the piano.

'Please carry on,' he requested.

'No.'

'I was enjoying it.'

'I'm not going to carry on with you watching me from the shadows like, like some kind of – some kind of piano pervert.'

Attis snorted loudly. 'Well, that's one I've not been called before. Nothing gets me going like a girl in a dark room playing sad songs on the piano. Oh baby!'

He was so ridiculous that Anna almost smiled but then remembered how angry she was. 'If you're not going to leave, I will.' She stood up.

'You're going to leave the piano pervert ALONE with a piano? Who knows what might happen.' He ducked as she threw a hymn book at him. He walked further into the room, the door closing behind him. 'What was the song anyway? It was . . . sad.'

'It was nothing.'

'You don't have any sheet music. Did you write it?' His eyes were on hers – persuading, questioning. She held them defiantly. He lifted up the top of the piano, peering inside.

'What are you doing?'

'I'd like to see how it works when you play it.'

'You're very odd,' she said sincerely.

He bent his head into the piano's insides and made a gesture for her to start playing.

'I told you. I'm done.'

He looked so disappointed she felt a pang of guilt. *No! He has a way of getting what he wants. This is what he does.*

'I've got to go.' She picked up her bag and moved towards the door. It was only the sound of the note that stopped her. She turned around, but Attis was standing a foot away from the piano. Another note played, the piano key pressing down without being touched – and then slowly, tentatively the tune of chopsticks filled the air.

She rolled her eyes at him but the magic held her in place. She asked the question she'd longed to ask her aunt. 'How are you doing that?'

Attis gave her a sly smile. 'I can teach you, if you'll play for me.'

'No,' she replied and he played a dramatic chord in response. He sat down at the piano, spreading his hands over the keys. His fingers were long and strong. He would make a good piano-player. 'My dad had a piano in the house. I never learnt properly but he was an excellent pianist.'

Anna had never heard him talk about his father before. His admission felt strangely intimate in the dark quiet of the room. She wanted to ask more but wasn't sure how.

'How are you feeling anyway, about the bindweed?' He looked up at her.

The question took her by surprise too, as did the concern in his eyes. They weren't eyes you could easily hide from – their attention so absolute when it was on you. 'Fine,' she replied abruptly. 'It is what it is.'

'Anna, your aunt poisoned you for nine years. That's not fine.' He stood up and the room felt smaller. She moved to the other side of the piano, placing it between them. He'd already heard her music, she couldn't tell him the truth about this – how her aunt had torn her heart, how alone she felt, how afraid she was. *Why would he care anyway?*

'I never thanked you,' she said. 'For, you know, uncovering the whole thing. At least now I can see if magic is a possibility for me. Not that it's looking promising,' she mumbled, as if it didn't mean the world to her.

'Of course it's possible. I can see it clear as day. Your magic is rising to the surface. I just heard it.'

Anna didn't know how to reply. She was deeply thankful for the sound of the bell. 'Come on. Class.'

'Yeah. I'm not sure I'll go.'

'Come on.'

'I have tromboning to do.' He poked at a trombone hanging from the wall.

'Attis, you're this close to being kicked out of school. You barely do any work. Why do you come here at all?'

'Because my father wanted me to. He said school was an extremely necessary waste of time and that I was to see it through. So I shall. I can't help it if some of the teachers in this school don't like me, it's only because I don't talk like I have a stick jammed up my arse. And I'm smarter than them.'

'Failing school is not smart.'

He shrugged.

'Do you not intend to do anything with your life when we leave this place? What do you want to be?'

'Exotic dancer,' he replied with great seriousness.

Anna snorted and shook her head. 'I think you have to be human to be an exotic dancer and, as was established that night on the roof – you're not human or a witch. You might have tentacles hiding under your shirt for all I know.'

He frowned. 'Ohhh, is that what they are?'

If he was going to ask his questions then she would ask hers. 'Quit joking. What are you if you're not a witch?'

'A vampire.'

'Really?' She narrowed her eyes. She'd not been privy to the magical world; she wasn't entirely sure what was possible.

'No. But that would be sexy, right?'

She glowered at him. 'Are you a warlock? Is that different from a witch? Or a wizard, is that a thing?'

Attis shook his head.

'A fairy? A shapeshifter? A shapeshifting fairy?'

He laughed. 'That's definitely not a thing but by all means keep guessing.'

'You're not going to tell me, are you?' she said, frustrated.

'This is more fun. Now, what do you intend to make of your life, Anna Everdell?'

'I'm going to be a doctor,' Anna replied.

'Huh,' he responded, as if the answer had surprised him.

'It's a good job. I want to help people,' she added defensively. 'Hence I'm going to class, because some of us want to pass our exams.'

'Hey, don't go, Dr Everdell. Play a bit more. You should perform. Do you ever play to the school? You're exceptional.'

'I don't play for others, I play for myself.' She picked up her bag. Aunt had never encouraged her to perform, had told her in the past that she wasn't good enough for that sort of thing.

'It's an injustice to keep your talents from the world. We have a responsibility to share them, just like I share my wit and charm with all my fellow people.'

'I thank my lucky stars every day that you do.'

'It must be so hard being you,' he said mockingly. 'So talented, so much angst, unable to share it.'

'It must be hard being you, so charming and such an arse-hole at the same time.'

'Oh no, that comes easy.'

'You know what else comes easy?'

'What?'

'Leaving.' Anna turned around with a flick of her hair. She shut the door on him, alarmed to find she was grinning. She quickly replaced it with an angry pout, reminding herself that he'd barged in there, disrupted her playing, side-stepped her with magic and confronted her about performing. *What's it to him if I play my music publicly or not?* She'd had to protect her music for so many years against Aunt; the last thing she wanted to do was share it with the pupils of this school, the people who'd ridiculed her and ignored her for years. It was one of the only things in the world that truly belonged to her and she wasn't about to reveal it to all on the advice of a boy whom she didn't trust and didn't understand. Especially when he would reveal so little of himself to her.

'We're going to Lydia's party,' Effie announced at lunch.

'I really can't—' Anna began to say but Effie thrust a poster in her face. It was for a science fair in Reading at the weekend.

'Not even my idea,' said Effie. 'Manda found it. Turns out she has more scheming in her than I could have hoped. It's perfect, Anna. You tell your aunt you're going to this fair and Manda's mum has offered to drive you both there. Your aunt can ring her mum to confirm. They can discuss how you've both been going to these study sessions after school, to back up your back-up story. Of course, the real plan is you and Manda get driven to Reading Saturday morning, hop back on the train into London where we'll meet. You can stay at mine and head back Sunday for the pick-up. You're welcome.' Effie took a bow.

Manda gave her an apologetic look. 'Effie said it's time that we start being seen out. This is our chance.'

'I'm not so sure—' Anna began. There were too many things that could go wrong.

'Selene got back last night,' said Effie.

Anna's heart lifted. 'Really?'

'She's desperate to see you. She's worried.'

'Worried?' said Anna. 'Did you tell her about the bind-weed?'

A guilty look flashed across Effie's face. 'Do you mind? It just sort of slipped out – we'd had wine. Selene went ballistic of course and was going to go round to your aunt's there and then but Attis and I managed to convince her not to. She's come round to the idea of the antidote now. She said only subterfuge will work with your aunt.'

'It's fine.' Anna tried not to sound annoyed. In some ways she was relieved Selene knew already. It was easier than telling her herself. Selene confronting Aunt certainly wouldn't have helped – there was nothing Selene could really do. *Is there?* Anna fleetingly entertained a dream of running away with Selene, Effie and Attis, going to New York or some other distant destination, becoming a permanent part of their world. She reached for her Knotted Cord and let the dream go. *Ridiculous.* She couldn't abandon her life and, despite everything, she couldn't leave Aunt. She needed to see Selene, that was all – perhaps Selene could help; perhaps she would have some answers. Anna just wasn't sure what the questions were.

'Did I mention Peter's going too?' Effie raised an eyebrow.

Rowan nodded officiously. 'I've had it confirmed by several sources.'

Anna rolled her eyes, but couldn't help smiling. 'We better
hope Manda's mum can convince my aunt then.' She brushed
away the feeling of foreboding with thoughts of the weekend
ahead. *Peter. Selene. Time with her friends. Normal teenage stuff.*

'YES.' Effie fist-pumped.

'Effie,' said Rowan. 'You know we're not actually invited
to this party, right?'

'I know, but I make a point of going to every party I'm
not invited to.'

When Anna woke on Saturday morning a kind of memory
tugged at her. It was hazy and distant, but recalling its exact
shape and meaning felt somehow critical. Images came back
to her: an apple – she'd been handed an apple. By whom?
Effie. She'd bitten into it and tasted blood. It had poured out
of it, down her mouth and chin, onto the floor forming a
pattern – seven circles. The seeds inside had been crow's eyes,
blinking, knowing. She could still taste the blood in her
mouth, but it was an impossible memory. It hadn't happened.

Anna realized with a start that it had been a dream. It had
been so long she'd almost forgotten how it felt to have one.

She looked up at the dreambinder – it was densely
knotted. *Did a dream slip through?* A dream had never made
it through, not in all the years it had hung there. It had
been disturbing and the seven circles spun round her mind,
but she relished the sensation of the dream anyway: its
delightful absurdity, its ominous potency. *Can it be the tisane?
Is it finally working?*

Eager for the day, she got herself ready and went down
to the kitchen. Aunt was in the shower. The urge came over
her suddenly. She lifted herself onto the counter and searched
through the cupboards, carefully and quickly. Eventually she
found it – in the small cupboard at the top of the oven among
various oils: a bottle with no label or name containing a

faintly green liquid. She unscrewed the lid and smelt a strong alcoholic aroma: *bindweed.*

She felt like smashing the bottle, upending the cupboard, but she placed it back and twisted her Knotted Cord. She couldn't show her anger. She needed everything to go to plan today. Somehow Aunt had agreed to Manda's mother driving them to the science fair. Anna had listened to them speaking on the phone and when Aunt had started discussing the school's inadequate parking provisions she knew it was a good sign. Manda's mother was Aunt's sort of woman – on the school's parental committee, upstanding in the community, believing in a strictness akin to her own mould of parenting. But now the day had arrived, Anna knew Aunt could easily find some reason for her not to go. She waited nervously at the kitchen table, counting down the minutes.

'Anna, don't wear your hair down like that, it looks slovenly. Are you packed?' Aunt's voice marched ahead of her entrance.

'Yes, Aunt,' she replied. 'All packed.' Anna feared telling her lies but not as much as she savoured them in that moment. *Yours, dear Aunt, are locked away in that cupboard and mine are setting me free.*

'Here, you can have this.' Aunt placed one of her old phones on the table. 'It only allows calls and texts, no internet. I want you to text me when you get to Miranda's, text me when you get to the fair, text this evening before you go to bed and another tomorrow on your way home.' Anna took the phone and Aunt grabbed her hand. 'I know I'm over-protective, but what do you expect? You're my sole responsibility in life; keeping you safe is all I have ever tried to do.'

Aunt's words were a pinprick through Anna's mood. She felt the creeping guilt returning. *No. You lied to me. You took away my magic.* But if Aunt truly believed magic would only lead her into danger – *is she simply protecting me?* Anna couldn't think about that now. She pushed the guilt down somewhere deep inside of her.

'You'd better go. I don't want you turning up late.' Aunt ushered her towards the door. 'Walk to the station and then a train to Richmond.'

'I know, I know. I'll see you on Sunday.'

'And, Anna?'

'Yes, Aunt.'

'Make sure you beat this Miranda at the science fair. I'll enjoy gloating to her mother.'

Several hours later Mrs Richards dropped them outside the science fair building. Miranda had inherited her mum's heart-shaped face but beyond that they didn't look much alike. Where Manda was small and thin and serious in expression, Mrs Richards was imposing, full of implacable smiles and relentless cheerfulness. She'd spent the entire car journey informing them about her various church committee duties, asking Anna direct questions about her grades and ambitions – while implying heavily she ought to attend an introductory meet-and-greet at her church – and singing along to loud choral music. Anna was glad to see her wave an enthusiastic goodbye. As soon as she was out of sight they turned to each other and laughed giddily.

'This is the worst thing I've ever done,' said Manda, looking at the science fair building ahead of them. They turned in the opposite direction.

Before they knew it they were waiting in the agreed location in central London for Rowan and Effie, who were late. When they finally appeared, Anna and Manda were frozen.

'Come on, girls, what are you doing hanging around? We're going in there,' said Effie, looking up at Selfridges, one of London's most expensive department stores.

'Why?' asked Manda.

'We're going shopping.'

'I can't afford anything in there.'

Effie shrugged and pushed her way through the rotating doors. A lady offering perfume samples looked her up and down snootily. They made their way through the cacophony of noise and conflicting scents into the centre of the store. It rose shiny and pillared above them, criss-crossed with escalators. They rode them up, past rows of sultry mannequins, hips thrusting, hands resting on impossibly small waists, draped in brightly coloured faux fur, structured lace, labels blaring, sequins flashing . . . up to the sixth floor where noise bubbled over from a restaurant. They peered over the edge of the balcony, the heads of shoppers below them wriggling like centipedes.

'Did anyone see anything to wear to the party?' asked Effie.

'I know I said I do this sometimes but I would not advise shoplifting in a store like this,' said Rowan.

'I can't steal clothes!' Manda protested. 'I look guilty even when I'm doing nothing wrong.'

Effie produced a feather from her pocket. It was white and perfectly shaped, like a smile.

'Everybody touch the feather. You all have to be holding it if you want to be part of its spell.' She leant over the balcony, holding the feather out; the others stretched to touch it too. Then Effie let go. The feather began to flutter down the six floors. Feathers do not move fast, but this one moved slower – impossibly slow – as if it were sinking through water. Anna had been so distracted by its gentle, rocking movement she didn't notice that the racket in the store was suddenly diminished. The noise reduced to a subdued muffle, as though the whole place was underwater too.

'Why's no one moving?' Manda cried.

'They are, just slowly,' Effie replied.

It was true. The crowds below them were still moving, but

in slow motion, as unhurried as the feather's fall – heads just beginning to turn, a foot lifting, a mouth opening slowly as the petals of a flower.

'It's impossible to control time, but there are ways of . . . bending it a little. That feather is one of Selene's most prized possessions and she would not be pleased if she knew I had it, so let's keep this to ourselves, yeah? We don't have long to take what we want; when the feather lands it'll all go back to normal time.'

'Is the whole of London moving like this?' said Anna, lost in wonder. 'Aren't we stealing time from them?'

'No, time has only slowed down for us; for everyone else it's still moving at the same speed. It's hardly going to affect the laws of the universe – much. We're just borrowing ten minutes. Come on.'

'Won't we get caught? There are cameras . . .' said Manda.

'What are they going to see? We'll be a momentary blur. And don't give me any moral crap about stealing either; this place makes more money in one day than half of London. If anything we're taking from the rich and giving to the poor.'

'Are you poor?' said Rowan sceptically.

'I don't own a Louis Vuitton bag and therefore I am poor. Like time, it's all relative. Come on.'

Time and all the people trapped in it moved inchmeal but for them it was a whirr of noise and action – running wild and free, drunk on the hedonism of their mission: Effie whirring through rails of perfectly lined clothes; Rowan wrapping herself in scarfs; Manda pawing rows of clutch purses, shiny as sweet wrappers; Effie stuffing dresses and tops into her never-ending bag, jumping on the beds, scrabbling at the costume jewellery, putting bright pink lipstick on a group of boys with a cackle. The Binders would have combusted at the sight.

Anna stared at the green dress on the mannequin with desirous eyes.

'You like that one?' said Effie.

It was velvet and as emerald as a dragonfly's tail. Anna nodded.

'Take it.'

'It's on the mannequin – it would be very obviously stolen.'

'So?' said Effie, getting up onto the display and unzipping the dress. Anna laughed and joined her. They pulled it off ungracefully, leaving the mannequin naked.

'It's yours now,' said Effie, stuffing it in her bag. 'Go choose some shoes.'

Anna ran over to join Rowan among the legions of shoes. She selected a pair of strappy black ones with the kind of heel that would make Aunt tut until her tongue turned blue.

'Two minutes!' Effie shouted. 'Hide your wares!'

They rushed downstairs and met her on the ground floor, stuffing the final few items into her bag as the feather touched the ground. The shop erupted with noise and suddenly everyone was buzzing around them once more. They looked at each other and fell about laughing and then promptly exited the store – the perfume lady looking down her nose at Effie for the second time.

'I take it back. *That* was the worst thing I've ever done,' Manda whispered to Anna.

# POTION

*The moon's power is too changeable, too unpredictable, too given over to passion.*

*Banned Languages, The Book of the Binders*

They took a train to Hackney and followed Effie down a higgledy-piggledy residential road to a line of Georgian buildings of faded grandeur. She stopped at a house with a bright yellow front door and a garden full of weeds. The door wasn't locked.

Effie took them through and into a large, high-ceilinged kitchen with white walls, dark floors, vast cupboards, busy shelves and heavy lamps hanging overhead. Selene stood behind the kitchen island looking entirely out of place in a kitchen – chopping limes in a sheer pink floor-length dress with ruffled sleeves. She dropped the knife as they entered and sashayed over, lips painted a showstopping red, the colour of theatre curtains. The curtains parted and revealed a smile which Anna was sure people would pay to watch.

'Effie, darling.' She planted a kiss on Effie's cheek and then swirled to look at the rest of them. 'Effie's new friends, such a pleasure! I'm Selene, her long-suffering mother. Tell me your names.' Effie rolled her eyes and wandered deeper into the kitchen.

'I'm Rowan and she's Manda.' Rowan stepped forwards, looking at Selene as if she wasn't quite able to believe anyone's mother could resemble such a woman. Selene adorned them with kisses.

'Miranda, actually,' said Manda.

'Oh, you look so young. How old are you? You're making me feel positively mummified.'

'Manda's sixteen going on forty-five,' said Effie, perusing the countertop.

'Sixteen – those were the days! I want to hear all about what trouble you're getting up to in school.' She swivelled to Anna, her smile faltering. 'My little matchstick.' She folded Anna into a deep hug. It smelt like fresh flowers on the wind, cloves and cinnamon. Anna sank into it. Selene eventually let go and an uncomfortable, hesitant silence fell between them. Anna wondered if Selene might bring up the bindweed or whether she ought to ask her if they could speak privately, but then Selene said brightly, 'Well, you're looking healthier than when I last saw you. More flame in those cheeks, more light in those eyes. This coven is doing you good. I think you need a margarita!'

A margarita was a long way from bindweed, dead parents and curse symbols, but Selene had pulled her into the kitchen before Anna could say any more.

'How was your trip?' said Rowan, descending on them. 'Effie said you've just got back from Russia!'

'Fabulous start, catastrophic end.' Selene made a dramatic gesture. 'Put it this way, I'm off Russian men and vodka for at least ten years. Now who wants a margarita?'

'But we're only sixteen,' said Manda.

'The perfect age for tequila, fresh and clean, before it gets all the bad memories associated with it. Effie, your friends seem a lot sweeter than the ones you were hanging out with in New York.'

'You sent me to an all-girls private school in Dulwich: what did you expect?'

'Don't worry, cherub.' Selene cupped Manda's chin. 'Just one drink. I've got a client due.'

'What client? What kind of magic do you do?' asked Rowan eagerly.

'Love potions – the only currency I deal in.'

Perhaps it was a kitchen for potion-making because it certainly didn't look like food had been cooked in it for a long time: wine bottles, lipstick-stained glasses, books and piles of unopened post covered the surfaces; the oven was full of takeout boxes and the smoothie maker was being used as a hat stand. Shelves along the back wall wheezed with books and pots and pans and hundreds of glass jars and bottles of all shapes and sizes, shimmering with so many wondrous colours it looked like the inside of a kaleidoscopic cave. A glinting copper cauldron sat on the hob amongst it all like a dragon's eye blinking out through the chaos.

Rowan pointed at it. 'Is that for your potions? I've never seen a cauldron so beautiful.'

'Are cauldrons beautiful?' Manda asked doubtfully.

Selene and Rowan looked at her as if she'd just insulted their own mothers.

'All cauldrons are beautiful.' Selene reached to stroke its bright edges. 'They are a window into a witch's soul.'

'Well, mine is blackened, dented and leaks, which is about right.' Rowan giggled. 'Can we make a potion, pleeeease? I have several men who it would be highly convenient to have fall in love with me . . .'

Selene laughed. 'Ah, but my sweet, there is no spell for love.'

'But I thought that's what you did?' said Anna. 'Love spells?'

'I do and they cover every permutation of love – lust, longing, obsession, infatuation, jealousy, heartbreak, revenge

– everything really, except true love. Maybe once upon a time . . . but no. That kind of magic is long gone.'

'So what you're saying is, we're screwed,' Rowan moaned.

'Of course not! Who needs love? You girls don't want to find the man you want to be with forever – now! Keep searching your whole life, I say, it's far more interesting. Passion. Now there's a more interesting proposition. Much more thrilling – volatile, impermanent, ever-changing. Love in motion. How about we add a little passion potion to our margaritas?'

They nodded vigorously and she turned to a book with a purple velvet cover on the counter and flicked it open to a page stained with multi-coloured splotches. 'Cherub, you read from this,' she directed Miranda and then threw the summer hat off the smoothie maker and dragged it to the centre of the counter. 'We don't have much time so today, ladies, this shall be our cauldron! It is the hour of Venus: let us begin! What do we need?'

A flustered Manda ran her finger down the list of ingredients. 'Er – ok – I don't know what these symbols mean, but it says we need apple blossoms, lavender, red hot chilli flakes, midsummer honeysuckle . . .'

'Come on.' Selene ushered the rest of them to her shelves and began fetching items from her store and throwing them into the smoothie maker with zeal. She seemed to be adding a lot more than the items Manda was reading out. Anna joined the hunt but was distracted by the names on the bottles and containers – 'Violet Blossoms', 'Liquorice Root', 'Myrrh Resin', 'Powdered Mandrake', 'Benzoin' – they tasted exotic on her tongue, whispering of distant places, hot sands and feverish spices. Others were stranger, darker – 'Numbing Water', 'Goofer Dust', 'Rainfall (downwards)', 'Rainfall (upwards)', 'Hangman's Ash', 'Devil's Shoestring', 'Blood of a Broken Heart' . . . She could have spent all day exploring every last bottle, wondering at the colours and textures, breathing in the different landscapes of their scents.

'. . . cherry stones, yarrow, cinnamon and cloves – it says to grind together for four hours.'

Selene laughed, twirling around the kitchen. 'We don't have four hours!' She pressed the button and the smoothie maker whirred into life, pulverizing the ingredients into a small hurricane of colour. 'Beautiful! A potion begins and ends with its cauldron. It mixes, transforms, dies, sparks once more – just like passion a potion is never still, it is always renewing. What more?'

'A quart – I think that means quart – of red wine and we have to distil rose petals—'

'Anna darling, pass me the rose water, that will do, and someone get me catnip!'

'Catnip?' Manda cried.

'Oh yes,' Selene replied seriously. 'A love-potion essential.'

The kitchen was veering wildly out of control. Various glass bottles were open along the surface, releasing strange and clashing scents and plumes of powder, while colourful drips and drops covered the surfaces; the mixture in the smoothie maker had begun bubbling and spitting up the sides and the crooning tones of retro love songs gushed from the radio. Anna felt transferred, as if she had entered some other, more vivid world. She played the melody with her fingertips, reaching for the rose water. Her hand moved towards the bottle as if she had known it was there all along, like the next line of the song. This was magic without bounds, without rules, magic fed by something else entirely.

'We need dream dew too for lust feeds on dreams,' sang Selene.

'I can't keep up!' Manda cried. 'You've missed half the ingredients and added a whole load more.'

Selene flicked the book shut. 'A potion doesn't need exacts, darling, it needs energy: grinding, powdering, boiling, brewing, stirring.' She raised her hands into the air and the smoothie maker responded, whirring the ingredients with colourful frenzy. Selene grabbed Effie's hands and the next moment they were dancing. Effie's unwillingness faded as Selene spun her in and out, giggling with an abandon Anna had rarely seen in her.

'Someone get me the powdered heart and feathers of a black cockerel,' said Selene.

'For a love spell?' Rowan replied, voice uncertain.

Selene spun Effie away. 'Ah, but there is darkness in love. Love is never complete without death.'

She sprinkled in a dark black powder and the mixture smoked pink, releasing a frisson of bubbles, smelling of wine and spices and something hot and unsettling. Anna breathed in deeply and felt her cheeks grow warm.

'Now, I want you each to give it a mix and add the name of the one you desire! The potion wants your stories! There's nothing more powerful than a story.' Selene threw her head back, laughing. Anna decided she was a little mad when she did magic.

They gathered around the smoothie maker, giving each other giddy if not wary looks. Effie stepped forwards first and pressed the button. The potion whizzed. 'Laurence Ellerton. Tonight.'

'My turn!' Rowan bounded her way to the front, almost knocking the whole thing over. She cleared her throat and held down the button, shouting over the sound: 'David Jones from band practice. Bryn Sawbridge in the year above. Adrian Martinez, son of a family friend. The guy I see on my bus to school and occasionally stalk. Leonardo Vincent—'

'He's a movie star,' Manda pointed out.

'I know! Attis Lockerby, I mean, who wouldn't? Any boy tonight at the party who takes my fancy – I think I've over-stirred this thing?' The mixture was bubbling so much it was almost overflowing and the air in the kitchen was tinged pink.

'I think you might have given the potion too many names, darling,' said Selene, stepping swiftly between Rowan and the makeshift cauldron.

Manda stepped forwards; her round face set itself into an expression of pained concentration as if she was about to take an exam. 'Karim Hussain,' she sighed, giving the mixture a quick, self-conscious whirr.

'Anna?' Selene nudged her forwards.

*Passion.* The idea of it had been fun, but now that it applied to her – Anna wasn't so sure. To Aunt passion and love were in the same bracket of deeply volatile, extremely dangerous emotions that Anna had always been ordered to avoid, but she was tired of Aunt's interpretations. Perhaps it was the scents stirring the air, the colours stirring the potion, but the thought of Peter's lips on hers sent shivers into the pit of her stomach.

Anna pressed the button and said it: 'Peter Nowell.' It wasn't as though she had any intention of chasing those feelings.

Rowan burst into song, not helping her embarrassment.

> 'Anna and Peter sitting in a tree,
> K – I – S – S – I – N – G!'

'Peter who?' Selene interrupted with a hint of accusation. 'Why haven't you told me of this boy before?'

Anna shrugged nonchalantly. 'Don't worry, I don't stand a chance with him.'

> 'First comes a kiss, then comes love,
> Then comes a spell and a pinprick of his blood!'

Rowan finished the song with flourish.

Selene raised an eyebrow at Anna and then switched the heat off. 'Well, you are all so young, hearts flit from one thing to another in less than a beat. Come on. It's time for a drink!'

They took up residence at the breakfast bar as Selene began preparing the cocktail. At the end she added a little of the smoothie mixture to the cocktail shaker. 'Just a few drops.' She winked, hips wiggling as she shook it. She poured the rosy-hued mixture out into their glasses, the sharp tang of lime stirring the air. 'To passion!' Selene raised her glass. 'May it be yours tonight and in the year to come!'

Anna and Manda coughed immediately after their first sip, making everyone laugh. The liquid burned its way down Anna's throat, through her body, making every limb tingle and bringing a flame of blush to her cheeks.

'To passion and the Goddess of the Dark Moon!' said Effie.

'Passion and the Goddess of the Dark Moon,' they chimed in, laughing again as Manda missed her next sip, tipping half of it down herself.

Someone knocked on the door. 'Ah,' said Selene, finishing her glass. 'My client is here. Can I trust you all alone? No more potion or tequila. Although I shall be disappointed if you don't steal something from the cocktail bar to take to your party.' She smiled wickedly and squeezed Anna's shoulder tightly as she left. Anna watched as Selene walked away, only then realizing she'd been so distracted with the potion and the cocktails and the sheer joy of everything, they hadn't had a chance to speak.

'I think I'm in love with your mother,' said Rowan.

Effie rolled her eyes. 'You and the rest of the human race.'

'So Karim is your secret crush.' Rowan elbowed Manda.

Manda blushed and stood up to look at the nearby shelf of books. 'It's silly. He's not interested in me. It's just – he came to Pen-a-Poem Club once and we ended up talking. He's Muslim and I'm Christian and I sometimes imagine us like Romeo and Juliet, fated to be together but torn apart by our families . . . but in reality I think he's just not interested in me.'

Rowan looked up from her phone. 'Looks like he's going to be at the party.'

Manda's eyes widened. She grabbed several books from the shelves and began flicking through them as if they could offer her protection from the oncoming night.

Rowan turned to Effie. 'And Laurence, hey? Apparently Olivia lost her virginity to him although he was going out with Rebecca most of last year.'

Effie laughed. 'You're like a human dating app.'

'I have my uses.'

'I thought you were with that other one, the big guy?' Anna asked.

Effie rolled her eyes. 'I am not *with* anyone, Anna. I don't do relationships. Plus he was an impatient kisser and, turns out, it translated to other areas too.' She looked down suggestively. 'Laurence is my new favourite. I'll be testing out his skills tonight.'

'You inspire me,' said Rowan, laughing. 'So – er – you and Attis . . . you guys really aren't – you know, a thing?'

'We are what we are,' Effie replied with a hint of a smile. 'We're not together. As Selene said, where's the fun in that?'

'Yeah, but there's Attis and then there's the rest of mankind. You girls know what I mean.' Rowan looked at Manda and Anna. 'He's got that look. Like he's undressing you with his eyes – no, he's already undressed you and he's deciding what to do with you.'

Effie nodded. 'Oh, I know the look you mean.'

Anna knew the look they were talking about too: those mismatched eyes – as though he'd seen right through you; as though he'd discovered all the parts of you that weren't whole and all the while had the answers but refused to give them up.

'I guess you just can't see past Peter's eyes, can you?' Rowan elbowed her.

'Something like that,' said Anna, supplanting Attis's eyes with Peter's intent stare. She imagined what it would be like to have it directed at her.

Rowan frowned. 'Are you sure about him? Isn't he just like the rest? He *is* with Darcey.'

'He doesn't know what she's really like,' Anna protested. 'You've seen her, all smiles and sweetness—'

'And double-D-cup breasts.'

'Peter isn't like that. I remember the first day I met him. I was in year eight; we had to go to this talk at the Boys' School. I just wanted to sit down and disappear as quickly as possible, but there weren't many seats left. I spotted a couple of spare ones at the end of one row but there were a group of boys in the way. The first couple stood up and I tried to get past but then the rest wouldn't stand so I was trapped between them. They started taunting me, just being idiots, but I was humiliated. Then I heard him – a voice from further down the row telling them to let me pass. They listened to him straight away and let me go. I looked at him to say thanks and he smiled at me and I'm not sure if I said anything at all . . .'

'And you've wanted to shag him ever since,' Effie cackled.

'I was twelve!'

'Lord in Heaven,' said Manda, looking up from a large tome, eyes glowing with fascination. 'It seems if we can't find boyfriends, we can just make one.'

'What's the spell?' said Effie.

'It's for something called a golem. It's a translation from an old Arabic spell.' Manda's fingers trailed down the page, past stains that looked disturbingly like blood.

'What's a golem?' Anna asked.

'According to this it's an artificial man created from a handful of earth. There seems to be a very long and specific spell for bringing it to life . . . names of power . . . heat and fire . . . you need the blood of whoever you want it to resemble.'

'I've heard of them,' said Effie, 'but I've never seen a spell for one before.'

Rowan narrowed her eyes. 'Does that mean if I can get some of Leonardo Vincent's blood, I can just make my own?'

Manda turned the page. 'I think you have to sustain it with fresh human hearts and blood.'

'That's going to be more tricky.'

A sound below them made Anna jump.

'That'll be Attis. He's back,' said Effie.

'Wait. Attis lives here?' Manda gawked.

'Of course. Where did you think he lived?'

'Can we feed him some potion?' Rowan pleaded.

Effie shook her head, smiling. 'Come on, let's get ready. Grab the tequila.'

They made their way upstairs. Effie returned the feather to Selene's bedroom, placing it in a space on the mantelpiece where it proceeded to float gently, an inch off the surface. They went up to the next floor and into a room with mirrors for walls. 'My dressing room,' Effie explained, though she needn't have – there were piles of clothes everywhere. 'Right. Makeover time!' Effie lifted up a pair of scissors with a dangerous smile. 'Manda, come here. I need to cut your hair.'

'What? No!' Manda objected. 'Don't you think my mum will wonder where I found a hairdresser at a SCIENCE FAIR?'

'Don't worry, these are temporary scissors. It'll grow back by tomorrow, promise. I use them all the time.'

'But surely people at school on Monday will wonder how my hair has grown back overnight?'

'They'll just think they've remembered it wrongly. Cowans will convince themselves of anything except the impossible.'

'Effie, I really don't think—'

'Pretty please. I promise you'll turn heads, including Karim's.' Effie put her chin on Manda's shoulder and made a pleading face.

Manda whimpered. 'You promise it'll grow back by tomorrow?'

When Anna returned from the bathroom, Manda was squealing at herself in the mirror. 'I don't look like me at all! What have you done to me? Although I like it – I think . . .'

Her hair now skirted her shoulders in a sharp, tousled cut which suited her heart-shaped face and made her eyes pop. Manda stared at herself, moving her head from side to side and pouting. Anna had never seen her pout before. Rowan had already put on her new playsuit and was shimmying at herself in the mirror. She kissed the mirror, leaving a red lipstick mark.

'I've been living in a magical household all my life but it never occurred to me that magic could apply to hair and make-up. Then again you've met my mum. She thinks a manicure is scrubbing the dirt from under your fingernails.'

'You do know there are magical beauty salons in London?' said Effie.

Rowan's jaw dropped. 'This is why I need you in my life.'

Effie clicked her fingers at Anna. 'You're up.'

'I don't really wear make-up—'

'Just trust me,' said Effie, sitting her down and retrieving a tube of beige liquid from the pile. 'Same colour skin as me – this foundation gets rid of spots as you put it on.' She took a sponge-like object and began rubbing it into Anna's face. A pimple that had been gathering speed on Anna's forehead disappeared as the sponge brushed over it. Anna leant forward and found no hint that the spot had ever existed.

'I need to get some of this stuff.'

'Sit back. Now do you want bigger eyes? I have some contact lenses that double their size.' Effie rummaged through the pile.

'I think I'm OK with my own eyes.'

Effie studied her. 'You're right – they're already pretty. Just a little of this . . .' She added some soft eyeshadow and darkened Anna's eyebrows. 'This mascara makes new eyelashes grow.'

The next moment Anna was pinioned in place by a torturous-looking contraption Effie referred to as an *eyelash curler*. Anna struggled to keep her eyes open as Effie gripped her chin and applied mascara. Anna watched as new eyelashes sprouted along her eyelid and her existing ones separated and lengthened. The effect was immediate: her almond eyes were suddenly black-lashed explosions, the green in them flaring.

Effie dusted blush across her cheeks. 'Anti-blush blush – it'll stop you going bright red when Peter talks to you.' Anna gave Effie a withering look, but she was too busy perusing a collection of lipsticks. 'How about this one? It makes your lips grow bigger with every kiss? Or this one makes your lips taste like your lover's favourite dessert . . .'

'Anything not to do with kissing?'

'This one enhances your natural colour.'

'That one.'

'Go on, you do it, you need to learn.'

Anna took the lipstick and opened it; it was completely translucent like a solid stick of water. As she followed the line of her lips in the mirror their hue did not change, but simply grew richer, more concentrated, collecting colour like the centre of a rose.

'Sinfully red,' said Effie, taking a comb to Anna's hair. It had a similar effect to the one Selene had given her, smoothing her hair and drawing it into curls, only with added volume. Anna moved and her hair bounced. Without the frizz she could see its colour – it still wasn't the golden red of her younger years, but there was more life in it than there had been for a long time. She could hardly believe she was looking at herself in the mirror.

'Anna!' Rowan spun her round. 'Wow. Is that you? You look smoking.'

Manda nodded enthusiastically.

'Still me, just heavier eyelids.' Anna grinned. 'You two look incred—'

'OK, can we stop the flattery party now? It's my handiwork anyway.' Effie broke into a smile. 'You do all look better than I ever imagined was possible.'

Rowan laughed. 'I think that's as close as she's ever going to get to a compliment.'

Rowan and Manda disappeared to show themselves off to Selene while Effie stripped off her T-shirt and jeans. Underneath she was wearing a black bra and thong. Anna went to look away, but noticed something on Effie's shoulder blade.

'What's that?' she said, peering more closely. It was a tattoo of a spider, just as Darcey had described, only Darcey had said it was on her arm . . .

'Touch it,' said Effie. Anna put her fingers out to touch the spider on her back, but as she did so it moved, climbing higher up her shoulder blade.

'What the—' said Anna, moving to touch the spider again. It crawled to the base of Effie's neck.

'It moves.'

'Darcey . . .'

Effie laughed. 'That was brilliant. The look on her face when she found nothing there.' It was a strange tattoo to have – a spider creeping all over your body – but somehow it suited Effie.

Anna guiltily picked up her green dress; the velvet was shamefully soft. She turned away from Effie and changed into it.

'Nice underwear,' Effie snorted at Anna's white polka-dot pants and unmatching pink bra. Anna made a face at Effie and zipped up her dress.

She felt self-conscious even looking at herself in the mirror; let alone other people looking at her. The dress was not particularly revealing but it attracted attention, the way it hugged her figure, the shimmer of its deep emerald. Anna could hear Aunt. *Just like those who wield magic openly and flagrantly – women who wear short skirts and redden their lips are asking for trouble!*

Effie threw a see-through top on, her bra showing through beneath. She belted her high-waisted black shorts, stepped into clompy heels and pulled her hair into a high ponytail, tendrils falling around her face and neck. Anna felt even more awkward in her dress next to Effie – it was too much, it tried too hard; Effie's outfit didn't care at all, it was rebelliously sexy.

'I never even knew you had curves,' Effie joked, poking at Anna's hips. 'And boobs!' Anna crossed her arms over her chest and Effie laughed. 'You're going to attract attention tonight! Come on.' She grabbed Anna's hand. 'Let's find Attis.'

Effie led them all to the lowest floor of the house, below ground, into a bedroom which seemed absurdly tidy compared to everywhere else. Anna had never thought of Attis being particularly neat and then she realized it wasn't that the room was impeccably organized, but that it had almost nothing in it. A bed, a table next to it with an iron lamp, a picture of Attis with a grey-haired man Anna presumed must be his father, a wardrobe and shelves stacked with books – so many books; Anna would like to have looked through them all. The room smelt like him, smoke and warmth, clean soap and pine.

'He must be in the forge,' said Effie, leading them down the corridor, the smell of smoke growing stronger.

'The what, sorry?' said Rowan. 'Whoa . . .'

Anna followed Rowan into what was definitely . . . a forge. It was brick-walled and smoke-stained; vivid flames came from a furnace on the far side. Attis was hammering in front of it, shaping a curved piece of metal on a large block, sparks erupting. He was wearing jeans and a blackened white top rolled up at the sleeves, the muscles in his arms flexing like a cable as the hammer slammed down. Equipment hung from the ceilings and weighed down the shelves; the remaining patches of wall were hung with horseshoes of varying sizes and shapes. The far side was open to the garden, a breeze pulling the smoke outwards.

'Attis!' Effie shouted. 'ATTIS! He hates it if I get too close or surprise him.'

He looked up, his face lighting up, sweat dripping through his smoke-smudged visage. Anna finally understood why his fingernails were always so black. He stopped hammering and put the piece of metal into a bucket of water next to him. It sizzled and steamed.

'I think I need to lie down,' Rowan whispered and Anna had to admit it was hard to take her eyes off him. She'd never seen him look so alive, as alive as the fire itself.

Attis walked towards them, looking Effie up and down, the grey in his eyes sparking like the metal he'd been hammering. 'Well, you look sensational.' Anna felt Attis's eyes land on her next. *That look like he's already undressed you and he's deciding what to do with you.* She tried to hide away in the darkness of the room but his gaze rebounded off her curves. It was unnerving. 'I'll be damned, I really get to walk into the party with you four on my arm? When are we leaving?'

'Ten minutes ago, get ready.'

'Give me thirty very long seconds.' He rushed past them, smoke lingering around his body.

They explored the forge and then headed out of the door, up a set of stone stairs into the garden. A strange sound startled Anna – a bleat. Two horns and a white blur came at her from the hedge. 'Gahhh,' she cried, but the creature stopped before it reached her and began sniffing her shoe. It was a goat.

Anna steadied herself. 'You should probably let guests know before they go into the garden that a goat might run at them from the darkness.'

Effie laughed. 'It's not mine.' She nodded towards the house where Attis was. *Of course.* Anna reached out and patted it on the nose; it nuzzled into her hand, then tried to chew at her dress.

'So this is where Dallington School's mascot has got to. I knew Attis had stolen it!' Rowan cried.

'His name is Mr Ramsden,' said Attis pointedly, jumping up the stairs two at a time. He was wearing the same jeans, still pock-marked with black stains, and an unironed T-shirt; his hair was dripping wet.

'Good to know you put as much effort into getting ready as we did,' said Effie.

'You know it's important for me not to try too hard or it becomes overwhelming for the women. Now come on. Mr Ramsden should be sleeping. I'm driving.'

'You're not old enough to drive,' said Manda.

'It's fine. I have a way with the police.'

Manda narrowed her eyes. 'A way that involves magic?'

Attis smirked. 'I can't reveal my tricks, but I can promise you a very smooth ride. Just don't judge a car by its cover. . .'

They walked around to the front of the house where a small, dilapidated Peugeot 206 was waiting. They clambered inside and sped off into the London traffic – windows down, radio on – Anna wedged in the back seat, enjoying her first taste of freedom in the cold night air.

*All going well. Going to bed now. Night x.*

Anna sent the text to Aunt. It was half past ten: bedtime. She was far from bed.

# PARTY OR DIE

*Any activities that excite the emotions should be avoided or detached from their emotional connection. This includes storytelling, singing, music, dancing, indulgent feasting and sexual pleasures.*

*Binders' Training, The Book of the Binders*

They ascended the steps to Lydia's vast, double fronted house. Effie banged on the door. After several further, impatient knocks, it swung open. Lydia stood in front of them, eyes popping like a mouse caught in a trap. 'Oh, Effie – hi – I—'

'Can we come in?' said Effie, stepping inside.

'Er, of course, yes, come in. Wait, these guys too?' She looked at Rowan, Manda and Anna with unmasked disdain.

'Yes,' said Effie coolly. 'That a problem?'

'It's just it was an invites-only party . . .' Lydia replied, weakly making her point while they stepped past her into the hallway.

'Ours must have got lost in the post.'

The hallway was crammed. Faces turned towards them – assessing, judging, greedily drinking in Effie and Attis. Attis raised a plastic bag above his head. 'I bring beer,' he bellowed and the crowd swallowed him up, carrying him off in a wave of noise and laughter.

Effie turned to them. 'Remember, parties are do or die. You make a name for yourself or you sink forever. I'll get the drinks; you guys hang.' She cut a line through the bodies like a hot knife into butter and was gone.

'She's left us. I'm sinking already,' said Rowan, backing up against the wall to make way for another group of people entering. She leant into Anna and whispered, 'I've never been in a room with so many people I've stalked online before.'

'What are we meant to do?' said Manda, looking around in panic. 'How do we hang? I'm not going to survive this.'

'We could start by going inside.' Anna moved them towards the stairs. She recognized some faces from school, but there were many she didn't know at all; eyes watched them pass, questioning, frosty, faintly curious. *What's the Nobody doing at a party . . .*

'Manda. MANDA,' Rowan called. 'Five o'clock. Don't freak out but it's Karim.'

Manda squealed. Two girls in front of them turned around, recognition dawning in their eyes. 'Oh my God, it's Miranda Richards. Shouldn't you be, like, in church or something?'

'I will be in the morning, praying for your salvation.'

They laughed in her face and wandered off – towards Karim. One of them hooked arms with him and Manda glowered.

'Manda, you're going to have to tone down the prayer chat, OK?' said Rowan. 'We're at a party. We're hanging.'

A loud rumble came from behind them. Anna looked back to see a group of guys storming down the stairs, chanting and whooping, beers in hand. She was caught in their path. A particularly drunken one fell against her as he passed, knocking her head against the wall.

'Are you OK?' Eyes blue as winter skies. *Peter.* Peter was talking to her.

Anna reminded herself how to speak. 'The stairway may

not have been the most sensible place to stand.' She stood up and their eyes met. Peter's showed a flicker of recognition.

He went to say something but Digby jumped over the banister and hit him on the head. 'Come on, apparently girls are taking their clothes off and jumping in the pool. It's heated!'

'All right, all right.' Peter started down the stairs. 'Make sure you put some ice on that,' he said firmly, his eyes lingering on her again.

Once he'd left, Rowan's face bulged between the banisters. 'Well, thirteen moons, Peter Nowell just exchanged words with you! Real-life words! Feeling the passion?'

Anna smiled at her dreamily.

'I bring sustenance.' Effie returned with a handful of paper cups, ushering them further into the party. Anna had only taken one sip of the sickly concoction when Darcey rounded the corner – ravishing in a small sequinned dress and impossibly high heels – abruptly reminding Anna that she had no chance with Peter.

'Oh, look, it's the Whore, the Virgin, the Beast and the . . . dear God, the Nobody is at a party.'

'I love your dress,' said Corinne, stroking down the front of Anna's dress.

'Are we all having fun?' said Darcey with deep condescension.

'It's dull. I imagine this is the sort of thing you live for though? Getting to walk around, feeling important at a school party, reminding everyone you have breasts.' Effie looked down at Darcey's on-display cleavage.

'Attis was looking just as intently as you are – perhaps I'll go find him . . .'

Effie laughed. 'By all means.'

Darcey looked past her to Manda. 'Miranda Richards, I do wonder if your mother knows you're here. I'm not sure she would entirely approve.'

Manda looked immediately stricken. Darcey smiled and walked off with Corinne.

'You don't think she would do anything, do you?'

'No, Manda, she's just messing with you. She wouldn't have your mum's number! Come on.' Effie dragged them into the crowd.

The next hour was a blur, Effie attracting waves of attention – both good and bad – and Anna speaking to more people than she'd done in her entire life. Not everyone knew her, which meant she wasn't always *a nobody* but a *friend of Effie's*, although plenty of people made it clear they were unwanted there too. There were catty stares, whispers, laughter; one girl pushed past, coughing *slut* not so quietly in Effie's ear.

Nose-job Lucie approached them with a group of girls and splurged on the party gossip. Apparently Darcey wouldn't leave Attis alone and now she and Peter had got into a fight, and Darcey had stormed off and Peter hadn't bothered to follow! Effie smiled at Anna and Anna read her thoughts exactly.

Before long they were dancing in a hot and crowded room, music booming from mammoth speakers.

'I FEEL LIKE I'M BEING WATERBOARDED BY MUSIC,' Manda shouted. 'I DON'T KNOW HOW TO DANCE. LIKE PHYSICALLY.'

Anna had never danced outside her bedroom before, but Effie forced her into it, pulling her forwards and backwards, shimmying against her – *Come on, when Peter sees you shaking it in that dress he won't be able to resist!* Effie topped Anna's drink up with something that made her head swim and before long she was dancing with abandon. They all were, Rowan threatening to take eyes out. Effie beckoned Laurence over. Head swirling, Anna realized she was going to be sick. She needed some air . . . or a bathroom . . .

'I'll be back in a minute,' she said, but Effie was too busy kissing Laurence to notice.

Anna wandered into the crowd, finding that the doorway ahead was not staying still. She managed to get to the stairway and pulled herself up it, stumbling over a couple who were making out. 'Sssorry,' she muttered. The upstairs smelt strongly of smoke and sweat and something sour. It made her feel worse.

She opened a door which she thought was the bathroom but revealed itself to be a bedroom. It was dark; a lava lamp vomited bubbles in the corner. There were shadows on the bed, tangled in each other.

'I'm sorry—' she stammered, backing out.

A giggle and then Attis appeared above the sheets. A girl's head popped up behind him. Then another. A messy-haired Attis grinned. 'Do feel free to join,' he said as nonchalantly as if he had been asking Anna to take a spare seat next to him in a taxi.

Anna slammed the door shut, her stomach rolling more than before.

'A real gentleman, isn't he?'

A voice behind her – smooth and flat, like a calm sea stretching out to meet the horizon. It balanced her. She turned slowly to Peter.

'I hope you're not one of those girls who finds him utterly irresistible? I suspect you've more sense than that, unlike those two in there.'

'I'm managing to control myself.' Anna made sure there was an appropriate level of sarcasm in her reply. *How could the girls in there not see he was just using them?* She pushed herself away from the wall, feeling steadier under Peter's unfaltering gaze while still completely unable to comprehend that Peter – was – gazing – at – her. Her dress had no pockets otherwise she'd have reached for her Knotted Cord.

'Are you a house-party virgin then?' he said.

Anna didn't hear him properly. 'A virgin? Er – I—' She

felt the blood run to her face and thanked Effie silently for the anti-blush blush.

'A *house*-party virgin,' he repeated more loudly, a smile settling on his face.

'Oh yeah,' said Anna, looking away. 'Well, I've been to some parties, but none in a house. No. So yes.' *Stop talking.*

'You don't know the rules of survival then?'

'Definitely not,' Anna laughed.

'Come with me.' He put his arm around her and, at his touch, she felt the shivers return to her stomach in waves. He led her down the stairs, steadying her.

She wasn't sure what to do about the arm: *Lean into it? Let it be?* She was acutely aware that several people at the bottom of the stairs had seen them and were whispering. She half expected him to turn around and reveal that talking to her was all a big joke, but he simply smiled back up at her in a camera-flash of white teeth and steered her into the kitchen, the floor sticky, glass crunching underfoot. Anna thought of Lydia and wondered if the popularity points she was earning were worth her house being trashed. *Probably.* A group of people were playing some kind of game involving chanting and banging on the table.

Peter leant into her. 'There are three things you need to know at a house party. Where the wine is.' He opened the fridge and took out a bottle tucked at the back. 'Where the bottle opener lives.' He put his hand behind a pot on the top shelf and pulled one out. 'And where the secret food stash is.' He opened the oven door to reveal a few slices of pizza on a tray. 'Here you are, my lady.' He handed her a glass of wine and a piece of pizza. Anna put her handbag down on the surface and took them. *He's only being kind, just be cool.*

'I never expected this level of service at a house party,' she said, biting into the pizza and realizing she was starving.

They clinked their glasses together and Anna drank the wine. It was sour.

'Don't we have a class together?'

'Yeah. English.' *Twice a week. You once said my name.*

'You look different. Is your hair a different colour?' He caught a lock between his fingers and studied it. *If Darcey sees me now I'll be dead forever.*

'I had an enforced makeover. I don't recommend it.'

'Sounds painful.'

'It was for my eyebrows.'

He laughed and took a sip of wine. 'And who carried out this makeover then?'

Someone bumped into them from behind, sending her glass toppling and the wine spilling out across the surface.

'For God's sake,' said Peter, pushing himself away from it, a wet line across his white shirt where he had been leaning. He turned to find the culprit – a greasy-looking boy who'd been participating in the drinking game.

'Sorry, mate,' the boy slurred.

Peter put a hand on his chest and pushed him back firmly. 'No harm intended,' he said rigidly. 'Did it get you?' he asked Anna, searching through a set of drawers and finding a tea towel. He dabbed at his shirt, tutting.

'I'm fine.'

'You sure?' He offered the towel to her.

Anna nodded.

'Good. We wouldn't want to ruin that beautiful dress, now would we?' His mouth softened into a smile. 'Onward with the survival tour?'

He offered her an arm. Anna took his again, her mind entering a space somewhere between panic and elation. They were walking through the maze of the house together – publicly. 'This place is huge! It's ridiculous,' she exclaimed. Peter nodded, pulling her closer to him as they wove through the crowd. Anna realized, feeling immediately idiotic, that the house wasn't out of the ordinary to him – his own was probably bigger. He led her into a slightly quieter room with several opulent sofas containing various writhing couples.

'Chill-out zone. An easier place to talk,' he said.

'I see,' said Anna, heart hammering as she watched a rogue hand creep up the jumper of a girl on the nearest sofa.

She'd never liked crowds but at least they had the advantage of anonymity. Standing here with Peter was entirely different; this crowd was aware – drunk and slurring, but mindful. They gathered around them with the interest of wasps. *Darcey's going to find out.* Anna finished her wine, a bubbling rising up inside of her – excitement or fear – it didn't seem to matter any more.

'Where's Darcey, Peter?' A girl with mascara halfway down her face appeared in front of them, looking back and forth between them.

'I have no idea,' Peter replied, irritated.

The girl laughed and raised a phone out of nowhere taking a picture of them – the flash temporarily blinding Anna.

'Shall we go outside?' Peter whispered in her ear. 'Then you can finally tell me your name.'

Anna nodded, her head spinning.

'There you are!' A hand on her shoulder. Effie's voice. *No! Not now!* Anna turned to find a significantly more dishevelled Effie. Her hair had fallen down and was wet on one side; she was clutching a glass in one hand, which was steadily spilling liquid onto the floor, and wearing a large blazer that didn't belong to her. Rowan was with her, holding a teapot.

'Peter.' Effie said his name with slow relish. 'I see you're looking after my Anna.'

'Effie,' he said stiffly. His gaze took in her revealing outfit.

'You got something on your shirt,' she slurred, drawing her finger across the red wine stain.

'I was aware, thank you.'

'Sorry to interrupt your mooooves.' Peter's jaw tensed – he did not like to be teased. Anna made furious eyes at Effie. 'But I'm going to have to borrow Anna.' Effie began pulling her away.

'Can't it wait?' said Anna.

'No. Come on.'

Anna turned back to Peter, mouthing *sorry* before she was dragged into the crowd.

'Anna, you were with Peter! All the cups have gone so I've been drinking out of this teapot. Works quite well.' Rowan tipped the spout up into her mouth. 'Manda's been stalking Karim but I think it's finally worked. They're making out in the other room. Where's *my* passion, people?'

Anna was still focused on Effie. 'Why did you have to wind him up like that? And why did you drag me away?'

'I was rescuing you. Darcey's on the hunt for him. Anyway, there's still plenty of time to stick your tongue down his throat.'

'That's not what was happening.'

'I forgot, you're far too puuuure for anything like that.' Anna glared at her. 'Point is he was calling all the shots. We don't want you waiting for his kiss, we want him begging for yours. Plus, I was bored.'

'What happened to Laurence?' said Rowan, offering them the teapot.

'He's the reason I was bored.' Effie took a gulp from it. 'Rowan, that girl who called me a slut earlier . . .'

'Oh yes, Charlotte.'

'Is her boyfriend still here?'

Rowan scanned the room. 'Yes, he's that one over there. Tall, dark brown hair.'

'Perfect, come dance.'

'I'll come in a minute,' said Anna. 'Need some fresh air.'

'Suit yourself,' said Effie, making a beeline for the man Rowan had pointed out.

'I guess that's Charlotte taken care of,' said Rowan with a mixture of admiration and disbelief.

Drinking the wine had brought back the earlier feeling of nausea. Anna stepped out into the garden, lit by waves of light rebounding from the pool house which was filled with splashing shadows. She moved to the side and leant against the wall. Her mind was full of Peter's face, of his lips whispering in her ear; everything in the garden seemed to dissolve into the colour of his eyes.

'You do know you're shivering?'

'Not now, please.' Anna rolled her head in the opposite direction.

'It's cold out here,' said Attis.

Anna didn't reply, her breath forming a momentary cloud.

'Do you know where Effie is?'

'Inside. Preying on an unsuspecting victim: male, brown-haired, tall.'

'That's my girl.'

'Are you OK with that?' she asked sharply, turning to look at him.

He shrugged and looked down.

'Well you can hardly condemn her,' Anna added defensively. 'You were up there with your own victims – two if I recall.'

Attis laughed, his breath joining hers in the air. 'Victims? That's an interesting interpretation. For victims they seemed to be enjoying themselves an awful lot.'

Anna felt the bile turn in her stomach. She bent forward, her head swimming.

'Are you OK?'

'Fine.' She breathed in for a few moments. 'If they're not victims, then they're misled.' She couldn't quite make the point she was trying to, with the force of conviction inside her.

'Not all girls are looking for love, Anna.' He looked at her in such a way that she couldn't help feeling utterly patronized. 'Some are just looking for a good time. It's a little sexist to presume otherwise, is it not?'

Anna considered his words, finding him right but feeling him to be wrong. 'But how do you know they weren't looking for love?' She pointed a finger at his chest.

'What? At the same time?' He smiled infuriatingly. 'It's just good fun. For them and me. Are you going to be sick?'

Anna steadied herself against the wall. 'What about that look?'

'What look?'

'The one you have, the undressing-with-your-eyes one. You shouldn't—'

'Undressing with my eyes?' He laughed, turning his eyes on her. 'I find women beautiful, I won't apologize for that, but I don't undress anyone with anything unless they want to be undressed. You're still shivering – look, here . . .' He leant forwards and touched her shoulder with his hand. She flinched away.

'I don't know where those hands have been. What are you doing?'

'This will help, trust me.'

She rolled her eyes and held her arm out to him. He traced a pattern on it with the tip of his finger – a symbol. Almost immediately a melting warmth spread from her arm across her body and she realized just how cold she'd been. Anna looked up at him, momentarily lost for words as the feeling travelled through her. 'What is that?'

'The magic touch.' He grinned. 'So have you had any fun tonight?' His eyes sang with amusement. 'I saw you with Peter.'

'Perhaps. It's not for you to know.' She gave him a knowing smile of her own. She could play his games too.

'And are you sure he knows your rules of engagement?'

'I don't like to reveal my rules of engagement until it's too late,' Anna teased, finding the nausea had settled with the wave of warmth.

He laughed. 'Who's the victim now then?'

'I'll guess we'll just have to wait and see.'

'I guess so.' He leant closer.

Anna backed away. 'Fire demon?'

'What?'

'Is that what you are? If you're not a witch . . .'

'No. That sounds cool, but no.'

'A werewolf?'

He laughed. 'No.'

'Come on, let's go back in. I promised the girls a dance.'

The air inside was a hot wall after the garden. Anna spotted Effie dancing with Charlotte's boyfriend, with Rowan and Manda alongside. She knew she should still be mad but she just wanted to dance with her friends.

'Anna! Attis!' Rowan called. 'Thank the Goddess you're here. We have a code red. Tell them what you've done, Manda.'

Manda turned to Anna, big eyes unfocused. 'Karim sent his friend to tell me to stop following him. That I was freaking him out.'

Attis released a laugh from behind. 'Don't worry, Manda, some men can't handle a girl with spirit.'

'I think it was when I followed him into the toilet that did it. Oh, but we kissed. My first kiss and two minutes later there's basically a restraining order against me and I've been sick, even though I've only had two drinks and one of them might have been water.'

'Meanwhile I've had two whole teapots and I'm fine,' said Rowan, pulling strange dance moves against the wall.

Anna started to laugh and found she couldn't stop. Manda looked hurt for a moment and then began giggling too. Effie abandoned the guy and came over. 'What's going on here?'

'We're just not very good at parties,' said Anna, blinking through her tears.

Effie smiled. 'Well, I'd gathered that.'

She put an arm around Anna and they danced, forgetting the angst, the dramas, the crowds and whispers; feeling nothing but being young and alive. And then Tom Kellman arrived. Attis had gone to get them water and Tom had obviously sensed the opportunity open up.

'I like your top,' he slurred in Effie's ear. 'I can see your bra.' He was wearing a bright red velvet jacket – now ripped down one arm.

'How fascinating,' Effie replied. 'Please give me more insights into the depths of your psyche.'

'You can have all the insights you want. Let's go upstairs.' He took hold of her arm.

'Get off me. I'm dancing with my friends, fool.' She pulled herself away.

'Cooooomme onnn,' he whispered in her ear.

Effie threw her drink in his face.

'HEY!' he shouted. 'You bitch!'

Attis had him against the wall within seconds. The noise of the crowd around them hushed.

'If you say anything like that about her again, I will kill you,' said Attis and the look on his face was terrible: a sudden inferno. Tom tried ineffectually to headbutt him.

'Get off him.' Peter grabbed Attis's shoulders and yanked him away. Attis made a face at Peter that was half-smile, half-snarl.

Tom threw back his shoulders and stuck out his chin. 'What? I can't be the first person to point out she is a massive, cock-teasing bitch!' Attis turned around to hit him but Peter pulled him away again, so Attis punched Peter in the face instead – and then again. Peter fell to the floor, blood pouring from his nose. Attis got on top of him. There were screams now, the music pulsing, egging him on. Anna was shouting at Attis, pulling at his shoulders, but he didn't seem to notice.

'ATTIS,' shouted Effie. 'HE'S NOT WORTH IT.' At the sound of her voice his arm froze in mid-air. Peter struggled against him on the floor and the next moment Tom had jumped on Attis from behind, knocking Anna in the process. The scuffle continued for several more moments, until Attis had thrown Tom off again. Effie smiled at Attis, who smiled back, blood on his cheek and a mania in his eyes.

'It's all good fun,' he laughed wildy, putting an arm around Effie.

Peter clambered to his feet and put a hand out to Anna to help her up. 'Are you all right?'

'Fine.'

'Fucking idiots, both of them,' said Peter, still holding her hand. Blood trickled from his nose, which was beginning to swell.

'Get out of the way.' Darcey parted the crowd. 'What's going on?'

They all turned to look at her. Anna saw the exhilaration in Effie's eyes. She was relishing every moment: the fight, the blood, the chaos . . . Anna's hand resting in Peter's . . . Darcey noticing.

'Nothing,' Peter spat. 'Just a loser trying to ruin a good time.' He let Anna's hand go.

'Speaking of,' said Darcey, her eyes landing on Anna like a feast she was about to tuck into. Corinne raised her phone towards Anna. 'You left your bag in the kitchen. Your phone was ringing so I picked it up. It was your aunt. She's terribly worried about you. Don't fret – I told her exactly where you are. She's on her way.' Darcey gave Anna a concerned smile and handed her bag back to her. 'It's well past your bedtime.'

Anna took the bag in shock, the crowd around her laughing.

'Darcey . . .' said Peter disapprovingly.

'It's not my fault! The phone was ringing, I thought I was being helpful—'

Darcey suddenly fell to the floor with a shriek, her ankle twisted. Anna could see that one of her heels had broken. Peter and Olivia rushed to help her. The look on Effie's face was all Anna needed to know that she'd done it. And the way Darcey was looking up at her suggested she knew it too.

'Come on.' Effie smiled, pulling Anna through the clamour of the crowd.

They wove back into the hallway, which was quiet now.

'Effie! What did you just do?' said Anna, finding it hard to speak, to move. *She's on her way.* Aunt knew she was out, knew she was at a party, knew she wasn't at a science fair in Reading.

Effie laughed. 'Come on, Darcey deserved it.'

'In front of everyone. You shouldn't have—'

'Anna!' Manda appeared in front of Anna, face wild with fear, 'If your aunt knows you're here then she'll tell my mum too. Lord! That's my life over. Over!'

Anna tried to find a way through. 'Look. I'll tell my aunt you're at the science fair, that I used you and went to meet Effie in London. Selene can back up my story, she can say that it was just Effie and me at the house.' She wasn't sure how her voice sounded so calm when her heart was beating so fast she could hardly breathe. 'You don't have to be dragged into this. Better that one of us gets to stay in the coven.'

'Anna, no, don't say that,' said Rowan.

'I've got to go.' The sick feeling was back with intent this time.

'Let me come out there. I'll give your aunt a piece of my mind,' said Effie, but Attis held her back.

'Effie, no, it'll just make it worse. You have to stay here and call Selene, make sure she agrees with the story. I've got to go.' Anna stumbled out of the front door onto the lawn.

'Look – the Nobody has to go home early, boo hoo,' she heard someone call out of a window. It sounded like Olivia. They'd all be watching her humiliation. None of it seemed to matter any more. Anna found it difficult to feel anything at all. Her entire world had been swallowed up by a fear so deep it was as if she'd sunk into the depths of a gloomy lake and was viewing everything from below.

She must have left her bag in the kitchen when she was with Peter, but there was no way her phone would have rung. It had been off. She took it out of her bag and searched the call list. There it was – not a call from Aunt, but a call *to* Aunt. *Darcey.*

A car door slammed. Aunt approached, her face devoid of emotion – a mirror of Anna's feelings. 'Get in the car. Now.'

Anna felt herself propelled towards it. Faces watched from the windows of the house. A nest of wasps. The sting had released its poison. Anna almost made it to the car door but then stopped and threw up on the lawn.

# EYES

*Like a row of knots in a cord, the Dark Times are fated to return over and over. We must remain vigilant. We must be prepared. The Ones Who Know Our Secrets are only waiting, ready to light the fires that will see their shadows rise.*

*The Return, The Book of the Binders*

The car was filled with a silence of such intensity Anna had never known anything like it. It was like watching the readings before the earthquake hits – a silence that threatened to break at any moment, but didn't, the waves of it growing more severe. Anna knew how to interpret Aunt's silences, but she didn't want to know the meaning of this one.

'Aunt, I—' Anna's mouth snapped shut against her will, cleaving her weak explanation in two. It beat against her mouth.

Anna did not attempt to speak again until they arrived home. 'Aunt, please, let me—'

Aunt made a knotting movement in the air and Anna's mouth snapped shut again, this time painfully.

'Please, it's not as—'

Aunt twisted her fingers and Anna's tongue twisted in response. Anna tried to call out in pain but the sound forced its way back down her throat like a block of cold air.

She tried to find other words that might break through, but the more she wanted to speak the harder it became to breathe – the words lodged in her throat. Aunt watched her struggle. *Please,* Anna thought and then tried to think no more. She held her Knotted Cord and let go of the desperation inside her.

Aunt followed her up the stairs. Anna walked into her room braced for the worst telling-off of her life but Aunt shut the door behind her. Anna heard Aunt's footsteps disappearing down the corridor. She turned the handle gently – it was locked. There was no lock on her door but it was locked nonetheless.

Anna didn't want to think, she didn't want to wonder what Aunt would do to her, she didn't want to remember the faces looking at her from the windows, nor bring to mind Darcey's satiated smile or – worse – the blue of Peter's eyes. She took off the green dress and left it in a pile on the floor.

She tried to fall into the nothingness of sleep, but sleep was different now. Dreams came to her.

They laughed at her. Laughed at her like a thousand faces laughing from windows that went on and on forever. They pushed her off a cliff, let her fall and then jolted her awake, heart pounding. She was holding her silver handheld mirror – Attis and Effie stood behind her, their hands over her eyes, then around her body, embracing, suffocating. Attis's fingers forming symbols on her skin. Seven circles. Effie turned the mirror around and the whole school was before her, waiting for her to speak – only the faces were changing, becoming the Binders, chanting, chanting, chanting; rose petals flying.

The dreams woke her again and again, her pillow damp with sweat, her sheets a twisted prison. *Dreams are torture. Let me be.* Then noises in the night. Footsteps on the floor above her – the third floor. *Is it Aunt? What time is it? Am I dreaming?* Then she was locked in the third-floor room, the curtains drawn and the walls drawing in around her, turning to water, to blood, drowning her in a green velvet dress.

When Anna woke in the morning she was exhausted. The dreambinder was tightly knotted. She took it down and began to undo the knots, hoping the action of releasing them might release her mind.

She waited for Aunt to knock, but she did not come. Anna went to her balcony doors. Dark clouds lay across the sky in lines like a ribcage, a frail, breathy breeze passing through the gaps and stirring the trees, knocking off the last few leaves. She tried to open the door but the key rattled against it ineffectually. Everything was locked.

She waited, aware of her growing hunger and fear. She waited all day.

Evening came and Anna's heart jumped as she heard the door open – *finally*! Aunt did not look at her. She placed a small plate of food and a glass of milk on the dressing table and closed the door again. Anna felt like throwing the glass against it. *She can't do this! She can't keep me locked up in here like this!* Anna snatched up the glass and stormed to her bathroom, emptying the milk down the sink – she'd had enough of Aunt's poison. She ate the food greedily; the last thing she'd eaten had been the pizza with Peter.

The night soon came, full of dreams again, disturbing and lucid.

When Monday morning arrived, Anna expected to be released – Aunt never let her miss a day of school even when she was ill. She woke thinking about how blissful it would be to take a shower. When six came there was no knock on the door. By seven, she was going out of her mind. By nine, she'd resigned herself to the fact she was not going to school, that she may never be let out of the room again.

She began to feel that she might go insane. She tried to study, she tried to read, she gave up and stared out of the window, watching the December evening come on inch by inch, the light disappearing to nothingness without a trace of it ever having been there at all. She longed to speak to Rowan, Manda, Effie, Attis, to hear them laugh about her psychotic aunt and make her life somehow feel as if it was copeable with, escapable. *Are they missing me too?*

Aunt dropped off her dinner but when Anna attempted to protest her tongue was twisted and her mouth was locked shut once more. Aunt left and Anna banged against the door ferociously and desperately, knowing she was only making it worse. Eventually, she had nothing left. She took herself to bed and ran her Knotted Cord through her hands, loathing every single knot.

When she fell asleep the dreams were waiting. Aunt was brushing her hair, but then the face in the mirror was her mother's, the two interchanging, blending into one face, feature-less as the Six Women. The mirror in her hand began to melt, running out of the frame like a river in moonlight. The river flowed across her floor, turning the carpet to shadowy grass, small, pale flowers growing among the blades and blossoming – bright as fallen stars. It ran beneath her bookcase, which began to transform into a tree, the wood of the shelves wrap-ping around themselves, wrinkling with deep lines of bark, spreading branches from which silver fruit began to grow . . .

Anna walked towards it, feeling the river run over her feet. She reached out to pluck a fruit from the tree but it fell before she could reach it and made a thud as it hit the floor. She woke.

Her toes under the sheets felt distinctly wet. The moonlight was pouring through her window – she'd left the curtains open. It streamed onto her mirror and cast a reflection which fell over her bookcase. A book had fallen onto the floor.

She stepped out of bed and walked over to it. It was the medical encyclopaedia Aunt had given her last Christmas.

Anna picked it up and then remembered what she'd done: she quickly peeled the dust cover off the book and there underneath was the collection of fairy tales from Selene. After her birthday, Anna had put the encyclopedia cover over it to hide it from Aunt and then had promptly forgotten about it. The engraving of a tree and its upside-down reflection caught the moonlight and shone like a pearl in the creamy oyster fabric. It was beautiful. Perhaps its old words would be a comfort, or at the very least lull her back to sleep. She crept into bed and opened the book to the first story.

## The Eyeless Maiden

Once upon a time there was a young maiden who lived on the edge of the forest with her mother. She longed to explore the forest but her mother would have none of it. An old spindle-seller who had once visited the house had said there was a lake deep within that, when the moon rose in the sky, revealed all truths.

One morning the maiden was picking berries in the garden when a little bird hopped down from the tree above. She put her hand out and the bird jumped onto it, pecking at the berries. It jumped from her hand and down the path into the forest. The maiden unlatched the wooden gate and followed. She looked back at the house. The chimney was puffing away: her mother was cooking. The maiden would not be gone long.

She stepped into the cool shadows of the forest. She walked deeper and deeper still, the darkness thickening, stealing the bird away until she could not see it any more. She became afraid. The trees grew closer; the shadows loomed. She swore they were moving around her, prowling, snarling – beastly, wolfish outlines behind the trees, watching.

A clatter of hooves made her scream, but it was three men on horseback passing her by: one dressed in red, one in black and one in white. She ran after them but they disappeared quickly. Still, their movement and action had chased away the shadows and the trees began to clear. The girl came across a strange house.

It was squatting on four scrawny chicken legs and whirring around and around in a mad dance. It stopped and sat down. The maiden saw with horror that the bolts of its doors and windows were made of human fingers, toes and teeth. She turned to run but heard a voice from within. 'What is it you seek, little girl?'

She didn't like to be rude so she replied: 'Good day to you. I seek the forest lake.'

The old woman cackled and it sounded like the ground was breaking in two. 'Why should I help you?'

'Because I asked.'

'That is the right answer. Come in.'

The girl stepped into the strange cottage. It was a sorry state inside, such a mess and a tangle you could barely move.

'If you wish to know where the lake is you must clean the house all over by the end of the day!' said the woman and left with a slam of the door.

Knowing the task was impossible, the maiden sat down and began to cry. But then the little bird hopped through the window and began to tidy. They worked together and soon it was done.

The old woman returned and seeing the maiden had completed her task shrieked with rage. She gave the girl food to eat and a key of silver, then fell asleep on her bed in the corner and snored loudly. The maiden tried the key in the locked door but it did not work. She lay down and slept.

The next day the old woman pointed at a pile of clothes as high as a mountain and said: 'If you wish to know where the lake is you must wash them all by the end of the day!'

Once she had gone the maiden sat down and began to cry. But the little bird appeared once more and began to take the clothes to the well. They worked together and soon it was done.

The old woman returned and seeing the maiden had completed her task jumped up and down with rage. She gave the girl food to eat and a key made of water, then fell asleep on her bed in the corner. The maiden tried the new key in the locked door but it did not work. She lay down and slept.

The next day the old woman pointed at the clean pile of clothes and said: 'If you wish to know where the lake is you must sew and mend them all by the end of the day!'

The clothes were as holed as blocks of cheese and the maiden sat down and began to cry. The little bird appeared once more with needle and thread in its mouth and began to sew. They worked together and soon it was done.

The old woman returned and seeing the maiden had completed her task laughed with rage. She asked to see the maiden's finger. The maiden held out her hand and the old woman chopped her finger clean off. She returned with a key made of blood.

The maiden asked about the three men on horseback.

'They belong to me,' said the old woman. 'They transform day to night and night back to day. Do you wish to know more?'

The maiden said she did not.

'Good, for to know too much can make one old too

soon.' The old woman led the maiden to the back door. 'Go that way with your three keys and you shall know the truth.'

The little bird hopped ahead and the maiden followed, travelling deeper into the forest until she reached a clearing in the trees. Before her was a vast ditch. She took the keys from her pocket and threw them into it. The ditch filled quickly with silver water and when the moonlight shone above the lake it became a mirror.

The maiden leant over and looked into the lake. She saw a beautiful apple grove, the grass speckled with daisies, the trees full and green, the apples red as blushes. Her eyes widened in wonder and the little bird flew down and pecked them right out. Her eyes fell into the lake and the girl could see no more.

Aunt had told her a version of the tale when she'd been young. *You see, little girls should do as they are told or else . . .* She could almost hear Aunt's warnings now, waiting like shadows in the wake of the story. She wondered if her mother would have read it to her. Selene had said the tales had been her mother's favourites. Anna closed the pages and held the book tightly – it was something then, something that connected them.

She reached into the back of her drawer and took out the photograph of her parents. It was full of sunlight compared to the darkness of the night. *Who are you?* Anna thought. She'd always avoided the question, but now, staring at her mother's smile, she wondered at all the other things that had brought that smile to her face – what she'd liked, what had made her laugh, whom she'd loved. Anna found herself smiling back. She looked beyond to the green lawn behind, the tree spreading its branches.

Her heart lurched. *The branches . . .*

She knew that branch, the way it curved almost back on itself. She knew that tree.

Anna sat holding the photograph until morning arrived. It took a long time – the winter light did not come quickly. She went to her balcony.

The branches of the tree in the centre of their back garden were plain to see, the thickest and lowest curving back on itself. She held up the photo and compared them but she was already sure. It was the same sycamore tree. She knew its leaves when they came in summer and the photo was full of them.

She let the idea of it sink in slowly, sinking to the floor.

*My parents were here, at this house. Did they once live here?*

Aunt had said that they had lived in London but she'd never said where. Surely she'd mention if it had been *here*. *Another lie, perhaps, or a truth conveniently forgotten?* Anna had never considered before how Aunt had even afforded their house on a nurse's salary – it had just always been their house. *Had it?*

She looked out to the garden again and imagined her mother sitting beneath the tree. It was another connection. A connection that was too much to bear.

The tears came from nowhere. She couldn't remember the last time she'd cried but now they poured out of her, hot on her cheeks, a surrendering deep inside her body. Everything threatened to overwhelm her – being locked in the room, missing her friends, fearing her aunt and the Binders, love, magic, longing for a mother she'd never known.

She cried until she had nothing left to give, shuddering to a stop, lying down on the floor and falling back into a deep and blissful sleep upon a grassy, starlit bank near a silver river.

\*   \*   \*

The rest of the week passed in slow torture. At first, Anna's discovery kept her occupied. She spent hours looking at the photo, wondering about Aunt's lies, her parents, the room on the third floor above her – *Does that hold secrets too?* – obsessing over what it could all mean – if it meant anything at all. But as the days rolled by, her desperation, without anything but hopelessness to sustain it, began to wither. She wasn't drinking the milk but she wasn't taking her tisane either and she could feel the tendrils of the bindweed still inside her taking hold. The dreams began to slow and then stopped altogether. Her thoughts slowed too; her sense of purpose dispersed like the clouds beyond her window. *Will I ever escape?*

Late on Thursday a banging on the front door disturbed her gloom. Voices. *Selene.* Selene was shouting. Anna ran to her door and pressed her ear against it.

'She's sixteen! She went to a party, for Goddess's sake, she didn't kill someone! How dare you keep her locked up there! You're insane, Vivienne, you're—'

Then Aunt's harsh tones. Anna couldn't quite make out the words – their voices turned to a bickering murmur and then disappeared. Anna listened for what seemed like forever until she heard the front door slam shut. Selene was gone. *Don't go!*

The next day came and went. Hearing Selene's voice had made it all harder again, had run like a river through her defences. When Aunt brought dinner Anna was close to falling on the floor and begging, but then she noticed that Aunt didn't have a plate in her hand at all. Instead, she opened the door wider. 'You can come downstairs.' Her voice was as strained as a spring pulled out of shape.

*It's a trick. A trap.* Anna didn't care.

'Shower first or you'll ruin dinner.' They were the best words Aunt had ever said.

Anna felt almost human again, entering the kitchen. The food was dry and flavourless but she ate eagerly. Aunt watched the speed at which she consumed with transparent contempt but said nothing. As soon as Anna had finished the queasiness set in; she realized that she might be out of her room now but that she was probably safer locked inside.

Aunt beckoned her into the living room. The glow from the lamp couldn't quite permeate the room. The fire remained bare, the tapestries glared down at them remorselessly, garrulous, muttering verses of fear and protection. Aunt patted the seat beside her. Anna sat down, ready for the worst.

'Do you know that the skin around your mother's neck was black and blue?' said Aunt matter-of-factly. 'The strangulation had been so intense she'd bled from her mouth.'

Anna thought of her mother's face in the photograph, full of life, her smile inescapable. She held the Knotted Cord in her pocket, worried the tears would come again.

'They asked me to identify the body. I had to look at my sister like that.'

Anna needed her to stop. 'I only went to a party.'

'She met your father at a party. One chance meeting and that was it. She fell for him. I'll never know if it was magic that supplied the poison and love that dispensed it or the other way round. It doesn't matter. Love, magic, they feed off each other – they are both poison in the end.'

*Poison!* Anna clenched the cord at Aunt's use of the word. *How can she speak of poison?* She wanted to scream but the walls of her room reared up in her head – she couldn't risk being locked away again. 'But surely not all magic is harmful? Surely there can be—'

'All magic is harmful! All. You must listen to me.' Aunt grabbed Anna's chin, her green eyes trembling, urging. 'I'm not trying to ruin your life. I'm trying to save it.'

Anna couldn't look away from her. Aunt was so convincing;

she had a way of transferring her beliefs into you until they were all you could see, the same way Effie could.

'From what?'

'Magic is a danger to our family!'

Aunt had always cast the net of danger wide, across all witches, but now it was around Anna like a trap: *our family.* 'I thought magic was a danger to all?'

'I—it is . . .' Aunt stuttered. 'There are dangers close and far. Especially now.'

'What do you mean now? Is this to do with the Faceless Women? The Seven?' Anna knew the questions were risky but she had to ask.

Aunt's eyes narrowed. 'What do you know of the Seven?'

'Nothing really – I overheard Effie. Just that they are some great witch grove.'

Aunt snorted. 'The Seven. The First Sinners who brought the sins of magic upon us all. We, the Binders, don't care that they were killed, only what their deaths mean. It is a statement. A statement of power. Whoever did it wanted to sow the seeds of fear. Was it another grove? Internal warfare? Or are our old enemies stirring? The Ones Who Know Our Secrets.'

Anna shivered though the room was not cold. 'Aunt, surely it's nothing that drastic, it could be any—'

'The Hunters never forget, Anna,' Aunt said forcibly. 'History has shown us that they always return. When we relax, when we stop looking behind us, when we think we are finally free – that is when they strike. We do not forget. The fire never dies; beware smoke on the wind.'

'But that was so long ago, a different time—'

'Is it? You think people have changed so much? Fear is an instinct. It never changes. We tried to warn them all and now look what's happening – cowans beginning to believe again.'

'But cowans don't see magic . . .'

'Oh really,' said Aunt, seizing her laptop. She opened it and drew up a news story from only the day before: 'Cult being investigated for links to harmful "witchcraft" practices'.

Anna read it quickly. It seemed nothing more than a bunch of crazy people carrying out strange acts. 'Are they witches?' she asked.

'Probably not, but it doesn't matter, does it? They are linking them with witchcraft. Have you read the news recently? All doom and gloom – the economy nosediving, cutbacks, terrorist threats, climate disasters, racial tensions – but, oh, these new stories are something different. Something deliciously, horribly distracting. Whispers are spreading.'

Aunt flicked to the next tab. 'Items of sorcery discovered in illegal immigrant hideout'.

Then another tab: 'WATCH: Disturbing new video of Six Faceless Women'.

'Look at the comments beneath,' Aunt snapped.

Their faces are so creepy, definitely something not right here . . .

How did a bunch of women break through Big Ben's high security?

Why are police revealing so little about the case? We're being lied to.

Bet they're naked under those robes.

Old Hags. Better dead than alive!

'The hangings have opened a door and magic is starting to creep out. If cowans believe again – then they fear again.'
'These are just rumours—'

'It only takes a few sparks to light a fire!' Aunt's eyes were distant – lit with something: *Terror? Thrill?* It ran through Anna too and she could feel the force that had been growing within her falter. *What if Aunt is right?*

Aunt closed her laptop and picked up her embroidery, suddenly calm and collected. 'You should be ashamed of yourself. Witches who flaunt their magic without shame or prudence put us all at risk. I can only imagine the sort of illusions Effie is filling your head with – boys and sex and spells and power.'

Anna winced at Aunt's words; they were uncannily accurate. She thought of Effie's cantrip – Darcey's heel breaking in front of a room full of people. She waited for it, waited to be told she must never speak to Effie again, to stay away from boys, that she was to be removed from school.

'Selene tells me you like a boy called Peter.'

Anna stifled her gasp. The last name she'd expected to come out of Aunt's mouth at that moment was Peter's. She felt a sting of betrayal. *Why did Selene tell her?*

'Oh, don't look like that. Selene was trying to convince me that you're just *young*, just *having fun*, that it's all harmless enough, you want to hang out with your friends, that you like some Peter – *shouldn't Anna be allowed to date at sixteen?*' Aunt began to sew. 'I don't blame your father for what he did, you know. I blame her. Your mother chose it. She knew he was having an affair and she stayed with him. She was stupid and weak, but I believe you are strong, Anna. You're like me, you see through the illusions of things, you see people for what they are. That is why I have decided to let you decide for yourself.'

The silence that followed was delicate. Anna knew if she said the wrong thing she might break it. 'What do you mean?'

'Whether to become a Binder or not.'

Anna could not comprehend her words. Impossible. Her

whole life had been leading towards the Binders. It had never been a discussion, but an inevitability, an unbreakable knot in the thread of her life. 'But why?'

'Because I trust you.' The word trust stung like an open cut. 'I'm not going to stop you seeing Effie. I have come to an agreement with Selene. You may stay at her house on the occasional Friday, at my discretion and under Selene's supervision.'

'Let me stay with Effie . . .' said Anna, bewildered. Now nothing made any sense.

'I want you to know the alternative so when you join the Binders – the choice is yours and not mine.'

Anna looked into Aunt's eyes and found them strained. It didn't make any sense. Aunt did not offer choices. Minutes ago she'd been ranting about Hunters and chaos and danger and now she was allowing Anna to spend time with *Effie* of all people. Anna knew Selene was persuasive but this was too much. *What did she say? Does Selene have more power over Aunt than I know?*

'I believe you will come to see the harms of magic and love for yourself and then you will understand why the Binders do what we do. In your heart you are a Binder, I know it as I know myself. There are conditions, of course. All other nights of the week you must be home by six. If you grow closer to this Peter I must know about it. You will not practise magic.' *She doesn't know about the coven then.* 'And if you deceive me on any of these points again I will arrange your Knotting immediately and your choice will be gone. Are we clear?'

Anna was completely unclear. Was Aunt just taunting her? Was it some sort of test? Would her answer end up locking her back up in her bedroom indefinitely?

'Yes,' said Anna, waiting for the trap door to fall but Aunt simply nodded.

*What else can I say?* If Anna didn't agree she would have

no freedom at all. At least this gave her something – an opening – even if it was all a trick. *It's always a trick.*

'I hope I choose the right path.' Anna turned away, Aunt's vulturine look already hunting for the lies in her eyes.

'You will.'

'So – I can go back to school?'

'After the holidays. Until then you're grounded – no leaving the house, no seeing friends, no Effie, until you return to school. And you must still be punished for your prior actions. Here.' Aunt reached over and picked up Anna's embroidery. 'Sew.'

*Anna's stomach clenched. It had all been too easy.* Anna took it and pulled out the needle which she'd left in the fabric. Aunt was watching her. Anna's mouth had gone dry. As soon as she put the needle into the material she felt the pain. She cried out and pulled down the neck of her jumper. There on the skin just above her heart was a pinprick of blood.

'I didn't say to stop sewing.'

'Aunt, please.'

'Sew or you will become a Binder tonight, no questions, no decisions, no say.'

Anna began to sew, feeling every stitch above her heart as if she were sewing directly into her skin. *Stitch in. Stitch back. Stitch in. Stitch back.* The pain became a constant until she could barely think straight. She regretted the image she'd chosen for the embroidery: a blood-red flower. It slowly took shape.

Anna looked in the mirror before bed and saw the rose stitched into her skin, raw and red. It would heal and fade, but she would never forget the half-hour she'd spent sewing it. She thought of the pattern of circles she'd seen sewn into Aunt's own skin – had Aunt sewn them there herself with the same spell? She thrived on punishment, both to others and herself. *What did it mean?*

Aunt walked in and winced at the sight of Anna's injury.

She came over and kissed her on the forehead. 'I needed you to know your behaviour won't be tolerated again. My father was always too soft on us and look where it got his daughters. One dead and one—' Aunt looked at herself in the mirror and winced again. 'I just need you to trust me.' She placed the glass of milk down on the dressing table. 'Now let me brush your hair.'

# GRIEF

### Twelve Years Old

'She used to sneak into my room at night and we'd read fairy tales under the covers. Marie always wanted to be the prince, the princes were always wearing hats in the pictures and she loved hats. I remember a straw one that she refused to take off for a whole year. She'd go to the front door wearing it and announce she was going on adventures . . .'

Anna tried not to listen but it was impossible. She was hungry for information about her mother and these small details felt of huge importance. Aunt continued her torrent of gentle stories.

'Do you ever wonder how it would have felt to have her arms around you?'

The way she said it all – so soothingly – that's what made it hard, what hurt so much. Anna felt the tears come to her eyes as if they had always been there, waiting.

'She loved you so much.'

Anna cried out, reaching for her eyes: her tears burned. They burned her eyes and cheeks with acid pain. She screamed again and scrabbled at her face but her cheeks felt the same as always. It was just a sensation. Just a sensation.

'Her laughter was always sudden. I remember—'

*'Stop. Please stop.' The burning was too much. She couldn't bear it. She rubbed at her eyes but they only watered more.*

*'Only you can stop it, Anna. Grief hurts. You must let it go.'*

*Anna tightened the third knot in her Knotted Cord. Aunt wiped a burning tear from her cheek and stroked her hair comfortingly. 'Your mother would have sung to you like this, Anna, she loved to sing . . .'*

*Anna tightened the knot until her fingers bled and her cheeks dried and the ache inside her was a distant thing that couldn't hurt any more.*

# SATIN

*Lover's Knot: To break off a romance/suppress sexual desire.*

*Knot Spells, The Book of the Binders*

Christmas approached slowly and silently. Anna was stuck in the house without any way to speak to or see her friends. But she was out of her room and taking the tisane again, every sip of it a satisfying act of rebellion. Aunt didn't have time to get them a tree so their only decorations were some recycled paper chains from the previous year. The front garden was of course adorned with tasteful lights for the neighbours to admire. There was a strict itinerary of chores and revision in accordance with her ongoing grounding.

As Anna worked she thought about Aunt's offer. No matter what angle she examined it from, it didn't feel right. She couldn't believe that Aunt was letting her choose whether to become a Binder or not; was prepared to let her spend time with Effie. It was absurd. She couldn't trust it. She couldn't say no either. *Perhaps she knows she can't control me forever, she needs the choice to be mine – or the choice is an illusion like all her other tricks . . .* Either way Anna needed to know the truth – and quickly.

Time was running out and there were so many secrets. How were her parents connected to the house? Why still live here, beneath the room in which they died? Why was magic a danger to their family? Why was her Knotting so impera-tive? What was she meant to sacrifice? What was in the third-floor room? *Why keep it locked?* Anna had started listening out every night and was surprised to find that Aunt went to the room more than she'd realized. Twice last week. Once already this week. *What are you doing in there?*

One day when Aunt was out Christmas shopping, Anna stole her laptop. She'd never researched her mother's death before, had never wanted to or felt as if there was any reason to, accepting all she'd been told in good faith – but things had changed. She typed 'Marie Everdell death' into the browser but as her fingers hovered over the enter key, she could feel her paranoia rising. She could feel Aunt over her shoulder. She spun around but there was no one there – only the rose bush on the piano watching her with red malice.

*If she finds out – I'll be locked away for good.*

Anna pressed enter, stomach rolling, but the search brought up no results. It had been sixteen years ago and she doubted the death had been national news, just a run-of-the-mill, if somewhat grisly, domestic. Anna tried a variety of other search terms but nothing appeared.

She eventually located a newspaper archive site. She found scans of several London and local newspapers from the week of the death and began to read through them exhaustively. Eventually she came across the headline: 'Man strangles partner and takes own life'. Her heart stopped. The words were a bolt through her middle. She didn't want to know any more. She had to keep reading . . .

In the quiet southwest London neighbourhood of Earlsfield, a woman has been found strangled to death in her own home by her partner of three years, who then stabbed himself in the heart.

Police received a distress call from Dominic Cruickshank, 28, around 11 p.m. last night, admitting that he had killed his partner Marie Everdell, 25. He claimed she had been having an affair. By the time police arrived at the scene Mr Cruickshank was already dead, having inflicted a stab wound to his own chest. The couple were found lying next to each other in their bed on the top floor of their London home in Cressey Square. Their baby of three months was in the cot beside the bed.

Metropolitan Police Inspector Ian Munro has confirmed that they are not looking for anyone in connection with the deaths. 'This is a truly tragic incident. It's understood the woman was violently attacked before the offender took his own life.'

Dominic Cruickshank had been a PhD student and research assistant in Psychology at the University of Edinburgh when he abruptly left his position just before completing his studies. Marie Everdell was working as an HR assistant at a local recruitment firm.

Ex-colleague Sanvi Sharma, from the University of Edinburgh, told the police she understood Mr Cruickshank had left his post to be with Ms Everdell in London. 'I didn't know where they were living. It was as if they had gone into hiding. He was a good man; it seems completely out of character. Dominic was no murderer.'

Neighbour Patricia Smith said: 'We weren't even aware that the couple had a baby. I'd never seen one leave the house. They kept themselves to themselves. It's a complete shock. This is a quiet, family neighbourhood. Nothing like this ever happens here.'

Anna stared at the screen until the words lost all meaning. She'd always known about her parents' death but it had been like a story – a dark and twisted fairy tale. Reading the matter-of-fact print, the unyielding details, for the first time, it felt real.

She found the words again: *Cressey Square* – they had lived here, in her house. The *top floor* of the house – they'd died in the third-floor room. She thought she might be sick. Her mother had been strangled two floors above her. The residues of her father's blood might remain, even now, woven into the fibres of the carpet. She leant forwards, taking deep breaths. Surely it was no coincidence that Aunt kept that room sealed off from her. *But why?* If she simply wanted the memories of it locked away – *why go there at night?*

*Dominic Cruickshank.* Anna had never known his full name. How had a *good man* turned into a murderer? There was a picture of him next to the article, more serious than the one she had of him, frowning and dark-browed, menacing even. She knew her mother's name but she was a stranger. *Who was this woman who had lived in hiding with a man who controlled her? Who'd given birth and told no one?*

She found a few other articles, most of which said much the same thing, and then came across one which revealed a further detail from the case. Police had uncovered a message from a woman on Dominic's phone: *When can you come and see me? Can you get rid of HER tonight? Carmenta x.* The police postulated that Marie might have seen the message and confronted Dominic who had then retaliated. They'd not been able to trace the number or determine who Carmenta was. There was no mention of the message again and the stories petered out altogether.

The case was simple: adultery, domestic violence, *a crime of passion*. A label that covered all sins of love, that meant they didn't have to dig deeper; a story they could close shut. A dark and twisted fairy tale.

Anna closed the laptop and went to the piano. She sat

down and started playing – a dark, stabbing tune, fingers like knives upon the keys, slicing the song into angry, staccato notes and short, sharp refrains – letting the melody bleed out. Aunt liked to take her joy from her as she played; well, she couldn't take her anger and there was no one she hated more in this moment than Aunt.

After that, all Anna could think about was the third-floor room. As she polished the silverware for Christmas – she thought about it. As she stirred chutneys for Aunt's gift collection and smiled sweetly at Aunt – she thought about it. As she hoovered the carpets and stood, vacuum in hand, staring up at the staircase to the third floor – she realized it had consumed her mind. She listened to Aunt going up there at night until she could take the questions no longer. Only one thing had the answer.

One day, after waving Aunt off to work, Anna stood in the hallway and glared at the key on the rack. Aunt's key. She reached for it hesitantly. The blade immediately began to morph and change, never fixing on one state. Anna wailed in frustration. She put it back knowing that it would not work but marched upstairs anyway, only slowing when she reached the stifling quiet of the third-floor staircase.

She felt for her Knotted Cord and tied her dread away. *I shouldn't be doing this. I have to do this.* She carried on up the narrow staircase, winding around at the top to the third-floor landing; all was quiet, all was dark, the door before her plain and ordinary. In her imaginings it was bigger – looming – locked with bolts and chains like the lair of a giant. But in truth the only thing that stopped her getting inside was the small keyhole by the handle.

She moved closer and studied the handle – there was a mark on it, only faint but the colour was distinct. Dark red. *Blood? Why would Aunt have blood on her hands?* Anna tried to turn it but the door seemed to shudder against her. Locked.

Then the handle moved beneath her hand.

Anna jumped back with a yelp and stared at the handle – it was perfectly still. *Am I the one going insane now?* She stepped forwards again and put her ear against the door. She was met with nothing but silence.

She watched the handle for several minutes until her frustration grew too much. She went downstairs and stopped outside Aunt's room. If the third floor would give her nothing, perhaps there would be something in there that could help. It wasn't entirely breaking the rules – she sometimes went into Aunt's room to change the sheets . . . *I could be changing the sheets* . . .

She stepped inside.

She searched Aunt's bedside tables first, moving methodically through each drawer: contact lenses, books, cords, sleep masks, a box of trinkets and old jewellery. Under the bed were drawers containing no more than bed sheets and towels. She opened the wardrobe. It was precisely organized – dresses hung in colour order, jumpers tightly folded, shoes tucked into slots. She opened the drawers in turn – socks, tights, underwear, white and functional, and then . . . her hand touched silk.

She opened the drawer wider and there, at the back, was something red. She pulled it out. The bra was all lace, its softness at war with its brash colour. Anna dropped it to the floor with shock as if some wild creature had landed in her hands. She searched the drawer deeper and found a pair of matching pants and then another set – green satin. They didn't belong. They didn't belong in this clean and white and lifeless room. She tucked them back into the drawer.

She'd been hoping to unearth a diary, or photographs, or something that might reveal more about her mother's life, her parents' death. She would sooner have expected to find a firearm or a severed limb than provocative lingerie. She

couldn't imagine Aunt's bony body wearing something so
. . . soft. *Why would she even own them?* Aunt was vehemently
against everything to do with love and love-making; she'd
never shown interest in a man in all Anna's life.

*Perhaps there's someone at work?* Perhaps there was no one
at all, the lingerie simply jewelled relics of a past life that
Aunt no longer led and Anna had never known. *I gave my
life up for you.* Aunt had said it so many times before. Anna
ignored the guilt. Had Aunt given up love for her too? But
Aunt hated lust and love and everything in between . . .
*doesn't she?*

Christmas Day was a carbon copy of every other Christmas
Day. Sensible gifts (socks and textbooks), a small roast chicken
(a turkey was too big), over-boiled vegetables, crackers and
soon-forgotten paper hats. In the afternoon they drove to
Richmond Park for a walk, watching deer cut through the
fading light with antlered silhouettes. Snow had been anticipated but it didn't come, the sky remaining an obstinate grey.
They returned to the house and put on a black and white
movie and Aunt laid out a puzzle for them while they watched
it. The fire finally crackled but it couldn't chase the loneliness
from the house, the loneliness that comes from the space
between two people who have nothing left to say to one
another. *Two people are not quite a family.*

When Aunt left her room that evening, Anna looked at
herself in the mirror, pulling at the skin on her face. It was
definitely brighter, and the green of her eyes was too. Even
her hair had grown stronger in colour, finding the reds and
golds of its old life. Perhaps the tisane was truly working at
last. Although she couldn't pinpoint any sudden change,
Anna felt different as well. She hadn't had any nosebleeds,
she wasn't so hungry all the time, she was sleeping better.
There was a growing agitation too, a kind of roving urgency

within her which longed for release, but what that was she couldn't say. It made the silent prison of life with Aunt even harder. It made her need for escape greater.

She went to close her balcony curtains and stopped. Something was glinting on the floor outside – a package? She opened the doors and picked it up. A gift. It was wrapped in festive paper covered with goats wearing Santa hats. The tag read:

Merry Christmas, Anna. I thought this book might help along your musical genius. Just put it on the piano and it will capture the notes you are playing. Don't worry if you go wrong, it will correct itself as you refine the song. It'll never run out of paper either. Attis x

Anna almost dropped it in shock. She ran to the edge of the balcony and looked out over the quiet gardens – there was no one to be seen. *When did he come?* She laughed with sudden delight and went back inside. She sat on her bed and eagerly unwrapped the music book. It had a plain blue front, her name appearing on it in silver script as she held it, making her squeal with excitement. She silenced herself and opened the book, finding empty musical staves, ready for her compositions. It was unexpectedly thoughtful. She hugged it tightly, desperate to run downstairs and try it. *Could I . . .?*

She crept out of her room and tiptoed up the stairs. She stood in the dark hallway and listened until she could make out Aunt's slow, heavy breathing – she was asleep. No third-floor visitation tonight. Anna made her way down to the living room. She knew it was risky but she would only play gently.

She sat down at the piano and placed the book in front of her. A frail moonlight webbed its way into the room from the window; the book glowed white, empty as snowfall waiting for footprints. She pressed a key and watched as the note wrote itself upon the stave in a shiver of black script. A treble clef appeared beside it, curved and dark as a cloaked stranger. She let out the first joyful laugh of the day and then clapped her hands over her mouth.

She began to play then, softly. The book responded, threading the tune through the staves before it flew away into the darkness. The notes were shadows, rising and falling, growing from one another, entwining, as if Anna were sewing the fabric of night itself into the pages. She began to feel something like magic. She stopped playing. The notes broke off – waiting.

She'd been avoiding it all holidays. Magic. She was taking her tisane daily but hadn't attempted casting, in case, *in case it's no different* . . .

She went over to Aunt's stash of cords and selected a brown one. *For focus.* She took it back to the piano. She held the cord in her hands and focused on the C key. *My Hira is twine and thorn.* She formed a Weaver's Knot – *for weaving together* – and pulled it tight. Nothing happened. Anna shifted the cord along her hands and focused harder, forming another knot. *Come on. My Hira is twine and thorn.*

The piano key remained still.

She thought about how Effie, Attis and Rowan had talked about their Hiras: sharp as whetstone, strong as fire, nourishing like soil – she tried to embody each of their descriptions in turn, with no success. A fear gripped at her heart. *What if I'll never be able to do it?*

She grew tired, but refused to go to bed. She sat forming knots along the cord – undoing them, tying them again – drowsy eyes on the keys, trying to feel something until her arm ached and her eyes grew sleepy. Her mind began to wander, drifting like the clouds towards the edges of dreaming. The moonlight lit up the C key and her fingers made a knot in the cord without thinking.

The sound broke the silence of night. A clear C note.

Anna wasn't sure if she'd imagined it. She quickly made another knot in the cord and the sound came again. She did it again and this time watched as the key pressed itself down, as if some invisible finger of night were playing it.

She could feel something – the steady strength of the cord, the chill of the endless moonlight, the pure sound of the note, the silence between it all. Worlds colliding. *Magic*, like twine – no, like threads, tying them together, forming a pattern . . .

Anna tied the knots more quickly, a small and simple tune playing in response: a melody of knots. She'd never known cord magic to make anything beautiful. She knotted faster – different notes, different rhythms, a travelling octave. Her thoughts broke through. *I'm doing it! Magic! I can feel something.* As her mind lost focus the music petered out. She could feel the strength of the magic wane and then disappear altogether until the knots were no more than knots once more.

Anna tried to recall how it had felt but it was like the translator had left and the feeling she had been so certain of was now in another language she didn't understand. It didn't matter. Magic had beckoned its hand and she had followed. It was a beginning – the door was ever so slightly ajar.

# SALT

*A Binders' Circle is formed with the vine of the Closed Rose. May its thorns protect as they punish.*

Binders' Magic, *The Book of the Binders*

Anna began practising magic every day, like a thirst she could not quench. When Aunt was out she played the piano – assigning different knots to different keys – until she could manage several basic tunes. She learnt how to draw a marble to herself with a Heave Knot until it came to her every time and she could spin it in circles. She took the bulb out of her lamp and lit it up, unknotting a cord in a burst of energy. She'd been so ecstatic the first time she'd managed it that she'd run around her room and Aunt had come knocking. With the feeling of magic running through her she wondered what she'd been so afraid of – it lifted the fears from her heart, released the knots in her mind, made her feel powerful in the face of all her powerlessness. She whispered the secret she was afraid to admit into her nanta bag:

*I never want to let it go.*

It was already January. Would she be Knotted by summer? Or did she really have a choice? Perhaps Aunt truly wanted the decision to be hers. Deep down Anna doubted it, but even so, if she was expected to make any kind of decision over her future, she had to understand her past. She would speak to Selene. If anyone knew any more about her parents' death or the secrets Aunt might be hiding, it was she. A few days before returning to school Aunt agreed in her most threatening tone that she could spend Friday at Selene's house, which was the ideal opportunity – not to mention *a whole evening of unlimited coven activities.* Anna was desperate to see her friends; it had been so long – she just hoped she could prove herself to them, at last.

She'd been so excited arriving back on Wednesday, she'd forgotten school's cruelties. She was met with a notice-board of mock exam times and panicked faces reviewing it nervously. She should have done more studying, but she'd been distracted . . .

Then there was the chitter and the chatter. As she walked down the corridor towards her locker she could hear it – the holiday gossip being unfolded like paper, examined and refolded into something sharp, designed to puncture. Only now she was the target; she heard her name, felt the laughter.

The whispers stopped suddenly. Anna spun round to find Attis approaching, onlookers temporarily silenced as they watched him pass. 'Anna.' He searched her face with some-thing like concern. 'You've had us worried.'

'Worried for my safety, were you?'

'No, your aunt's. I thought you'd smoked her and done a runner.' His face broke into a wide, uneven smile. Anna had forgotten just how contagious it could be.

'It's good to see you, Dr Everdell.'

'It's er – good – to see you too,' she said, looking away.

'Come on, we've got Mr Ramsden. I'm sure he's missed me terribly over the holidays.'

Anna shut her locker and made her way down the corridor with Attis, trying to ignore the stares that followed them.

'Attis,' she said uncomfortably. 'I wanted to say thank you – for the music book.'

'Oh, that old thing.'

'Attis, really, it was so unexpected . . .'

'Sorry I didn't use the front door. Selene explained the balcony procedure to me.'

'I mean if my aunt had caught you, you'd probably have been hanged from the balcony, but the book is really amazing. I've already recorded a bunch of songs and—'

He wasn't listening; he was peering at her closely, like a doctor assessing his patient. 'You look different. What is it? Cut your hair? Pierced something? Changed your name?'

She raised her eyebrows. 'I've done none of these things.'

'I know, but I'm not joking about you looking different. Your eyes are brighter, like a beech leaf in sunlight. You're still taking the tisane?'

Anna nodded, her cheeks reddening.

'It's working!' He beamed. 'Want to try out your magic on Ramsden? I had some good ideas over Christmas.'

'Attis . . . no. No.'

When Anna entered the common room at lunchtime something came hurtling towards her. She was almost tackled off her feet. 'Anna!' Rowan released her from the hug. She was with Manda. 'Is it really you? What in thirteen dark moons happened? Are you OK? You weren't really locked away though, were you? Effie said you were but you know how she likes to exaggerate.' Anna's look must have disturbed Rowan because her voice turned sober. 'You weren't, were you?'

'No,' said Anna, trying to sound casual, 'Aunt was just mad is all. I was heavily grounded.'

'I swear by the maiden, mother and crone, I'd like to sock that aunt of yours.'

Anna laughed. 'I'd love to see that.'

'We really missed you.' Manda gave her a hug in an uncharacteristic display of affection.

'I've missed you all too – you have no idea.'

'Well, you look good,' said Rowan. 'Did you do something? You look different.'

'Nope,' said Anna.

'Someone's been skiving.'

Anna turned to find Effie. She didn't know if Aunt was right about her – if Effie was leading her into doom and despair, if she could be trusted – but as their smiles met, her doubts faded. It was one of Effie's true smiles.

'Good to have you back. Selene told me what the bitch was doing to you. She's a lunatic, Anna. We've got to get you away from there.'

'I know,' said Anna, surprised to find she meant it.

They took a seat at their usual table in the corner. Anna cast a few glances around the common room and found half the room watching them. 'OK, why has everyone been staring all day?'

The table went silent. Effie smiled faintly.

'Well.' Rowan chewed her cheek. 'Everybody's been talking about your exit from the party. Corinne kind of filmed it and Darcey's made sure everyone's seen it.'

'Great,' said Anna and then remembered. 'But, Effie, you did magic. Darcey's heel . . .'

Effie laughed. 'You think anyone has noticed *that*? They're all far too distracted by the bit where you throw up on the lawn . . .'

Anna groaned.

'Well, everyone thinks Karim and I slept together at the party! He hasn't come out denying it either!' Manda cried.

'Why would he? Makes him look good,' said Effie.

'Well, it makes me look bad. I'm saving myself for marriage, you all know that. Do you know how many people have signed up to Bible Study this term? One! The others have presumably decided I'm not fit to run it any more.'

Effie laughed.

'As usual Effie is taking this all very seriously.'

'All I can see is that you guys now have a reputation. A month ago you were walking vacuums.'

'I didn't want *this* kind of reputation.'

'Are we talking about Manda's threesome?' said Attis, sitting down beside them. 'I heard it was steamy, literally. You guys did it in the shower? How did you all fit?'

'We didn't do it anywhere!' Manda protested loudly, drawing looks from the adjacent table. 'If anyone had a threesome at that party, it was you.'

'I can neither confirm nor deny anything.'

Anna remembered Attis in bed with two giggling girls. She glared at him. 'Why is no one talking about Attis and Peter's fight? Attis punched him, surely that's bigger news.'

Attis laughed fondly at the recollection.

'Because no one cares when men fight, only women,' said Effie. 'And all this means is we've got everyone's attention now. The Dark Moon is rising.'

'But how are we going to do any magic now Anna's been caught by her Stepford Aunt?' said Rowan.

'About that . . .' Anna smiled and so did Effie, in a way that implied she knew already. Anna explained her new agreement with Aunt. 'So now we'll have the freedom to do whatever we like.' Anna watched Effie's smile widen and added, 'Within reason.'

Rowan stood up. 'Well, this calls for a celebration! Sod it, I'm going to get some bloody tart.'

They spent the rest of lunch dissecting the remaining gossip from the party. Anna was pained to learn that Peter and Darcey had made up. She discovered that Manda had got off scot-free. She'd told her mum Anna had been taken ill during the fair and had gone home early. Her mum had called to check and, thankfully, Aunt had confirmed the story. *She wouldn't have wanted to lose face, to have Manda's mother think I'm the wrong sort of girl.* Anna also discovered that Selene had taken Effie and Attis back to New York for the holiday season and they'd had *the best time.* Remembering her own Christmas locked away, she couldn't help feeling a prickle of resentment. She'd have given anything to go away with them.

The others departed and Anna sat with Effie, filling their free period with her tales of New York at Christmas. Darcey's voice cut through their laughter. Effie appeared delighted at the sound, turning around – but Darcey was looking at Anna.

'Oh, Nobody! So good to see you back!' She spoke loudly, making sure all those around were listening.

Anna froze, one hand reaching instinctively for her Knotted Cord. *Do nothing. Say nothing.*

'How was Christmas with your lovely aunt? She seemed awfully perturbed when she turned up at the party. Such a shame you had to go home so suddenly – in front of everyone, as well. Peter included. He knew you were a freak but he didn't realize just how much—'

'Still feeling threatened, are we, Darcey?' said Effie.

'Coming to her rescue as always, Effie?' Darcey replied. 'She's about as threatening as a wet mop.'

'I don't know. I could do some pretty decent damage with a wet mop right now. Run along now, no one is listening.'

'On the contrary, Anna is listening, aren't you?' Darcey prodded Anna's back, stepping closer, speaking more quietly. Anna gripped the cord tighter. *Do nothing. Say nothing.* 'You'd be smart to take a leaf out of her book, Effie. She understands the essential truth—'

'Which I'm sure you're going to tell us.' Effie yawned.

'That she's nothing and I'm everything she'll never be. I pull the strings of her sad, pathetic life—'

'So pull the damn strings, Darcey.' Anna was as surprised as everyone else to find that she was the one speaking – plainly and calmly – with the kind of slow coldness Aunt specialized in. 'Call me names. Send me home from the party. Tell Peter lies. Ruin my existence. Whatever you do, believe me, I've been through worse. I've been through things you can't even imagine. You are honestly the least of my worries.'

A few people around them began to laugh.

Anna exhaled, feeling the weight of years of silence lift from her shoulders. She'd meant every word. Aunt's punishments, the threat of the Binders, the violence of the third-floor room – these were the dark places that occupied her mind now. Effie hooted with laughter. Darcey blinked several times; something around the edges of her eyes showed Anna that she was furious. Then her mouth twisted in a small, razor smile.

'I think you're right, Anna Everdull. There's nothing I can do to you that I haven't already done. Been there, broken that. But there are so many other victims to choose from. How about that one you love to defend – you know, large, easy target . . . the Beast.'

*Rowan.*

'I just want you to know that when I break her – it's on you.'

Anna floundered for words, panic tightening her throat. *Why did I have to speak back to her?*

'You seem to have lost your voice again.' Darcey gave Anna a final smile and left, laughter trailing behind her.

'Well hello, Anna. Good to finally meet you.' Effie grinned.

'Rowan,' said Anna. 'Darcey's going to make her life hell.'

Effie made a bored noise. 'She was going to make Rowan's life miserable anyway. She's just trying to get to you.'

'Well, she's got to me.' Anna raised her voice and now

Effie was the one who looked surprised. 'I know it's all fun and games to you, Effie, but people are going to get hurt. On my account.'

'Let's do something about it then.'

Anna had been looking forward to their first coven session on Friday, to flexing her magic, but now she watched guiltily as Rowan added new objects from her bag on and around the altar: pot plants, a witch ball, a framed picture of Leonardo Vincent . . .

'If we're going to start a revolution, then our magic needs to be more powerful. We need to learn how to protect ourselves,' Effie commanded, drawing everyone's attention towards her. She looked around the sewing room, her eyes stopping on Anna. 'Have you been practising?'

'Yes,' Anna replied, finding her magical confidence had suddenly fled. 'It's coming along . . .'

'Well, *I* scheduled magic practice into my revision time-table,' said Manda. 'I've been reading all the books that Rowan lent me.'

'You don't learn by reading,' Effie scoffed. 'You have to find your own way. Any languages calling to you yet?'

'I've tried several,' said Manda, as if she were being tested. 'Earth magic, some symbol work, word spells. I was feeling quite drawn to the latter—'

'Anna?' Effie interrupted.

'Er – just knots and cords at the moment.'

Effie rolled her eyes. 'You need to break free of your ties.'

Anna touched the Knotted Cord in her pocket. It was easy for Effie to say, but she hadn't been raised to fear all other languages. She longed to tell the coven everything – about the secrets and lies of her life; but she couldn't. The secrets were hers to bear. *If I end up becoming a Binder, they'll hate me, hate me for how weak I am.*

'Well, do you know *your* language yet?' said Manda to Effie.

'No,' Effie snapped. 'But it'll be powerful, as powerful as the Seven. Mark my words.'

'Can't have been *that* powerful if they got themselves killed,' said Manda. 'Does anyone know who did it yet?'

'No.' Rowan shook her head. 'Mum seems to think they should have returned already.'

'My aunt believes it was the Witch Hunters,' said Anna, remembering the look in Aunt's eyes.

Effie laughed. 'She's really not letting that go, is she?'

'It's why she doesn't want me practising magic, drawing attention . . .' It was as close as Anna could get to the truth.

'I'm sorry,' said Manda. 'Who are these Hunters that Anna's crazy aunt keeps going on about?'

'You know the witch-hunt era?' said Rowan. 'It didn't go so well for our kind – burnings and pitchforks and all that jazz.'

'Everyone knows about witches being hunted, but that was a different time,' Manda responded.

'But what if it wasn't just that period?' said Rowan. 'There's evidence of hunting outbursts throughout history, further back, and some of the old stories suggest they go back even further.'

'Well, witches have always been scary, it's no surprise' said Manda. 'I'm still scared of them and apparently I am one.'

'But the old stories and legends don't believe the hunts are random, but that they're planned – like a cycle. That there's a sect behind them. Five founding members. The Wolves, they call them in the old tales, destined to return again and again to bring doom and destruction on us all.'

Effie began to chant:

'Beware, beware, the wolves are here.
There's smoke, there's smoke, in the town square.
Red thread and boots, prepare the noose.
The big bad wolves are roasting goose!'

Effie snapped her arms around Manda and made her scream.

Rowan chuckled. 'Exactly. They're just nursery rhymes and stories conjured up to scare little witches when they're misbehaving and doing magic they shouldn't be. E.g. me, during my entire childhood. Realistically, the last witch hunts happened because of war and economic strife and religion, and what do people worship now? Celebrities and designer brands. What are they going to do – pelt us with shoes?'

Anna joined in with the laughter. It did sound ridiculous when you spoke about it out loud. Aunt thought magic was a sin and love was evil – she couldn't be trusted. 'I know you're right,' she said. 'I've just got a lifetime of trauma to overcome.'

'And a lifetime of magic to embrace.' Effie clapped her on the back.

'Exactly,' said Anna, tired of the darkness and paranoia. 'What are we doing today then? I'm ready for anything.'

Effie grabbed a glass bottle from the altar with relish. 'Upstairs. We're going to need space.'

They were getting to know their way around the school at night and sneaking into the old sports hall was easy in spite of Manda's objections. The walls were a utilitarian green and the yellow floor was scuffed from decades of use. It was large and echoey and reminded Anna of best-forgotten gym lessons.

Attis was waiting for them with a large duffel bag. He dumped it onto the floor and unzipped it. He pulled out two hefty bags. 'Salt,' he announced. 'One of the most powerful protective substances on earth, as incorruptible and pure as all of your souls.' He tore the tops off the bags and decanted the salt onto the floor. He walked to the centre of the room, his presence, as always, strangely eclipsing, diminishing the world around him. 'Now, we all know my purpose in this coven is to provide eye candy; however, my main concern is your protection and the best way to protect you is to show you how to protect yourselves. Have you ever cast a magic circle before?'

Manda and Anna shook their heads.

'Mum taught me her version, but to be honest, when I'm casting spells, I never bother,' said Rowan.

'Exactly. It's a basic of magical work but as a basic it's all too often forgotten, yet it's imperative. Children of witches used to be taught it at a young age. You know the old nursery rhyme Ring o' Roses?'

Rowan sang:

> 'Ring a ring o' roses,
> Lined with salt and ashes.
> A shadow! A shadow!
> We all fall down!'

'Exactly. Well, it has its roots in casting circles – a way of encouraging them to practise.' Attis stood still for a moment, eyes shut. Anna felt a shift in the energy of the room, a drawing in towards him, as if he were a magnet turned on them. She studied his face in the half-light, shadowed lines and soft lips and eyes; he looked younger with them closed, and strangely vulnerable. *That's how he reels them in, looking as if he's the one who needs rescuing . . .*

She gasped as the salt on the floor began to rise up and disperse. It swirled around him, filling the room like a snow storm, beautiful and surreal against the mundane backdrop of the hall.

He opened his eyes. 'There are many different kinds of circle. The simplest will focus and amplify your magic, keep dark energies at bay and deflect an oncoming attack. Effie, if you will.'

The salt swirled faster, a blizzard of white. Effie stood up excitedly and threw the glass bottle at him. It hurtled towards him but stopped just before it reached him, shattering into pieces. Manda screamed. Effie laughed delightedly. *The games they must have played as children.*

The salt fell to the floor.

'As you can see, if that had been a hex coming at me, my circle would have acted as a barrier, blocking its path. You can see its shape in the salt on the floor.' The salt had formed a distinct pattern on the ground around him: a solid, thick circle with short lines coming away from it, like the dials of a compass or the rays of the sun. 'It's more than just a useful visual aid though. You can draw on the protective power of the salt to help cast your circle. Rowan, you go first as you've done it before.'

Moments later, Rowan was standing at the centre of her own salt storm. She closed her eyes and the salt pushed away from her, as if an invisible hand were brushing it aside. It started to fall, quietly and serenely, until it formed a pattern around her: a large and wavy circle, looping in and out like petals. If viewed from above Anna was sure it would look like a flower.

'Good work,' said Attis.

'Dang, my magic is pretty.'

They repeated the experiment, Attis helping Rowan to cast her circle more quickly and with more solidity. Her pattern grew clearer and more flower-like each time. Manda was called up next.

'Now, you and Anna haven't tried this before. There's no easy way to explain it really and every witch has their own technique – I just want you to visualize a circle around you and to interlace your magic with it. Imagine it however it appeals to you – as light, as colour, with neon strobe lighting, whatever you want. And draw on the power of the salt. It's there to help you. We'll try as many times as you need, so don't worry.'

It didn't take Manda long. She was almost lost in the salt surrounding her and as it fell it formed a new pattern on the floor: a circle about a metre from her and then another around that, lines zigzagging between the two.

Attis assessed it. 'It's very protective, with a double, interwoven barrier. I think we just need to work at the size.'

Anna suddenly felt flustered. *What if I can't do it? I don't know how to cast without my knots* . . . and then Attis was calling her name. She took her place at the centre of the room. He stood opposite, going over the instructions again. She hated that magical instructions were always so hazy.

Attis retreated and the salt began to swirl around her, its sea sharpness on her tongue. She closed her eyes and tried to find the magic in it. She visualized a circle of white light around her, but as the salt fell she knew it wasn't enough. She opened her eyes and saw that it had formed no pattern at all. She shook the salt from her hair.

Attis stepped forward. 'I thought it was a good look,' he said and she laughed at the absurdity of her situation. 'Effie, come here.' He beckoned. 'Right, let's hold hands. Now close your eyes.'

They formed a circle.

Attis began to sing.

> 'Ring a ring o' roses,
> Lined with salt and ashes—'

'Attis. . .' said Effie.

'OK, focus. So we'll create a circle of power and I want you to try and feel it, Anna.'

Anna closed her eyes again. With their hands in hers, the pulse of their magic running through her, she sensed it almost straight away. *Magic.* She let herself sink into it and found the different parts of it – the hush in the air, the purity of the salt, the push-pull force from Effie and Attis on either side. She imagined a circle of light around her . . . not quite a circle, more like strands interweaving, forming a net, her Hira a needle joining it all together.

'Can you feel it?' said Attis.

'You can't just go and ask a girl that,' said Anna.

Effie burst out laughing.

Attis tutted playfully. 'Who's not taking this seriously now? Right, I want you to try on your own, quickly.'

He and Effie backed away and Anna, feeling more relaxed, closed her eyes. She felt the salt lift around her and sank back into the feeling of a moment ago, a smile on her lips. She held the circle in her mind and pushed it out from her, weaving a lattice of light as if it was no more than an embroidery, threads of protection and security – nothing would break through it.

When she opened her eyes she did a small jump of joy. The salt had formed a circle and another circle after that and another after that – filling the entire hall like a storm and she the eye . . . Anna counted them. There were seven.

'You did it! Lots of circles!' Manda clapped. 'I think mine may technically have been better in terms of protection. Attis, comparisons please?'

But Attis's eyes were roving over the circles on the floor. Rowan and Effie stared too. Anna didn't know what to say.

'What's going on?' said Manda.

'Er – Anna's pattern,' said Rowan. 'It's a bit reminiscent of . . .'

'Of?'

'The Eye.' Effie turned to face her. 'It marks the magic of witches who are cursed.'

Anna couldn't look away from the pattern rippling from her, her fears rushing back at once. *I finally manage to achieve magic and now it's broken. Cursed?*

'But it's not that simple. Magic is a complex beast,' Rowan said gently. 'This pattern could mean any number of things or nothing at all.'

Anna looked around for similar support but Manda viewed her warily, Effie with intrigue and Attis didn't look at her at all. 'Rowan's right.' He cleared the salt from the floor with one push of his hand. 'Just a coincidence. You get all sorts of patterns with these circles. Maybe we call the salt quits for today. I'll try and fire a simple spell at you and see if you can deflect it with a circle.'

They practised for another hour until Anna's mind was tired and her body ached as if the magic had been seeping out of her muscles. It had taken her a while but she'd eventually managed to block one of Attis's oncoming spells. They hadn't celebrated – the curse mark was still hanging over them, full of questions that Anna was too afraid to ask.

*A shadow. A shadow. We all fall down.*

# STARS

*Ask no questions; seek no answers.*

*Tenet Five, The Book of The Binders*

Anna tried to put the circles out of her mind. Perhaps she was only searching for meaning, for paranoid connections, where there weren't any. The magic had felt good, hadn't it? It had felt more than good. And now, for the first time in her life, she wasn't going home, she was going back to Effie's house, a den of magic. *To Selene.*

Selene was nowhere to be seen.

Effie hopped up onto the kitchen counter and rifled through takeaway leaflets. 'I'll order us pizza.'

Anna nodded distractedly. 'I'm, er, just going to find Selene . . .'

She side-stepped out of the kitchen into a room done up like a retro lounge with a cocktail bar. A light was shining from the stairway. She made her way up. Steam and the sound of Selene singing was coming from a door, slightly ajar: 'If I gave my heart to you, I'd have none and you'd have two . . .' For someone with such a sonorous voice she was not particularly talented at singing, but what she lacked in tone she made up for in volume. Anna smiled and knocked on the door.

'Come in.'

Anna peeked her head into the room. It smelt sublime, like the lair of an Egyptian queen: warm spices, sylvan resins and sultry incense. Through the steam she could make out Selene reclining in a freestanding bath surrounded by candles and steeped in a liquid that definitely wasn't water. It was a bright, shimmering liquid gold. A small yellow duck bobbed along it.

'Sorry, I didn't realize you were in the—' Anna backed out of the door.

'Don't be such a pickled old prude and get in here. I love nothing more than a good conversation while I'm in the bath.'

Anna walked back into the room, eyes transfixed by the liquid. It moved slowly, creating dizzying reflections on the marble walls. Selene picked up a handful and it ran in compact globules down her arms. Anna took a seat on the toilet lid. 'What is it?'

'Liquid amber. My secret beauty elixir.' She pulled her wet hair over one shoulder, twisting it round and wringing it out, the liquid threading through it and running off in pearls of gold.

'Does it stop ageing?'

Selene let out a tinkling laugh. 'It washes away a few wrinkles but no, unfortunately I don't have that kind of power.' She looked at her slender hand while she spoke, waggling her fingers and watching the bones and veins underneath – a little more prominent than Anna's perhaps, the skin a little looser. She put it back in the water. 'I intend to be defiantly beautiful in my old age.'

Anna giggled. 'I can imagine you at eighty, long, golden-white hair, dressed to kill, winking a wrinkled eye.'

'I shall have eight toy boys, one to celebrate every decade of my life! Anyway, enough about me, how is your roster of young men? Is this Peter after you yet? Or perhaps another has caught your eye?' She searched Anna's face.

'I think Peter's running in the opposite direction.' She leant her head against the wall, finding it painful to think about him. 'I think we're not meant to be.'

'Meant to be, my wet arse.' Selene thumped the water, her fist sending golden sparks flying. 'There's no such thing. There's just a woman who knows what she wants and goes out and gets it. Until she gets bored.'

Anna laughed and then asked something she'd always wondered. 'Did you ever love anybody, Selene?'

'Love?' Selene raised a bubble to her lips. 'Ah, such a romantic notion. I've loved people, but in terms of men, there was just one, once. I was determined not to, mind you. I intended to keep my heart all locked up, but it found me out . . . love, who laughs at locksmiths.' She blew the bubble away until it popped.

'Who was he?'

'I barely recall.'

'Did my mother love my father?'

Selene sat up again, breasts bouncing in the molten water. 'Why do you ask?'

'Did she?'

'They loved each other very much.'

Anna shook her head, the questions tumbling out. 'Why did he kill her then?'

Selene seemed taken aback. 'My little matchstick, you can ask me anything about your mother but how she died – there's nothing there to ask.'

'Was he having an affair? Was there more to it? Did my mother tell you anything? I know about the house too, our house – they died there, Selene, in the room on the third floor. Aunt won't let me in—'

'Anna, Anna,' Selene said, her voice soft as the lapping water. 'My darling, I don't know what to tell you. I heard something about a supposed affair after their death but Marie had never mentioned anything. All I know is your father killed her in a moment of anger that we will never understand. It is best not to try. Love is the world's most powerful emotion and its mysteries hold depths that we can never know, both light and dark. What matters is Marie chose love anyway. Your mother chose to open her heart to the world, while Vivienne closed hers forever.'

'But she goes there. Aunt goes to the room on the third floor.'

Selene sighed. 'I never wanted you to know that was the house they died in. I didn't want you to have to suffer that. I told Vivenne to bloody well move – I don't know why she chose to stay after she inherited it.'

'She inherited it, then?'

'Well, actually, you did, I think, but as your legal guardian Vivienne has control until you turn eighteen. Anyway, I would have locked the whole place up and never looked back and what your aunt does in that room I can't say.' Selene's voice soured. 'Probably just punishing herself.'

'For what?'

'I know what she's like but I'm sure on some deeply buried level she feels guilty for your mother's death, for not being there for her, not finding some way to stop it.'

'But she hates my mother.'

'Hate is merely one of the depths of love.'

'Is that why she became a Binder?'

Selene stilled, turning slow circles in the bathwater with her finger. They did not speak of the Binders, of her future among them – they spoke of things light and delightful as bubbles.

'You don't think Aunt had any reason for giving me the bindweed, do you? That something might be wrong with my magic?' Anna asked quietly, watching the ripples, thinking of the curse mark.

Selene looked up, distraught. 'No, my darling. There is nothing wrong with you! The only wrong thing is what Vivienne did to you. She doesn't know how to cope with the hate and the fear inside of her. Sometimes it's easier to take it out on you than herself. It doesn't mean there's anything wrong with you or that she doesn't love you. She does. In her own way, she does.'

'But what's she so afraid of? The Hunters?'

Selene laughed bitterly. 'That's their excuse, yes. It was how the Binders began, you see, during the Dark Times, when there was something real to fear. Women who misguidedly believed that witches had brought the hunts on themselves, as if we were somehow to blame for the magic inside of us. But now? They're afraid of nothing but themselves. It's no way to live.'

'PIZZA!' Effie shouted.

'Ah. Our feast has arrived! Go on, let's not ruin your first visit with all this talk of Binders.'

'But—'

'Come on, there's fun to be had.' Selene nodded to the doorway, planting a fresh smile on her face. 'I'll be with you in a minute.'

Anna left the steam of the bathroom more confused than when she'd gone in. Selene was just as evasive as Aunt when it came to her parents' death. Why would neither of them give her anything? *Perhaps because there's nothing really there, just shapes in mist, patterns that don't exist.*

Effie and Attis passed her on the stairs with pizza boxes. 'To the roof!' Effie declared, leading them to the top of the house and out onto a small patch of roof furnished with mismatched chairs and sun loungers. It was January and freezing. Anna walked to the edge, the jagged skyscraper horizon of London close and glinting, the sky cloudless, faint with stars.

She felt a blast of warmth behind her and spun round to find a roaring fire suddenly burning from the metal drum. Attis smiled. They laid out the pizzas and ripped open the garlic bread, dripping with oil. It was the sort of food Anna was never allowed to eat. Selene joined them and they talked about their Christmas antics in New York. Anna sat back and listened and laughed, her troubles feeling as distant as the sky. She was barely able to believe her newfound freedom.

'So how do you like your first night in our world?' Effie asked, taking the final slice of pizza.

'I love it. It's amazing up here. You can see all of London, the whole sky, so many stars, more than I've ever seen.'

'More than you've ever seen,' Selene scoffed. 'Honey, I think most of those are planes.' Her smile dropped. 'Anna, have you seen the night's sky outside of London, away from the lights and pollution?'

'Remember in Wales, Attis used to take us on moonlit walks using only the stars for guidance?' said Effie.

He laughed. 'And you'd run off and get lost anyway.'

Anna remained quiet but Selene prompted again. 'You have, haven't you?'

'We went to St Albans once, that's outside London, but it was in the day.'

'You've never been on holiday? Never travelled?' said Attis, spinning round to look at her, the fire reflected in his eyes. Anna shrugged and looked away.

'I could kill Vivienne,' Selene growled, taking a large gulp of wine.

Attis jumped up. 'I know!'

'What?' Selene snapped, turning her annoyance to him. Anna hadn't noticed much warmth between them.

'What about those candles? You've got those candles, haven't you?'

'Oh. Oh yes! The inside-out candles.' Selene clapped her

hands delightedly, leaving the wine glass floating in mid-air. She waved a hand at him. 'Go and get them then!'

Attis hopped between his left and right foot. 'Where are they?'

'I don't know, somewhere. Just look. Maybe in the basement, with the boxes I brought back from New York, by the thingamajigs.'

'Helpful,' he said, disappearing back into the house.

'Is this really necessary?' said Effie. 'It's just some stars.'

'Ignore my as ever enthusiastic daughter.'

'What's happening?' Anna asked.

'These candles, incredible things. Hugely popular in New York, as you can imagine.' Anna could not, for she hadn't the faintest idea what they were. 'When you light them, instead of emitting light, they absorb it. I discovered them when I was dating Jack Torres. He laid out a blanket in his back garden and lit these candles and POOF.' Selene snapped her fingers. 'Like that, all the lights of New York disappeared and it was just him and me and total darkness.'

'What does that have to do with the stars?'

'Well, very distant light can still get through, so once you've removed all the light pollution, you can see the night's sky in all its pinpoint glory. We made wild love under the stars for hours.'

Effie groaned.

Attis appeared in the doorway, childlike excitement on his face. 'Close your eyes, Anna! No peeking.' She heard them moving around her. Then his voice close to her. 'Ready.'

Anna looked up and let out a gasp.

The night's sky had always been a hazy, grey thing: overworked stars and a dominant moon. Not this one. Here, the moon was part of a greater network, a vast, incalculable network. For the first time, she had some vague notion of infinity. She tried to focus on one area of sky – to count the stars within it – but the closer she looked the more there were, and more behind, smaller again, like mirrors of infinite reflections. It wasn't still either. There was somehow movement – passing planes, ceaseless twinkling, the faint shifting colours of galaxies. Anna felt as if she should hear something from all the life and commotion above them – the sound of stars burning – but there was nothing. Their power existed in their absolute silence.

'There's just – there's so many . . .' She looked back at them and Attis was beaming at her.

'You've got a little drool there.' Effie pointed at her chin.

Anna shut her mouth. They'd lit the candles around the perimeter of the roof. She walked to the edge and looked closely at one. The flame was merely the outline of a flame. Inside there appeared to be nothing at all – a hollow centre. London was a vast darkness. She stuck her head out beyond the candle and the city she knew reappeared, electric and agitated. She pulled her head back in and it disappeared again, as if someone had simply flicked a switch. 'The moon is so much brighter than I've ever seen it.'

'The Goddess wove the language of the seven old planets but the moon rules them.' said Selene, her voice a lullaby. 'It shows us the truth that can't be handled in the light of day.'

Anna watched the sky change overhead as they talked and ate thick slabs of cheesecake. She was more relaxed than she'd been since she could remember, the warmth of the fire, fanned every now and then by Attis, constant and comforting. And then they got onto the topic of magic.

She tensed. She'd forgotten about their circle practice earlier – the pattern of the salt. *The curse mark.*

'I can't do it,' said Effie. They were talking about something called a *chimera*.

'It'll come,' said Attis, chasing her spider tattoo up her arm.

'What's a chimera?' Anna asked.

'It's an illusion, like . . .' Attis looked around and settled on the fire. He focused on it. After several moments it wasn't a fire any more: the flames had turned to water, shivering and smoking like flames but blue and transparent and rippling.

'Do you see that?' said Attis. Anna nodded, hypnotized. 'It's not real. It's a chimera, an illusion I've created with magic. If you were to put your hand into those watery flames, they'd still burn you.'

'Like a hologram?'

'Sort of.'

'It's bloody hard is what it is,' Effie huffed.

'It's hard because it's not really a spell, you're not really changing anything in the physical world. A chimera belongs to some strange half-world between reality and a spell.'

'How do you cast one?'

'There's no one way, no exact method . . .' Attis grappled with his own vagueness.

'I don't understand this new world of magic! There are no rules, no formulae, no tables of bloody correspondences. Aunt would have several small fits.'

'Oh, you will have to unlearn everything Vivienne's taught you,' said Selene, as if it was nothing. 'Her methodology is limiting.'

'Limiting,' Anna repeated, thinking of the days of her life spent learning every correspondence, practising every knot.

'Magic is not a mathematical formula. It's not an encyclopaedic study. Can you learn to dance by studying the biological mechanics of the muscles?'

'But there are certain rules, surely?'

'No. No rules, my dear.'

Rules. They were the grid lines of her life. They gave things a framework for measurement, for meaning. In her head the grid lines began to rise up, criss-crossing, entangling, floating off into space – but what was left? A rootless, drifting world.

'There aren't rules, but there are patterns. Patterns is a

better word, it's open-ended, growing, full of possibility.' Selene gesticulated to the night's sky above them. 'We find patterns in the heavens whether they are there or not.'

The wine bottle lifted in the air in front of her and poured Selene another glass.

'OK, how did you do that?' said Anna, exasperated. 'Everyone's always doing magic without casting at all. Aunt casts magic by making knots in the air with her hands and no cord. I thought you needed a language to cast?'

'Did you know that there were seven original languages of magic?' said Selene.

Anna shook her head.

'Planetary. Elemental. Botanical. Verbal. Imagic. Symbolic. Emotional. All of them need something, a translation – except the last one. The language of emotions. To cast a spell with nothing but emotion alone, that is the most difficult kind of magic and an extremely rare language. When I light a candle without word or movement, I am drawing on nothing but what is inside me.'

Anna's world continued to open, drifting free of its restraints. 'But surely there's no end to that? You could cast any spell with nothing but your mind?'

Selene smiled. 'It's not your mind, Anna, and no, the possibilities, unfortunately for most witches, myself included, are limited. As a language, emotional is by far the most diffi-cult. Why do you think I can only pour myself wine or light candles using it? I could never cast a love spell using emotions alone; the demands of it would be far too intense and complex. I fall back on my potions for that is the language which speaks to me and which I understand.'

'My language is going to be one of the original languages,' Effie declared. 'Like the greatest witches.'

'There are great witches in every language, Effie,' Selene tempered.

'The most powerful then.'

'How will I find out which of the seven languages is mine?' Anna asked, hoping she could master just one in her lifetime.

'Seven? Anna, you're limiting things again. I said there were seven original languages, not seven in total. Think of those seven as the main constellations in the sky, drawn and labelled. Now look up and tell me just how many more stars there are.' Anna was overwhelmed again by the depth of the foreverness above her. 'However many stars you see doesn't come close to the number of languages there are.'

'But there are potentially an infinite number of stars.'

'Exactly. I've met people in my life who work magic through the patterns of willow bark, hand shadows on a wall, the sound of raindrops, computer circuit boards, through tracing the flight of birds across the sky. I knew a group once who cast spells through synchronized swimming, another through orgies . . .'

'I met a guy who could only cast while skydiving. Apparently the act of falling was a powerful generator,' Attis added.

Anna's head was swimming with stars.

'Now where are your rules? Where are your categories?' Selene's voice was bitter and Anna sensed the words weren't directed at her any more.

Anna looked at the sky again. *What if magic really could be like that – endless connections, endless possibilities.* 'I want to learn it all.'

Selene's smile faded. 'You will, one day, you will. Right, I'm going to take myself to bed. All this talk of magic is exhausting. To be young and starry-eyed . . .'

She left and Anna found it strange to be alone on the roof with Effie and Attis, as if she were somehow invading their space. They were complete without her, a whole already. *I don't belong.* Effie snuggled into the crook of Attis's arm and

Anna yawned. 'You know what. I think I'm going to go to bed too. Thanks for the dinner and the candles . . .'

'Don't thank us, you're part of us now,' said Effie.

Anna smiled at her and left. She wanted nothing more than to stay with them, but she wasn't sure if she was meant to. There were no rules when it came to Effie and Attis either and she didn't know how to navigate them.

She waited up for a while, but Effie did not come to bed. She imagined the candles on the roof burning low, the stars gradually disappearing. *Attis chasing Effie's tattoo.* She fell asleep and dreamt more vividly than she had ever done before, no dreambinder above to catch a single one.

# BLADES

*The body is not a vessel for magic but an instrument for control. Pain must not be sought for pain's sake but to attain freedom from that which pulls at our vanity, threatens our weaknesses and puts the self before the Goddess of Silence and Secrets.*

*Binders' Training, The Book of the Binders*

Anna woke early, unable to shake off Aunt's schedule. She showered. Dressed. Made the bed. Effie's door was shut so she went downstairs – no one was in the kitchen and there appeared to be nothing edible in the fridge. She could hear hammering coming from the basement. She dithered at the top of the stairs and then walked down, into the heady aromas of burning and smoke. The door to the forge was ajar. She pushed it slightly and promptly stepped back into the hallway.

The hammering stopped.

'Anna?'

'Yes.'

'Why are you hiding?'

'I'm not.'

'Why are you standing outside the door hidden from view then?'

Anna reappeared in the doorway. 'I just wasn't sure if it

was a good time.' Attis was topless, his body dappled in flame, a distracting, dark grey symbol of a horseshoe in the centre of his chest. 'Aren't you going to get yourself burnt?'

'I don't burn easy.'

'Forged in the fires of hell and all that?'

'Something like that.' He grinned and put down the hammer. He dropped his hands into a bucket of water.

Anna moved past him, occupying herself with his shelves. Her eyes landed on the white key, the key she'd seen many times before. The right side of her body suddenly felt warm – Attis had appeared beside her, still emitting the heat of the fire.

Anna picked up the key. 'You used this to open those doors at school?'

'Yes, my skeleton key. Opens any door.' The greys of his eyes were as changeable as the smoke in the room as he watched her.

'A skeleton key . . .' Anna held it closer. It weighed almost nothing and yet – *does it hold the weight of the third-floor room within it? Could it open the door at last?* She studied the smooth, white material with fascination and then added with shock, 'Is it made out of bone?'

'Yes.' Attis smiled. He took it from her and put it into a jar of keys on the shelf.

'Your tattoo is interesting,' said Anna, keeping her eyes on his face.

He looked down and Anna took the opportunity to glance at it. Up close, it didn't appear to be an ordinary tattoo. It gleamed in the light as if threads of wire were woven into his flesh.

'Is it magic?' She resisted the urge to reach out and see what it felt like.

'Yes. An iron tattoo. For protection.' He turned away and reached for a T-shirt on the back of the door. He threw it on, the white of it stark against his tanned and sooted skin.

'Is it some sort of rite of passage to get a magical tattoo or something?'

'Only the coolest witches have them. There's a club and everything.'

Anna rolled her eyes at him.

'I'll do you one if you want? An iron horseshoe on your arm. Here.' He reached out and his fingertips brushed the top of her arm just below her shoulder. 'For protection.'

Anna pulled away. 'Why would I need to be protected? If my magic is cursed then it's everyone else who needs protecting from me.'

'Your magic won't hurt anyone unless you want it to,' he said, his eyes growing serious and dark. Anna preferred it when he was grinning.

'What were you working on then?'

'Want to see?' He was suddenly animated, leaping back towards his anvil.

Anna couldn't help smiling. 'Yes.' She watched the fire stretch and strive, flexing its limbs – never still, like him. He drew a piece of metal from its depths to show her. It looked long and thin and sharp.

'What's it going to be?'

'A blade.'

'Oh.'

He reached into his back pocket and pulled out a wooden handle. 'For my knife of many blades.' The wooden handle was covered in intricate markings – symbols.

'What are they?'

'I work with the Warders, a grove who specialize in protective magical symbology. The symbols give my blades their power.'

Attis held up the knife and flicked it down quickly; a small but sharp-looking blade appeared from the end of it. 'That's my go-to knife, covers all bases.' He curved the handle through the air and the blade coming out of it transformed. It was now startlingly long with a curved belly. 'A machete.' He crossed the handle through the air and, although Anna still couldn't pinpoint the moment when it happened, the blade changed again, shorter now with a fierce curved tip at the end. 'A hex-cutter.'

'The blade changes depending on how you move it through the air?'

'Exactly. The movement corresponds with one of the carved symbols and switches the blade.'

Anna raised her eyebrows. 'And how many blades does this knife have?'

'Twenty currently. It's got blades for every use from combat to cutting wood to carving meat. Then there are some magical blades . . .'

'What are the magical ones?' asked Anna eagerly.

'There's one that can cut through anything. A throwing knife which always hits its target. A fire blade, of course. An invisible blade – very useful. Plenty more.'

'What's the one you're working on now?'

'It's for sacrifices. Pierces true and quick. It can slice through bone and always finds the heart.'

'And what do you intend to sacrifice?' Anna asked, perturbed.

'Nothing specific.' Attis turned away, putting the blade down. 'But it's good to be prepared.'

'Are you secretly a dwarf? Aren't they always blacksmiths?'

'Bit tall for that, aren't I?'

'Goblin?'

'Too beautiful for that.'

'Maybe a goblin then . . .' Anna mused. Her stomach rumbled.

'You're hungry. What do you want for breakfast?'

'I'll grab some cereal.'

'Cereal's bad for you. What do you want? I'll make you something.'

'I don't know.'

'You don't know what you want? Is this a chronic problem?'

'I want an omelette with red peppers,' said Anna without thinking.

He nodded seriously. 'An omelette with red peppers.'

Anna shook her head. 'You don't actually have to make me an omelette, honestly. I'll have a piece of toast.'

'You're having an omelette.'

'Are you going to have some?'

'Sure.'

'OK.'

Anna stood awkwardly in his forge and then backed out of the door. 'To the kitchen,' she said, unsure why she needed to point out where they were going.

He laughed. 'To the kitchen, sergeant.'

Attis popped to the corner shop to pick up ingredients and returned with several bags full of food. 'I've got eggs. I've got peppers. Goats' cheese. Orange juice. Bread. Muffins. We're having a feast.'

The smells of his cooking must have woken Selene. She wandered into the kitchen in search of coffee. 'I've already brewed it,' said Attis, pouring her a cup.

Selene took it and sat down. 'Come, elixir, awaken me.'

'Where's Effie?' Anna asked.

'You won't see her until midday. She hates sleeping until she's asleep and then she loves it,' Attis explained, sprinkling herbs on the omelette in front of her, red peppers shining like ribbons, goats' cheese oozing.

'Thank you,' she said, tucking in.

'My brain is defogging. Work to be done,' Selene announced. 'I have a client in half an hour.'

'What's the spell?' asked Anna, wishing she could join in.

'She's been in love with a man who she works with for some time. He's single but uninterested – we need to turn his head.'

'A love spell?'

'Not love, seduction.' Selene smiled. 'With a little help from magic, of course. He won't stand a chance.'

'Is that fair on him?' Anna asked.

'Doesn't really matter if it's fair on him, does it, Selene?' said Attis through a mouthful of omelette.

Selene ignored him. 'Seduction is seduction, Anna. All women do it. A little dab of perfume here, a little cleavage there, a sway of the hips, a bite of the lip. Magic is just another helping hand in our repertoire.'

'You forgot ass-shaking. A personal favourite,' said Attis.

'You mock, Attis, but you're as clueless as the rest.' Selene picked up her mug and walked over to the sink.

'Some Cupid kill with arrows; some with traps,' he said, stabbing his fork through a pepper.

Anna soon made her excuses and left. She was relieved to be away from them. She'd never been alone with Attis and Selene before and it was uncomfortable. Selene was often dismissive towards men but when it came to Attis it no longer felt like a generalization: it felt charged, hostile – specific. Perhaps it was simply an extension of her feelings towards the male species, or was their relationship more complicated than she knew?

The next month passed quickly, hectic with studying and exams and magic. The coven began meeting every Friday, finding their flow, sharpening their languages, savouring the taste of new ones. Anna had been worried at first but with no further signs of the curse mark she let herself relax into it. She could feel her magic stretching and strengthening. Her Hira was not twine and thorn, it was unwinding – not twine but threads, strong and fine; not thorn, but a needle, wielded by her mind. *Stitch in, stitch back, stitch in, stitch back . . .* the dreamy state her head fell into when she was sewing. Only now she was sewing the thread of things.

Anna tried to ignore the fact that the thread might soon be snapped. There had been no more threats about bringing her Knotting forwards, but even so it was getting closer and Aunt still seemed on edge. Aunt had no idea about her secrets and she still didn't know Aunt's either. She listened to her at night, visiting the third-floor room, while she stared at the photograph of her parents. The more she thought about their death the less she understood. Why would her father kill her mother if he loved her? Who was this Carmenta he was with? If he wasn't a witch how had he even managed to overpower her mother? Perhaps he'd caught her unawares while she slept – but why hadn't she fought back? *Why didn't you fight back?*

Anna normally ended up nothing more than frustrated. At her mother. At Aunt and Selene for giving her so little. At the fact she had no one else to turn to. Her grandparents on Aunt's and her mother's side were dead and she'd searched but couldn't locate her father's parents – they'd probably changed their name after all that had happened. She doubted they would want to know her and what help would they be anyway? The curse was magical, which meant it had likely come from her mother's side. She needed a new line of enquiry or she'd have no choice but to try to break into the room on the third floor. Time was running out and Anna was acutely aware that the Binders could snap at any moment.

'Look at this!' she exclaimed, nudging Rowan and Manda. They'd been in the common room revising for several hours. Effie hadn't shown up.

Rowan looked up, eyes somewhere between manic and blurry. 'Erghh, what? Sorry, I don't think I've thought about anything other than the functions of mitochondria for the last hour.'

Anna thrust the phone in front of their faces.

'Anna, you were meant to be borrowing Rowan's phone for revision,' Manda chided.

'I was. I just, kind of, came across this – ' The news story was only short:

## Animal entrails found in luxury flat construction site

Animal entrails in the shape of seven circles were found within the Whitechapel construction site of much contested luxury flats. The entrails, which included intestines, feathers and a heart at their centre, were discovered by builders and are reminiscent of the mark discovered on the back of the Faceless Women's necks. The items have been linked to occult practices and may have been used as part of a ritual to 'curse' building work and disrupt the project.

'What about it?' said Rowan.

'Well, it's about magic. Curse magic!' Anna whispered, disturbed by the graphic image of a curse mark it conjured. 'It's on a news site.'

Rowan laughed. 'Not a reputable one! Look, the next story is about a man who cured his cancer with cosmic rays. Probably just some entrails dragged in by a fox and now people are imagining shapes and rituals in them!'

'Do foxes drag in whole hearts?' Anna cried. 'Besides, whether it's real magic or not, or linked to the Faceless Women or not, the fact is it's been noticed. Don't you think there's more coverage of magical activities in the papers since the summer?'

Rowan frowned. 'I don't know. I haven't been looking. I'm guessing your aunt has though?'

'Maybe . . .'

'Look, Anna, I love a good study procrastination, but I really don't think chasing crazy rumours is worth your time. How about we consider the fine qualities of Bryn Sawbridge instead?' Rowan nodded towards the other side of the room.

'How about we study!' said Manda.

'I am studying! I'm considering how his mitochondria work . . .'

Manda elbowed her and Rowan slumped back over her books. 'You don't even have to study, Manda. Look at your notes! Those are the notes of someone who is going to pass these mock exams with their eyes closed. How many high-lighters *do* you own?'

'Fifteen,' said Manda proudly. 'And I can't risk failing anything, even mocks. Do you know how competitive law schools are?'

'Not competitive enough for the likes of you, Manda.' Anna smiled. 'You'll have your pick. If I don't get into medical school, however, Aunt will keep me at home forever.'

'At least you all know what you want to do,' Rowan groaned. 'I'm taking Psychology, Biology, Geography and Economics – why did I do Economics again? What can I even do with these subjects, except, possibly, fail them. Maybe I'll take the Effie stance of zero revision . . .'

Rowan continued but Anna had become distracted by Bryn and the group of people he was with. They were looking over and laughing in their direction. She'd grown fairly used to the laughter but they weren't looking at her, they were looking at Rowan. One of them raised a phone towards them. Anna went to say something but Manda made eyes at her and shook her head quietly.

'Hell's feathers! I have to go, I'm late!' said Rowan, bundling her stuff together. 'Wish me luck!'

Anna watched her leave the room, the group laughing as she passed. Fortunately, Rowan, in her haste, hadn't noticed.

Anna turned to Manda. 'What's going on?'

Manda's mouth hardened into a flat line. She took out her phone and showed Anna a picture of Rowan caught red-faced, mid-pose playing tennis. The caption read: *Beast spotted on courts. Girl or animal? Share your thoughts.* 'I saw some people laughing over it yesterday. Apparently, it's a game going round in certain circles. Without Rowan noticing you have to try and take the most unflattering picture of her possible, share it and rate it. I don't think Rowan knows yet but it's only a matter of time.'

Anna wanted to smash the phone to pieces. Darcey had been sharpening her blade and now she'd finally made the incision. It was too cruel, too horrible . . . *and all my fault.*

'Come on.' Manda sighed, packing up. 'We'll have to deal with it once exams are over next week. For now, we just have to stop Rowan discovering it.'

But the next week Anna spotted Rowan running from the common room in tears. Anna followed her to the nearby bathrooms. Sobbing was coming from a locked cubicle; only barely though – more a sound of shaking than a sound at all. 'Rowan?'

The sobbing shuddered to a stop. Eventually the door opened and Rowan exited, red-eyed. Anna handed her a tissue.

'I'm fine, I'm fine.' Rowan gave a wobbly smile.

'What's wrong?'

'I'm not stupid, Anna. I know what's going on. I know what they're doing. I've seen it—' She choked back a sob.

Anna's head fell forwards; Rowan knew. The guilt rolled heavy through her. 'I'm so sorry.'

'It's not your fault. It's Darcey and her lackeys. This is what she does. She finds the weakness in people. That's why Effie's so brilliant, she doesn't give Darcey anything, but I can hardly hide my weakness, can I?' She looked down at herself. 'I know that I shouldn't let it get to me and that, you know, I pretend everything's fine and given half a second I'd be dating a hundred different men' – she laughed faintly – 'but I don't love the way I look and when people are talking about you and taking photos and the guy you fancy in the year above just whispered Beast as you passed . . . well – it makes it kind of hard . . .'

'Rowan, it's not everyone.'

'I know, but it's enough.'

'It's not true either. You're gorgeous.'

'Let's be realistic: I'm hardly a bikini model.' She looked at herself in the mirror. 'And besides, once a rumour takes hold, it's more powerful than reality. I'm the Beast now and forevermore.' She was still staring at herself.

'I'm going to put a stop to this.' Anna gripped her Knotted Cord. 'I promise you.'

Anna hadn't spoken to Peter since the party. Goddess knew what he thought of her now – what lies Darcey had been feeding him – but she had to put her feelings aside. She needed to talk to him.

She waited until the end of their English class and just as he was leaving she took a deep breath. 'Peter . . .'

He turned around, surprised to see her standing there. 'Anna, hi.'

*He knows my name! Focus, Anna, focus.* 'I need a word.'

He seemed even more surprised by her directness. A couple of the boys he was leaving with started making stupid noises. 'Sure.' He elbowed one of them. 'All right. Go on, shove off, you lot.' He held the door open for her, his look inquisitive but his smile softening. 'How have you been?'

'Good thanks. Surviving exams – but, actually, I need to talk to you about something.'

Peter stopped and turned to her. 'Of course.' A line appeared between his brows. 'Tell me.'

'Have you heard of this game going around about Rowan? You have to take a picture of her and share it?'

'Who's Rowan?'

'The girl in our year. Wild hair, loud voice. She's being picked on for her weight.'

'Oh. Maybe. I might have been shown something. There are always stupid games going on; I don't take much notice. I certainly haven't joined in, if that's what you're asking.'

'I didn't think you would have. I just wanted to see if you could use your influence to try and stop it.'

He pulled himself up straighter. 'Of course. I'll see what I can do, although these kinds of things are hard to control once they start. People are idiots.'

Anna nodded in agreement. 'Well, if there's anything you can do.' The bitter words rose to her lips: 'Talking to your girlfriend might help.'

'Why do you think Darcey had anything to do with this?' he replied quickly, the smooth tone of his voice hardening.

'I just know she did.'

'That is hardly evidence, Anna.'

'Darcey is behind all kinds of bullying and if you don't see it then that's because you don't want to.'

Peter's frown deepened. He breathed heavily. 'I'm not stupid. I know she can be cruel sometimes. But she wouldn't stoop that low . . .'

Anna held his gaze. 'We'll have to agree to disagree there.' She'd spent years unable to utter a word to Peter and now here she was on the edge of an argument with him. A tense silence stretched between them, his clear blue eyes on her, studying her with an attention she wasn't used to.

'You sure it's not Effie behind it?' He said her name with distaste. 'She seems the type.'

'No, definitely not,' Anna replied just as defensively. 'Rowan's her friend.'

'Are you her friend?'

'Yes.'

'Well, I'd be careful there.'

'OK,' said Anna, not wanting to get into a row with him over Effie.

'Anyway, it's good of you to look out for your friend Rowan,' he continued. 'Most people in this school wouldn't bother. They're far too concerned with their own popularity.'

Anna met his eyes. 'Not you?'

Peter shook his head slowly. 'Popularity. Gossip. Games. Even lessons, exams, university . . . Sometimes it all feels so meaningless, you know? Sometimes I just want to get away from here, do something – purposeful. Something that actually makes a difference.'

Anna had always been fascinated by the depth of his eyes, but she'd never seen such intensity behind them. She smiled to soften the moment. 'You will.'

He smiled back, shaking his head and clearing the look from his eyes. 'I like your confidence in me, Everdell. I shall have to make sure to talk to you again.'

'Well, that would be – I can – I'll see you next class.'

He laughed at her incoherence. 'For sure. Right, I've got to get to Politics. See you soon.' His eyes lingered on her and Anna almost began laughing giddily as he left, before remembering the point of their conversation.

She tracked Attis down that afternoon and told him to put an apple in their lockers. She explained what was going on and he agreed immediately. They needed an emergency meeting. She wasn't sure if she was meant to have control over coven meetings but she didn't care.

When they met later, Rowan's face was buried in her phone, her shoulders hunched, her usual smile wiped from her face. Attis looked on with concern. Effie was lighting a candle on the altar without touching it – on and off, on and off, a bemused look on her face.

Anna walked into the centre. 'I called this meeting because of the Juicers. Darcey, Olivia and Corinne: they've—'

'I know what they've done, Anna,' said Effie. 'Continue.'

'It's time we did something about them. I'm not sure what yet but we need to do something.'

Manda jumped in. 'I found a spell on the internet to bind their cruelty. We just need a poppet, some masking tape, a rope—'

'You sure you're not planning a murder there, Manda?' said Attis.

'Perhaps we ought to look into something that ups our own protection?' Anna suggested. 'Dispels the attention, somehow.'

Attis nodded. 'I could help with that.'

'I would like anything attention-dispelling right now,' said Rowan, head still downcast. 'Any invisibility spells?'

Effie flicked the candle on. 'Child's play,' she said, moving to stand by Anna. 'Bindings. Protection spells. All child's play. You can't find anything worth doing on the internet. Darcey and her little friends have gone too far; it's time we stopped them for good. We're going to need an older kind of vengeance.' She smiled with dark delight. 'I know just where to find it. The Library.'

Rowan looked up from her phone.

Manda frowned. 'I've never seen anything even remotely magical in the library.'

'Not the school library!' Effie laughed. 'The British Library. We need a spell to take care of Darcey once and for all and the Library always provides. You're staying over tonight, right, Anna? Let's go tomorrow morning.'

'That sounds great fun,' said Manda. 'Mum won't mind me going out if a library is involved. I'll dig out my British Library membership card.'

'You won't need a membership card where we're going.'

Manda looked perturbed.

'Where *are* we going?' said Anna.

'I promised I'd take you to a magical library, didn't I?'

'You're going to love it, Anna,' said Rowan, smiling at last. 'Once my brother got lost in it for three days.'

'How big is this place?'

Effie and Attis looked at each other with infuriating, knowing smiles.

'Just bring breadcrumbs so you can find a way out.' He winked.

# THE LIBRARY

*Rest gentle and in silence deep,*
*Let not dreams disturb your sleep.*
*Shut tight your eyes and wipe your tears,*
*For the darkness knows your fears.*

*A Binders' Lullaby, The Book of the Binders*

Anna looked around in paranoia at the rows of faces coming up the escalator, seeing Aunt in every one of them. She knew it was a bad idea to leave Selene's house. If Aunt found out where she was . . . but she had to help Rowan and she had her own motivations too. If this library was the vast and wondrous place that Effie promised perhaps it could give her the answers she craved?

The British Library rose up in front of them, full of jolting angles and imposing might. Aunt had taken her once and Anna had loved it – its clean, open foyer, its modern glass centre rising high with old books, the reading rooms silent with focus. Every part of it seemed to work together, like a quiet, ticking mind in the centre of London. *How many secrets live within its walls?*

It wasn't busy inside: a few drowsy-looking students and milling staff members.

'We've got to go up to come down,' said Effie, cutting a path through the foyer and taking the stairs up to the top floor. No one was around. She walked to the glass centre of the building. Anna had always thought it impenetrable, but now before her, amidst the books, was a rather dilapidated-looking lift, its brown doors barely noticeable. Effie pressed the button and they waited. It arrived with a barely audible *whoosh* and they stepped inside.

It was small. They shuffled together and the doors squeezed themselves shut. The buttons went down to minus five. Anna wondered if they were going that deep. Effie reached out and pressed the intercom instead; there was a buzzing sound. She leant forwards and stated: 'Eneke Beneke,' into it clearly. The lift made a metal groaning sound and began to descend through the heart of the library, hidden from view by the wall of books around them. The electronic display followed their descent: *minus one, minus two, minus three, minus four, minus five . . . minus six, minus seven . . .*

Attis leant into her. 'There are five official underground floors at the British Library. The rest are unofficial.'

The lift gained speed. *Minus ten, minus eleven . . .* Anna's stomach began to do several tumultuous stomach flips.

He continued: 'The underground site was actually a library of magical texts long before the British Library ever existed. Later it made sense to build the public library on top as a sort of cover.' *Minus fifteen, minus sixteen . . .* 'Many members of the British Library board are witches. They oversee the cowan library too but their real job is guarding the collections that lie beneath.'

Manda and Anna looked at each other, a similar excitement jumping between their eyes. *Minus twenty, minus twenty-one . . .*

'Mum says we're lucky we have access to so much know-ledge,' said Rowan. 'That during the Dark Times witches had to bury it much deeper. It was too dangerous to put down in books. They hid it away instead, in folk songs, nursery rhymes, tarot cards, works of art . . . our secrets are everywhere.'

'Are there librarians down here?' asked Anna. *Minus twenty-five, minus twenty-six . . . How deep are we going?*

'No,' said Effie. 'No one works down here. For that reason, it can be dangerous. Just don't stray too deep.'

The excitement in Manda's eyes had now turned to fear. *Minus twenty-nine, minus thirty . . .* The display went blank but the lift kept hurtling downwards until it stopped suddenly with a dull thump. It pinged open and several books fell in front of the doors. Stepping out, Anna wondered how it had managed to arrive at all. The lift appeared to be embedded in books. The doors shut and it was no longer possible to see where it had been.

The room ahead of them was dimly lit and full of swirling dust. Anna's eyes took a moment to adjust. She looked down at her feet and saw that they were standing upon . . . books . . . a patchwork of covers and pages, puddles and streams of words, compacted with footprints and dust.

She lifted her gaze. The room around her was vast – corridors of books spread out around them as if they were in the centre of a wheel, spokes extending in all directions. Faded light trickled through some of the corridors while others seemed to swallow the light whole. Anna looked more closely at the shelves and realized that while they held books, they were also made out of books – stacks and stacks of them – forming the spines and ribs of each shelf. She tilted her head further again – it was hard to make out the ceiling, it was so far away. It was formed of books too, tightly knitted together, but some were falling loose, dripping pages and words over their heads.

'Watch out for the loose ones,' said Attis, smiling at her face. She wasn't even sure what expression she was pulling.

'It's all books . . . everything . . .' She lifted a foot and saw she'd scuffed the pages beneath it, crumpling the words. More books than she'd ever seen, that she'd ever been able to comprehend. It was beyond wonderful. The room was dark and crowded and heavy with words and yet Anna felt herself lifted, freed by the worlds waiting to be discovered all around her – the old, damp, dusty secret scents oddly comforting and strangely delightful.

There was no floorplan, no categories for the maze surrounding them. Only one sign, which appeared also to be made out of books. It read: 'A story, a story, let it come, let it go'.

'Where has the lift gone?' Manda asked with controlled panic.

'We'll find it again. Come on.' Effie moved forward.

'I'm not so sure about this, I think I want to leave . . .' Manda's panic escaped and the books gobbled up her echo.

Anna began wandering down one of the corridors. She could locate no floorplan or categories for the maze surrounding them.

'Hold your horses there, bookworm,' Attis called out to her. 'We need a plan or you will not be home by midday and your clothes will turn back into rags.'

Anna walked back to the centre. 'How does it work then? How do I find the section I want?'

'The Library is far too vast to be ordered in the traditional sense; instead it's run by magic,' Effie explained as if it was obvious. 'You need to state your intention clearly, what it is you're seeking. The Library will hear and guide you – unless it has other ideas . . .'

Rowan sniggered. 'It *always* has other ideas. Just wait for the books to come to you. It's best not to go digging or you could end up, you know, irrevocably damaged in some way. Try to avoid the really dark corridors. A lot of magic in here, both good and bad, some very old . . .'

'I think I'll just stay here and peruse the immediate area,' said Manda, looking back hopefully as if the lift might appear again. 'Anyone want to stay with me?'

Rowan laughed. 'I'll stay with you. I feel like Effie knows what she's looking for and I'll probably just get in the way or lost or injured or all three.'

'OK, well, the rest of us should state our intention,' said Effie. She stepped forward and narrowed her eyes. 'Library, I'm seeking spells of vengeance – spells for those who deserve all they get. You know who I'm talking about.' The light flickered in one of the corridors and darkened. 'Guess I'm going that way then.'

'Greetings. I'm seeking ancient symbols of metallurgy. New subject matter, please. Also a fun read, something with a spy and an irresistible love story.' Attis turned and settled on the corridor he wanted to go down.

Anna wasn't sure what to state. She didn't want to bring up her parents' death or a fear of curses in front of everyone. She stepped forward, opening her mouth to speak to a room full of books, feeling entirely insane, and yet, as she began, she felt them bend towards her like ears, eager and hungry. 'Library.' She cleared her throat. 'I'm seeking information about my family. The truth.'

The room around her was silent but she swore she could hear something – the whisper of words buried deep, stirring, stretching out their letters towards her like a finger unfurling. She turned and caught a whisper coming from a corridor to her left – it was dark but not as dark as some.

'I'm this way.' She pointed, unsure but trying to trust the sensations around her. Effie was giving her threateningly curious looks. Attis's eyes were narrowed and unreadable in the semi-darkness.

When Effie made off down her corridor, he stepped back towards Anna. 'I don't think you ought to go into the Library alone, not as a first-timer.'

'I want to go in alone.'

'Well, unfortunately, the Library is now telling me to go the same way as you, so . . .'

Anna narrowed her eyes. 'That seems convenient.'

He shrugged, an implacable expression in his eyes. Anna shook her head and made her way into the web of books, Attis's footsteps behind her. The corridor was long and full of small sounds on the edge of hearing. She continued down it, feeling the heavy press of knowledge on either side, the rows of books on books within books narrowing around them. She reached a crossroads and took a right because it felt right. She walked deeper, noticing a large gap in one of the shelves which was filled with paper debris as if a book had exploded. The light overhead flickered. She almost screamed when she came across a woman sitting atop a pile of books, another pile on her lap. The woman shook her head and threw the one she was reading behind her; it was about to land on Anna's head when Attis batted it out of the way.

'Oh, sorry!' the woman said. 'Didn't see you there.'

Anna nodded in return and continued down the corridor. Half of her was glad of Attis's presence and the other half wished she could break away – her mission was not one for sharing. She took a fresh turn, following the whispering that disappeared as soon as she stopped to listen to it . . .

They passed a corridor of books all bound in red, another where all the titles were written backwards, another in which every book was tiny – no bigger than the size of her palm. Several corridors were lost in complete darkness, one releasing a strange gurgling noise which made her run in the other direction.

'Anna, wait up!' She heard Attis call from behind her, but the whispers were drawing her onwards. They grew louder and she took a sudden turn. 'Anna—' She turned again down a narrow corridor and the sound of his footsteps behind her stopped abruptly. She swivelled around to see where he'd gone but the turn she'd just taken no longer existed – there was nothing there but a wall of books.

'Attis!' she called, but there was no reply, no sound. 'Attis?' She felt suddenly very alone amidst the towering shelves, but alone was exactly what she needed to be . . .

She carried on down the snaking corridor, ignoring the tingle up her spine. She took in the many peculiar titles as she passed: *Ancient Magical Mirrors. Topiary for Hedge Witches. Vasalisa and the Burning Skull. Magical Radios and Inhuman Frequencies. Symbology of the Taliswomen.* Many were in other languages: French, Latin, Arabic, Greek; others she couldn't place; some were not formed from words at all but strange images and symbols. Not all were still either: many moved, shifting and transforming. She stopped to stare at a gilded snake wriggling up and down a book's spine. Others had no names at all.

Anna couldn't resist opening a few, finding the pages old and dry, crackling under her fingers. She swore one yawned as she opened it. In another the ink was still wet and began to run when she held it up, ruining the words.

She soon had the distinct feeling she was walking in circles and was surely lost. Time felt as warped as the corridors – she wasn't sure if minutes or hours had passed but she couldn't stop. Something was pulling her onwards, books watching her pass, the light becoming even more emaciated, as if it had been trapped in the pages for too long.

The title of a book caught her eye: *Whickstamp*. She stopped and read the surrounding titles – they were all surnames. She reached for the *Whickstamp* book. Inside was a family tree spread across its pages, covering every Whickstamp who had ever lived, all the way back to 1376. Anna's heart somersaulted with excitement. *Family histories!*

But the books were in no particular alphabetical order and

there were thousands of them. 'Where are you, Everdell?' she said aloud, walking along the row. *How is this library meant to work?* She stumbled on a book underfoot and reached out a hand to steady herself. She turned and saw the book she was holding: *Everdell!*

'Apologies – you do work. Thank you!' she cried out to the surrounding silence.

She sat on the floor cross-legged and placed the book on her lap, finding her heart was now the loudest thing in the vicinity. The lighting overhead grew stronger as if to aid her reading. She opened it—

It was blank.

Anna turned the page – blank again – and the next, and the next. Feeling desperation take hold of her she rifled through the whole book, but all of it was the same – blank, blank, blank. She tipped the book up and shook it as if hoping the words might somehow spill out, but the pages remained stubbornly empty.

She grabbed at other books along the shelves and searched them in case they suffered from the same phenomenon. *Gooderidge. Greene. Hedgel. Pike.* They each contained full family trees. A word began to write itself into one of the pages making her stop midway through her frantic search. The word: 'deceased'. It appeared next to one of the recent names in the family tree along with a date. *Today's date! Has the person just died?* Anna closed the book and threw it away, realizing with a mixture of awe and horror that the family trees were alive . . . tracing the families they recorded in real time.

'Then why is mine a magical black hole?' she cried out to the Library, as if they had been in conversation.

She continued to look through the books desperately in case there was another *Everdell* book hiding from her, and then, fretting about the time, she put the one she had under her arm and set off in search of the way out, full of frustration.

*Why is everything a dead end? Like the third-floor room – closed off to me forever.*

She tried to retrace her steps but either she'd forgotten or the corridors had moved because she was soon utterly lost. The Library seemed to be getting darker, as if night was setting within it. She walked faster. 'Library, I'd like to leave now . . .' Surely she could find a way. She turned down a well-lit corridor she thought she remembered. The end of it forked into three. She turned left; halfway down it the lights stuttered out. She swallowed a squeal and tried to get her bearings but the darkness was complete.

*Stay calm. You've coped with darker places.* One hand reached automatically for her Knotted Cord, the other out in front of her. She tried to feel her way, the shelves guiding her – tripping on books and stilling herself, heart beating, breath loud in the darkness. She thought she heard footsteps pass her by and stopped.

'Hello? Attis? Effie?' She heard the strange whispering in the air again, on the edge of hearing . . .

A narrow corridor to the right was releasing a dim light. Anna turned down it and realized immediately it was a corridor she shouldn't be in. The books were bound in black and red and from the titles on the shelves and images staring up at her from open books on the floor she could tell they weren't dealing in a good kind of magic. *Mortuus Cantus Carnium. Black Hen Magic. Blood and Boils: A Hex Compendium. Hekate's Grimoire* . . . Many were sealed shut with thick chains and rusted locks.

She stood in something that squelched and looked down to see a dark red, sticky liquid beneath her feet. She screamed and put a hand on the shelf to steady herself, finding the shelf just as sticky and realizing with horror that the blood was oozing out of the books themselves.

She ran.

The end of the corridor was a dead end. She heard footsteps

again . . . and then a book caught her eye. It was bound in black leather and locked shut – no title, just a symbol: seven concentric circles. *The Eye*. It beckoned her forwards. As she reached a hand towards it, the lock unclicked. She opened it and words began to fly up off the page, disappearing. A hand reached out from behind her and slammed it shut. A body, crouched and grey, wrestled with the lock. 'I would not. I would not. Lock the Eye back up.'

Anna jumped back against the shelf, away from the creature. She screamed as her hair began to be sucked into one of the books behind her. She wrenched it free and stumbled forward again. The creature put its hands over its ears and screamed too, knocking books everywhere.

Anna realized then it was a man. A bundle of bones. He straightened up to look at her. She wasn't sure whether to smile or run . . .

His face was long, the cranium large and hairless and his eyes deeply sunken as if they had been winched into the back of his skull. He wore only a vest and a pair of trousers that finished a few inches above his ankles; his feet were bare. The rest of his body was not skin at all. It was grey as ash and covered in words, as if he'd fallen asleep in a pile of books and left with their print marks all over him. It looked deeply unhealthy, much of it peeling off and flaking away like old paper.

She could make out the words 'Veritas vos liberabit' across his forehead and across his heart: EWORHEN – but as she read the word the letters moved, shifted into a new formation, alive on his skin. He blinked and Anna saw that even his eyelids had words on them.

He began to pick up the books he'd knocked over, putting them back on the shelves. 'Little girl, getting lost in such a loquacious tomb, straying into the cimmerian plains of your imagination.' His voice was a kind of dry wheezing.

Anna helped him in his task.

'Be most careful,' he said, taking a stack of books from her.

'Where am I?' asked Anna, unable to look away from him, the words writhing along his skin as he spoke. 'What was that book that I tried to open? The locked one. . .'

'That book is a mean book. Cursey. Induces cacodemonomania. Let the words free and you will be lost in the aphotic depths of your nightmares forever. Silly, silly to open.'

'Thank you for saving me. What's your name?'

He twitched and a sheaf of skin fell away from his arm, words and all. 'Will you stay with me here, little girl?'

'I need to get back to my friends . . .' Anna backed away.

'But you still seek, you still seek. Your expiscation has so far been most unsatisfactory. Though perhaps there is something in nothing.' He looked at the *Everdell* book in her hands and his eyes twitched. 'Why do you have that book? Explain.'

'Well, my name is Anna Everdell and my mother was Marie . . .'

His eyes widened, retreating further into his skull. He took several steps closer to her and studied her face. He reached out a flaking hand and brushed it along her cheek. Anna stood frozen. 'Yes. Marie's daughter.'

'You knew her?'

'She was my friend.'

'How did you know her?'

'She came here. Searching, fossicking among the books, among the curses, as you have. Trying to find answers.'

'What was she looking for?'

'She did not say. I don't believe she found it here but I know where she went. I will tell you if you will be my friend.'

'I'll be your friend,' said Anna, as encouragingly as she could.

'She went to see the Curse Witch.' He began to sob, wetting the paper-skin of his face. 'Nana Yaganov.'

'Nana Yaganov.' Anna repeated the name. It was difficult to say, full of sharp angles. 'Who's that?'

'The greatest Curse Witch who ever lived.'

'OK,' said Anna, swallowing her fear. 'How do I find her?'

He shrugged his skeletal shoulders. 'How do you find a shadow in the dark? Now stay with me. I can't remember what I'm searching for.' He wiped a tear away, smudging a word. 'Stay with me.'

'I really need to get going . . .' But Anna found her foot was stuck – a black vine had crept out of one of the books on the floor and was wrapping itself around her leg. She cried out and the man cracked open his shrivelled mouth and began to wail.

Anna wrenched her leg free and ran blindly.

She heard wailing and whispers behind her, but couldn't stop. She fled down the corridor, taking turns at random, hoping she was going the right way. She collided with a large figure.

'Anna.' Attis held her by the shoulders. 'Where did you go? You look pale as a sheet.'

'I – I—' She tried to catch her breath, finding herself holding onto him. 'I got lost.'

'Are you OK?' He searched her eyes. She met his for a moment and then pulled away. 'Did you find anything?' he said, looking at the book in her hands.

'I – No, not really.'

'Come on, we're only two shelves from the entrance.'

They broke free of the corridors, back into the centre where they had arrived. Anna couldn't understand how they had been so close; it felt as if she'd walked miles away. Manda was sitting reading a book, while a bored-looking Rowan tore strips of paper from the ground.

Effie was pacing. 'There you are! I found the perfect grimoire, full of suitably vengeful revenge spells. What's that?'

She grabbed the *Everdell* book from Anna's hands.

'It's my family history, but—'

'It's blank.'

'Yes.'

Effie frowned. 'That's so weird.'

The others gathered around. Effie, like Anna, shook the book upside down as if the words might drop out of it.

'That doesn't make any sense,' said Rowan. 'Those family trees are living records and you're standing here in front of me. *You* should be in it at the very least. Are you OK? You look a bit spaced . . .'

'I – I – met a man in there. He was scary and . . . sad.'

'A witch?'

'I don't know what he was. He was covered in words, like they were part of his skin.'

Rowan dropped the books she was holding. 'Maiden, mother and bloody crone! You met Pesachya! No one ever meets Pesachya. My brother and his friends went on a mission in here once to find him, trying to prove his existence.'

'Who?' said Effie.

'They say he arrived here when he was just a young teen. Some say his family died in the Holocaust and he came here seeking answers and revenge, but he never left.'

'The Holocaust?' Anna exclaimed. She tried to think how old he was, but his face was impossible to place, he could have been forty, he could have been eighty, or older still.

'That's one of the stories anyway; there are lots. They say he's part-man, part-book.'

'That's definitely true,' said Anna, remembering his papery skin with a shiver.

'How can he possibly live down here? That's ridiculous. How does he eat?' Manda scoffed.

'He lives off words,' Rowan replied as if she had it on good authority.

'I want to find him. Which way was he?' Effie looked back towards the corridors.

'Not now,' said Attis, guiding her arm. 'We'll come back and bring him some McDonald's or something. It's gone half eleven, let's get these guys out of here.'

Anna had forgotten the time. She would be late. The empty book in her hands and the name of a curse witch from a madman probably wasn't worth the punishment coming.

By some miracle, when she got home, Aunt was still at work. She ran upstairs to hide the *Everdell* book. She opened it hopefully, but it was still blank. She tried to think logically about the situation. Either the book's magic had failed to record her family history, or the contents had been purposefully removed, by someone who didn't want anyone discovering what it might contain. 'Please!' she begged the book, hoping talking to it might help. She opened it again but the pages remained maddeningly empty.

She threw it across the room, suddenly furious. It landed with a loud bang. She shut her eyes and breathed against the frustration ripping through her. She quickly fetched it and put it under her bed. She lay down thinking about the name Pesachya had given her. Nana Yaganov. The Curse Witch. Why was her mother searching among the curse section of the Library? And searching out curse witches? *She went to her and after that she never came back . . .*

Anna shivered, recalling the dark corner of the Library's curse section, the wet sounds of blood beneath her feet – the curse mark, like a maze you can't get out of once you enter.

*How do you find a shadow in the dark?*

# FLIES

*Whispers divide; in secrets we thrive.*

*Tenet Six, The Book of the Binders*

Effie banged the large and tattered grimoire she'd taken from the Library on the altar. 'It's time! These wrongs need to be righted. These hierarchies broken. Justice served and punishments delivered. The Juicers need to be poured down the drain and left to rot – and I have just the spell.'

Anna had never seen her look more alive. She had the feeling this was what Effie had been waiting for since they started the coven.

'Shouldn't we technically report the bullying to Headmaster Connaughty?' said Manda, looking a little afraid. 'Surely there's enough evidence to prove Darcey is harassing Rowan . . .'

Effie baulked. 'You think this school has a proper justice system? You think Darcey wouldn't find a way of turning it all around? No. I am talking about a different kind of justice. Nature's justice. A woman's revenge. Wild and lawless, measured out by moonlight, exacted by the Dark Moon itself. We need to bring it.' Effie opened the book and announced with restless flourish: 'It's a rumour spell.'

'More rumours?' said Rowan.

'Why not fight fire with fire? Either we're controlling them, or they are. It's an old spell and a powerful one, originally intended for gossipmongers and spiteful chinwaggers. Apparently it was the inspiration behind the old nursery rhyme "There was an old lady who swallowed a fly" . . .

'There was an old lady who swallowed a fly.
I don't know why she swallowed the fly – perhaps she'll die?
Oh why, oh why, did she swallow a fly?

'The book states it was written by a witch whose daughter was hanged for witchcraft after someone in the town spread malicious gossip about her. The spell gives the caster power to turn the gossiper into the gossiped-about, to twist their rumours back on themselves. We just need to decide on the rumours.'

'What will they do?' Anna asked.

'They will hound them, chase them. They won't go away easily.'

The fear in Manda's eyes had turned to excitement. 'I'd love to see them get a taste of their own medicine.'

'I don't normally live by the concept of revenge, but come bane or boon I've got to make an exception for the Juicers,' said Rowan.

Anna thought of Rowan drying her tears in the bathroom, of Darcey's laughter which poured out of her as easily as her cruelty. Rumours could be nasty but they couldn't cause any real harm. She turned to Attis, who was sitting on one the desks in the corner of the room. 'What do you think?'

'I think let Darcey chase her own tail for a while.'

*He's never going to disagree with Effie.*

'She can choke on her tail for all I care,' said Effie. 'Anna, if we don't do this, it'll just get worse for Rowan. You don't want that, do you?'

Anna shook her head. It was the last thing she wanted. 'I'm in.'

'Good. I've thought of a few rumours already.' Effie smiled slyly. 'Thought we could say Corinne's a nymphomaniac.'

'I think she might already be known as that,' Rowan pointed out.

'Any other ideas then?'

Manda stepped forward. 'Corinne's whole reputation is built on the fact that she's, you know, chilled out – all about the *free love*, pretending to be your friend. Makes me sick. What if we took that away from her? We could say she actually suffers from acute rage issues and all that yoga and drug-taking is just to keep her mellow, but at any moment, she might just . . .' Manda clicked her fingers. 'Snap.'

Effie considered it. 'It's a curveball, but funny. I like it. I, of course, already have one prepared for Darcey.' She cleared her throat theatrically. 'She may have boys running after her, but she's only got eyes for one man and, hell, what a man: Headmaster Connaughty.'

Rowan spluttered. 'What? That's insane. No one will believe that.'

'Well, under normal circumstances, no, but these are magical rumours.'

'He's so – so' – Manda shuddered – 'old and large and ugh. I can't in a million years imagine them together.'

'You'll be able to soon. What about Olivia?'

'I've got one,' said Rowan. 'She wants to be Darcey. She's obsessed and jealous of her and will go to any length to be her, in every way.'

This one was just within the boundaries of reality. Olivia knew she didn't quite live up to Darcey and poured all her efforts into her looks and clothes to make up for that fact.

'Appropriately twisted.' Effie steepled her hands.

'Well, she's the one who made up the name Beast,' Rowan added defensively, as if ashamed of her suggestion.

'So we're agreed? Corinne suffers from rage episodes, Olivia is obsessed with Darcey and Darcey and Connaughty are having an affair. Ta-da.'

They nodded and Anna did too. Hearing them expressed like that they seemed more ridiculous than anything else. Surely no one would really believe them. They waited while Effie wrote out the rumours and the wording for the spell before handing it to them to learn. Anna muttered the words over and over, committing them to memory. She didn't want to be the weak link this time.

'Ready?'

Effie held up a glass container. Inside three flies whirred around, large and angry, butting themselves against their glass prison. She held it to her eye. 'Three flies for three rumours.' She placed the container in the centre, followed by three cups. 'Their juices from this morning,' she explained, 'and put your phones in the centre too.'

'Why?' said Rowan.

'We need the rumours to travel everywhere and most of the gossip in this hellhole of a school lives inside them.'

Attis began shaking salt out around the perimeter of their circle, then back into the centre forming a pentagram shape. Once he'd finished, Effie stepped forward. They turned to look at her. Her eyes flashed in the light and she held up her hands.

'Energies joined, joined we stand,
May none enter our ring of hands.
Between the worlds we now roam,
Take us there and safely home.
As above so below, as within so without,
Weave our circle without doubt!'

Anna imagined a circle surrounding them, powerful and protective. They repeated the words until she didn't have to visualize it any more, she could feel it, solid and whole, cutting them off from the world beyond, placing them somewhere else that could have been anywhere else: a dark forest, a high mountain, a wasteland.

Effie looked at Manda and she stepped forward, nervously. 'I call to the watchtowers of the North, to the element of Earth. Bring forth your justice which is strong and sure.'

Rowan stepped forward. 'I call to the watchtowers of the East, to the element of Air. Bring forth your justice which is cunning and true.'

Effie's turn. 'I call to the watchtowers of the South, to the element of Fire. Bring forth your justice which is force and fury.'

The words came out of Anna without her needing to try, as if they had been waiting for her to find them. 'I call to the watchtowers of the West, to the element of Water. Bring forth your justice which is passionate and pure.'

They spoke together. 'By pentacle, wand, blade and chalice, charge our spell with nature's justice.'

Effie opened the jar of flies; they flew out but remained in the centre, chasing each other in circles, buzzing madly. Effie placed the pieces of paper on which she'd written the rumours inside the container.

> 'Curdle and coil, serpents of spite,
> How you hiss and rattle, with tongues that bite.
> Gossip and spoil, rumour fly and infest –
> Swallow them whole at our behest.'

As their chant grew the flies began to buzz with a demented energy. Anna felt the same energy coursing through her. It was different to magic she'd experienced before, which had come almost by accident, gentle and tentative, dream-like. This magic was certain, forceful – within her and beyond her. It was the elements; the whirr of flies; the dark rumours and the darker words – the threads binding tightly together into a web that quivered and shook with dark delight. Their voices rose. Anna felt torn between exhilaration and panic – the feeling you get standing on the edge of a cliff, looking down.

'Gossip and spoil, rumour fly and infest –
Swallow them whole at our behest!'

The power of the spell expanded, threatening to pull them apart – they held tight, raised it up into the air, flies reaching the ceiling like a storm cloud. Effie laughing. Candles sputtering. The sewing machine on the altar bursting to life, needle chattering: *Ticker. Ticker. Ticker!* Anna felt as if her head would explode, as if water were filling it, as if it were buzzing with flies. They called out the words – louder, louder, louder – and then, suddenly, the flies were released, flying away, disappearing.

'By pentacle, wand, blade and chalice, elements be released. As below so above, as without, so within. Close our circle but leave it spin.'

The candles went out and they were plunged into darkness. Anna felt herself returning from wherever she'd been, her head flying in different directions. She'd never experienced magic so intense before. Effie stepped into the centre and sealed the jar of rumours with relish and placed the empty cups on the altar.

'That was good. We can do better, of course, but that was good.' Her eyes were wide, otherworldly, still high on magic.

Rowan dropped to the floor. 'I'm exhausted.'

Manda slumped down next to her. 'I didn't even feel like myself for a while there, it was . . . intense.'

Attis entered their circle with a smile. 'It was. I was terrified.'

Effie put her arms round him. 'I told you, didn't I? I told you this would work.'

'I never doubted you, as I never do.'

'I'm always right.'

'I bow to Queen Effie.'

'Oh,' said Rowan who had just picked up her phone from the floor.

'What?' Effie turned to her.

'Er . . .' Rowan turned her phone around to face them.

The screen was glitching – static – *no, not quite* – a pattern was beginning to form through the noise. Circles. *Seven circles.* Anna's heart lurched.

Slowly, they all turned to look at her.

'It might not be seven circles.' Rowan squinted at it. 'It's hard to make out – could be six. Could be, er, eight.'

Manda and Effie picked up their phones to investigate and turned the screens round – they were filled with seven circles too. Anna didn't know what to say.

'I hope it's not broken,' said Manda with a touch of accusation.

'Point is,' said Attis, 'the spell worked. Job done. Let's go.'

'We need to keep an eye on this,' said Effie, drawing their attention back to the static.

'I don't know why . . .' said Anna. 'I didn't do anything.'

'Let's go,' Attis repeated.

They cleared up and gathered their things. Their phones went back to normal after restarting them, but the pattern of the seven circles was not so easy to erase from Anna's mind. *Cursed. A dark explosion of the heart.*

She left last and, before turning the lights off, looked around the room – along its windows, into its corners. There were no flies. *Where have they gone?*

# FEAR

*Thirteen Years Old*

*Anna pushed against the cupboard door. It was locked.*

*It wasn't completely dark inside; more like twilight, when the sun has just sunk below the horizon and the world is not so sure of itself. She knew the cupboard well. She was in and out of it several times a week for cleaning appliances, but it was different now – its familiar outlines morphing in the darkness, shadows appearing. She tightened the knot in her cord.*

*She pushed on the door again. Still locked. Her heart jumped and the darkness of the room was constricting. She couldn't see so much now – only faint silhouettes – as she pulled the knot harder, but the panic was making her fingers shake. She tried to look at the dark space behind her: Empty. She spun back around: More emptiness.*

*The fear opened up like a dark hole in which anything might live. It had no edges to it, nothing to hold onto.*

*Anna began to beat against the door madly, shrieks erupting from her. 'Let me out! Please let me out! Aunt! Aunt! Oh please!' She dragged her fingernails down it.*

*The cupboard was now a darkness that she could not comprehend. The kind of darkness that was alive, with claws and fangs and a gaping mouth. A deep nothingness, threatening to swallow her forever. Anna had dropped the Knotted Cord and could not move to find it. There was an awful sound, strangled by darkness – she realized it was her own moaning.*

*The door opened and light flooded back in. She gasped at it as though desperately thirsty, crawling out on hands and knees.*

*'Pull yourself together,' said Aunt.*

*Anna looked back at the cupboard and saw that it was nothing out of the ordinary at all.*

*'The more you fear the darker it grows. This should be easy; fear is not a complex emotion. Like darkness is the absence of light, fear is the absence of reason. You merely need to learn how to switch it off.'*

*But Anna had not felt fear to be like that. Like darkness it had no beginning and no end – it was a circle that surrounded you. It knew exactly what it wanted with the precision of a needle.*

# SNOWFLAKES

*Emotions must not be engaged nor understood, only recognized and silenced.*

Binders' Training, The Book of the Binders

Anna went back with Effie and Attis to the house. All was quiet; Chinese takeaway half-eaten on the table alongside a bottle of wine.

'I see Selene's already had a feast to herself. How nice,' Effie huffed, shovelling a leftover spoonful into her mouth.

'I'll be back in a minute,' said Anna, heading upstairs. It was time. She had to speak to Selene about the curse mark. Selene had always been such an advocate of her magic and she didn't want to disappoint her, but she knew no one else could help and she couldn't ignore it any longer. The static of the phone screens crackled in her mind. Something was wrong with her magic – her family's magic – and whatever it was might contain the truth about her mother's death.

'Selene?' The bathroom door was ajar again, steam escaping, anointed with deep herbal scents. Anna smiled and pushed the door open. 'I was just hoping to – oh—'

Selene was not alone. Another head rose from the water next to her. A young and pretty head.

Selene laughed and lay back in the water. 'Anna, would you like to meet my new bath toy?'

The man nodded, mildly embarrassed. 'Henry. Good to meet you.'

'Er—' Anna panicked but, halfway out of the door, not wanting to be rude, she stopped. 'Anna. Good to meet you. I'm, right, well, have fun . . .' She pulled the door shut and could hear them laughing behind it.

She trudged up to the roof. Attis and Effie were lying in deck chairs, the sky was piled high with clouds, full of wintry promise. It was a fiercely cold February night and even Attis's fire failed to warm up the surrounding air. Anna settled onto the sun lounger next to them.

'Speak to Selene?' Effie asked.

'She was occupied.'

'Has a new man, does she? What's the spec, old and gentlemanly? Middle-aged and married? Young and fawn-like?'

'A young fawn in the bath with her.'

'That's my mother. Never there for you when you really need her.'

'Yeah.' Anna tried to hide her disappointment. 'Maybe we should go in? It's freezing.'

'Nonsense, it's beautiful. It smells like snow,' said Effie.

'Anna's right,' said Attis. 'You're both shivering and I can't make the fire any hotter than it already is without it melting the container.'

'Warm me then,' said Effie, reclining yet further. 'Anna, Attis has this magical trick of warming you—'

'I've shown her before,' said Attis.

'Oh. When?'

'At the house party.'

'It was when I was outside, after Peter left me,' said Anna quickly.

'Well, do it again,' said Effie with a frozen smile.

'What?' Attis asked, confused now.

'Warm Anna again.'

'I thought you wanted to be warmed.'

'Guests first.'

'I'm fine,' said Anna, stilling her shivering with effort.

Effie ignored her. 'Warm her.'

Attis wandered over to Anna's chair and sat down on the edge. Anna felt trapped between them.

'You have to take your jumper off,' Effie instructed. 'For him to get to your skin.'

'He can just do it on my hand,' Anna protested.

'Take your jumper off,' Effie insisted, clearly in her most obstinate sort of mood. The grey sky pressed overhead. Anna yanked her jumper and long-sleeved shirt off – she was wearing a vest top underneath. She put her arms around herself, unable to stop the shivering now.

'Come here,' said Attis, eyebrows meeting. Anna moved down the sun lounger towards him and presented her arm. Attis took it, his hand so warm against the cold air it felt as if it were burning her. With the other he drew a concise pattern on her arm and she felt the warmth of it spread like a ripple across and down her body. She stopped shaking almost immediately.

'Better?' he said.

Anna nodded, fingers brushing against the spot where he'd touched her. She reached for her jumper and shirt and pulled them back on, crossing her arms around her knees.

'Isn't he wonderful?' said Effie. 'Come, Attis, warm me all over.'

She pulled up her top revealingly. He shook his head and then sat down beside her and drew a mark on her goose-pimpled skin.

'Works every time,' said Effie. 'Now you can keep me warm the old-fashioned way.' She shuffled forwards so there was room on the chair behind her. Attis sat down behind and wrapped his arms around her. Anna could still feel the warmth he had generated circulating around her body, as if his arms were around her too.

They sat that way for a while until Effie jumped up suddenly. 'It's snowing,' she announced, delighted as a child. 'Hail to Mother Holle, I love snow!'

Anna looked up and saw the flakes falling, as if the sky had grown so heavy it had shattered. Effie spun round, grabbing at them. The only time Anna ever saw her this excited was when she was doing magic. The snow suited her, settling on her black hair like fallen stars; her cheeks were turning pink. She'd never looked so young.

'Come, Anna, come,' said Effie, pulling her up. They tilted their heads back to the snow, laughing. It felt as if it was reaching them first and the rest of London after. Attis lay back on the sun lounger, watching them.

'Check this out.' Effie caught a snowflake on the tip of her finger. 'It's beautiful, right?' Its intricacy seemed almost impossible, a pattern of six little trees joined together – a tiny forest of ice.

'How's it not melting?' said Anna, entranced.

'Magic. You try.'

'I haven't really nailed the magic with my mind thing yet.'

'This is as easy as it gets. Just hold out your hand and believe the snowflake won't melt. Feel it.'

Anna put out her hand, finding it easy to sink into magic under the open night's sky in a snowstorm. She felt her thoughts shift from the logical world to some other hazy place. *My Hira is needle and thread.* She drew the strands together – the night and the snow, her palm a frozen landscape, but the snowflakes continued to melt. *Feel something . . .*

She looked at the sky and felt a yearning, a yearning for something of beauty in her life and the sadness that came with it. She pulled at the strands of feeling and wove them into the spell. She couldn't have said how much time passed amidst the gentle ticking of snowflakes before one landed on her palm and remained – a pattern of everything she'd felt.

'I'm doing it!' she squealed.

Effie caught her own snowflake and they held their fingers together, excitement jumping between their eyes. Effie peered more closely. 'They're identical . . .'

Anna studied them. It was true. The snowflakes on their fingertips were a mirror of one another – every ridge, curl and frond.

'Impossible,' said Attis. 'There are over a trillion water molecules in a single snowflake, meaning there are almost an infinite number of potential arrangements.'

'Well, smart-ass, get up out of your chair and look,' Effie rebuked him.

Attis jumped up and walked over. He scrutinized the snow-flakes but Anna found her magic couldn't fight the heat radiating off him and her flake melted.

'See,' said Effie, letting hers melt too.

'They were very similar,' he conceded.

'Men are infuriating, never willing to believe what they deem impossible even when it's in front of their eyes.'

'You're right.' Attis nodded. 'I just hate science.'

'Whatever. Let's go out,' Effie pleaded. 'I know a club in London that reflects the weather outside. We can dance in the snow.'

'I can't,' said Anna, wanting nothing more. 'If Aunt found out . . .'

'She'd what? Lock you in your bedroom for a few days? Trust me, it'll be worth it.'

'She'd do a lot worse than that.' The words slipped out. Anna had been careful to reveal as little as possible about her life with Aunt.

'What do you mean? What would she do?' said Attis, rounding on her.

Anna laughed lightly. 'Well, I might never be let out for one thing.'

Effie moved closer, studying her face. 'Does she hurt you?'

Anna wasn't sure if it was the snow or the way they were looking at her, or the fact she was desperate to talk to someone, but something made her sit down on the sun lounger and put her head in her hands. She tried to hide her tears.

'Anna.' Effie sat down beside her. 'You have to tell us.'

Anna pulled at the Knotted Cord in her pocket. 'She does have her little punishments . . . but it's not the physical stuff. How do you say no to your own mother when they've planned their whole lives around you?'

'She's not your mother,' said Attis sharply.

'She's as close as I've got. She has my whole future mapped out. She pretends to give me choices but I don't see I truly have any. I know she's going to make me become a Binder.' As she said it she was sure of it. Aunt had never given her a choice before – why start now?

'What's a Binder?' said Effie.

'Selene never mentioned them?' said Anna, surprised.

Effie shook her head.

'They're a grove my aunt belongs to. They don't agree with magic – believe it will bring the downfall of all witches. When you become one, your magic is bound.'

'What the fuck?' Effie cried. 'That's insane. Wait there, I've seen your aunt cast . . .'

'The Senior Binders have their magic released. They believe they need it, in the name of duty.'

'How convenient for them,' Effie snapped. 'They sound like maniacs. You can't join them, Anna. It's madness to remove your magic.'

'Is it? I don't know. Aunt can lock my mouth shut, stick me with needles like a pincushion, and I can deal with it, but she has other ways of convincing me she's right, that there's only one way. My mother's death . . .'

The words were coming up now, spilling out of her.

'What do you mean, stick you with needles?' Attis dropped to the ground next to her. 'What does she do to you?'

'Nothing permanent, don't worry.' She looked away from him.

'What about your mother's death?' Effie asked eagerly. 'At the Library, you said you wanted to learn more about your family. What do you want to know?'

Anna took a deep breath, calming herself, wondering how to relate something she'd never related to anyone but herself. 'Well, supposedly my father killed my mother because she found out he was having an affair. Aunt always says it was love and magic that truly killed her, led her on a path, as if my mother's magic was somehow wrong, dangerous.'

'Your psychopathic aunt would say that – she thinks all magic is dangerous,' Effie spat.

'But what if there's something there? What if there's more to my mother's death she's not telling me? What if there was something wrong with her magic and it's the same thing that's wrong with Aunt and . . . me? Is that why Aunt hates and fears magic so much? You've both seen the curse mark . . .'

Attis paced away from them.

'Curses *can* run in families,' said Effie.

'It's extremely rare,' said Attis, his voice strained with cynicism. 'Anna, I know it's not what you want to hear but it's much more likely your dad was simply a murderer.'

'Maybe,' Anna replied, taken aback by his resistance. He was normally so open to all possibilities. It riled her up even more. 'But I've spent my whole life accepting what I've been told. I'm tired of it. Isn't it my right to finally question it? Why does Aunt tell me so little? Why is Selene so cagey? Why did neither of them tell me my parents died in the house I live in now? Why did my parents not tell anyone I existed? Why was my mother researching curses? Why did she go to a curse witch called Nana Yaganov?'

Attis span round. 'Who?'

'The man in the Library said he knew my mother, that she'd gone there searching for something and that she'd found this woman, Nana Yaganov. So I'm going to find her.'

'Wait,' he said. 'A crazy man in the Library claims he knew your mother and then gives the name of a potentially crazier old bat. None of that makes any sense.'

'Nothing about this year makes sense, but maybe I have to follow the patterns.'

'You're chasing shadows that aren't there.'

'It sounds suspicious to me,' said Effie.

'Everything sounds suspicious to you,' Attis retorted.

Anna dried her tears in the wind. 'I just feel like, even if there's nothing sinister there at all, if I can understand what happened, who my mother was, then it'll give me the strength to become a Binder, or . . . to find a way out.' *I have to find a way out.*

'I'll find this Nana,' said Effie, fired up. 'I know a lot of witches; I'm sure someone will have heard of her. You're not becoming a Binder. Your aunt will have to go through me first.'

Anna smiled briefly. She looked at Attis but he had stalked away to the edge of the roof. Effie rolled her eyes. 'Attis, go and get us a drink. Something strong.'

He nodded and disappeared down the stairs into the house.

Effie's mouth curved. 'I knew there was a lot more to you than meets the eye, Anna Everdell.'

Anna didn't know how to respond to that. 'Well, you know, it could be nothing, but I can't ignore the curse mark any more.'

Effie caught some more snow in her hand. 'Ignore Attis. He just needs time. He has this thing about protecting people. He's probably just annoyed that he didn't see it sooner – how frightened you are of your aunt. I saw it the first time we met, but, Mother Holle, I didn't know how bad it was or what she's planning to do to you. You can't let her—'

'It's not that easy,' Anna interrupted.

'It is.'

'No. She's not like Selenc. You can't just get your way with someone like my aunt.'

'You think I get my way?' said Effie, irritated. 'You don't get your way with Selene; she just makes it feel like you do.'

'But Aunt took me in, raised me, I can't just—'

'You're in so fucking deep you can't see how deeply fucked it is.'

They sat breathing heavily, cradling their own hurts.

'Look. Let's just start with Nana and go from there. I'm not giving up on you yet,' said Effie forcefully.

Anna nodded, glad of Effie's strength. She would need it. 'But can we just keep it to ourselves for now? Don't tell the others.'

'Your secrets are safe with me.' Effie twisted an imaginary key to her lips as the sound of Attis's footsteps came back up the stairway.

He put their drinks down on the table. Effie picked hers up and swallowed most of it in one go. 'Thanks,' Anna said to him, taking a sip.

'Come out with us now,' said Effie, jumping to her feet. 'It'll cheer you up. I promise.'

'Ah. I don't think so – I'm going to head to bed.'

Effie looked as if she would argue but then nodded with

something like understanding. 'Come on then, Attis. Let the snow take us!'

They wound back into the warmth of the house. Anna went to the spare room and listened to them leaving, unsure if divulging her secrets had made her feel better or not. As soon as her head touched the pillow she fell asleep. She dreamt of snow – her and Effie catching snowflakes, all of them beautiful and identical, Attis reaching inside his heart and pulling out a shard of glass, Effie eating it, blood running down her chin, then the snowflakes growing darker, a flurry of black spots which Anna realized were flies – clouds of flies, like static, forming patterns, seven circles . . .

Anna woke, thrashing around the bed. It was four in the morning. She crept into the hallway making her way towards the bathroom.

Noises stopped her. Giggling, insistent giggling, and then heavy breathing, knocking – something falling – a moan of pleasure. Anna rushed into the bathroom and shut the door. Had the noise been coming from Effie's room? Was Attis in there? Or had it been upstairs? Selene and her fawn?

She quietly poured herself some water and sat on the edge of the bath trying not to imagine Effie and Attis together. It was hard not to; they were already moulded to one another – two halves of one whole. *I don't belong to either of them.*

Anna woke early. She pulled up the blinds and saw that snow had settled across the roofs and dusted itself across the roads; the trees clutched at it as if they too had been hands reaching for snowflakes all night. Someone was battling with a half-frozen car windscreen.

Effie's door was shut and there was no sign of Attis. She checked his forge but it was empty, the ash of the fire still twinkling with old heat. She could smell him in the smoke.

She walked to his shelf – to the jar of keys – but the white key was not in it any more.

When she got back home the house was cold and empty. She sat down with a cup of tea and looked out across their ordered garden. Anna wondered if Aunt had left her somehow incomplete, like one of her plants, snipped and sheared into submission, moulded into a shape of her choosing – growing more inward than outward, the secrets between them buried under thirty feet of snow. Aunt would ask her about her evening and Anna would lie, as always. She'd become adept at filtering the truth of her visits. She would not mention the drinking, or Selene in the bath with a man, or catching snowflakes on the roof, and she was careful never to mention Attis at all.

Restless, she threw her coat back on and headed for Cressey Square garden. It was a fairy tale today, ringed by a frozen iron fence, snow wreathing the bare hedges and bracken of the flower beds, the air frosted and fresh compared to the sterility of the house. Anna made her way down the path to her usual spot, past the water fountain turned off for winter to the small patch of trees at the end. She put her coat down on the ground and sat beneath the old oak tree. Despite the cold, she could somehow feel the warmth inside of it: life trickling deep within its thick and sturdy trunk.

She picked up the bones of a leaf from the floor, remembering her spell the night before. It had been a small spell, small as a snowflake. *It felt so right.* She took two red cords from her pocket and tied them together with a loop in the middle: the Ankh Knot, *Life Knot.*

She focused on the leaf and envisioned it bursting back to life – uncurling, growing strong, reclaiming its brightness. The knot in her hand quivered with sudden, unknown energy. She pulled it free, feeling a release. Anna gasped. The leaf was whole again: green and fresh as a summer's day. She held it up like a trophy – it blazed green against the green leaves behind.

Anna turned slowly around. The entire oak tree above her was green. The floor beneath her feet was swathed in grass. She spun around to find the other trees of the garden swaying green in the breeze, the bushes cloaked with leaf, the flower beds an eruption of colour. The water fountain had sprung to life. The entire garden was in the throes of summer. A bird began to sing above her.

Beyond the fence it was winter still. The contrast could not have been more stark, or noticeable. Her magic was plain for all to see.

*The neighbours! And Aunt! She's due home any minute . . .*

Hands shaking, Anna formed a Choke Knot. She tightened it, trying to constrict the magic she'd released, but the tree remained stubbornly tree-like. *Please!*

She sank to the floor, chanting, tying, pleading to the Goddess of the Dark Moon and every other kind of moon. She couldn't have said how many minutes of terror had passed when, to her sudden, unbearable relief, the leaves began to fall . . .

She pulled the knot tighter and the garden slowly died around her: rotting, freezing, the snow beginning to fall over it once more, covering the scene of her crime.

*Thank you. Oh thank you, Goddess.*

She scanned the neighbourhood – all was quiet – and then she made for the house, unable to shake off the cold or the fear of what she had just done. As she approached, a movement caught her eye in their own house. The curtain of the top-floor window. The room on the third floor. Anna stopped in her tracks and stared up at it. Had the curtain moved? But all was perfectly still, the room dark as always. *Just a trick of the light – or I've finally cracked.*

Still, Anna found herself hurrying inside, to the safety of the house that was no safety at all.

# WHISPERS

*The control of another's will should only ever be utilized for their own good. We are here to guide and to mould, to bring out the greatest potential in every Unbound.*

*Binders' Magic, The Book of the Binders*

As the week progressed Darcey and the others were forced to turn their attention from harassing people to some small but strange rumours wiggling their way into the school's consciousness.

*Darcey's been spending a lot of late nights at school with Headmaster Connaughty . . .*

*I heard Olivia had that chin reduction over the summer so she'd look more like Darcey . . .*

*Did you see the way Corinne looked at Katy yesterday when she was late for yoga class? I thought she was going to strangle her . . .*

And that was how it began. Innocuous little comments appearing out of nothing. Whispers stirred. Phones vibrated. Darcey laughed them off, as if she were merely batting a fly away, but they quickly returned, until the whole school was buzzing.

*Did you hear? Darcey was in Connaughty's office for over an hour today . . .*

People laughed at them disbelievingly and yet, the next day, they found themselves repeating what they'd heard, exaggerating, beginning to believe it themselves. Anna could sense the rumours as she walked through the corridors of the school, as if they were threaded into the air, forming faint suggestions on the tip of her tongue, waiting for release.

When the coven met that week they couldn't contain their delight.

'You're welcome, you're welcome.' Effie bowed to the row of mannequins.

'Read this one, read this one. It's too good.' Rowan shoved her phone under Manda's nose.

Manda put a hand over her mouth, giggling at whatever she'd read. 'Darcey looked so mad in class today. I've never seen her like it; she was snapping at everyone,' she said.

'I haven't spotted anyone taking a picture of me for days,' said Rowan. 'Everyone is too busy whispering about Darcey, Olivia and Corinne. Their reign is coming to an end!'

Effie laughed. 'Step up Queens of the Dark Moon.'

They spent the coven session reading all the rumours they could find, laughing until they cried. It felt good – it felt so good to watch Darcey fall into the web of her own making. When the session was over, Anna hung back, waiting for a moment alone with Effie and Attis.

She tried to sound casual. 'Anyone find anything about Nana?'

Attis breathed out, nose flaring, eyes sparking. 'I told you that line of enquiry was pointless.'

'I know. I didn't listen.'

'Well, I've heard some things, but nothing solid yet,' said Effie. 'There are rumours about a crazy homeless witch in London who goes by the name of Nana. One guy said she was the oldest witch in the country, descended from a line of ancient Russian casters. Another swore she was from New Orleans. No one knew how or where to find her though.'

'Ah,' said Anna, trying to hide the disappointment in her voice.

'I can ask Selene?'

'OK, but maybe don't tell her why you're asking. I don't think she'd be happy with me looking into my mother's death like this.'

'Of course she wouldn't be happy,' said Attis. 'This woman claims to be a curse witch. She's probably more deranged than Effie.'

'All the more reason to find her,' Effie responded.

They walked back through the school, Anna relating the incident with the snow and the garden and her panic as it had bloomed. She made light of it, hoping the story might soften Attis, but he did not smile or say goodbye when they parted ways. Anna sat on the train and grew more angry at him.

The following week the rumours continued to spread at an alarming rate. Darcey was not taking it well. She was angry, lashing out. Anna had heard that Corinne and Darcey had had a falling-out and now they weren't speaking.

*I saw Connaughty put his hand on her knee under the table during the council meeting . . .*

*She'll do anything to make sure she gets a good reference for Cambridge . . .*

*She likes her men with lots of meat on them . . .*

When Anna met the others for lunch in the common room, the whispering had taken on a life of its own, voracious and buzzing. She watched as a fly landed on a girl's face and crawled towards her lips. She moved and it flew off to join others clamouring at the window.

'Speak of the devils,' said Effie, pointing openly at Darcey and Olivia, who had just entered.

Darcey held her head high, striding into the centre as if to dare anyone who would talk about her, and yet there was a slight tremor in her eyes – the look of a hunter realizing they have become the hunted. The whispers quietened but did not stop.

'Disappear,' said Darcey to a group of girls leaning against one of the high tables. They scattered and Darcey took their place. She clicked her fingers at Lydia to come and sit with them. Darcey began a conversation as if she hadn't a care in the world. When Peter entered she called him over and pawed at him, playing with his hair, his ears, until he looked mildly irritated and left.

Only when Darcey was leaving did she look their way, trailing past their table.

'Pudding, Beast, was that wise? A moment on the lips, a lifetime on your fat arse.'

'You wish you had my arse, Darcey,' Rowan replied, relishing another bite.

Darcey's eyes narrowed imperceptibly. A fly landed on her smoothie cup and crawled onto her finger; she shook her hand free of it. It returned. She flapped her hand again, growing more irritated. It clung to her finger. 'Ugh, trust your table to attract the flies.' She tried to brush it off and it flew into the air and then landed on her hand again. She made an irritated noise, slapping the fly and crushing its body into her skin. She brushed the debris off and looked between them with suspicion – a suspicion she obviously didn't know how to pin down or put into words, but was there nonetheless.

'Let's get out of here, Olivia, it's disgusting.'

Olivia linked arms with her and they flounced out.

'She knows it's us.' Manda was reeling. 'She knows.'

'So?' said Effie. 'She's going to be so busy fighting fires she's not going to have time to light any new ones. We've got her now and the school is ours for the taking.'

Manda giggled slightly hysterically. 'She can't do shit any more.'

'Manda, did you just say *shit?*' Rowan laughed.

'Lydia,' Effie called. 'Yoo-hoo, over here.' Lydia looked around and hesitated. She knew talking to Effie would be crossing enemy lines, and yet Effie had her own form of influence. She walked towards their table.

'Come sit with us. Did you hear this thing everyone's been saying about Darcey and Connaughty?' Effie made a shocked face and then leant in conspiratorially. 'Do you think there's anything in it?'

Lydia hardly needed any encouragement; she began to betray Darcey at once, spilling all the gossip she'd heard.

After lunch Anna went to the music room to play. She'd barely sat down when a song began to free itself from her fingers. It opened low and foreboding, followed by a series of high notes chasing one another, up and down. She wasn't sure where the music was coming from, her or the piano: it felt as though they were playing each other.

After several minutes she became aware of a shadow in the doorway. The notes jarred to a halt. 'What are you doing here?'

Attis closed the door behind him. 'I have just as much right to be in this room as you. Perhaps I want to practise myself.'

'Practise what?'

'The, er, bongos.' He grabbed some off the shelf, pulling them onto his lap.

Anna fought the smile on her lips. 'You came in here to practise the bongos?'

'Yes. Please continue. I'll play quietly.' He began to tap them gently until Anna laughed.

Attis grinned back at her, but then his smile dropped. 'Anna. You have to tell me if your aunt hurts you. It's not OK. I don't think you understand – it's really not OK.'

Serious Attis always unnerved her, his face was not designed for frowning.

'She doesn't hurt me – not really.'

Attis nodded, sadly. 'Just tell me.'

'I will.'

'So . . . I asked around about Yaganov.'

Anna had presumed he wouldn't help. 'And?'

'*Nada*. I'm sorry. I think that Library guy was a loon.'

Anna played a few irritable notes. 'Maybe.'

He sighed. 'What are you trying to find? Confirmation that your magic is cursed, somehow special? When we're afraid, sometimes it's easier to look for patterns, deeper meanings—'

Her fingers went rigid. 'You think you know everything, Attis, but you don't.'

'You don't have to do what your aunt says for the rest of your life. Humour her, become a Binder, then when you're old enough you can leave. Escape.'

'Escape!' Anna laughed, spinning round on the chair to face him. 'We can't all be like you, drifting, relying on no one, doing exactly what you want, whenever you want.' Her raised voice rebounded in the quiet acoustics of the room.

'You're going to get yourself hurt! Don't you see that?' His own voice rose to meet hers. Anna had never heard him sound like that before, the music of his voice flattened out like a piece of wire.

'Why do you even care?' she cried, exasperated. He didn't reply and Anna didn't know what answer she was looking for – that he was doing it out of some sense of coven responsibility, because she was Effie's friend, or . . . for her.

He let a low, pained exhale escape his lips. 'Just play the sodding piano, OK?'

'I don't want to while you're here.'

'Well, I'm not going anywhere.'

'Fine.'

'Fine.'

Anna turned around and began to play because if she

didn't she was going to throw something at him. The song returned immediately, rumbling like thunder, flashing with high notes of lightning. Her fingers moved, quick as rain, up and down the keys. She didn't want to think. She just wanted to play until her thoughts drained away. Attis watched quietly. She lost track of time as the anger drained itself away. *Maybe he's right. Maybe I'm being paranoid – just like Aunt.*

She heard a faint beating from behind her, the sound of bongos. Her mouth twitched with a smile. *You, Attis Lockerby, are an idiot.*

She spun around accusingly. 'Enjoying yourself?'

'Very much so. Nothing like a good bongo session.'

Anna managed to glare and smile at him at the same time.

'Just tell me,' he said. 'Tell me if it gets worse at home and we'll find a way to get you out of there.'

'OK.' Anna nodded, knowing that if she was going to get out of there, she had to do it her own way. She closed the piano lid and stood up, but Attis moved towards her.

'Now, have you thought about this?' He produced a piece of paper.

'What's that?'

'A sign-up for the Performance Assembly.'

'And why are you showing me that?'

'Well, you write your name down on it, you see, like this . . .' He took a pen out of his pocket.

'I am not signing up for that.'

'OK. I'll sign it for you.'

'You will not,' she said, snatching the paper from his hand. 'You're not the boss of me, Lockerby!'

'When are you going to show people your music?'

'I'm letting you listen, aren't I?'

'I mean real people, not piano perverts like me.'

'Oh, in that case, my answer is still never.'

'And it's still a disappointing answer. Why do you insist on disappointing me?'

'It's better than leading you on.'

'I'd much rather be led on.'

They stood watching each other in the dark room. It was too dark and too warm. He was too close.

'Come on,' said Anna abruptly. 'We'd better get to class.' She stuffed the sign-up sheet into her bag and dragged him towards the door.

'Who's the boss of who now, Dr Everdell?' He laughed as they left.


Anna was careful not to play the piano as she'd played it earlier with Attis watching. Her fingers moved methodically, the notes falling into perfect line, while Aunt sat beside her. The metronome was more maddening than ever: *tick, tock, tick, tock . . . I'm running out of time!*

How had Effie and Attis found nothing out about Nana at all? Effie had been trying, at least, but Anna wasn't so sure Attis had truly tried, no matter what he claimed. She had no idea where his resistance was coming from. The boy was impossible to understand. *Impossibly frustrating.*

'Keep in time.'

Anna focused back on the ticking and let her mind sink into the song. She thought of the one she'd played earlier, so charged and freeing. She smiled imperceptibly as she wondered how Attis's bongo-playing might fare against the metronome. Her mind began to lose itself in its wanderings and the gentle beckoning of the music; Aunt and the ticking faded away. Some feeling rose up, a feeling she couldn't put her finger on, but the music took hold of it, the melody softening, the notes melting into one another, then quickening like a heartbeat, lighting up the dark places of her mind and bringing a heat to her cheeks—

A sharp pain pierced Anna's finger, slicing through the song. A line of blood ran down the white piano key. Anna lifted her finger – blood was running from its tip. A thorn had dug deep into it as she played. She looked at Aunt, incredulous.

'Curious how the metronome began to tick in time with you and not you with it,' said Aunt, ignoring the injury. Anna felt her stomach drop; she had not even noticed. 'But then you were so carried away, weren't you? By the beauty of the song . . . the beauty of the music, the magic of it. I've never heard you play that way before.'

Anna tried to find words to explain herself.

'Neither have the roses, apparently.' Aunt nodded to the rose bush atop the piano. It was tightly closed up – except one rose. One had bloomed, red as her own blood. Anna looked at it in horror. She had lived with those roses her entire life and not a single one had ever opened. It was beautiful – a deep, alluring red, the petals folded with never-ending questions, a centre dark with whisperings.

'The Binders will be visiting over the Easter break.' Anna tore her eyes away from the rose, trying to take in Aunt's words. They only deepened her horror.

'They want to see how you're getting on. If you're remaining in control of your magic. It will be extremely embarrassing for me if they see that you are not, not at all.'

'I am. I . . .' Anna thought of the garden blossoming, seven circles in static, rumours spreading. *Am I?*

'Don't trust magic.' Aunt reached for the rose. 'It looks beautiful, doesn't it? Smells like the first stirrings of love – but all the while it's wrapping its thorns around your heart and before you know it, well, you know how your mother ended up. Whispers are spreading in the news. The Binders are tense. I don't want to give them any reason to worry about you too, do I?' She made a knotting gesture and the rose closed back up without a sound.

For a moment Anna almost told Aunt about the curse mark. The words were on the tip of her tongue but she held them back. Aunt would not be understanding – she'd know that Anna had been practising magic; her anger would probably spill over and leave Anna with more to deal with than a single line of blood on a piano key.

It was a miracle that Aunt sent her to her room without further punishment as it was. Anna lay in bed thinking over the Binders' upcoming visit and running her Knotted Cord through her hands, feeling its six knots – strong and tight and secure. *Weakness in feeling, strength in control. Am I in control? Or is my magic in control of me? Can curses be controlled? Perhaps it's better if I am bound.* But no. Anna knew she couldn't give up yet. She just had to find another way to understand what was happening to her.

She fell slowly into disturbed dreams: she was playing the piano, petals were falling, but thorns were wrapping themselves around her hands, piercing her fingers, vines winding around her body and throat; the notes on the page in front of her unfolding, reshaping into circles – seven circles – the music growing louder, louder, louder – reaching a climax and then – a loud thud.

Anna jerked upright in bed, suddenly awake, the music fading from her ears.

She saw that the book of fairy tales had fallen from the shelves onto the floor again. She crept out of bed and picked it up, taking the cover off. 'How did you get there?' She was growing used to talking to books.

It answered only with a gleam of moonlight across its front, catching the tree engraving. She took it back to bed and read the second fairy tale, hoping it would be happier than the first.

## Little Red Cap

In a faraway land beyond sky and smoke, mountain and lake, a maiden lived on the edge of the forest with her mother. Her grandmother was sick and her mother told the maiden she must pay her a visit. She gave her a basket of apples, a cake and a vessel of wine to take as gifts. She put the little maiden's best red cap on her head and told her not to stray from the path.

Little Red Cap set off into the woods. She was careful not to stray from the path, until she heard a terrible moaning from among the trees. Whatever was making the noise sounded as if it was in a great deal of pain. She left the path and discovered a big black bear in a big black rage, roaring and growling and holding its paw. It had a thorn embedded there. Its anger was a terrifying thing but the maiden stepped forward and in her most gentle voice offered to remove it. The bear turned to her and roared, blowing her cap right off her head, but she stood her ground. Then he dropped to the floor and offered up his paw. She removed the thorn and the bear was happy. He gave Little Red Cap a present: a bag to wear around her neck containing twig, coin, needle and thimble. He guided her back to the path and she continued on her way.

Before long she heard a voice calling her name from among the trees. She stepped off the path once more and came upon a wolf. He asked her where she was going. Little Red Cap explained she was off to visit her grandmother, who lived in the old cottage by the three elder bushes. The wolf told her she ought to pick some flowers to cheer up her grandmother's old, frail heart. Little Red Cap thanked the wolf and began to search the forest for flowers.

The cunning wolf ran swiftly ahead and found the

old cottage. He quickly killed Little Red Cap's grand-mother, gobbling her up, leaving only a little flesh which he put in a dish in the pantry and a little blood that he drained into a bottle. He put on the grandmother's clothes and got into bed.

When the maiden arrived the wolf called out in a croaky old voice: 'Come in, my child.'

Little Red Cap stepped into the house. 'Grandmother, I have come with apples, cake and wine for you and flowers for your home.'

'Put the food in the pantry and the flowers in a vase, my child. Are you hungry?'

'Yes, I am, Grandmother.'

'Then take the meat you find in a little dish in the pantry and cook it in the cauldron. Are you thirsty?'

'Yes, I am, Grandmother.'

'Then drink a small glass of wine.'

The young maiden ate the meat and drank the wine, which was truly her grandmother's flesh and blood. Once she had finished the wolf said something in a whisper that she could not make out.

'What did you say, Grandmother?' asked the maiden.

The wolf whispered again and the maiden drew closer.

'I still can't hear you, Grandmother.'

The wolf whispered again and the maiden stepped even closer.

'Speak louder, Grandmother.'

The maiden sat down on the edge of the bed and put her ear to the wolf's mouth.

This time she heard it: 'Now, I'm hungry!'

But Little Red Cap sprang from the bed before the wolf could catch her. She took the twig from the little bag around her neck – it turned to wind and blew the door open. She ran out.

The wolf followed and began to catch her up.

Little Red Cap took the coin out of her little bag and threw it behind her – it turned into a mountain of earth which slowed the wolf down for he had to run up and down it.

Little Red Cap continued to run but the wolf again began to catch up with her. She pulled out the needle from her little bag and threw it behind her – it turned to fire and set the forest alight. The wolf was caught among the flames.

Little Red Cap ran and ran but the wolf leapt high over the flames and began to catch up with her again. She pulled out the thimble from her little bag and threw it behind her – it turned into a great river. The black bear appeared from the forest and told Little Red Cap to jump on his back. She held on tight and he swam across, delivering her safely on the other side.

The wolf leapt into it after them, but the river was too deep. He sank and drowned.

At least this one had a happy ending. Aunt had always preferred the other kind of story, the one with retribution: There are no happy endings in real life, my child, and stories will not protect you. The wolves will always be waiting in the woods. Anna shivered at the recollection of her words and closed the book of fairy tales. She couldn't spend her whole life fearing shadows. 'If you can't protect me, then I have to protect myself,' she whispered.

The book did not reply.

# LETTER

*Word spells are not secure; they are too open to interpretation and misuse. A Binder must only ever employ a single word of power and even then it should only be written or spoken in anagrammatic form.*

*Binders' Magic, The Book of the Binders*

Flies knocked against the windows of the school. Anna held her Knotted Cord tightly as she walked down the corridor. That morning she'd watched one crawl out from inside a girl's ear in assembly. Yesterday she swore one had flown out of the innards of a phone.

Anna had tried to deny it to herself, but she knew – it was their spell. It was all their spell. She'd expected it to have lost its power by now but it was getting worse – growing and spreading like a voracious mould, taking on new forms . . . As the weeks passed it was starting to become harder to know what was rumour and what was real any more.

Olivia seemed to be changing, becoming a grim caricature of Darcey. She was getting skinnier, her hair lighter – she'd grown it out of her bob and was styling it exactly like Darcey's. Corinne genuinely seemed angrier, although of course it could be no more than the fact that the rumours were driving her crazy. And then Darcey . . . Anna had been watching her during assembly and could have sworn she kept giving Connaughty lingering looks. *Did she really spend two hours in his office last night or was that just a rumour?*

A fly circled about her head. Anna tried to escape it but it returned, *buzz, buzz, buzz,* sticky as static. *What if it's me? What if there's something wrong with my magic? My curse is bleeding into the spell?*

At lunch their own table was buzzing with more than flies. As Darcey's standing had fallen, Effie had made sure theirs had risen – people surrounded them. Even the school's most popular had begun to switch allegiance.

'The evidence is undeniable.' Effie laughed, handing around her phone. It was a picture of Darcey looking longingly at Headmaster Connaughty, cartoon hearts rising from her head. *I'm not the only one who's noticed then . . .*

Manda giggled and passed the phone to Lydia. Anna noticed just how much make-up Manda was wearing. She'd had Effie cut her hair short too, permanently this time.

'That's so gross.'

'Maybe she likes them old?'

'Maybe she likes the headmaster's cane . . .'

'I heard she didn't leave after the student council meeting last week . . .'

Anna caught Attis's eye. He was the only other person who didn't seem riveted by the conversation. He knew Anna was worried about the rumours – he'd been coming to the piano room more and more to watch her play and to talk. She'd become used to his presence and found the music flowed from her just the same, more even.

'Peter!' Effie called. Anna looked up and saw that he had just entered. He looked disdainfully at Effie but assessed their table, seeing that it was full of his friends. 'Don't worry, I'm not going to make you sit on my lap. I thought you could sit over here – by Anna.'

A few people sniggered. Anna glared at Effie, feeling the blood rush to her cheeks. Peter approached their table cautiously. 'Effie. Still causing havoc and destruction?'

'Still refusing to join in with the fun?' Effie replied with a provocative sneer. 'To be fair, you might need to get rid of that girlfriend of yours first. We were just talking about her.'

'I'd rather you didn't.'

'Come on, mate, it's just banter,' said Tom.

Peter shook his head and took the seat next to Anna as the rest of them continued on with a new line of gossip. Peter turned to her. 'I'm sorry about this lot.'

'I'm sorry about Effie.'

They smiled at each other. They had only spoken a little since Anna had asked for his help with the game against Rowan. That seemed a long time ago – their own game had taken over and the stakes were much higher.

'We'll just have to stick together, hey?' He nudged her, just slightly. 'That's a terrible choice of dessert there, Everdell. Everybody knows the rice pudding is more gloop than rice, plus there's a fly in it.' He scooped it out with a spoon. 'There you go.'

'Thank you,' she said, feeling instantly guilty and finding it difficult to look into his searching eyes.

'Bloody pests, I thought they were meant to have been dealt with by now.' He slapped another out of the air and dusted it onto the floor. 'We should eat lunch at the café. I never see you there – you're so elusive.' His smile deepened and Anna felt herself blushing profusely.

'I'll see what I can do,' she said.

'Uh-oh,' Anna heard Effie say amid sudden laughter. Anna looked up to see that Darcey had entered. Her eyes landed on Anna – Peter – Effie's smile. Several flies buzzed towards her and the laughter grew louder. She looked at them with a venom so potent that Anna could feel it, laced with hatred and rage. Darcey spun on her heels and left. Their table burst into laughter again.

'I'd better go,' said Peter, but his voice was flat and impatient. 'See you soon, Everdell.'

Anna had been looking forward to the coven session that evening, where it would only be them, but when she opened the sewing-room door, she staggered backwards in dismay. The room had always smelt stale, like a stagnant pond, but now it smelt as if they had sunk to the bottom of it. The altar was festering with flies.

Effie clapped her hands together, catching one. 'Attis, can you go and find some spray or something?'

'Hell's feathers!' said Rowan, flicking the lid off one of the smoothie cups. Inside it had filled itself with sludgy grey water. 'Where in Mother Holle did that come from?'

'Is it our spell?' said Manda.

Effie shrugged. 'It's working and if things get a bit wild, so be it. Nature's justice is wild.'

'Darcey's gone into hiding,' said Rowan gleefully, tipping out the smoothie. 'Although did you see what she's saying about us now? It's so pathetic.'

'What?' said Anna.

Rowan handed Anna her phone. Darcey had posted a picture of them along with the caption: *DO NOT TRUST THESE GIRLS. THEY ARE EVIL. THEY ARE TRYING TO RUIN MY LIFE.*

Anna gripped the phone tighter. 'Do you think she knows what we've done?'

'What? Magic?' Effie laughed. 'Oh, she suspects us – of something. But what? Spreading rumours? That's hardly a crime.'

'*Evil* has quite strong implications.'

'Everyone just thinks she's losing her mind, Anna,' Rowan

reassured her. 'And no one seems to care what she has to say any more. I still can't believe people actually want to sit with us. Not just people. Boys. Karim was definitely giving you eyes today, Manda.'

'He was not,' she retorted. 'Wait – was he?'

'Manda, you need to start being seen going out if you want to seal the deal with him,' said Effie. 'Come out this weekend.'

'I'm there!' said Rowan.

'Same,' said Manda. 'I'll find a way.'

'I thought popularity was for the feeble-minded, Manda?' said Anna but Manda looked annoyed.

'Look, for the first time I'm not being actively shunned by everyone and I'm going to enjoy it, OK? This is our chance.'

'Don't be jealous, Anna,' said Effie. 'We'll get Peter to seal your deal too. We're almost there.'

Anna found herself flustered. 'I really don't think Peter is interested in me. Anyway, you taunting him all the time doesn't help.'

Effie laughed. 'He's in my Politics class – what else is there to do? He loves it really, beneath all that moody seriousness. Anyway, come on, admit it: you want it.'

'Of course I want it – him,' Anna snapped. 'But he's with Darcey, so—'

'Can't find any bug spray,' said Attis sharply from behind her.

'Gah, begone!' Effie spun around and clapped her hands once – hard. Every fly in the room dropped dead.

Anna watched them twitch on the floor. 'Effie. When do you think this spell will end? The rumours have worked already.'

'When it decides justice has been served.'

'What if it gets worse?'

'All the better.' Effie smiled. 'Can we move on?'

'Did the original spell come with any warnings? Can we see it?'

'No, a revenge spell from the seventeen hundreds did not come with warnings and you can't see it because the book has gone back to the Library.'

'So you took it back?' said Anna accusingly.

'No. It left of its own accord.'

'The Library takes its books back once it's decided they have served their purpose,' Rowan explained. 'So useful, actually, as I always forget to return them. I've been banned from the school library – twice.'

Anna wondered about the *Everdell* book beneath her bed – why had the Library not taken that back?

'Now, can we drop this?' said Effie. 'We've got magic to do.'

At the end of their session, Anna was sitting with Attis, who had been teaching them some of the different magical properties of metal, when Effie approached. Even though Anna was still annoyed at her, she had to know if she'd discovered any more about Nana. 'So, have you guys found anything out about you know who?'

Effie understood what she meant. 'Nope. Well, I've heard plenty of rumours but none of them helpful. A friend of mine from the Wild Hunt said their father knew of her, that she's mad and you'll never find her.'

'That's that then,' said Attis.

Anna shot Attis a look. She had no intention of giving up that easily – the Binders were due to visit, her Knotting was looming. 'Rowan!' Anna called. Rowan skipped over, untangling a cord she'd managed to knot into her hair. 'Have you ever heard of a witch called Nana Yaganov by any chance?'

'Yaganov, Yaganov . . . Yaga. Nov. No. I know a Yosovich?'

'Do you think you could ask your mum?'

'Sure. Who is she?'

'Just someone I need to find. Unfortunately I don't have any more than a name.'

'Hmmm,' Rowan considered. 'If you only have a name you could try sending a letter.'

Anna narrowed her eyes. 'But I don't have an address.'

'You don't need an address with a Futhark Stamp.'

'What's a Futhark Stamp?'

'Rowan, you're a genius!' said Effie, grabbing her shoulders. 'Well, obviously.'

'What's a Futhark Stamp?' Anna repeated.

'I've heard of them, but I've never actually used one,' said Effie.

'There's certainly no harm in trying,' Rowan continued. 'Except, you know, if she's dead and the letter invites her spirit back into the world, or you get a hex in return, or something like that.'

'It's madness,' said Attis. 'You can't just go around sending letters with a Futhark Stamp if you don't know who you're sending to.'

'We used to send all sorts of things when we were kids and nothing happened.' Rowan shrugged. 'Except that one incident when my brother received a letter back with some sweets that took his voice away for a month.'

Anna held up the cords threateningly. 'I'm going to silence you all in a moment if someone doesn't tell me what a flipping Futhark Stamp is!'

Rowan took a deep breath. 'It's a runic symbol that draws on the magic of the Runic Witches. With it your letter can contact anyone within the magical world – you don't need an address, just the stamp, a name and a clear intention. It's considered a little dangerous because it doesn't just deliver letters to our world—'

'I'll do it,' said Anna.

'Who are you trying to contact?' asked Manda, wandering over.

'Just an old relative.'

Anna ignored the suspicion in Rowan's eyes.

'I have letter-writing paper and envelopes in my bag,' Manda offered and then added in response to Effie's eye-rolling, 'What? You never know when you'll be required to write a thank-you note. Do you need a pen?'

'Futhark Stamps require nothing more than your blood,' Effie taunted, making Manda yelp.

'She's kidding,' Rowan reassured Anna. 'Although people do sometimes form them with their blood, for added force.'

'I'll just go with ink,' said Anna, taking herself off to one of the desks to write it.

Dear Ms Yaganov,

I am Anna Everdell, daughter of Marie Everdell. I was given your name by a man known as Pesachya who lives in the Library. He informed me that my mother went to see you before she died, sixteen years ago. My father strangled her to death when I was just a baby and then killed himself, if that rings a bell. I wondered if you had any useful information that might help me to understand what happened that night.

Please.

Yours sincerely,

Anna Everdell

She folded the paper over and put it into the envelope. She wrote the name 'Nana Yaganov' in big letters on the front. 'So, how do I do this?'

'You need to make this symbol on the back, like a seal. Here.' Rowan had sketched it out for her to copy. It was similar to the letter R but the lines were more severe, the top of the R triangular.

'A runic R,' Rowan explained. 'Can't remember what it means.'

'Raidho. It means journey,' said Attis, his voice flecked with irritation.

Anna drew out the symbol carefully. 'What do I do now?'

'You post it, of course,' said Rowan.

'What? A normal postbox?'

'Well, sort of. It needs to be an old one. Come on. I think there's one near Dulwich Village.'

The letterbox was certainly not easy to spot. They made their way down a cobbled side street off the village centre and there it was, buried behind some brambles and embedded into the stone wall. It looked quite normal, although old and weathered, its red paint peeling, its delivery hole narrow, like an eye half-closed against the wind and rain.

'How do you know it will work?' asked Anna, looking it over.

'You see that,' said Rowan, pointing to the V and R engraved along the top, the English crown stamped between them.

'That's Queen Victoria's royal cypher,' said Manda.

'Yeah, but look more closely at the R,' said Rowan and Anna scrutinized it, finding it was not like the V on the other side, but more spindly and pointed, like the R Anna had drawn on the envelope. 'See – a Futhark Letterbox. They're all over London, hiding in plain sight.'

'Cool,' said Anna, tracing the symbol. 'So I just post it?'

'What do you think?' Rowan smiled. 'You do a ritual dance around it?'

'It's highly possible.'

'Kind of wish I'd said that now.' Rowan laughed as Anna stepped forwards.

She peered into the hole but was met with nothing but

darkness. Where would the letter go? She made a firm intention in her mind: *Please send this to Nana Yaganov, the woman who can help me learn about my mother and the curse.* She pushed the letter into the box and turned around.

'Right, that's done.' She didn't want to think about it or get her hopes up. 'Wait,' she said alarmed. 'How do I get a letter back?' Aunt would be suspicious of any post delivered to her directly.

'Don't worry. These letters don't use the front door.' Rowan shook her head, as if Anna had suggested something absurd. 'If she sends one back, it'll come to you. Only to you.'

Manda was studying the letterbox slot, searching for signs of magic.

'I wouldn't get too close,' Effie whispered in her ear, making Manda cry out again.

But Anna was distracted by Attis's vexed expression. She turned away, refusing to indulge him. He took his role as coven protector far too seriously for someone who rarely took anything seriously at all. Anyway, she didn't need his approval – she just needed a reply.

# NECKLACE

*In sacrifice, may our hearts be pure.*

*Tenet Seven, The Book of the Binders*

Anna had spent the first few days of the Easter Holidays relieved to be out of school and away from the guilt of the worsening rumours. But now the dreaded day had arrived and she would rather be anywhere but at home. The Binders were due. She was a tangle of nerves.

What if her magic escaped again? What if they sensed its darkness? What if it revealed the curse mark? Would they waste no time? *Will I be forced to join their ranks today?* It was strange – she'd never had to worry about having too much magic before. Part of her relished the thought of turning it on the Binders, watching their puckered faces burst open in shock, but the rest of her knew it was imperative that she revealed nothing, risked nothing.

The doorbell rang at midday on the dot.

'Helen, do come in.' Aunt's voice feathery, welcoming.

Anna listened as they arrived one by one, exchanging polite greetings. She picked up the cakes and forced a smile, entering their lair. They cast critical gazes at her – the usual nine pinched faces, looking as if they'd been sucking lemons all night. There was a new face among them. A girl her age, big-boned with bristly auburn hair. Anna recognized her vaguely. *Rosie. Mrs Bradshaw's daughter.* They had met once before.

'Hi, Anna. Good to see you again.'

'Rosie,' Anna replied warily.

'Anna, Rosie has recently gone through her Knotting,' Aunt explained. 'We thought it could be good for you to talk. Let Rosie put your mind at ease.'

Rosie smiled obligingly at Anna, wedged next to her mother on the sofa, her hair cut in exactly the same unflattering bob. They'd been much younger when they'd met before. Rosie and Anna had been sent to Anna's room while the Binders conducted one of their meetings. Rosie had immediately tried to coerce her into doing magic, suggesting they send paper aeroplanes from the balcony into the wind, that they could write rescue messages on them to save them from the tedium of their lives. Anna had been too afraid to comply and Rosie had grown exasperated. Anna couldn't imagine her becoming a Binder.

'Would you like some cake?' She offered the plate to Rosie.

Rosie looked at her mother. 'No, thank you.' She rested her hands back on her lap.

Anna continued to take the orders, trying to sift their babble from her consciousness and avoid any sudden movements or eye contact. If she could just escape to the kitchen, talking to Rosie wouldn't be so bad; it could even prove useful.

'Your hair looks lovely, Anna.' Mrs Withering's smile snapped around her like a trap. Anna froze. She'd hoped they wouldn't notice her hair. Mrs Withering took a biscuit from the tray. 'Homemade this time, I see? What an improvement. I've heard troubling news from your aunt that you are not yet sure about becoming a Binder. We're all very concerned.'

Anna tried to keep steady. 'Aunt has presented me with
the decision and I am still weighing up my options.'

A few of the Binders began to laugh – high-pitched spurts.
Mrs Withering's smile screwed itself tighter. 'Weighing up
your options! How idealistic. The youth of today are presented
with too many choices, if you ask me. Are you not aware of
tenet nine, Anna?'

'The fire never dies; beware smoke on the wind.'

'You think we say it for fun? Wear our necklaces as acces-
sories? Bind witches for our entertainment? No. We are here
for a purpose. They say the Seven protect all witches but this
– as we are seeing – is a fallacy. We, the Binders, are the
ones who know what true protection means, who may be
the only hope the magical world has left. Whispers divide;
in secrets we thrive.'

Anna nodded. She had been treated to such speeches before
over the years.

'Have you ever heard the story of our founder?'

Anna shook her head. That she had not heard.

'How about a demonstration?' Mrs Withering clapped her
hands together with delight. 'Rosie, stand up. You can play
the part.'

Mrs Bradshaw nudged her forwards and Rosie walked,
without question, to the centre of the room.

'Introducing: Agnes Mandilip.' Mrs Withering pointed at
Rosie, who pretended to tip an imaginary cap in response.

*What the hell is going on?*

'It is 1640. The town of Bury St Edmunds. Agnes is the
town healer, famed across the county for her skills, revered
and respected. *Witch,* they whispered, but no one probed too
deeply; it was better not to know. Agnes took others on in
secret – apprentices to learn her arts – gathering herbs,
preparing ointments and tinctures, casting spells of healing.
But times were changing. The Hunters' influence was

growing stronger, spreading across the country like black storm clouds from village to village, winds rising, smoke stirring – releasing their poison. The whispering grew louder. *Witch,* they said, *witch! Witch!* Fingers began to point, accusations bubbled up . . .'

In response to Withering's words the Binders around the room raised their fingers towards Rosie, whispering, muttering. Rosie cowered and Anna could no longer tell if she was acting.

'When they arrived they arrested Agnes and tortured her for nine days straight.' Mrs Withering smiled. *'Confess,* they said, *confess! Confess!'*

The Binders began to chant: *confess, confess, confess.*

'They wanted names! They wanted more witches to torture! Agnes tried to resist, but their methods were terrible and she screamed and howled . . .'

Rosie's mouth sprang open and she began to shriek as if she were suffering the very tortures now. The performance was convincing – *too convincing* . . .

'Stop it,' Anna cried 'Stop!'

But Mrs Withering ignored her and raised her shrill voice above Rosie's. 'In the end Agnes gave them the names of her apprentices. They hunted them down and brought them to her. She had to listen to them being tortured day and night. It was then, lost in the din of their screams, that she realized the error of her ways. It was her magic, her prideful magic, that had drawn the Hunters to their town, that had unleashed chaos and brought suffering on all those she loved. All she had was the cord her wrists were tied with. She managed to free them and with one last anguished wail she tied a knot in the cord and drew her emotions inside of her. Forever. She locked her magic away so tightly and so deeply that the Hunters would never get to her again.'

Rosie's mouth snapped shut, slicing her scream in half.

'No matter how they tortured her after that she remained silent. The whole town turned out for her hanging and as she dropped to her death – her feet kicking, her body writhing – Agnes did not make a sound.'

As Mrs Withering said the words, Rosie reached for her neck, fingers scrabbling – her clamped mouth shut. It took a moment for Anna to realize what was happening. *They're hanging her. They're hanging her right here, right now!*

'Rosie!' she cried. 'NO! Stop! What are you doing?' The women around her sat docile, stirring their tea and nibbling on biscuits. She looked to Rosie's mother but she did not stir. *They are all mad!*

Rosie's eyes bulged wide, her face becoming red, contorted. Anna could feel her pain as if it were her own. She raised her hands towards her and let go of her magic with a wail – Rosie fell to the floor, retching and gasping, her breathing returning in shuddering waves. Anna looked up and saw that every rose on the rose bush in the corner had opened – silent screams.

All eyes turned to look at her. Anna reached a hand into her pocket, clutching her Knotted Cord, trying to calm herself.

'How curious,' said Mrs Withering. 'I felt something like magic emanate from you then, dear Anna. Not a knot in sight, either.'

*I can feign confusion at least.* 'I – I didn't know what was happening. I panicked and – and – that happened.'

'I hardly think that counts as magical talent,' said Mrs Dumphreys disparagingly.

'Not talent, but some power.' Mrs Withering eyed Anna. She turned to the room. 'How can we be sure she will remain in control during her ceremony? That she will be ready to make the necessary sacrifice? Vivienne, I thought you said she was under control.'

'She won't panic,' Aunt snapped. 'Anna will be ready.'

Mrs Withering took a sip of tea, looking doubtful.

'Now, are we done with this little demonstration? I think we have more urgent matters to discuss.'

'Considering everything going on right now, Vivienne, I think there is little more urgent than teaching Anna the importance of our history,' said Mrs Withering. 'You see, Anna, before she was hanged, Agnes passed on the secrets of her silence to her apprentices: how she had come to see the sin of magic, how she had bound it inside of her, how all the Unbound must be bound in their turn. Only one apprentice survived but it was enough to carry on her teachings and the noose that hung around Agnes's neck became our symbol. Our Binders' necklace. To remind us of her pain and dedication. We have carried her secrets for centuries, binding our magic, bringing witches into our fold and trying to prevent their return. But the magical world hasn't listened and now the storm clouds are brewing again. But don't worry, Anna.' Mrs Withering smiled sourly. 'You take your time. You make your decision. It's not like it's important, is it?'

Anna took a moment to speak. 'Thank you. You've given me a lot to think about.'

'Well, think fast. Summer is approaching. You don't have long.' Mrs Withering looked at Aunt with significance. 'Silence and secrets.'

'Silence and secrets,' the room replied in unison

'Go on, Anna. Take Rosie to the kitchen,' Aunt instructed sharply.

Anna only just made it to the kitchen table before her legs buckled beneath her. Rosie poured herself some water from the jug, smiling cheerfully as if nothing had taken place. A few minutes passed in silence before Anna spoke.

'Are you OK?'

'Oh yes, fine.' Rosie was still smiling.

'Rosie, you know what happened in there wasn't right. It was messed up.'

'Pain paves the way.'

Anna breathed deeply. If the girl she'd known before was in there, she was buried deep. 'You're a Binder now, then?'

'I am,' Rosie replied. 'The lowest of ranks, of course, but we must all start somewhere.'

'What about your magic? Do you remember when we met before and you tried to get me to cast a spell with you, but—'

'You wouldn't. That's why I told my mum that they didn't have to worry about you. You've always been so disciplined, you've always had such self-control.'

'But surely there's no harm in the odd spell.'

Rosie's smiled dropped and she spoke with a lowered voice. 'Anna, no, magic is dangerous. Life is much simpler without it. You'll be happy, trust me. It's not like you can't feel things any more, you just don't care as much. It's like looking upon the world with a new level of maturity. I'm very happy now.' The smile returned, her eyes steady – blank.

'The Book of the Binders says that during your ceremony you must be ready to make the necessary sacrifice. What is the sacrifice?' Anna said urgently.

'Wind,' Rosie replied.

'What?'

'During the ritual the Binders have to generate magical energy that mirrors your own and then use it to bind the magic inside of you. For sin drives out sin and magic must be bound by like magic. My language was the wind and so they used that to bind me. I remember them drawing on the wind – windows banging open, a hurricane of air around me, petals flying . . .' There was a flicker of excitement in her eyes as she recalled it. 'And then – it was Knotted. Gone. Deadly still.'

'Did it . . . hurt?'

'Pain paves the way.' Rosie smiled. 'If you stay in control that will help. Weakness in feeling, strength in control.'

Anna couldn't take any more tenets. 'But I don't know my language, so how will they bind me?'

Rosie frowned. 'I don't know. Presumably there's a way of dealing with that scenario. Are you sure you don't know your language?'

Anna shook her head, thinking of the seven circles. *Is a curse my language?* 'No. Can they bind any language?' *Can they bind a curse? What will they sacrifice?*

'Yes. Any language, I think. Maybe they won't bind you until you know what it is.'

Anna nodded sceptically. That was not how it felt when she was surrounded by the Binders. There was a hunger in their shrivelled gazes; they wanted to bind her, and soon. They knew something she didn't. 'So your magic is gone now?'

'No. It lives here.' Rosie reached inside her jumper and pulled out a Binders' necklace from around her neck, just like Aunt's. Anna could see the bruises blossoming beneath from her earlier strangling. 'Or at least this represents the magic bound within me.'

'Can you not still access it somehow?'

'Oh no, it would be incredibly difficult for me to practise magic. If I tried to cast now this cord would strangle me and – as you've seen – that's not a pleasant experience.' She put the cord back under her jumper and joined her hands on her lap. 'Of course, during training it is sometimes necessary.'

Anna stood up from the table, her insides recoiling. She didn't want to be here any more, talking to this girl with her contented expression and her glazed eyes.

She began to pack the cakes away. 'Do you know what they're talking about in there?'

Rosie joined her. 'Maybe I'll just have one,' she said, looking towards the doorway. She bit into a cake and then

leant into Anna's ear, icing on her lips. 'They're talking about
the latest news stories. The questionable events around the
capital.'

'Have there been more?'

'Oh yes. They've been keeping track. Only last week a local
eco-pagan group were accused of carrying out perverted acts
in Epping Forest. It wasn't a big story, mostly covered by the
local paper, but still, people were talking. Then there was a
dispute between two neighbours in Hampstead Heath, one
claiming the other killed her dogs with 'black magic'. There
are a couple of articles beginning to notice the pattern of
strange events too – suggesting that the Faceless Women and
their deaths might somehow be behind it all.'

'But that's not true. The Seven protect us.'

'Supposedly, though they seem to be failing, don't they?
Anyway, it doesn't matter if it's true or not. The Seven's
deaths drew attention to the magical world and now cowans
are noticing. That's what matters.' A piece of icing fell from
Rosie's lips. She leant forward again and whispered, 'I overheard Mum on the phone. Apparently the seventh, the one
who escaped, has returned . . .'

Anna's eyes widened. 'Has she said what happened? Who
killed them?'

'I don't think so. The Binders will not be the first to find
out anyway; they are not in direct communication with the
Seven, of course. Why would we be? The Seven are a disgrace
to the world of magic, the First Sinners; their actions may
yet bring terror on us all.'

After that Anna could get no more from Rosie. She made
strained conversation until she could take it no longer and
pretended she had to leave to do homework. Aunt would be
annoyed but that was the least of her worries – she had
revealed her magic in front of the Binders. The punishment
would be severe.

But Aunt did not mention the incident during dinner. It was there nonetheless, their every word stepping around it delicately. They sat sewing in silence and Anna couldn't help glancing at the rose bush, the roses sealed once more.

'Your magic showed its face again,' Aunt said.

'Yes.'

'Are you lying to me?'

Anna's needle halted. She thought of the coven, the spells, the letter to Nana Yaganov. 'No, Aunt, about what?'

'About this boy you like. Peter. You aren't together are you?'

Anna hadn't been expecting that. She shook her head, not having to lie for once.

'You must tell me if you are.'

'Of course.' Anna had no intention of telling Aunt anything of her heart. *Why does Aunt care?* She'd always hated love as much as magic, *but why?*

'Good. I will know the man who breaks your heart.' Aunt continued to brush her hair. 'These are dangerous times, Anna. *If* you decide to become a Binder, you must be ready. You must be in control.'

But she'd never felt less in control in her life.

Anna was losing hope. No letter from Nana had arrived. She'd spent most of the holidays cooped up inside the house with Aunt who was more suspicious than ever since the Binders' visit – forcing her into emotional control sessions almost every night. Anna wasn't sure she could take any more and time was running out, one knot at a time. Then one morning, a few days before returning to school, her hand landed on something crumpled in her sock drawer. She pulled it out and turned it over in confusion, realizing it was an envelope with her name on it. She tore it open.

Dear Ms Everdell,

You're lucky I saw your correspondence – I receive a
lot of fanmail. I'm busy from now until next year.
However, I may be able to squeeeeeze in a visit this
weekend. Find me at Cutz and Clips, Brixton Station
Road, Brixton. Dress smart.

Nana Yaganov (the First)

This weekend! After languishing the days away in self pity
Anna suddenly had no time to waste. She went straight to
Aunt and asked if she could see Effie – *please, I've done all my
work, I've done all my chores, I haven't been out all holidays, just
one visit before school starts.* Aunt took her time to decide, all
day in fact, before angrily assenting and calling Selene to
arrange.

Of course they were not meant to leave Selene's house
but when Anna arrived and showed Effie the letter, they left
immediately for Brixton. Attis insisted on coming too: *because
the letter is clearly unhinged!* Brixton was mayhem: a choppy
sea of commuters, criss-crossing and colliding, motor-mouthed
ticket touts, a man on a microphone preaching about Jesus
the Saviour and a steel drum band brightening the evening
with hot metal sounds. Effie cut through it all, as if crowds
merely existed to part for her.

'That's the one.' Attis pointed at a shop beneath the railway
arches. Its sign was an electric lime green and its windows
were cluttered with posters and special offers and a list of
services. 'Weaves, bonding, ponytails, cornrows, braids,
plaiting . . .'

'You sure?' said Anna, trying and failing to imagine an
ancient witch in a Brixton barbers. The door was open, a man
standing on the threshold smoking. There were several men
inside, talking and laughing. No one seemed to be cutting
hair. Music blared.

'Well, it's the name on her letter, which doesn't mean to say that it is correct.' Attis stopped outside the shop.

'You guys wait here,' said Anna.

'I'm coming in too,' he said.

'No. I think it'll be better if I go in alone. I'll be fine.'

Attis frowned. 'I'm watching from the window then.'

Anna approached the man in the doorway. 'Is a woman called Nana Yaganov inside?'

He gave Anna a long, hard look and then stepped aside. Anna walked into the rabble of loud voices and music, feeling entirely out of place.

'Er, does anyone know a Nana Yaganov?' she said, but no one appeared to hear her. A dog jumped off one of the men's laps and barked at her. Someone turned the music down.

'Boys, this girl is trying to say something,' he yelled. The room quietened.

'Does anyone here know a Nana Yaganov?' Her voice sounded small.

'Who's asking?' A cracked voice came from the corner. One of the men stepped aside respectfully and revealed an old woman sitting in one of the chairs. She was so small and stooped and wearing so many ragged layers of clothing that Anna would probably not have noticed her even if she'd been in sight. She spun round to face Anna, narrowing her eyes, which cut through her face like two deep crevasses in a mountain range of wrinkles.

'I'm Anna Everdell. I wrote you a letter . . .'

'Everdell.' Yaganov said the word as if she were biting into it. 'Yes.' She turned back around, facing the mirror. Anna waited, growing more uncomfortable. One of the men stepped in front of the doorway, blocking her exit. 'Are you here by your own free will or by compulsion?' Yaganov croaked.

'I don't entirely know,' said Anna. 'Are you Nana?'

Anna could hear Attis trying to get through the door.

'Nana Yaganov. The oldest witch in Europe and a curse expert, having cast numerous in my own lifetime and plenty in other lifetimes too. Come and brush my hair.'

Anna walked up to the old woman, the men's eyes following.

'Go on, don't be shy.'

Anna picked up a brush, reflecting on whether this was the most absurd moment of her life so far. The old woman lifted herself up in the chair and Anna ran the brush through her hair – or what was left of it. It was grey and long and sparse, a purpled scalp peeping through. After she'd pulled the brush through carefully it tangled again almost immediately. She could see Effie peering through the glass window with a what-the-hell-are-you-doing look on her face.

Nana cackled wickedly. 'One strand of my hair can break a man's neck, do you know that? What pretty hair you have – maybe you can lend me yours?'

Anna looked at herself in the mirror, but now she was the one sitting in the chair and Nana was brushing her hair; with each stroke it was falling out – golden-red strands clogging the brush, dusting the floor, her own scalp beginning to show . . .

Anna screamed and Nana laughed silently. Anna looked away from the mirror and realized that she was still the one brushing and her hair was still intact on her head.

'Oh, you're making heavy weather of it,' said Nana, pulling the brush from Anna's hand, 'and I'm hungry. I've been starving since 1978. I need a good feeding before I tell you what you want to know.'

'What do I want to know?'

'Oh everything, everything. The dark side of the moon. Come on.'

With great difficulty, Nana stood up from the chair. Anna

put a hand out to help but was batted away. Nana walked bundle-like through the room of men and out into the night.

Attis grabbed Anna. 'You screamed.'

'I thought I saw something – it was nothing—'

'Where shall we go for breakfast?' Nana interrupted.

Attis looked down at Nana; he must have been twice as tall as her. 'You must be—'

'No introductions. I know who you all are, knight in shining armour. Did you steal my trolley?' She looked around, her eyes passing over Effie as if she wasn't there. Effie frowned. 'Oh, there.' She dawdled over to the alleyway by the side of the barbers and pulled a large trolley from it. It was piled high with what were either her possessions or garbage; a fishing rod stuck out of the top.

'This way, this way,' she said impatiently, as if they hadn't been waiting for her. She pushed the trolley down the street and stopped outside a murky café which on its sign claimed to provide 'Genuine British Food'. Inside, it smelt of grease, the windows were dirty, walls wooden and bare, the tables utilitarian – their only decoration bottles of ketchup and mustard.

'They serve the best shepherd's pie since Ailis McConville's in West Kerry, 1843.' Nana descended into a seat. She was small and shrivelled but not frail; there was flesh on her bones and, despite her slow movements, there was a robustness to her. The waitress came over.

Nana scowled. 'I'll have a bowl of Cheerios and tea, black as a nun's habit.'

The waitress smiled, looking unsurprised by the breakfast order at nine o'clock at night. The rest of them ordered drinks.

'We've heard a lot about you, Nana,' said Effie.

'Well, I've heard nothing about you.'

Attis laughed.

'Don't know what you're laughing at, pretty boy. You've got nothing to be cheerful about.'

He stopped. It was hard to do anything when Nana turned her eyes on you. They were dark caves, deep wells, black as a crow. Her face was shifting sands, one moment all chin and nose, mouth tucked up in gummy laughter, the next it had latched onto you, shrew-like and scornful, scissored with wrinkles. Anna had no idea how old she was – ancient, perhaps.

'Nana,' said Anna gently. 'I take it you read my letter and you know that I'm here to find out more about my mother, Marie Everdell . . . and her death.'

'The past is dead. Hurrah.' The waitress placed a bowl of Cheerios in front of her. 'Now this is life, look at them.' She held a small Cheerio up to her eye. 'Each a little germ of being.' She put it in her mouth and sucked.

Anna pressed on. 'I have been practising magic recently and I fear there's something wrong with it. It points to a sign—'

Nana leant forward and sniffed Anna. 'HO! CURSED!' She held up her spoon and banged it down onto the table. 'CURSED SHE IS. CURSED. Cut to credits. Cut to credits.' Her eyes were focused behind them, as if she were talking to an invisible director. She made cutting motions across her neck. 'It's why your mother came to me. About her curse. Just like this. Begging. Afraid. CUT TO CREDITS.'

Anna could see nothing but the snarling face of Nana, the words erupting from her mouth. *It's true. I'm cursed . . .*

'Come on, Anna, let's go,' said Attis. 'She's a nutter.'

Nana chanted:

> 'Jack, be nimble,
> Jack, be quick,
> Jack, jump over
> The candlestick.'

A Cheerio slid off Nana's thin, hairy lip. 'Why don't you take her' – she made eyes at Effie – 'and go have a smooch in the alleyway? It's what you really want, isn't it? Is it?'

Attis snarled and then pounced across the table, his hands pulling Effie's face towards him and then they were kissing – their mouths hungry for each other, his hands tearing off her shirt.

'I'm not going anywhere,' said Effie. Anna blinked and saw Attis still sitting next to her, looking pale.

'Oh, you're going somewhere, Effie Fawkes, nowhere good. Fear drives you even now. I see it inside you like a mad clock. Will his arms be there to hold you? Or will they hold another?' She smiled a black smile.

'Just tell us what you know. Unless you truly know nothing at all.' Effie jutted her chin out defiantly, but then her eyes went wide, her mouth slack. *What are you showing her?*

'Now she's getting clever. Bright and sharp as a mirror, ho!' She looked back to Anna.

'Do you know something?' said Anna, hanging onto her questions like dinghies in an ever-expanding sea. 'About this curse? Please.'

'Curse. Not a fluffy word, is it? It's endless, deep as the earth itself. A tiny prison. I know every curse that has ever been made, Everdell. I see them even now, drenching this world like black rain, nourishing the soils of our nightmares.'

Attis exhaled loudly. 'This is pointless, Anna.'

'You're pointless. Your whole existence is pointless,' Nana snarled at him. 'But you know that already, don't you?' She smiled a terrible, pitying smile. Attis looked down at his hands.

'Count out my change,' she snapped at Anna, emptying her purse all over the table, copper and silver coins running everywhere. 'Little piles, please, little piles. Orderly as soldiers.'

'They say you know the Seven,' said Effie, as Anna began to organize the coins. Anna didn't recognize half of them;

one was definitely a shilling and several were from foreign countries.

'They say a lot, these people:

> 'The more he saw the less he spoke,
> The less he spoke the more he heard.
> Why can't we all be like that wise old bird?'

'Are they dead? Are they going to come back?' Effie pursued.

'Protcctresses of heaven. Nature in female form. Keepers of the languages. The good within us all.' Nana cackled. 'Oh, the Seven will be back. Too late now though, isn't it? They've really messed up this time.'

'What do you mean *too late*?' Effie asked.

The coin Anna was holding burned suddenly into her flesh, leaving a brand there. She called out in pain. Attis reached out to her, but then it was gone, nothing there at all.

Nana turned to her, eyes feeding greedily on Anna's fear. 'We should all be afraid, for they are returning.' Her voice was low and slow now, as if it were coming from somewhere else. 'All of us. Witches. Women. Souls who question the way things are – free-thinkers, deep-thinkers, the cows who hoped to jump over the moon. All are at risk. Especially the cursed.' She pointed a spindly finger. 'Your red hair is enough to mark you out.' She leant forward and grabbed a chunk of it. 'If the dark days come again, shave it off, shave it all off.'

Anna felt a pure terror take over her soul.

'Fear not, dear. You have the bone structure for baldness. Must be off.'

'Wait. Who are returning? The Hunters? Why are the cursed at risk?'

Nana began to laugh, smacking her tongue against her lips. 'You already know, Anna. A story. Just a small story. Small as a key. People think stories are harmless but they are the most dangerous weapon mankind has.'

'What story?'

'Ah! The usual kind. A prophecy. The Hunters have always loved a prophecy. Gives them a sense of purpose, a reason to shine their boots.'

'What prophecy?'

But Nana had stood up from the table, scattering the piles of money Anna had sorted. She gave the waitress a ten-pound note from her pocket and left.

'She's crazy. Don't bother,' Attis shouted, but Anna followed her out onto the street.

'Nana, what is my curse? I can't get anywhere until I know that.'

'How does the wolf know what its teeth are for?'

'How is that meant to help me?'

'If I help you, you won't learn.' Nana reached for her trolley. 'Study your dreams, then, for they are free. Follow them to the edge of the woods and beyond, where your name isn't Anna and curses croak like frogs.'

Anna grabbed the trolley with both hands as Effie and Attis came out of the café. 'I'm not going anywhere until you help me.'

Nana smiled a jagged tear of a smile. 'FINE.' She threw her hands up in the air dramatically. 'Three questions. You can have three questions for three truths, for truth is golden in these days of darkness. Soon all will be lies.'

Three questions hardly felt like enough but Anna took her chance before it was gone. 'What is my curse?'

'If I tell you now you'll never escape it. I shall give you a riddle instead.' She cleared her throat. 'The truth is within the leaves. The mirror within the mirror. The mirror is the key.'

Anna repeated the words in her head. They made as much sense as everything else Nana had said. 'How do I stop it?'

'Curses take but a moment to cast and a lifetime to live out – most probably a short one. There are only two things in this world which can break a curse. The magic of the one who cast it in the first place, or a spell more powerful. Sadly there is little as powerful as a curse.'

'Did my mother die because of the curse?'

'Oh yes, oh yes, as you will too. Play with love and you'll play with death.' Nana cackled and her open mouth was an abyss. Anna was filled with a fear she could not escape from – how could she escape from what she didn't know?

'What does love have to do with anything?'

'Oh, everything. All curses begin with love.'

Anna thought of Aunt's hatred of all things love, her warnings, her sudden interest in Peter . . . *Did their family curse begin with love?*

Nana shuffled closer and whispered in her ear: 'All you need you already have. Now let an old woman be.' Anna saw Effie and Attis reflected in the shop window behind her. He was strangling Effie to death, as her father had strangled her mother.

Anna spun around, begging that the nightmare vision would be gone.

'What is it?' Attis said.

'Nothing.'

She turned back around but Nana was already halfway down the street, people jumping out of the way of her trolley.

They walked away in stunned silence, Anna's mind still lost in the dark tunnel of Nana's eyes.

Attis began to chuckle, an unnaturally high sound compared to the deep river of his normal voice. 'I hate people who say I told you so, so I'll try and find a different way of putting it. I was right. The woman is bonkers. High-security institution bonkers. Curses and prophecies and riddles. Anyone can spout that kind of rubbish, Anna.'

'She was powerful, you have to give her that,' said Effie, glancing between them. She looked pale. 'Those chimera visions she did – did she do them to you guys too?'

They rounded the corner onto the high street to be met by a battery of people. Anna dodged out of the way, thankful for the distraction – she didn't want to answer Effie's question. She didn't want to have to describe what she'd seen. *What did Effie see?* Anna turned and found Effie's eyes. They stared at each other in a moment of silent battle. They would never say. Anna remembered Effie and Attis's bodies writhing as one, Attis's hands around Effie's neck – the kind of thoughts that did not go away.

'She had a flair for the dramatics,' Attis agreed grimly. 'Anna, I hope you're not actually considering the things she said.'

'What? That I'm cursed? That there's no hope? That I'm going to die?'

'In a nutshell.'

'*The truth is within the leaves. The mirror within the mirror. The mirror is the key.*'

'That riddle will send you on a wild goose chase, probably a dangerous one. Now, there's a great pizza place just inside the market, I suggest we drown our sorrows in melted cheese.'

'I'm going back home. I need to clear my head,' said Anna, beginning down the tube steps.

Attis grabbed her hand. 'Don't. If you go home now you'll be worrying all night.'

There was a loud cough from behind them. 'I'm going home too.' Anna dropped his hand and turned to find Effie, arms folded, at the top of the stairs, blocking a trail of people trying to get past. Anna didn't think she'd ever heard Effie say she was going home on a Friday night.

'I want to re-emphasize: melted cheese,' said Attis, but Anna was already halfway down, the splintered rumble of the train ahead bringing Nana's laughter back into her head.

# MAYPOLE

*Contract Knot: To make an unbreakable oath.*

*Knot Spells, The Book of the Binders*

'"With an increasing number of what can only be described as 'unnatural' events, police have to start looking at whether these acts are somehow related. What ritual were the Faceless Women trying to enact that night so many months ago? Were their deaths intended to unleash some kind of dark force that is now spreading outwards across the capital?" Halden Kramer, Head of Communications for the Institute for Research into Organized and Ritual Violence.'

Anna dropped the paper she'd been reading aloud from down on the table where they were sitting in the common room.

'Sounds like a nutjob to me,' said Rowan. 'I mean, what's the Institute for Research into Organized and Ritual Violence? There's a reason the police aren't listening to them.'

'But people are noticing.' *The Binders are noticing!* 'They're one step away from calling the Faceless Women' – Anna lowered her voice to a barely audible whisper – 'witches.'

'Actually a lot of people are already calling them witches.'

Rowan showed Anna her phone with all of the various comments in response to Kramer's latest statement. 'But an equally large number are claiming they're aliens. These are nothing more than conspiracy theories.'

'These are sensationalist sites and papers too,' Effie rebuffed. 'Not exactly serious news.'

Anna picked a fly out of her food with irritation. She was not in a good mood. Whether the threats had any credibility or were the ravings of lunatics, Aunt was still tense. Anna hadn't come any closer to solving Nana's riddle. And school was worse than ever. Anna had hoped that the rumours might abate over the break but they had merely stored themselves up and then unleashed themselves with renewed force, fuelled by fresh whispers. Flies were flying through the corridors, teeming at the windows; dying, rotting, multiplying; filling her mind like a dark fog. Pest control couldn't locate the source of the problem and had recommended the school be temporarily closed. It was only Headmaster Connaughty's stubbornness keeping it open.

'What about the school rumours?' Anna snapped. 'They're not going away either.'

'Things are finally getting interesting, if that's what you mean,' said Effie.

'Did you see what Darcey wrote about us yesterday?' said Manda.

'No.'

'FLIES AND LIES. FLIES AND LIES. THE WHORE. THE NOBODY. THE VIRGIN. THE BEAST. THEY ARE BEHIND IT ALL!' Effie recited with delight.

'Everyone just thinks she's jealous,' said Rowan. 'Which she is.'

'Did you hear Corinne's Yoga Club has been cancelled? She kept yelling at everyone.' Manda laughed.

'Is that a rumour?' asked Anna. 'Or true? If it's true then

don't you see, we're not dealing with rumours any more – they're real.'

'Good. Darcey and Headmaster Connaughty would be hilarious. Speaking of, what is this about Karim asking you out?' Effie elbowed Manda playfully.

Manda blushed. 'Maybe.'

'One hundred per cent he has. They're going for coffee,' Rowan confirmed.

'I'm just worried he's still in love with his ex,' said Manda. 'The last picture of them online together was only three weeks ago and she commented on something he posted two days ago, which suggests they're still in contact. I looked through her pictures – she's really pretty and she looks nothing like me and they've known each other since they were young. I found a picture of them hanging out when they were, like, twelve. How can I compete with that?'

Rowan laughed. 'Just how many pictures of her did you look through?'

'All of them. I looked at all of them. I think I'm in love with him. Can we cast a spell to banish her away?'

'I can look into something,' said Effie.

'No!' said Anna. 'We can't just go around banishing people.'

'It seems a *bit* harsh. Free will and all that,' Rowan agreed.

Manda spluttered. 'If I recall, a few days ago you wanted to cast an infatuation spell on trumpet-boy so he'd finally take notice of you. Free will didn't seem so important to you then.'

'Let's do both.' Effie gave Anna a challenging look.

Anna held Effie's eyes. 'We shouldn't be doing anything to attract *more* attention right now.'

'Anna preaching from her pulpit,' said Effie, 'but I've been told today that Peter has broken up with Darcey. You certainly had a hand in that.'

Anna went quiet, processing the news. *Peter's broken up with Darcey!*

'I didn't do anything.'

'Oh, you didn't think our rumour spell would result in that? Really, Anna, you aren't *that* naive.'

Anna's momentary excitement fizzled to guilt. *She's right.*

Manda raised her nose. 'Yeah, Anna, you've had your wish, now let me have mine.'

'Hey, me first,' said Rowan.

'Rowan, you don't need magic—'

'Girls, girls.' Effie raised her voice above them. 'Look at us bickering. We've finally got what we wanted: the Juicers' power decapitated, the school falling at our feet, magic at our fingertips, and all we can do is argue. This is not the time to fall apart but to come together. It's Beltane this Friday. May Day. The festival of new beginnings. Let's celebrate with a coven initiation ceremony, bind ourselves together as one. Forever. It'll be fun.'

'Beltane is my favourite,' said Rowan, bubbly again. 'The whole family gets garlanded up and we sow seeds in the garden until sunrise. Mum gets tipsy on hawthorn brandy and then ends up tipping it everywhere. Apparently she's "feeding the soil".'

'Initiation sounds painful. Will there be pain?' asked Manda.

'Only the pleasurable kind. Come on, it's going to be the best night of your lives.'

Anna did not want to back down but she couldn't risk any kind of magical exposure, not with Aunt so close to snapping. Their spell was out of control and she couldn't shake off the worry that her own cursed magic might be at the root of it. 'I'll come as long as we do something about the rumour spell.'

Effie exhaled loudly.

'Selene?' said Anna. 'I'll talk to her. Tell her what's going on and see what she thinks.'

'Fine! Saturday morning you're free to speak to Selene about whatever you want.'

Only once Effie had agreed did Anna allow herself to get excited by the thought of Friday. Anna secured permission from Aunt to stay at Effie's while Manda convinced her mum too, claiming they needed to work on a school project. Selene had been happy to lie to Mrs Richards on their behalf. Nothing was standing in their way. It was exactly what the coven needed and, after her week of control sessions, it was exactly what Anna needed too.

On Friday, they headed for the roof. The sewing room was inhospitable – the altar was littered with flies, dead and alive and somewhere between the two; the plants were dried corpses and the smoothie cups overspilling with rancid liquid; the witch ball had burst, black sludge running over the broken glass. The horns of the skull were forming a twisted spiral . . .

'We'll deal with it later,' said Effie.

Rowan had brought a collection of May flowers with her – hawthorn blossoms, cowslips, bluebells, daisies – and they sat in the fading light threading them through each other's hair.

Rowan handed Anna a dark bottle of something. 'I stole some of Mum's hawthorn brandy. May Day gold right there.'

Anna tried it. It tasted sweet and succulent, dizzyingly rich.

Effie took a swig and raised an eyebrow. 'I fully intend to go a-maying tonight.'

'What's a-maying?' said Manda.

'Traditionally it's when all the boys and girls went off into the woods and fields and made sweet love to celebrate the season of fertility and welcome summer in,' Rowan explained. 'Whole villages at it like rabbits.'

'That's disgusting,' said Manda, stifling a giggle.

'It's sex magic. Powerful stuff.' Effie pulled a lewd face at Manda. 'I've heard the Seven draw on it annually to replenish Britain's magic.'

Rowan sang loudly:

> 'Oh, do not tell the priest our plight,
> Or he would call it sin,
> But we have been out in the woods all night,
> A-conjuring summer in.

'The fun was ruined eventually – all the festivities got banned, even maypoles. A maypole never hurt anybody unless it fell on them.'

'These people were just fertilizing the crops. They were being practical,' said Effie.

Rowan nudged her. 'What crops are you fertilizing tonight then? Seeing as we're in London.'

'I'm sure there's a crop somewhere that needs me.'

'Can he be involved?' Rowan asked, looking towards Attis, who was swinging himself over the railings. He was dressed in green and wearing a mask of leaves. Horns protruded from his head.

'What beautiful May maidens stand before me. Salutations from the Green Man, plougher of fields, spreader of seed, bringer of new life.' He dipped into a low, embellished bow.

His mask didn't look like a mask at all, but as if the skin around his eyes had become an oak leaf. Rowan prodded at the curled horns. 'These are deep-rooted, they're coming out of your head! Wait, are you actually the Green Man?'

Attis considered her theory, then smiled his crooked smile, looking all the more roguish for his costume. 'I'd love to be, but alas, this is just a very good costume, helped along with a touch of magic.'

'The moon's almost up! We need to get dressed,' Effie

announced. She presented each of them with a white, gauze-like piece of cloth. Anna held it up and realized it was a dress, so finely woven it was hard to know where it ended and the moonlight began.

'Selene bought them for us. They're skyclad dresses,' Effie explained.

'What are skyclad dresses?' asked Anna.

'Wait and see.' Effie started to throw her clothes off.

Anna looked over at Attis, who gave her a smile and turned away. 'I shall stand guard and protect your virtues.'

They got themselves changed, goose-pimpling in the cool spring air. Despite their different sizes and heights the dresses fitted each of them perfectly. Once they were ready Attis stepped back out of the shadows. 'Fairer May Queens I never saw. You will end global warming with your fertility. Shall we proceed?' He held out an arm to Effie.

'Where are we doing this initiation anyway?' asked Manda as they walked back through the now-empty school.

'On the playing fields,' Effie replied.

'Are you crazy?' Manda's voice filled the corridors. 'We're not allowed on the school fields now.'

'We're only going to light a little balefire . . .' said Attis.

'FIRE? That's against every school rule ever written.'

'Therein lies the fun,' said Effie.

Manda clung to Anna's arm. 'How do we always end up in these situations?'

'Here, have some more.' Rowan offered them the bottle. 'We're going to need it.'

Anna considered the hundred repercussions there would be if they got caught but let the liquid spread and clog every sensible passageway in her brain. The lure of freedom was too much. She needed a release or she'd surely go mad.

Outside the moon was hiding its modesty behind clouds. Attis carefully laid out a pile of rowan wood he had lugged with him and struck two thin pieces of metal together. Although he was standing several feet away from the wood it burst into flame, spitting and snapping its hot fingers at the air. He laid a hefty plank across it. Effie made them all take off their shoes and the grass beneath Anna's feet was refreshingly damp. Mammoth trees bordered the field like shadowy guarding giants; black smoke spiralled into the air above them.

They took up positions around the fire and called on their elements. It was easy with the night winds around them; the cool earth beneath their feet; the fire warm on their faces. *So many threads, so many worlds.* Effie stepped forward, hands outstretched towards its heat, her skin dappled with flame, black hair glowing metal-bright. 'Ready for the initiation?'

Anna had been preparing for one initiation her whole life, to become one of the Binders – to be Knotted – the threat of being *ready* always hanging over her. This initiation wasn't a question. Despite everything going on with the rumour spell, Anna would have given everything to be a member of the Dark Moon forever. She was ready.

'I call to thee, Goddess of Spring,' Effie began:

> 'Mother and lover of the Great Horned One,
> The blossom blows, the flower opens,
> The earth swells under moons new.
> Join us tonight and forever as one:
> A coven brave, a coven true,
> Bring us joy! Bring us abundance!
> Bound by the fires of your womb,
> May we leap through flame,
> And give our hearts to you!'

She looked at them. 'Initiates, cast your circle of protection and then you must each pass through the flames to prove your allegiance to the Coven of the Dark Moon now and forever more. The Horned One will wait on the other side to seal your fate and ensure our everlasting abundance with a five-fold kiss. Go forth with hearts brave and true!'

The fire raged, crackling and popping and releasing dark wood scents and hot sap. *I have to pass through that?*

Effie stepped up onto the plank with bare feet and her ghostly form disappeared into the fire, flames engulfing her. She appeared as a shadow on the other side – a horned silhouette welcoming her. The others looked nervously at one another.

'Don't be afraid!' Effie yelled. 'Cast your circle and you won't burn!'

Rowan came forwards. 'This is madness!' she cried, stepping into the flames.

Anna returned to the moment and the magic, focusing on her circle and not the terror of the flames ahead. She could feel her circle around her: strong and pure; complete and impenetrable. *Impenetrable enough?*

'You go next,' Manda squeaked.

Anna nodded and stepped up onto the plank. She could feel the heat of the flames on her face. *Protect me.* She found Attis's outline on the other side and focused on it. *Protect me.* She half closed her eyes against the flames and walked onwards, encouraged by the fact that she wasn't currently on fire. *Protect me.* The flames swirled around her, beautiful and terrible. And then she was out on the other side, dizzy from the warmth but unscathed, Attis standing before her, offering her a hand. She took it and steadied herself, stepping onto the cool grass.

'I did it,' she said, hopping about. She could see Effie and Rowan dancing in the distance.

'All right, May Queen, stay still and let me finish,' Attis commanded, his eyes behind his mask in motion, spiralling, full of heat.

Anna stood still, unsure what the five-fold kiss entailed. He dropped to his knees and bent down to kiss her feet. 'Blessed be thy feet which stepped through the flames.'

She could have sworn his lips were just as hot as the fire. They sent small sparks up her body.

He kissed her knees. 'Blessed be thy knees that kneel before the Great Goddess.'

He raised himself up and kissed just below her belly button, through the fabric of her dress. Anna found she could not move. 'Blessed be thy womb, bringer of life and abundance.'

He half stood so they were eye level but she could not meet his eyes. He leant forwards and kissed above each of her breasts. 'Blessed be thy breasts, formed in beauty.'

He smirked and looked up at her. Before she could process what was happening, he rose to his full height and kissed her on the lips – his own a sudden flame and then gone. 'Blessed be thy lips, that shall utter the Seven Names.'

They watched each other. Anna's breath was quick and shallow, his lips still parted where they had touched hers. 'Forever,' he said. The flames crackled behind them. 'Forever a member of this coven. Run and be free, May Queen!'

Anna reminded her legs how to move. With one last look, she darted away, joining Effie and Rowan and running wild as she'd never run wild before. The school grounds seemed to stretch for miles around them. Their kingdom. They were the Queens of Summer and magic was threaded into every fibre of the air.

Effie grabbed her hands and spun her round. 'Forever!'

'Forever!' Anna whooped. Effie handed her the bottle and she poured the sweet brandy down her throat, hearing Attis's voice in the distance, coaxing Manda. Anna handed it to Rowan and then gasped, pointing at Rowan. 'Your dress! Where's it gone?' Rowan stood before her in her underwear, the moon on her skin.

'What do you mean? I'm wearing my dress!' Rowan looked down and cried out, covering herself with her arms. 'I'm naked! How the – No, look, I'm still wearing it.' Rowan moved the fabric and parts of it shimmered, barely there at all. 'Anna, you're naked too!'

Effie laughed thickly. 'They're skyclad dresses.' She pointed up to the moon, which had come out from behind the clouds. 'They disappear when the moon comes out.' Anna looked down and saw that she was just as exposed.

'Effie!'

'You both look like radiant wood nymphs.'

Rowan laughed. 'I'm a bloody radiant wood mushroom over here.'

Anna took another swig and decided to embrace it. They cheered as Manda finally stepped through the fire, looking as if she was about to faint into Attis's arms.

'You did it!' Effie whooped. 'Drink and be merry! Let's dance!'

They formed a moving circle around the fire, dancing like flames; the smoke tangling itself in Anna's hair; the moon drifting in and out from behind clouds, covering them up and stripping them bare. Attis dancing bare-chested, iron tattoo glinting, howling at the moon. It didn't seem to matter out here, under the stars, the earth charged beneath their feet – four shadows and one horned creature, moving as if the earth moved around them.

'Everyone call down the first rains of May!' Effie called out. 'Think of rain! Dance as if you are rain! The first rain of May keeps you young and beautiful all year!'

Anna imagined the rain on her skin. She let water fill up her bones and moved like liquid, slipping and sliding, hair like a storm, stamping her feet like raindrops. *Be the rain!* She was assured by the fact that everyone else looked like a lunatic too.

And then the rain came. A small and very localized shower just above them. They raised their faces to it, let it run over them. Attis howled. The fire sizzled out and they danced, soaked to their bones, covered in falling silver rain as if the moon itself were dissolving above them.

Somewhere between dancing in the rain, Effie handing her a new outfit to wear and several further swigs of hawthorn brandy, Anna found herself agreeing to go out. She couldn't stop herself – she didn't want to stop herself. It wasn't as though she was at Selene's, so if Aunt checked on her she would be dead anyway. *May as well die having fun.*

They took the tube to Oxford Circus. They wove through the crowded streets, handfuls of flowers in their arms, handing them out to confused and wary passers-by. 'Take a flower, make a wish! Flowers for wishes!'

'May love equals free love!' Effie shouted, throwing a bunch of blossoms over three middle-aged women who scattered in fear.

Anna gave a flower to a homeless man and told him to make a wish. It bloomed under her touch and he looked up at her as if she truly was a magical wood nymph. *Make his wish come true,* she whispered to the night.

'Where are we going?' asked Manda.

Effie jumped on Attis's back and pointed. 'To Mayfair, of course!'

'Mayfair was where they used to hold the huge May Fair in London every year, hence the name. Until it got cancelled,' said Rowan.

'Cancelled for cowans, not for us,' Effie bellowed.

They turned down a small alleyway between an Italian restaurant and a dark-windowed building that looked like offices shut up for the night. There was a wooden door, smaller than Attis. He ran his hands down the wood. 'An

Elder Door. They're made of elder wood and are all over London, all over the country. They interconnect, so if you pass through an Elder Door you are entering an Elder Door elsewhere. Somewhere else. Only witches can pass through so they're extra secure.'

There were no signs above it, nothing to suggest it was even open, and yet it opened at their touch. Anna walked through and found herself abruptly in a nightclub, although whether the club was in the building she'd stepped into she wasn't sure.

'Equinox,' Effie shouted over the sudden wall of music. 'One of the best witch clubs in the city and it goes all out for festival days.'

'I can't believe I'm in Equinox!' Rowan yelled. 'My brother has talked about this place but even he can't get in.'

'I think this might be the first time I've felt cool in my life!' Manda laughed giddily.

Anna had dreamt about the freedoms of the magical world for so long and now here they were before her. The room was huge and bell-shaped, garlanded everywhere with flowers and vines. Around its edges were cushioned areas and cosy alcoves in which groups and couples lounged. Dominating its centre was an enormous maypole, reaching all the way up to the high ceiling. Scantily clad men and women were dancing around it, weaving its brightly coloured ribbons into complex, mesmerizing patterns.

'Honeysuckle cocktail?' A woman with iridescent blue hair offered Anna a glass of amber liquid from a tray. Anna took one and sipped, suddenly understanding why bees liked climbing inside flowers so much – the drink was sweet nectar.

She looked more closely at the flowers camouflaging the walls – liquid was dripping from their centres, running down to the floor, which was soft and earth-like beneath her feet. Some of the liquid ran into ornate dishes along the wall. Rowan dipped her finger in one. 'Weird . . .'

'What's this?' Effie asked a guy leaning against it.

'Dew face wash, for beauty. Not that you need it, what's your name?'

'Wouldn't you like to know?'

'For beauty?' said Rowan, splashing it on her face. 'I'm going to need a vat.'

Anna rinsed her face with the cool water. She hadn't really expected it to do anything but when Rowan and Manda turned around they looked the same and yet not the same at all. They looked unreal, as if the reality of them had been stripped away, leaving something luminous – skin like rippling water, lips glowing dewy, eyes shining.

'Anna, your eyes are so green!' Rowan pointed at them, mesmerized.

Anna grabbed Rowan's face. 'You look incredible!' They weaved into the crowd. Attis had disappeared, as usual. *Doesn't matter.*

The centre of the club was a riot of colour, full of people in May Day outfits – faces painted and masked, wearing towering flower headdresses or antlers or fairy masks and wings, fluttering of their own accord. The ends of the hair of the girl next to her appeared to be on fire; there were more Green Men than she could count. Lights dappled colours over all of it, turning like sunlight through the petals of a flower. *Are these my people?* She realized with head-spinning wonder just how cut off she'd been, how blinkered her vision because of the Binders. Their world was dark but this one was full of light.

Anna danced, finding everything more vivid than it had ever been before – the people, the music, the colours. *If these are my people I never want to leave!* They were friendly, decking them with flower garlands and offering drinks and sweets: ginger strawberries, sugared bluebells and little maypoles made out of liquorice. Someone handed out glasses of champagne 'filled with the bubbles of clean spring winds'.

Effie joined them and Anna couldn't quite remember how but within an hour they were dancing on a table, a crowd cheering them on below – the maypole spinning around them or they were spinning around the maypole. *Everything is spinning.* Effie grabbed her and pointed. 'Do you see them?'

In a room of unbounded ostentation a medley of people had just entered, who somehow – impossibly – managed to stand out more than the rest. Anna wondered what it was. Their costumes were certainly more outrageous, the way they moved through the crowd bolder and more brazen, yet it was something else – they all had that same look about them, of mischief and mayhem, of people who don't live life quite where everyone else does, but instead at its edges, existing purely to test its limits.

'Who are they?' Anna asked, entranced.

'The Wild Hunt,' said Effie. 'One of the more unconventional groves. Everyone's young, everyone's mad.'

'What's their magical language?'

'Hedonism. Pure unbridled hedonism.' Effie cackled. 'I like to play with them. Now which one shall I have fun with tonight?'

'Which one?'

'I have several Wild Hunt lovers – see him there, Jeudon, he doesn't speak but he's an animal on the dance floor. Or Emilia, she looks sweet, right? She's not, she terrifies me. It's always fun though. But then there's Ivor, the one that looks like he could break a brick with his bare hands.' She pointed to a hulking blond man dressed in a floor-length green coat with gigantic antlers jutting from his head. 'Hmmm.' Effie began to move her finger between them. 'Entry, mentry, cutrie, corn, apple seed and apple thorn. Crossroads dirt and casket lock, seven geese flying in a flock.' It landed on Jeudon. She moved it across to Ivor and shrugged. 'Who am I kidding? He's my favourite. Come on.'

Effie jumped off the table, pulling Anna, who was thankfully prevented from falling on her face by the crowd. They approached the motley crew, Effie tapping Ivor on the shoulder.

'Effie,' said Ivor in a low rumble of a voice, looking her up and down. 'I could kiss you, you look so good.' He pulled her into his arms and did exactly that and then turned to Anna. 'Will that line work twice?'

'No,' Anna replied, laughing.

'This is my friend Anna,' said Effie. 'Now kiss me again.'

'Disgusting,' said a voice from behind them. Anna turned around to find a handsome, black-haired man with a smile that ran from ear to ear. He was wearing an unbuttoned gold shirt, red trousers and a crown sitting at a jaunty angle on his head. 'Get an alcove!' he shouted at them and then looked back to Anna, smiling. The smile felt genuine but his eyes were thick with trickery. 'Oliver Moridi, at your service.' He gave a deep bow. 'I am somewhere between an Iranian prince and an Iranian pauper and I've never seen a girl with such beautiful hair in all my life. Did you walk right out of Oz?' There was something androgynous about his movements; they were a little theatrical and strangely sexy.

'Good to meet you, Oliver,' she shouted. 'I'm Anna. Are you in this Wild Hunt too?'

'I am, sweet Dorothy. We pursue life's pleasures and drink of their marrows deep. I ask you now, in great seriousness, will you come and play games with me?'

'What does this game involve?' Anna raised an eyebrow as she'd seen Effie do, her head still light from the drink and Oliver's attention making her feel bolder than she normally would. It was strangely thrilling.

'Well, you choose—' He produced a die between his fingers. 'Roll it and see.'

Anna took the die from him with a wry look and assessed

the options: *Drink. Play. Dance. Feast. Fly. Leave.* She rolled it on the table next to them.

The dice stopped on *Kiss.*

*'Wait, that was not one of the options—'*

'Fate has spoken; we cannot deny it.' He put a hand on his heart.

Anna laughed. 'Not fair. It's a trick die!'

'Trickery is exceptionally fair.'

Anna rolled it again. It read: *Slap.*

She looked up and he bent forwards, puckering his lips. She slapped him playfully.

'Red-haired and feisty, my favourite.'

'Ollie.' Attis appeared from nowhere. 'You getting yourself slapped by girls again?'

'Not any girl, the most beautiful Dorothy I have ever met. She slaps so well.'

'I have yet to receive the pleasure,' said Attis. 'Although it has been threatened, often.'

'You two know each other?' said Oliver. 'I should have known. Where there's a beautiful woman, Attis is never far away. He's both my nemesis and my hero.'

'Well, I thought you were doing just fine on your own,' said Anna.

Oliver held out a hand. 'Shall we dance?'

'I think we shall.' Anna took it, glancing back at Attis with a playful look of her own.

She danced with Oliver, surrounded by the Wild Hunt, who were bedecked in ostentatious, bejewelled outfits and a ridiculous selection of hats and horns. Oliver spun around her, jigging and laughing and pulling her into swift, dizzying embraces until she barely knew which way was up or down. Effie disappeared to one of the alcoves with Ivor. Rowan danced her way between them all looking like a child in a sweet shop. 'Manda's gone a-maying,' she laughed in Anna's ear. 'Or at least she's kissing some guy over there. This bunch are great, aren't they? So bloody dapper. I like the one in the antlered top hat, but, Anna, I've had too much to drink and I'm not even sure if what I'm doing can be classified as dancing any more . . .'

Anna laughed. 'I'll get us some water.' She wasn't sure where exactly to find water – she hadn't seen a bar anywhere.

She wove back through the crowd and asked one of the people serving cocktails. They ran off and returned with two bottles of water which didn't taste like water, but faintly like the inside of a plant stem: crisp and clean. Whatever it was, it cleared her head. She looked back to the dance floor but couldn't locate Rowan. She walked up a curling stairway to a balcony overlooking the room and searched the crowd.

'Look who's returned from her soirée with the Wild Hunt.' Attis stepped forward from the balcony, swaying gently, a hazy look in his normally arrow-sharp eyes, a lazy smile on his face. 'You should beware, Oliver is quite the seducer.'

'It takes one to know one,' said Anna.

'Touché,' said Attis, trying to shoot his fingers at her but failing.

'Are you drunk?' Anna smirked.

'I don't know. I've forgotten.'

'This'll be fun to watch.' Anna folded her arms, assessing him.

'I know what you're thinking.' He sighed. 'What if he's so drunk he can't dance any more? I can see the anxiety in your eyes. Fear not, the more drunk I get, the better I dance.' He did a little tap step with his feet, one of which suddenly found itself tangled in the other. He fell against the wall beside her.

Anna giggled. 'Smooth.'

'Hey, you mean girl.' He twisted towards her with an exaggerated sad face. Anna laughed again before realizing how close they were, their faces almost touching, so close she could make out the freckles on the bridge of his nose. She thought of the warmth of his lips on the playing field. She turned away, trying to find Rowan in the crowd again.

'You have a lovely neck,' he said and she could feel his breath on it tickling the strands of hair there. Her own breath caught in her throat. She turned back to find his eyes tracing her. 'The way it curves,' he said distractedly. He moved a hand out as if to touch it but stopped himself.

'You're drunk,' she said, moving her hand over her neck self-consciously.

'And you're impossible to work out, Anna Everdell.'

'I wasn't aware you were trying to work me out.'

'So self-contained, closed up.' He made an inarticulate gesture with his hands, lost in thought. 'Like a flower in winter. This was all meant to be simple, but it's not any more.'

'What was meant to be simple?'

He turned his eyes on her, two mirrors, revealing something behind them. 'You.'

Anna was perturbed by what she saw, or what she didn't see. 'Hey, I'm not the one who can't stand up straight. If anyone is simple here—'

He took her by the shoulders suddenly. 'You should go. Escape. Leave your aunt and go. Don't come back.'

'Attis,' cried Anna, flinging his arms off her. 'What are you on about?'

His jaw tensed. 'Nothing.' He leant towards her but she turned to look out over the balcony, her heart beating with several emotions she couldn't pinpoint.

'Can you spot the others?' She would not look back at him. She would not.

'There.' Attis pointed. 'There's Rowan and there's Effie and – Ivor.'

'Doesn't that bother you?'

'Not really. Nobody owns Effie and I wouldn't want to, but we belong to each other anyway.'

'I'll never understand you two,' she said, more scathingly than intended.

'It's best not to try.'

'I won't, don't worry.' She wanted to shake him, wondering why, when pushed on anything he cared about, he always shrugged and pretended as though everything was fine. 'I need to go rehydrate Rowan. See you later.'

He didn't say goodbye, but she felt his eyes on her as she left and could still feel the grip of his hands, telling her to go, to leave. Escape. She wasn't sure she'd ever understand him.

Rowan downed the bottle of water in one go and then dragged Anna off to find Manda, who appeared to have lost the man she'd been kissing. 'WHERE IS HE?' she shouted into the crowd. 'HENRY? Wait, was his name Henry or Harry? I don't know but I think he might be the love of my life. I need to find him . . .' She stumbled and fell against Anna.

'I think we need to get you home. Come on.'

They found Effie and disentangled her from Ivor. 'The Wild Hunt have invited us back to their after-party. Want to go a-maying?'

'I need to go home, my mum is going to kill me,' said Rowan. 'And Manda is – well . . .'

Manda was stopping random people and asking them if they knew a Hugo. Attis appeared just in time. 'Come on, Manda, let's get you some fresh air. Meet outside in five?'

Effie rolled her eyes. 'FINE.'

'Goodbye, sweet Dorothy,' said a voice in Anna's ear. Oliver took her hand and kissed it. 'May we meet again.'

'You get that die fixed, OK?' She laughed and waved goodbye; his crown glinted under the lights.

They stumbled back out of the Elder Door and into the dark, abandoned alleyway. They looked a mess – faces sweaty, make-up running, hair everywhere. It had been the best night of Anna's life.

Attis went with Rowan to make sure she got home safely. 'Better make sure, she's a bit drunk,' he slurred. Anna bundled into a taxi with the others, recounting every detail of the night until Manda fell asleep. Back at Selene's they put her to bed and then danced around the kitchen, still soaring on the night's energy.

'So,' said Effie. 'You like Ollie? He seemed to like you.'

'He was – charming. I don't know . . .'

'No Peter, hey?'

Anna laughed. 'What about you and Ivor?'

'Ah yes, my Viking. I always go back to him.'

'Maybe you guys are meant to be.'

Effie burst out laughing. 'Meant to be! You're always so . . . romantic Anna. I'm not meant to *be* with anyone. Except Attis, of course.'

Anna wasn't sure if Effie was joking or serious or just drunk. 'I don't get you two,' she said carefully, 'you say you're just friends, or like brother and sister . . .'

'I think we all know that's not true. If there is such a thing as a meant to be – he's it. He's mine. But we're young, we want to be free. We have our own arrangement. All the girls fall in love with him but he belongs to me.'

Their eyes met and Anna wasn't sure what to say. It was true. He was Effie's. She'd known it all along but it still felt strange to hear it said out loud.

'Is he – human?' she asked. 'He said he wasn't a witch when he took the berries . . .'

Effie laughed dismissively. 'He was just messing with us. I mean, did you actually see him eat one of the berries? He won't have, he's not the opening-up type, but I've seen Attis and believe me he's all man.'

Anna thought of the noises she'd heard in the house at night, the giggling, the moans. She imagined Attis and Effie's bodies fitting together as if they'd always been two parts of the same whole. It was hard to remove the images from her mind.

'Come on. Let's dance,' said Effie, grabbing Anna's hands and pulling her up.

When Attis arrived home – damp and considerably less drunk – he found them singing at the top of their lungs and forcing a piece of pizza into the toaster.

'What's happening here?'

'We wanted to see if you can toast pizza. 'S gone cold . . .' Effie prodded at it.

He smiled, walking over and removing the knife from her hands. 'I'll warm it.'

They talked and ate and laughed and didn't leave the kitchen until the sun started to rise; only then did it seem right to go upstairs to bed – Effie led them to her room. It was in its usual state – black, postered walls, the floor covered with mountains of clothes and make-up and jewellery, a large magical painting hung up behind the bed, its chaos of colours moving in slow, hypnotic waves.

'SUMMER'S HERE,' Effie declared, pulling up the blinds. A soft pink light was rising from behind the houses, seeping daylight into the night above. 'I love sun and snow and nothing in between. Let's do magic.' She turned and gave them that look, that implacable look.

Attis gave her his own indulgent look in return. 'What do you have in mind?'

Effie bit her lip. 'Blood magic.'

'No, Effie. It's late—'

'The night is not yet over. Can't you feel it? The world is waiting for us to do magic!'

'I really don't think blood magic is a good idea.'

Effie ignored him. 'Anna, you're in, right? Blood is a powerful language. It contains the keys to a witch's magic.'

Anna felt herself grow excited at the energy building in Effie's eyes. She looked at Attis, who was willing her to say no, but she found she wasn't willing to give him what he wanted. Not tonight. 'Let's do it.'

Effie hooted. 'Anna and I are going to do it anyway, Attis, so you can either join or leave us be.'

He exhaled gruffly. 'Fine. Seeing as you're both equally mad.'

'Wait there.' Effie disappeared from the room.

Anna and Attis surveyed one another.

'I thought you were the sensible one, Dr Everdell,' he said.

'Sorry to have misled you.'

He laughed. 'I never really believed it anyway.'

'So am I about to be bled in some sort of May Day sacrifice?' Anna asked.

'I don't think so but I can't be one hundred per cent sure. Effie is drunk.'

At that moment, Effie appeared back through the door with a knife.

'Effie, you know you have to ask before you can touch my knife,' said Attis.

'I never normally have to.' She raised a provocative eyebrow and ushered them into a circle on the floor. 'We need the needle blade.' She handed it to Attis.

'I'd advise the painless blade.'

'No. The needle blade. What's the point in a blood pact without pain?'

Attis moved the knife through the air, spelling out a specific symbol, and a thin, fine blade appeared from the base. Its tip was glistening sharp.

'Perfect,' said Effie. 'Right, let's sit.' She cleared a space on the floor for them, kicking away the debris that covered it. 'Now, palms into the centre. Attis, I want you to carve the symbol for power into our palms.'

'I'd rather not hurt you.'

'Attis. Do we look like we can't handle ourselves?'

Anna tried to look as sure and strong as Effie, although the words *blood pact* and *carve* were going round her head.

'It'll be worse if I try and do it,' Effie threatened.

Attis shook his head and reached out, taking Effie's palm in his own. The blade was fine, but even so, as he began to draw the symbol across her palm the mark he left was finer still, fine as a needle, a whisper along the surface of her hand, but deep enough for the blood to well up in its path – the symbol bold and fluid and beautiful. Effie looked at it with ravenous delight.

Attis moved and put his hand beneath Anna's lightly. He drew the blade across her palm so gently that she only felt a slight sting, nothing compared to Aunt's punishments.

'I'll do yours,' said Effie, taking the blade and copying the symbol across Attis's palm. His blood rose up, the same deep raspberry red of his lips. Anna winced at the sight.

'Feel the power of your blood,' Effie commanded.

Anna didn't need to look at her hand to feel it – the warmth and vitality of her blood, the pain of the cut, the thrill of the moment, its unsettling intimacy. Magic was in the air and in her body, absolute and unquestionable, as steady and powerful as the beats of her heart.

'Now we join our hands—'

'Wait,' said Anna, her heart stuttering. 'I'm not sure we should blend our blood. I mean, not mine. I might . . . infect you guys – you know something might be wrong with my magic.'

Effie laughed. 'Stop stressing. It's hardly a lot and, anyway, we're in this together. That's the whole point.'

'But we don't yet understand—'

Effie grabbed her hand before Anna could protest any further. 'Together.' She pulled Attis's hand to wrap around theirs, their blood trickling to mingle with each other's.

Anna looked up into Attis's eyes and could see conflict there too, but he said the words with rough intensity: 'Together.'

'Together,' Anna replied, her heart welling over as the blood had done. They belonged to each other, but somehow – inexplicably – she was part of them too.

They released their hands, the symbol on their palms smeared, but the blood that had trickled onto the floor had begun to form its own pattern – spiralling into circles . . . *the curse mark.* Anna looked up, wild-eyed.

'It doesn't matter,' said Effie. 'That was likely to happen. We know your magic is connected to the symbol.' Anna went to speak but Effie stopped her. 'Do not even mention the word infected or I'll get bored and I don't do boredom in the early hours of the morning. Can't you feel the power of the magic?'

Anna tore her eyes away from the pattern of blood on the floor and tried to block out the fear. She wouldn't ruin the whole evening; it had all been too perfect. Instead she let herself relax back into the feeling of magic from only moments ago – the feeling that had been on the edge of all things, where everything had felt possible, where they had felt invincible. *Together.* The sun rose like a blood spot over the rooftops, drenching the room in light. They danced wildly until they had nothing left to give, falling onto the bed, finally tired, nothing but the sound of their breaths and thudding hearts.

'I'm gonna go,' said Attis, lifting himself up.

'No, stay with us,' Effie commanded. She patted the bed seductively next to her and Anna. Anna realized how much of herself was revealed in her dress. 'We could have some more fun . . .'

He looked at them for a moment, fiercely, and then laughed. 'The most tempting offer I've ever received but no. Get some sleep.' He closed the door.

Anna remembered his breath on her neck in Equinox.

'No fun,' Effie called after him. She turned towards Anna so they were face to face, eye to eye. 'Well, I'm not tired,' she said, her eyelids drooping.

Anna smiled and they found each other's hands and knotted their fingers together, the blood still on their palms.

'We're officially a coven now. We're going to do great things together. I just know it.'

'We will.' Anna wanted it to be true. She wanted to belong to the magical world forever. To Effie's world.

'You know, I feel like I've always known you.' Effie smiled sleepily, eyes half-closed, lined with a woodland of dark lashes.

'Me too.'

'I'm glad we found each other.'

'Yes,' said Anna, holding her hand and holding back tears. 'I love you, Effie.'

But Effie was already asleep.

# DESIRE

*Fourteen Years Old*

*Anna was hungry. She'd been hungry all day.*

*Aunt placed the chocolate box in front of her, each chocolate, bronzed and shiny, moulded into its own tempting design and slotted into a neat compartment, ready to be plucked. Anna's fingers itched to reach for one, but she knew these tests were about pain, not pleasure.*

*'Look at the chocolates, Anna.'*

*Anna's eyes darted from one to the other. Her stomach rumbled.*

*'Now eat one.'*

*Anna had not expected that. She looked at Aunt for validation. Aunt nodded. Anna selected a heart-shaped chocolate from the box. She bit into it. The inside was soft and buttery with tiny crystals of sugar. Her hand reached out and selected another. She popped that in her mouth too: creamy orange zest. She took another one: dark truffle. Another: thick, fudgy on her teeth. Another. Another.*

*'Anna,' Aunt chimed in. 'You are not controlling yourself . . .'*

*But Anna couldn't stop. Another. Another. Another. She'd eat the whole box and be done with it – only the more she ate the more chocolates appeared, the compartments of the box never empty, always ripening with a new one.*

*Another. Another. Another. Her stomach was hurting now.*

*'You must try harder.' Aunt's voice was growing sharper.*

*Anna understood the game now – the trick. She held onto her cord and tied the knot, trying to control the wanting inside of her, but they tasted too good – she couldn't stop . . .*

*Another. Another. Sweat broke out across her forehead.*

*Another. Another. Another. She pulled the knot tight and managed to resist the last one momentarily but it was too late. Aunt held out a bowl for her to vomit in.*

# FOOTAGE

*In capture we must never confess. By blood or flame, may silence be our only salvation, may death be our only freedom.*

The Return, The Book of the Binders

Anna must have only slept a few hours when she woke. Effie was fast asleep. Anna remembered the events of the night before as if they had been a dream; then she looked down at her dress, the blood on her hands and the curse symbol staining the floor. She counted seven. She felt distinctly less invincible in the light of day, not helped by the groggy feeling in her head.

There was no sign of Manda, but her bed was made. She must have gone home, hopefully looking as if she'd enjoyed a night of heavy studying rather than partying. The kitchen was a bomb scene of empty bottles and glasses and pizza. The house was quiet except for the distant sound of hammering. Selene was meant to be back already. *Where is she?* Though Anna wanted to run back into the fun and freedom of the night – she had to talk to Selene.

Anna padded downstairs to Attis's floor. The door to his forge was ajar. She took a deep breath and went in. He was hammering at the anvil, shoulder blades opening and closing through his T-shirt. She watched him for a while, making his music, just as he watched her make hers. She smiled at his concentration face, brow furrowed and tongue resting on his lower lip.

He turned around and jumped. 'Anna.'

She laughed. 'Who's the creep now?'

He broke into a smile.

'Do you ever sleep?' she asked.

'Not really. Though you've only had about three hours yourself.'

'I wake early.'

'Quite a night.'

Anna nodded, feeling self-conscious as she remembered the blur of the club, the wild dancing, the blood pact. 'What's going on there?' she said, pointing at a mess of wood on the floor behind him – what looked like piano keys.

'Oh, that.' He scratched his head. 'It's part of a piano. I took it apart.'

'Why?'

'I wanted to see how it worked. They're incredibly complex instruments. Do you know there are over ten thousand moving parts in a grand piano? Over a hundred in every single key.'

Anna nodded, bewildered. She knew the theory but she hadn't really thought much about how a piano actually worked; the sound of it had been enough for her and the rest was magic. 'And have you worked it out then, how they work?'

'Yes and no.' He kicked at some of the debris.

'Do you know when Selene is due back?'

Attis dried his face off with a towel. 'Do I ever know anything about Selene's movements? The woman barely speaks to me.'

'Yeah, I've noticed. Why?'

Attis shrugged. 'I'm just another man to her. Disposable.'
'You're not just another man though, you're Effie's . . .'
'Effie's what?'
'I don't know.'
'Well, in that case I still only exist in relation to Effie, don't I?'
'That's not what I meant.'
He sighed. 'I know.'
Anna walked closer to the furnace, the heat of the fire on her face.
'Don't get too close,' he cautioned.
'What are you working on?'
'Just finishing my blade. I'm shaping it at the moment.'
'Can you show me how it works?'
His tension disappeared at her request. He smiled and rubbed a hand through his hair, sending it flying in different directions. 'Of course. If you want to see?'
'I do.'
He leapt over to the furnace. 'Blacksmithery is a combination of tools, techniques, chemistry and artistry – but in many ways it is simple. It all begins with this.' He ran a hand through the flames. 'A true blacksmith knows how to speak with fire. Listening is the most important thing. The fire shouldn't be too large or burn too quickly – you want a clean, concentrated flame. You have to listen to its music, the colours of its flames, the shades of its smoke, the patterns of its sparks.' He raised his hands up and the flames grew taller. 'I do have the advantage of magic, however.'
He drew the long piece of metal he'd been working on from the fire, its tip orange and angry. He beckoned Anna over to the anvil, placing the metal onto it. He began to beat it with a hammer – working quickly and skilfully – turning the blade on its side and hammering down, turning it again and flattening it out, a clear and steady rhythm. 'I'm shaping

it,' he shouted, moving it from the flat part of the anvil to the horn-like end of it, twisting, turning, hammer singing, sparks flaring. He rubbed a bristled brush along it, hot scales peeling off the blade. 'Want a go?'

'No. I don't think—'

'Go on,' he encouraged.

'OK,' said Anna, stepping towards the anvil. He picked up the metal again and showed her how to hold it steady. She took the hammer from him and brought it down onto the metal, feeling the shudder up her arm. Sparks skittered. Attis waved a hand, dispersing them away from her. She smiled. 'I admit, hammering is fun.'

He placed his hands over the top of hers. 'You want to draw it out. Keep turning it like this.' He showed her how to move the piece of metal. 'And easy with the hammer, firm but gentle . . .'

Anna tensed up at the proximity of his body, the closeness of his touch, but his attention was so entirely on the fire and teaching her that she became lost in it too. She was amazed at how malleable the metal was, how easily it responded to the hammer and yet how hard it was to get it to do quite what you wanted it to. She couldn't imagine moving with the speed and precision Attis had. Slowly, the blade began to take form.

'You're picking it up quickly,' he said, beaming.

Anna brought the hammer down again and, this time, as the sparks leapt into the air, Attis brought up his hand and froze them mid flight. Not quite frozen – they moved in slow motion – a suspended eruption. Anna laughed. Attis smiled at her delight and moved his hands again: the sparks began to turn in a fast spiral around her. She wanted to reach out and touch them but she knew they'd burn.

'Show off,' she teased.

He smiled. 'I'm just a man who likes to flex my sparks.' He took the blade and put it back in the fire to heat again.

Anna reluctantly handed him the hammer, wanting to learn more, to understand what every tool did, the different techniques, how to speak with fire. Her yearning didn't stop there – it extended to all the magic that had woven its way through her life, a desire that burned within her as never before. She had nowhere to put it. She walked along the room to distract herself, surveying the horseshoes on the walls, the shelves heavy with curiosities – hammers and tongs and pliers – weighing his life down as if he was worried it might float off at any moment.

Her eyes landed on the jar of keys again – the white was one among them. 'Attis,' she began tentatively. 'Could I borrow your skeleton key?'

Attis walked over. 'Why?'

'There's a room in my house I need to get into. Aunt keeps it locked. I just need to know what's in there,' she said, downplaying the desperation within her.

'It's probably just where your aunt keeps her items belonging to her secret rubber fetish.'

Anna gave him a withering look. 'Attis, come on.'

'Or she's secretly into miniature railways? Or owns a ferret collection? Some people love ferrets.'

She wrenched her eyes from the key, irritated now. 'Attis, why do you have to make a joke out of everything? Like all my questions are just punchlines – they're not, this is my life. Please, I need your help.'

'All I'm saying is – ferrets require a lot of space.'

'Stop it. I'm serious. How can I know who I am without knowing who I came from? I have to. I'm running out of time!'

'I don't know my parents. Do you see me going around putting myself in danger?' The joking edge had faded from his voice.

'You knew your father . . .'

'He wasn't my real father.'

'Well, you never told me that,' she snapped. It was aggravating how little she knew about him, how much of himself he kept a secret. 'But why would you? You don't tell anyone who you are.'

'What's that supposed to mean?'

'You're a different person to everyone – no one really knows you.' She stepped closer to him. 'You know what the worst part is? You act like nothing matters to you, like everything's a big joke, but I don't buy it. You always ask me what I want but what the hell do *you* want? What do you want from this life? What are you? Who are you?'

'You wouldn't understand, Anna.' The way he said her name, almost dismissively, made her angrier.

'You know what I think?'

'What?'

They were shouting now.

'You don't know who you are or what you want and you hide behind this mask, pretending to everyone you're just fine, happy-go-lucky, when really, if you took it off, we'd all see you are nothing at all.' Her words came out in a tumble, red and hot, hands shaking.

'Well, I'm glad you've got me all worked out!' He fired in return. 'I'm glad you've realized what I've been trying to tell you – I AM NOTHING!' His face was inches from hers, contorted, his features twisted, but his eyes were shot with pain. It caught her off guard.

She wasn't sure what to do next. They were so close. The room so hot. Their anger alive and temporarily frozen like the sparks of only moments ago; Attis's breath fast and heavy and the scent of him suddenly dizzying. Anna looked down. He stepped closer and lifted her chin, his eyes a smoke behind which fire burned—

'What's going on?' Effie opened the door and they jumped apart.

Attis stalked to the anvil. 'Nothing.'

Anna felt her face burning red. 'Yeah, nothing. Just discussing keys.'

Effie looked at Anna with intensity. 'Selene is back. I thought you wanted to speak to her.'

'Yes.' Anna quickly made for the door, deciding the best thing she could do was to leave.

'You look more like your mother every day!' Selene cried when she saw her, taking her face in her hands. Anna's increasingly thumping head was still reeling from what had just happened. 'Effie said you wanted to talk with me. I've just deposited a client in the back room so I can't be long. Need to get a few ingredients prepared.'

'I only need a moment.' Anna tried to gather her thoughts – she didn't know how she could fit everything into a moment. 'I don't know if Effie has told you anything, but there are these horrible girls at school—'

'Effie tells me nothing.'

'Well, they are the worst. Bullies, through and through.'

'I abhor bullies,' said Selene, walking over to her shelves.

'They were threatening to do this awful thing to Rowan so we stepped in. Effie found a spell which would spread rumours about them that wouldn't go away. It worked. Only I'm worried they're working too well. It feels as if they're becoming real.'

'Sounds like they're getting their comeuppance.' Selene selected various bottles from her shelves.

'But the spell is getting stronger. It doesn't seem to be ending. What if it doesn't end?

'Darling, you do worry too much about everything. You're a new coven, you wouldn't have the power to do something that would get *that* out of hand. If you're really worried, then I'll talk to Effie, find out a bit more about it.'

Anna bit her lip. 'It's just' – *say it* – 'it's just my magic, it feels like there's something not right with it. This symbol keeps appearing, seven circles – the curse symbol. Perhaps it's me, perhaps I'm what's caused the spell to get out of hand . . . to become so dark . . .'

Effie entered the kitchen with Attis. Selene began to laugh. 'Cursed.' A high falling laugh, as if it were jumping off the edge of something. 'Anna, you're not cursed and, anyway, curses don't work that way – they don't affect spells like that.'

Anna breathed out, more frustrated than ever. 'But the symbol—'

'You're making patterns out of nothing.'

'I saw the symbol,' said Effie. 'It's not nothing. Anna's magic does seem a little . . . twisted.' Effie smiled at her coldly.

'Anna's magic is not twisted,' said Attis. 'There's no firm evidence that it's cursed in any way.'

'Attis is right,' Selene agreed, although she seemed to resent admitting it. 'There are no curses in your family's magic. If there were, I'd know about them. How could you simply become cursed? Who would be cursing you? Come on now, Vivienne is just getting into your head. We *know* she does that. Why don't you spend the day here? You and Effie can join my client session now. It'll be delicious fun.'

'What's the spell?' said Effie.

'A revenge spell. Her husband cheated on her with another woman. We're going to make him pay.'

'Aren't you currently seeing a married man?' Effie pointed out.

'All's fair in love and magic.'

'I thought you were with the man in the bath? Henry?' said Anna.

Selene waved a hand. 'Oh, I had to end it, he was falling in love with me and it was all getting rather dull.'

'Right.' Anna was growing tired of all this talk of love. 'Does this other man really deserve this punishment?'

'He's a man, Anna. They have done us enough harm across the ages that any harm we do to them now is insignificant.'

'String me up now,' said Attis darkly.

Selene looked at him and somehow looked right through him at the same time. 'Oh, come on, girls. It's just a little love spell.'

'Sure.' Effie joined Selene.

'Anna?'

Anna laughed incredulously. 'You really don't get it, do you, Selene?' She stormed from the room. She did not make dramatic exits but she couldn't help it. Selene was meant to be there for her, wasn't she? She grabbed at her bag and her coat, trying to untangle them.

Selene appeared in the doorway, full of sighs. 'Anna.'

Anna successfully wrenched them apart. 'I have to go.'

'Would you look at me?'

Anna spun to look at Selene, into the dazzling violet of her eyes. *Too dazzling.*

'I'm sorry, darling. I just think—'

'I'm going to become a Binder, Selene. Do you understand? Do you care?'

Selene closed her eyes, pained. 'Of course I care. It's difficult. I don't know how—'

'I guess we're both afraid of Vivienne then,' Anna spat.

'What do you want, my little matchstick?'

'I want to know the truth. Was there more to my mother's death?'

Selene stepped forwards and took her by the hands. 'No. Your parents' death was the greatest sadness of my life but it was not a mystery, no more than any love is. There is no secret. There is no hidden story.' Her eyes were as dark as the skin of a plum now. Serious. Urging.

Anna looked away, confused.

'I know how Vivienne is with you, matchstick. I can't imagine how hard it must be—'

'She wants me bound,' said Anna.

Selene's hands trembled in hers. 'I know. But I can't decide your future for you.'

'You really think I have a choice?'

'If you ever feel like the choice isn't yours then come to me. I promise you, I will help you. I'm not as afraid of Vivienne as you think.'

Anna gripped her hands tighter, holding onto Selene's words. 'Do you really promise?'

'By the waxing of my heart, by the waning of my life, I promise on the moon. A witch's promise. I will always be here for you.'

Anna watched as the flies crawled into the hair of the girl in the row in front of her. The prefects squirmed and shivered with them on stage. The hall smelt of rot, decaying flies and festering rumour. Headmaster Connaughty had looked defeated for weeks but this morning there was a new expression in his eye, something ravenous. His small eyes consumed the rows before him.

'I must start today's assembly with some troubling news. It appears that on Friday night the school grounds were broken into. We have obtained CCTV footage—'

Anna's heart stopped.

'—showing a group of five people – four girls and one boy – trespassing on school grounds. They lit a fire and . . .' He coughed. '. . . danced around it.'

Furious whispers rippled across the pupils. *And walked through it. He's not going to share that part . . .*

'QUIET, ALL. This is a serious matter. It was a disturbing display that flirted with extreme danger.' He leant forward threateningly. 'The perpetrators will be found.'

Anna clasped her hands together. *They don't know! They don't know it was us!*

'We'll be studying the footage in greater detail and are in discussion with local police. As the trespassers appear to come from inside the school we suspect they are students.' He scoured the hall again. Anna heard Manda whimper quietly next to her. Darcey glowered from the stage, eyes fixed on Effie. 'If anyone has any information they must come forward at once.'

At lunchtime it was all anyone could talk about.

'We're dead! When they study the CCTV they'll see it was us.' Manda cried.

Effie laughed. 'They've got nothing. He's just trying to scare us into coming forward.'

'Attis brought the fire to life within seconds. We ran through fire. We made it rain,' said Anna, berating herself for being so stupid. If they were caught it would not be for trespassing but for carrying out impossible feats. *Magic.* They would expose magic to the world. The Binders' worst nightmare.

'The CCTV is too far away. They won't be able to make anything out,' said Attis.

'Have you guys seen the playing field today?' said Rowan. 'The grass has grown a foot tall and it's covered in flowers – we didn't exactly cover our tracks . . .'

'Cowans have a peculiar way of explaining away the impossible. I wouldn't worry,' Effie said dismissively. 'The earth is flourishing and so are we.'

She was right. Whether it was their growing notoriety or the Beltane face wash, Anna had never received so much attention in her life. Before, any attention had always been at her expense, now it seemed as if people were simply . . . interested. They were drawing looks from all over the common room.

'Does this mean I have a chance of getting a date for the

ball?' said Rowan. 'I never anticipated this – do I need to buy a dress? Do I need to shave? Karim is definitely going to ask you, Manda.'

'No way, I'll die. Do you think he will?'

'Probably,' said Effie, 'but let's get a few more options on the table. Yoo-hoo.' She called to a group of boys who had just entered – Peter, Tom, Andrew and a few others. 'Peter, you haven't asked me to the ball yet. I'm devastated.'

Peter scowled at her. 'If I had all the choice in the world, you'd be the last person I'd ask.'

Effie put a hand to her chest in mock shock. 'Oh no. How will I ever get through this?'

'I'll take you.' Tom took a seat next to her. 'I'll take you all the way, any way you want to go.'

She made a disgusted noise. 'If I had all the choice in the world, I still wouldn't go with you. So, Peter, are you saving yourself for Anna, then?'

Peter ignored her and pulled up a chair beside Anna. The rest of them descended into stupid chatter. 'I still don't get why you tolerate her,' he muttered.

'She's just teasing you.' Anna smiled, hoping to soften the frown on his face.

'She makes one good point though.'

'And what's that?'

'Do you have a date yet for the ball?'

Anna choked on her lunch. She coughed, her eyes catching Attis's who was looking their way. She turned back to Peter, flustered. 'The ball? I mean, I'm – No, I don't.'

'Good to know.' He flicked at a fly on the table. 'That's if the ball goes ahead; they're talking about shutting down the school for a week, you know.'

'Well, at least it's a week off school . . .'

'Who are you kidding, Everdell? You love school. You're always reading away in the library. Or hiding away,' he teased, his eyes intent on her. 'No need to worry, my dad is a member of the London Library, very exclusive. I could probably get us in.' He sat back. 'Wow, did I just offer to take a girl to a library?'

Anna's laugh died in her throat. Olivia entered the common room wearing dark glasses. She'd been away for a week and it was painfully clear why. Her lips were horrific – puffed up and inflated into a gruesome pout, the skin bright red and taut. They looked raw and painful. The room looked on in quiet horror. Olivia didn't seem to notice, walking over to a group of girls who clearly did not want to engage with her. As she smiled at them, her lips split and started to bleed. She took a tissue from her pocket and dabbed it against them. Anna felt sick.

She looked at Effie, Rowan, Manda – none met her eye; Attis's expression was grim.

Olivia was thinner again too, her bony face only making her lips seem more absurd. The girls turned away and she was left standing alone in the centre of the room.

'What has she done to her face? To think she used to be hot,' said Tom.

Andrew smirked. 'Put a bag on her head and I probably still would.'

'I heard she's booked in for a boob job next week.'

Their table continued to dissect Olivia's humiliation with Effie stoking the fires. Peter listened but didn't join in. Anna made her excuses and left.

The gardener was out on the playing field mowing the grass that had grown wild. Anna saw them dancing around the fire, white dresses flowing and disappearing in the moonlight, binding themselves together forever . . . She'd hoped after that night things might get better.

\* \* \*

Over the following days, they got worse.

Corinne was suspended for pushing a year ten pupil into oncoming traffic. Fortunately the girl had not been seriously harmed. Corinne claimed she'd fallen. The school was investigating.

'We have to do something,' Anna urged Attis. She'd gone to the music room to clear her head but found that the music wouldn't come. Her fingers were tense, her mind tightly coiled. 'This has gone too far. Now teachers are beginning to talk about the Darcey–Headmaster Connaughty situation. Next thing you know they'll be calling for an investigation there too.'

'Have you spoken to Effie? Perhaps—' Attis began.

'I've tried speaking to Effie several hundred times. She's too distracted by her own triumph to care and the others are blinded too. Effie's denying it all anyway; she just says it's nothing to do with our spell any more, that if the rumours have taken hold then it's because they were good rumours. She's lying! I've hated Darcey longer than any of them. Losing her popularity is one thing but we're destroying her life and Headmaster Connaughty's.'

'Anna, calm down.' He walked over to her and put his hands on her arms. The warmth of them was comforting, grounding. 'Let's discuss it at the coven-meet tomorrow; everyone will be together.'

'Fine, but I'm not sitting around any more. I'm going to stop this, one way or another.'

'You can't stop it on your own; we have to do it together. Magic is always a lot harder to get back into the jar once it's out.'

They left the room and found Darcey on the other side of the hallway, watching. Anna looked at Attis. *Did she hear?* He shook his head a little as if he had read her thoughts. Darcey watched them go.

When Friday came Anna was more determined than ever to speak to the others – to put a stop to what they had started. Halfway through her first lesson of the day, it appeared she might be too late. A prefect knocked on the door and informed the teacher that Anna had to report to Headmaster Connaughty's office.

Anna was exceptionally good at hiding her feelings but, as she walked towards his office, she knew her fear was showing. Her hands were shaking, her voice was tight in her throat, and when she saw Effie, Manda and Rowan sitting outside the office, she wasn't comforted. *They know. They know it was us.* Manda was stripped of colour and Rowan didn't look much better. Effie was smiling as if she hadn't a care in the world.

The secretary led them through.

'Not laughing any more, are we?' said Connaughty, hands clasped together on his desk.

'Depends on what you have to say, I guess,' said Effie, taking a seat.

*Shut up, Effie! You're just going to make this worse.*

Connaughty's eyes widened and, with nowhere to go, disappeared into his face. 'I thought I told each of you that if I saw you in my office again we would need to have a conversation about expulsion.'

Manda squeaked. Anna reached for her Knotted Cord and tried not to think of Aunt.

'And yet, here you are, all four of you at once. So many bright futures with so far to fall.' He relished the silence as he looked at each of them in turn, leering with smugness. 'Now, can you all tell me where you were the night of the first of May?'

'At home, sir.'

'At home.'

'At home.'

Effie smiled. 'Visiting my sick grandmother.'

'I have received a very serious allegation from a student who swears that you four along with one Mr Attis Lockerby were the ones who broke into the school grounds and lit a fire and—' He stopped.

Effie sat back. 'I'm sure I would remember if I'd been dancing around a fire. Besides, what evidence do you have?'

Connaughty clasped his hands tighter, looking as if he'd rather they were around her neck. 'The student who has come forward is a highly respected, senior figure on the student council. Her word would be taken extremely seriously. She claims she was working late and saw the five of you walking the corridors after hours.'

'She was at the school late, was she? Practising her ballet steps?'

Connaughty's beetle eyes scurried around the room. 'I will not reveal the identity of the student in question. However, I do have further questions—'

'I'm sure it wasn't Darcey but it would make sense if it was, wouldn't it? She's often here late at night, working hard on her ballet. Just yesterday I was here late and she was still going at it in the dance studio . . .'

Connaughty's hands fell apart. His cheeks trembled.

'I'm not entirely sure, but were you helping her, Headmaster?'

Anna looked back and forth between Effie and Headmaster Connaughty. The air was tense. The red of Connaughty's large nose had begun to spread across his face as if it were melting. He dabbed his handkerchief at his forehead.

'I was not there and I am not aware of Darcey Dulacey's movements after hours.'

Effie frowned. 'So funny, I swear I saw you—'

'So.' Connaughty squirmed in his seat, his eyes avoiding theirs. 'You all say that you weren't on the school grounds on the night of the first of May?'

They nodded their heads.

'This will be taken into consideration. You may now leave. I will call you to my office again if any further questioning needs to take place.'

'Looking forward to it.' Effie stood up and took a sweet from the dish on his desk.

As soon as they were released they hurried to the empty toilets.

'What in thirteen dark moons was that?' Rowan cried.

Effie laughed. 'Did you see how much he was sweating?'

'How did we just get away with that? Did we just get away with that?' Manda gripped the sink as if to stay upright.

'Because of me. Watch what I filmed yesterday.' Effie presented her phone. They gathered round and she pressed play.

Anna wished she hadn't watched it. For the rest of the day she could not erase it from her mind. All she could see was Darcey and Headmaster Connaughty – together – against the wall, his hands around her, their mouths hungry for one another.

The sick feeling wouldn't go away this time.

At lunchtime Darcey made her way towards them. Anna tried to shake her head at her, to warn her off, but Darcey would stick the knife in even while she was bleeding. 'How was your trip to Connaughty's office?' Her smile was unbalanced, no Olivia or Corinne to laugh at her digs any more. 'It's time that everyone realized what you all are.'

'And what is that, Darcey?' said Effie with feigned interest.

Darcey's mouth opened and closed, looking for a word that could give shape to her suspicions. 'Sick. Twisted. Satanic. Strange things have started happening since *you* joined this school. Your disappearing tattoo. You broke my shoe heel – I know it was you! I've watched the party video over and over. Destroying my reputation; flies and lies – you're all behind this and you've tricked everyone else into believing you—'

'Darcey,' said Attis appeasingly. 'You know this makes no sense.'

Darcey snarled at him. 'I'm the only one who makes sense in this whole school and don't give me that smile of yours, Attis, you don't fool me any more. I know you're in on it too!'

'Why? Because he wouldn't sleep with you?' Effie laughed. 'And neither will Peter now either. I heard he has his sights set elsewhere for the ball . . .' She looked over at Anna pointedly.

'Oh.' Darcey smiled at last. 'But I think Anna might be too busy with Attis. I thought he'd be taking you but they spend so much time together these days. The number of times I've seen them coming out of that music room alone . . .'

Anna felt her cheeks burn as Effie glanced between them, for the first time knocked off balance. But then Effie laughed. 'I have many options, Darcey. I'm still thinking them all through.'

'I think that's the problem, isn't it? Perhaps Attis is looking for something less used.' Darcey looked Effie up and down. 'Anna sure has that purity thing going for her. Pretty and sweet – everything you're not. She might be a nobody but she's got some sense of self-worth left, which is more than I can say for you – but you know already, don't you? That you don't deserve him . . .'

*Stop talking, Darcey. Stop talking.*

'He's not the one getting late-night ballet lessons from Headmaster Connaughty,' said Effie – slowly, coldly. 'Is he taking you to the ball?'

Darcey fell forward, her hands catching on the table to hold her up. Her eyes went wild, her rage temporarily unhinged and flailing; she searched for words but, finding nothing satisfactory, turned and ran.

Effie smiled and put her hand on Attis's.

\* \* \*

*THESE ARE THE CULPRITS. THEY ARE MEMBERS OF A SATANIC CULT. DO NOT TRUST THEM.*

Darcey had finally flipped. Rowan had showed Anna the posts in Biology – pictures of them, accusatory words emblazoned beneath, burning with fury. It had all gone too far – the rumours, their horrific consequences – and now Darcey was as good as calling them *witches*. Anna still couldn't get the video out of her mind.

She paced outside the sewing room, drumming up the courage to go in. It reminded her of the first time she'd stood outside the door, trying to decide whether to join the coven or not. When she finally opened it, the room stank – the altar was ruined, overflowing with rot. No one even tried to clean it any more. The mannequins were turned away.

'This spell will give her a bout of severe acne. Perfect. Karim won't look at her twice.' Manda showed Effie the book she was reading.

'What's that?' Anna tried to get a look at it.

'Karim's girlfriend won't stay away. Effie says it's time to take care of her. We can cast it tonight before my date with him tomorrow. We're going for a drive.'

Rowan's mouth dropped open. 'That sounds less like a date and more like a hook-up.'

Manda giggled. 'We'll see what happens.'

'I'd get it over and done with,' said Effie. 'What do you think, Anna?'

'I thought you said you wanted to wait, Manda?'

'Love doesn't wait,' said Manda, as if Anna could not possibly understand. 'So long as we get rid of his ex . . .'

'I don't think we should cast any more spells until we've stopped this one.'

Effie swatted at a fly, ignoring her. 'It's horrible in here. Shall we go somewhere else?'

'No.' Anna stood her ground. 'Why don't we stay here and deal with what we've done? This.' She waved at the altar. 'Out there. That video. It's because of us. There was something wrong with that spell and we have to fix it.'

Effie went to speak but Anna stopped her. She had to get this all out.

'It's gone too far. You all can't deny it any more; the rumours have become reality. Corinne pushed someone into a car!'

'I heard they fell,' muttered Manda.

'We have a video of Headmaster Connaughty and Darcey – together. If that got out it would ruin their lives. It's sick. They clearly don't have any control over their actions. We've had our fun; we've scared the shit out of everyone, Darcey most of all. We have to delete that video—'

'Why would we get rid of our one piece of leverage?' Effie countered. 'That video would bring Darcey down once and for all.'

'We can't really share it though,' said Rowan. 'If that's our spell Headmaster Connaughty is implicated.'

'IF?' Anna cried. 'It definitely is our spell. We need to erase it and stop the spell now before it spirals further out of control. If we started it, we can finish it.'

Manda looked down at her feet. Rowan winced. Effie continued to stare at Anna.

'Anna's right,' said Attis, coming through the door to stand beside her. 'The spell was darker than we thought. I've been looking into a few anti-rumour spells we can do and there's—'

'There was nothing wrong with the spell!' Effie snapped. 'If it's out of hand, it's because there was something wrong with the magic.'

Rowan put a hand on Effie's arm. 'Maybe we should hear out Attis's options.'

'Why?' Effie snapped. 'If they're not hounded by rumours

you know what'll happen? The Juicers will re-form, they'll take over, they'll start making your lives hell again. You'll lose everything you've gained. You think Darcey has learnt her lesson? You're her number-one enemies now and she'll be coming for you.'

'Why should we feel guilty?' spluttered Manda. 'I suffered at her hands for years. If the video gets shared and she gets expelled and her perfect future is in tatters, well, so be it. Otherwise she'll spend her whole life bullying people. We've done the world a service.'

'Let's not pretend like we're trying to service anyone but ourselves,' said Anna. 'And what about Connaughty?'

'But how do we know they won't come after us? We could lose everything,' said Rowan.

'You mean lose our new so-called friends and – what? Getting noticed by boys? Is this really why we formed a coven and practised our magic so hard, so we could find dates to the GODDAMN SUMMER BALL? Don't you see, we wanted to change the rules, but we're playing by the same rules as everyone else!'

'Calm down,' said Effie. 'Where is all this anger coming from?'

Anna spun round to her. 'Stop pretending that everything's fine, Effie. You know this spell is fucked up—'

'Is it the spell that's fucked up, or your magic?' Effie began to circle Anna, wielding her words like a knife. 'I mean, it's your magic that's shown signs of darkness. We've all seen the curse sign, more than once. Then there's your family: your father killing your mother; your aunt making you give up magic, fearing it's too dangerous. Everything you don't understand about your mother's death – that she may have been cursed too . . .' Effie bared her secrets, just like that, as if they were nothing. 'The flies, the rot, the rumours becoming real. How do we know it's not all come from you?

That you haven't infected the spell? You're the only one whose magic is, well, rotten. I think we all remember the seven circles in static . . .'

She twisted the knife and Anna could do nothing to remove it, because she was right. The shame of it flooded through her.

'Effie, shut up, this isn't helping,' said Attis, his voice gruff.

'Attis, you've been keeping these secrets of hers too. It's not fair. We're a coven, we're meant to be honest with one another. She's trying to blame us all for something that's her fault.'

Anna found her voice. 'If it is me – my magic – then I'm sorry. But that doesn't mean we shouldn't put a stop to this. Let's destroy that video and cast a spell to end the rumours. There must be a way.'

'Fine,' Effie relented. 'I'll get rid of the video, but we don't have time to worry about ending spells, we've got new ones to cast. It'll fade.'

'No.' Anna wanted to reach out and shake her. 'We have to end this before it gets worse. Darcey's not going to stop raving about us—'

'So?' Effie yelled, her eyes unyielding now. 'No one cares what Darcey says. The only one I hear raving is you; I thought it was your aunt who was crazy but I'm not so sure any more. This spell is your mess, you clean it up.'

'I need your help.' Anna shouted back, looking to Rowan and Manda desperately. 'Come on, who's with me?'

'If any of you agree to this, you're out of the coven,' Effie challenged. 'Out.'

'I'm leaving if you don't help me,' Anna threatened.

'Perhaps that's for the best,' said Effie, suddenly gentle. 'Your magic should probably be kept at a safe distance.'

Anna felt herself floating then, untethered. She reached for her Knotted Cord and twisted it around her fingers. 'Rowan? Manda?' she pleaded. 'This is wrong. Come with me.'

Manda looked away. Rowan looked between Anna and Effie, dithering.

'You'll lose everything, Rowan,' said Effie. 'You want them to start up that game again? The Beast? And for what, to put Darcey back on her throne? To do magic with someone who's been keeping secrets from you?'

'This is madness. No one is leaving the coven.' Attis stepped between them.

'She is.'

'I am.'

'Go on then,' Effie dared. 'Attis, you stay here.'

Anna looked at him and then turned around and left. She fled down the yellow brick corridor, wiping angry tears from her eyes. No one followed her.

# ESCAPE

*In silence and secrets we are bound.*

*Tenet Eight, The Book of the Binders*

Anna took a deep breath and wrote her name down on the Performance Assembly sign-up sheet: *Anna Everdell – piano recital.*

Even writing it made her feel sick with nerves – she didn't know if she'd be able to go through with it when the time came, but she had to. There was no choice any more.

It had been a few weeks since she'd left the coven and it had been surprisingly easy to sink back into it, into being a nobody: going to school, keeping her head down, speaking to no one, having no one to speak to. In other ways it was the hardest thing she'd ever had to do. She'd never had friends before and so she'd never experienced the all-encompassing pain of losing them.

She'd thought Attis might try to talk to her – to say sorry for backing down so quickly – but it seemed he was too much of a coward for that too. She barely saw him anyway and Rowan and Manda avoided her. Effie didn't spare her that dignity, she simply carried on as always and acted as if Anna were not there at all. With Darcey, Anna had chosen to be a nobody, but Effie forced her to become one.

She heard about them through rumour only now. Manda and Karim had supposedly slept together. She didn't know if it was true. She discovered Rowan had been asked by David aka trumpet-boy to the ball. Anna smiled when she heard until she remembered she couldn't ask Rowan about it. Effie and Attis were going together, of course. For a few days she'd been whispered about too; the abrupt end to her friendship with Effie had been of some interest, but then, not belonging to her orbit any more, Anna was quickly forgotten.

Fortunately school was winding down, with only course-work to get through. Anna gravitated between the library to work and the music room to play – taking it all out on the piano in the only way she knew how. When it all became too much she put the rest into her Knotted Cord. She didn't have time to indulge her anger, to wallow in her sadness, to bleed and to ache – she had too much to do. She had to end the rumour spell. Corinne had been suspended, Olivia was off school again for an upcoming procedure and Darcey was . . . Anna didn't want to know but could vividly imagine.

She'd taken herself off to the Library when Aunt was at work. She'd got lost in its corridors once more, trying to find something that might be useful, half expecting to stumble across Pesachya again, but he did not surface from the papery depths. She returned home with books up to her chin. She ended up discarding all but one. The lengthy rituals, the potions, the binding spells – it was all impossible on her own, but a single spell buried in one of the books gave her the seed of an idea. She didn't know if it would work. She had to try.

When the day of the performance came round she could feel herself crumbling.

*I'm ready, I'm ready. I can do this.*

She walked quickly to school before her legs could carry her anywhere else, repeating the mantra to herself. *You have to be ready. There isn't a choice.*

It was busy behind the scenes of the school stage. The other performers rushed around her: the school choir, a trio of violinists, a band testing vocals, checking instruments, while she sat alone, trying to work out how to stop her hands shaking. *What in the name of the Goddess am I doing?*

The spell idea she'd found in the Library had dealt with the language of song – how a piece of music could be a spell. There had been nothing specific but it had suggested a witch could compose her own musical spell – 'infused with Hira and delivered with magic' – for whatever purpose was required. Anna had no real clue how to achieve this but she had to try. The Performance Assembly was the one time where the entire school would be together – the Boys' and the Girls' Schools combined.

She'd composed the spell with Attis's music book. As she played she'd imagined the rumours dying in the air, clean winds sweeping away the flies, mouths sealed, phones silenced. The song wrote itself across the pages; the musical staves – threads, the notes – little knots of silence. *Everyone's going to laugh at me – the Nobody – who does she think she is . . .*

'You're on last,' a prefect with a clipboard told her. 'The piano is already on stage. Where's your sheet music? Do you need someone to turn the pages for you?'

'No. I don't have any sheet music.'

'Whatever. Just don't mess up.'

Headmaster Connaughty was on stage already, introducing the assembly. *I'm not going to remember the song. What if the spell doesn't work? Or worse . . .* Anna couldn't think about that now. She had to try something.

The performances began. Anna could hear the violins going off with slight discord, a note wrong here, the rhythm out of time there. Loud clapping. Whispering. There were a lot of people out there. She imagined Effie in the audience, Rowan, Manda, Attis – the look on their faces when she stepped out to play. She didn't want Attis thinking she was doing this for him. It was in spite of him.

When her name was called she just stared at the prefect.

'Oh Christ, you're not going to bail on me, are you? I knew I shouldn't have let you play. Anna the Nobody.'

It was one of her old names. It made her feel stronger.

'I'm ready.' She pulled herself off the floor. Her entire body was shaking now, her mouth dry as a desert. She stood in the wings while she was introduced.

She stepped out. The lights were bright, but not bright enough – she could still make out the faces of pupils and teachers before her. She sat down at the piano. The silence, as they waited for her to do something, was the loudest silence of her life. She put her hands on the keys and they trembled. Suddenly her perfectly orchestrated plan crumbled – *What if the spell spreads the darkness of my magic? Curses everyone?* She couldn't remember the first note of the song. She didn't want to remember it.

She put one hand in her pocket, feeling the old fears in her Knotted Cord. She looked into the wings and saw the prefect mouthing something at her.

*I have to do something. I have to try . . .*

She put her hands back on the piano. She couldn't feel any magic or even remotely remember what magic felt like, but she thought of the rumours – Olivia's face falling apart, Corinne's suspension, Headmaster Connaughty's hands on Darcey, Darcey's accusations——

She began.

A simple series of notes, exposed and raw, trembling under her fingers, drawing together the silence of the room, gaining ground and pace: a melody floating like a white, silent sail through the dark seas of the crowd, rippling minor chords that spoke of anguish, remorse, forgetting.

The magic came to her then, quietly, unfurling in the spaces between each note. She threaded it into the music and found the song was different to the one she'd practised. What was coming out of her was new, painful to the touch, as if her fingers were leaving their usual bloodstains on the keys: she was locked in a dark cupboard; watching a picture of her mother curling in the flames of a fire; falling asleep, one hand in Effie's; Attis was reaching out to touch her neck; breaking up pianos in his forge, white keys scattered like bones; there was a small white key she wanted but could not have; a door that was locked, forever.

The song reached its crescendo, melody crashing, notes binding together, pulling tight, tighter – a moment of pause – the quietest of endings, a gentle warning, repeating over and over: *stitch up, stitch back, stitch up, stitch back.*

Anna stopped playing.

She was met with a wall of silence. No applause, no murmuring, not even a whisper. It was broken by a small sob, then whimpering sounds, a nose blowing. She stood up and looked over the crowd. The faces looking back at her were distraught. She could see teachers along the front row crying, tears rolling down their cheeks, dabbing eyes with sleeves.

*Has it worked? Or have I broken the entire school?*

One of the teachers dropped a head into her hands, shuddering.

A lone beat of applause from somewhere in the crowd. Attis. Others joining in and then they were clapping. It was not great applause by any measure. It was slow and startled and wary. Anna removed herself from the stage as quickly as she could. The prefect with the clipboard was sitting weeping in the wings. She wound her way through the backstage area and out of the door.

*What have I done?*

\* \* \*

Anna ran through the corridors. Students were beginning to filter out of assembly but no one was speaking, not even a whisper. *What is that sound?* Anna realized it wasn't a sound but a lack of one – dead flies littered the ground but not a single live one buzzed. She put her head down and made her way through the deafening silence to the library.

She'd been hiding out for a few hours when a low voice behind her spoke. 'I thought I might find you here.' For a moment she thought it was Attis, but the voice was too quiet, too finely composed. She turned around to find Peter. Since she'd been shunned by her friends, she'd been talking to Peter a little more – walking back from class with him. She was sure he was just taking pity on her. He was smiling at her now, a dazed look on his face.

She gave him a worried smile.

'Anna, this morning – your performance, that was incredible. Everybody is – I don't know what . . . stunned. I didn't even know you played the piano.'

'Do you feel . . . OK?'

'I feel fine.' He laughed, sitting down beside her, running a hand through his hair. 'I don't think you get it. You're incredible. I've seen what *Effie*' – he said the name gratingly – 'has done to you. Discarding you like that.'

'She didn't discard—'

'It's for the best. You're so much better than her. She's trash. You're an angel in comparison.'

'I'm no angel and Effie isn't trash, she's – complicated.' Anna sighed. 'We're just too different.'

'I like you different.' He lowered his head to catch her eyes. 'You're different from all the other girls here. I'm just sorry I hadn't noticed it sooner.'

'Don't worry.' Anna laughed, trying to hide from the intensity in his eyes. 'I don't think anyone noticed me.'

'Well, the world is a better place now you're in it.'

She wanted to reach out then, to hold him and to have him make everything better, but no – *he thinks I'm an angel, but I'm not: I'm as cursed as hell.*

A few days later she found the roses taped to her locker. A tag read: 'Everdell. There's no one else I'd rather go to the ball with than you. I hope you feel the same. Peter x'.

Anna pulled them free and leant against her locker, hardly believing that through all of the chaos of the year, the most unlikely thing had happened. Peter liked her. The boy she'd had a crush on for years actually liked her, when no one else did. The flowers were just beginning to open. She'd always promised to herself, to Aunt, to keep her heart at a safe distance from any *threats* of emotion – but she'd broken a lot of promises, and this one couldn't hurt. Peter wasn't caught up in the world of magic, he was normal, steady, decent; someone she could depend on.

Anna smelt the flowers and soaked up the wonderful quiet of the corridor. She was beginning to believe that her spell had worked – the flies had gone, the rumours had begun to peter out and Darcey hadn't posted about them in some time. She hadn't come to school either; she was apparently taking some time off. *To recover?* Anna hoped it would be possible and a worse part of her hoped she'd never return.

In class, she spent the whole time catching Peter's eye. Afterwards he came up to her: 'So did you like the roses?'

'I loved them.'

'And?'

She'd been set on avoiding the ball – it would be too painful to see them all there together, but looking into Peter's hopeful eyes, she knew she couldn't say no to him. She didn't want to.

'Yes.'

They laughed and then he moved closer and gave her a kiss on the cheek.

'They reminded me of you. Red.' He pulled at a lock of her hair. 'Delicate, beautiful . . .'

She felt herself blushing and switched off to his words, instead looking into the steady calm of his eyes. *Peter taking the Nobody to the ball!* It might have been the most absurd rumour of them all.

Rowan found her leaning on the wall behind the common room the next day. She approached tentatively. 'Is it true, then? Peter asked you to the ball?'

'Yes,' Anna replied warily.

Rowan's smile grew wider. 'I knew it! I knew he would! I'd hoped for it. You've liked him for so long, you deserve it and—' She stopped herself. 'I'll talk forever if you let me go on.'

'I don't mind,' said Anna, realizing how much she'd missed the sound of Rowan's voice.

'You don't hate me?'

'I don't hate you.'

'I've been too ashamed, I—' Rowan's smile wobbled. 'I'm sorry.'

'I'm sorry too.'

'I do not accept your apology.'

'OK . . .'

'No, wait, I mean, because you don't need to apologize. You were right. You were so right, those rumours – they were nasty but they weren't meant to come true. When they started to . . . I didn't want to admit to myself what was happening. I'd got so caught up with everything. I'd never been popular and suddenly people wanted to talk to me, to hear what I had to say and – I know, I know, it was Effie's attention they really wanted but it still felt good and I don't know . . . I lost it. Couldn't see the wood for the trees, the flowers for the bee stings, the—'

'I get it, Rowan.' Anna smiled.

'And what you did with the piano, I swear by my Hira that was the most beautiful thing I've ever heard. I was a blubbering mess, genuinely, tears, snot, dribble – the unholy trinity. Did Attis tell you we put gag root herb in all the school food?'

'No, I haven't spoken to him.'

'It banishes gossip. We wanted to make sure the spell was definitely over, but I don't think we needed to after what you did. It's been so quiet, hasn't it? And Darcey, she's disappeared. You were right about her too; we should have been more careful. I know people think she's lost it but even so, that footage and her spouting off about satanic cults and the like, it was not a good idea, especially right now.'

'What do you mean, right now?'

'I don't know.' Rowan sat beside her. 'I've been trying to deny it too, but maybe there's something going on. Mum still seems a little spooked and the Wort-Cunnings have been meeting more often. These conspiracy theories in the news aren't going away either. I checked out that Institute for Research into Organized and Ritual Violence. It looks like it only came into existence a year ago, not long before the hangings, and suddenly it's got all this sway in the media.'

'The media likes giving voices to the outspoken.'

'It just all seems weird. The magical world is such a wonderful place. It's free, you know?'

Anna remembered its wonderful freedoms all too well. She missed it more than she could put into words. Her future was likely to contain little of it.

'I don't know,' Rowan continued. 'If I've learnt anything from the past few weeks it's that there's no smoke without fire . . .'

'The fire never dies; beware smoke on the wind,' said Anna quietly.

Rowan gave her a quizzical look. 'What do you mean?'

'It's just something my aunt says. She's . . .' Anna hesitated. 'She's a member of a grove known as the Binders.'

'What are the Binders?'

'I thought you might have heard of them?'

Rowan shook her head. 'No, but I don't like how they sound.'

'They don't exactly tolerate magic. They use knot magic to control and manipulate it. They've always feared the return of the Hunters, but, honestly, their claims have stopped feeling like the usual fearmongering and started to feel real. I'm worried about what's going on too, and—' Anna stopped herself. She had almost told the whole truth, about what the Binders intended to do with her once the year was up, but she sensed Rowan would not take that calmly.

'Anna, you have to speak to my mum. These Binders don't sound like a legitimate grove and if they know something about what's going on we all ought to hear it.'

Anna shook her head firmly. 'The Binders don't work that way, trust me, and please don't tell your mum, OK? After everything that's happened, I'm asking you that. I need to deal with them – my beloved aunt – on my own.'

Anna couldn't trust anyone else. Not any more. She'd already said too much.

Rowan's heavy eyebrows knitted themselves together. 'I won't say anything, but I am here.'

Anna nodded, holding her Knotted Cord to stop herself relenting.

'So with all this fear in the news, do you reckon you could play the piano and silence the whole of London too?'

Anna smiled. 'We're going to need a bigger stage . . .'

Rowan laughed and then fiddled with a weed sticking out of the wall. 'You know Effie was impressed by what you did. Angry, but impressed.'

Anna shrugged, trying to seem indifferent.

'She talks about you a lot. Goddess knows I have so much to tell you . . .'

And that was that, Rowan didn't stop talking for the next half an hour. Anna listened and was late for class and didn't care.

That weekend, Anna escaped to Cressey Square garden. She leant her head against the oak tree and took out a book, listening to the hum of activity around her: birds flitting, bees frantic, breeze rustling and dusting off the leaves. The sun was warm on her face. Summer was in the air, like bubbles in a glass, rising to the surface through the earth below.

*Things are getting better* – school was going back to normal, Rowan was speaking to her again, Peter was taking her to the ball – *and yet nothing is OK* – the effects of the rumour spell, what they'd done, would never truly go away. *Effie isn't talking to me. Attis doesn't care. The year is almost up and I have to decide whether to bind my magic – if the decision is even mine.* After everything that happened Anna knew that the sensible thing to do was to proceed with the Knotting; she had more than enough evidence to know that there was something wrong – dangerous – about her magic, but with so many secrets still locked away, she couldn't help hoping that there was another way.

*The truth is within the leaves. The mirror within the mirror. The mirror is the key.* Nana's words were maddening, going round in her head every day like a melody she couldn't forget. She snatched a leaf from a nearby bush – *how can the answer be within you?* She held it up to the light – *there's nothing there. The mirror within the mirror. What mirror? What key? The key to the third-floor room?* The room was all she had left now. *Does it hold the answers to my questions?*

'There's a ladybug in your hair.'

She knew the voice and yet it was so incongruous to the setting, so inconceivable that he should be here, that it took her a moment to recognize it.

'What are you doing here?' Her words didn't come out as a shout, but slowly and icily.

Attis was standing above her, blocking the sun from the pages of her book. 'OK, it just flew away, we're all clear.' He sat down.

'Attis, go away.' She closed her eyes. *He can't be here.* 'It's a private garden. I have a key. You don't have a key.'

'I have a key.' He held up the skeleton key and then put it back in his pocket.

'You don't live here. You're not allowed in this garden.'

'Stickler for rules suddenly, are we?'

Anna knew she sounded pathetic but this was the one place she could be alone. Where she could escape. The one place that was hers.

'You're still mad at me then.'

She refused to look at him. 'If you're going to stay, can you go somewhere else? I need to read.'

'I like this tree though.' He patted the oak as if they were old friends.

Anna bit her tongue to stop herself from shouting: *IT'S MY TREE.*

'Could I just stay for a while? I won't speak,' he said. She made the mistake of looking at him. He smiled – a little hopeful, full of open-hearted willingness, a smile so adept to shaping itself to the requirements of the moment it could win awards. It pinned you to the spot while brushing your legs from underneath you.

'Fine.' She began to read. He lay back on the grass next to her and watched the sky.

Anna managed fifteen minutes before she broke. 'What do you want?'

He sat up. 'You were amazing.'

'What?'

'The piano spell. It was amazing. I . . .' She'd never seen him lost for words before. 'Mr Ramsden was blubbing everywhere. Best thing I've seen all year.'

'Why are you here?'

'I came to see how you are. I've barely seen you at school and when I do, it's like you're not there.'

'Ha! You're the one avoiding me, not the other way around. How's the coven going?' She tried and failed to hide the bitterness in her voice.

'It's on and off. Not quite the same really. Effie misses you.'

Anna turned away. 'She made her choice.'

'You and Effie didn't have to do that – draw a line between you.'

'I didn't; Effie did. Everyone chose their sides anyway.'

'There are no sides.'

'Really?' She looked back into his eyes.

'She needs you – you're a good influence on her.'

'Oh, but she has you.'

He smirked. 'I have some influence – I'm not sure if it's good. You still doing magic?'

Anna nodded. 'I've got to decide though. Soon.'

He lowered his head, understanding. 'What are you going to do?'

'I don't know . . . become a Binder, live with my aunt and maybe, one day, get my magic back. I'm too much of a coward to run.'

'You're not a coward, Anna, you're afraid. It's different. No one is exempt from fear.'

Anna shook her head at his words. 'Even after everything, I just – I don't know how to leave her. She's my only family.'

He frowned, his face peculiarly ageless, somewhere between

a young boy unsure what to do and a man tired of life already. She wanted to get up and leave, before he found a way into her head as he always did, but instead she found herself asking: 'Did you ever know your biological family? You said before your father wasn't your real father . . .'

He ran his hands through the grass. She thought he wouldn't answer but then he said: 'No. I was adopted by my father and his partner, though one passed away when I was ten and the other – well, I haven't seen him in a while.'

'I'm sorry, Attis. The one you haven't seen, is that the professor? Where's he now?'

'We had a falling-out. We're not – we don't speak now. I don't know where he is.'

'Over what?' Anna knew she was asking too much of a boy who never spoke about himself, but she was hungry to know more.

He took a while to answer, his eyes passing through several grey clouds of thought. 'Effie. Love. Fate.'

It was a bigger answer than she'd expected. 'Oh.'

'No matter. I'm ploughing ahead anyway. Live fast, die young, maybe get a dog – I don't know.'

'Right.' Anna could see he would give her no more today. She could only learn about him a little at a time. Perhaps it was better that way – all at once would be too much.

They sat in silence for a while, listening to the breeze, and then he said: 'So I heard someone's going to the ball with dreamboat Peter.' He made eyes at her. Anna kicked at him. 'Heard he got you flowers and everything.'

'He's a gentleman.'

'Roses, wasn't it?'

'Yes.'

'I'm terribly sorry to hear that.'

'Roses are a perfectly lovely flower.'

'They're boring. A rose is a rose is a rose . . .'

'At least he gets a girl flowers, what do you give them, an STI?'

He fell over on the grass as if she'd shot him down. 'Well, that was uncalled-for. Besides, I don't go on dates.'

'Of course, why bother with all the preamble when you can just go straight for the prize?'

'At least I'm honest about it. You're just annoyed he bought you generic flowers.'

'They're not generic. They're classic, timeless, romantic.'

'But, Anna, you are none of these things.'

'Thanks.' She gave him a look that could have withered any flower. 'What should I receive then – a bunch of weeds?'

'Good question.' His eyebrows met in thought. 'There's the daisy.' He picked one from the grass. 'Pretty, understated, undervalued, but no, too common.' He went quiet. 'There's ivy – strong, loyal, but too poisonous perhaps. Or the poppy – a redhead, mysterious, intoxicating, quite the death stare, matches the one you're giving me right now – but no, no.' He fell silent again.

'See, you've got noth—'

He sat up, excited. 'I've got it. Springwort.'

'Now that does sound like an STI.'

Attis snorted. 'It's not an STI. It's a flower. A flower few have ever seen. A flower that belongs to another world.' He leant forwards. 'Its stem is as green as your eyes, its petals like your hair – not red, not gold, but somewhere in the middle, bright as a fallen star. It grows only in wild places, hiding away in the dark and lonely shadows of the woods. Its roots are deep; its vines run free; it is rare. They say one drop of its nectar can kill a man or bring him back to life.' He moved closer to her, holding her gaze. 'It produces but a single flower, which blooms only once, but when it does the whole world falls on its knees for the beauty of it.'

Silence ensued and Anna burst into laughter. 'You expect me to believe that? And what is its intoxicating aroma? Bullshit?'

'No. It smells like a first kiss, like your skin right here . . .' He reached out a hand to the side of her neck and she froze.

'You try that one on all the girls?' she replied hastily, ignoring the melting feeling down her spine. 'Does Effie know you're here?'

Attis dropped his hand. 'I am able to do some things without her knowledge, you know.'

'Not much.'

Attis shrugged. 'She's my family.'

Anna nodded. *That* she could understand. Her heart was beating fast. She looked out beyond the park to the row of stern-faced houses beyond. 'I just wish – I wish I could escape.'

'I wish you could too.' He looked so sad then she wanted to reach out and touch his cheek, but as her hand fluttered, his eyes lit up in that way they did whenever he was charged with an idea.

'Take my hand.' He extended it towards her. She looked at him warily and, deciding to throw caution to the breeze, moved closer and took it, her skin bright against his smoke-stained fingers. He closed his eyes and focused. She felt the magic pass between them. It didn't happen all at once, but slowly, like falling asleep, and then suddenly the whole world was different.

The oak tree was still there, rising above them, and the grass beside them and the flowers, but the park . . . the railings were gone, the road gone, the houses gone. London was nowhere to be seen. Instead the green lawn of the park billowed out, becoming a meadow which extended in all directions, lit with flowers and dotted with trees, dressed up in blossom. Beyond, it extended outwards to fields and wooded hills, the landscape uneven and undecided, full of light and shadow. *Wild.*

'What is this?' she said, looking up at the sky, and then down at the grass beneath her, which looked and felt entirely real.

'It's a chimera.' Attis let go of her hand, but the illusion didn't falter. She was still here, in this paradise, in a park in London and yet a very long way from the city.

She breathed in. There were no fumes, no wet tarmac; the air was fresh as new grass, as if the green of a flower stem had been cut and spilt over the earth. She pulled a blade of grass and held it to her eye – beyond it the horizon glimmered in the warm, bright sun.

'It's not real, is it?'

'It is and it isn't. I've created it in my head, so it's as real as any thought.'

Anna smiled and looked at him. 'I like this thought of yours.' His eyes were softer here, one lighter, one darker, his smile somewhere in between. 'Am I in Wales? Is it your memories?'

'Some memory perhaps and something new too. Let's call it an escape.'

Anna sank back onto the grass, the sky blue and without edges above her. 'I don't care if it's real or not,' she said. 'Not now, not for a while.'

Anna stayed inside Attis's thought for as long as she could, watching the sky roll through different shades of blue. Attis didn't speak and she didn't know what to say that wouldn't ruin it all, so she was quiet too, watching butterflies and strands of grass fade in and out of focus.

Eventually she knew she had to leave. She was afraid Aunt

would come out looking for her and find her lying on the grass in the park in a daze with *him*.

'Attis. I have to go home.'

He turned his head to her as if he wanted to say something, but then nodded. The world shifted around them, the horizon diminishing to the park railings, the sound of traffic returning. The sun above them no longer seemed as bright and that scared Anna for a moment, as if somehow the real world would now always fall short.

'Thank you,' she said.

His smile was complete. 'I'll speak to Effie, OK? She just needs a push to get over her pride.'

Anna was still angry at her, but she missed her more. 'Would you?'

'I have some influence, minimal as it is.'

She smiled. 'Can you just go and see if my aunt's car is outside the house? I may need to sneak in.'

'Sure.' He jumped to his feet and walked to the fence.

Anna leant over and reached a hand inside the pocket of his coat. She pulled out his set of keys. Fortunately the skeleton key was on its own ring – quick and easy to pull away from the others. She slipped the keys back into his pocket just in time.

'She's there,' he said, returning.

She couldn't quite meet his eye. He'd given her a moment of escape, but she needed more.

He picked up his jacket. 'Don't take any shit from her now. Right, I'll see you Monday then.'

'Bye, Attis and – thank you.'

He nodded, sadly, and left.

She went back to the house, scents of disinfectant souring the air.

'Anna, is that you? I need your help.'

'Coming, Aunt.'

Anna wandered into the living room, remembering the sweet freedom of the sky extending in all directions. The rose bush in the corner began to open, one bloom at a time.

'NO.' Anna took a cord out of her pocket. 'NO.' She made little Choke Knots in it, fear coursing through her. The buds locked tight again.

'Anna.' Aunt rounded the corner as the last one closed. 'I said I needed your help.'

'Sorry, Aunt.' Anna bundled the cord up in her trembling hands.

Anna fretted all night that Attis would come back looking for his key. She just needed a little longer. Aunt would be off to work early and then she could do it. She could break into the third-floor room. She barely slept, talking herself into it and out of it and into it again.

In the morning she watched Aunt drive off from the window. She would wait half an hour, to be sure, and then . . . She pulled the key out of her pocket.

She paced the hallway until it was time. Stepping out in front of the whole school had been terrifying but this was a different kind of fear. A more absolute kind. It was not humiliation she was risking, but her past and her future. It was the sort of fear that was so great you couldn't look directly at it, but only glance from the side and hope you could still breathe after facing it. She'd been avoiding it for too long. It was time.

She walked up the stairs. The third floor was dark despite the sunshine outside. She put her ear to the door and could hear nothing from behind it. The room where her parents died. *I'm sure it's going to be full of Aunt's tax files and then I'll feel like an idiot.*

Without thinking, with a lifetime of curiosity urging her

on, she put the key in the lock and turned it. She heard it click open and her heart jumped, but then – the key began to bleed. The lock twisted back shut of its own accord and spat the key out onto the floor, blood seeping from the key onto the cream carpet.

She stood immobile, watching the blood spill out, before horror tore through her. She grabbed the key from the floor but the blood would not stop. She wrapped it in her sleeves and they began to turn red. She fled downstairs, blood seeping through her hands and onto the floor like footprints following her. She threw the key into the sink and left it to bleed down the plughole.

*Stay calm, stay calm.* Anna couldn't remember what calm felt like. Her heart was hammering, a pure black fear threatening at the sides of her vision. She poured water into a bowl, grabbed a cloth and cleaning products and ran upstairs. Back outside the third-floor room, she wiped the blood from the door and scrubbed furiously at the carpet. The blood did not come away. She poured water on it, sprayed it with every spray at hand, scrubbed it and scrubbed it, and still it did not budge.

Aunt would be home in two hours. Fear coursed through her uncontrollably.

She ran back downstairs; the key was still bleeding out into the sink. She looked up and saw the rose bush in the corner of the room had opened – every single rose – like sirens going off. She ran blindly into the dining room – they were all open too. She ran to the living room – the same: roses looking back at her, agape and laughing.

She felt as if she would faint and fell to her knees, fear edging her mind with darkness. The wall of embroideries looked down at her, but they weren't the embroideries she'd sewn; the pretty borders, the Bible verses, the flowers had turned, were turning . . . turning into the sign of the curse . . . threads reweaving themselves into seven circles, the centre a dark hole, into which her mind was descending . . .

She looked at her hands. They were covered in blood.

The darkness took over.

# CHOKE KNOT

*From Thorn Bindings, to Knot Lashings, to Death Knot Stances, there are a range of tools, techniques and knots that can be employed for various acts of penance. Pairing the correct method to the weakness in question requires careful self-examination and ongoing assessment.*

*Binders' Training, The Book of the Binders*

She was drowning. Water in her mouth. She coughed and opened her eyes. Aunt was standing above her with an empty glass. What she'd done came back to her all at once. She looked at her hands – they were still stained with blood.

'The guilty are marked,' said Aunt. 'Up.'

Anna stood up without thinking. She went to speak but realized she couldn't. She couldn't do anything.

'You don't like that sensation, do you?' Aunt held a cord in front of her face, a knot in the centre of it: the Choke Knot. 'I've bound your free will. I had no choice. You've betrayed me again, but it's for the last time. Feels most unpleasant, doesn't it, like you're trapped in your own body?'

It did and yet it was worse. She wasn't trapped, she was empty. Her body was no more than a shell, her life force was elsewhere, hidden somewhere she couldn't get to.

'The room on the third floor is just a test, an empty test, and you failed. You had to go in there, didn't you? I don't even want to know where you got that key. I trusted you, I treated you like an adult and you have responded like a child.' Each word was drawn out with a slow, shuddering disappointment. 'From now on you will do as I say. You will speak my words, you will think my thoughts and you will become a Binder. This knot.' She held up the cord. 'This knot is the end.'

Anna could not move or speak. She tried to panic but even that was denied her.

Aunt compelled her to scrub the blood from the carpet all afternoon until her fingers bled into the cloths. The blood still did not budge. Aunt had known it wouldn't, that only magic would remove it. Then Anna was sent to her room, not knowing when she would see the outside of it again.

Not having control over her own body was the strangest, most terrible sensation and yet it wasn't just the physical aspect that disturbed Anna, but how peculiarly hard it was to tap into your thoughts and feelings freely when your body did not belong to you. When sadness overwhelmed her, she could not cry; when anger came, she could do nothing but sit and stare at the wall; she could not laugh, if she ever had a reason to laugh again; it was impossible to think straight about the questions that held her just as captive. She felt as if she were drowning inside of herself.

After a paralysing day and night of emptiness, Aunt loosened the knot enough for her to move around, enough to do her school work, but not enough to formulate any plan of escape.

Aunt informed the school she had glandular fever and Anna lost track of the days she was locked away. It didn't really matter any more; her body was the prison now. Of the many punishments Aunt had carried out over the years, this beat them all. Sleep. Wake. Work. Sit. Long to cry. Sleep. Wake. Work. Sit. Long to cry.

Would Selene come? Would she save her like she'd promised? After two weeks, Anna lost the distant hope of even that.

One night she heard quiet knocking on her balcony doors. She got up and saw Attis behind them, looking at her through the glass. She looked into the grey rain of his eyes and then turned around and went back to bed. She couldn't open the doors; she couldn't want to open them. She wondered if he might break them down, but he didn't.

Several hours later she got up to see if he was still there but he was gone.

Another week passed and time lost all meaning without meaning to give it substance. She lost the will to work and retreated to bed, watching the daylight come and go.

She couldn't say exactly how long it had been when Aunt came into her room. The light was low – it was evening. Anna sat up, limbs weak. Aunt smiled at her. Anna couldn't even hate her.

'I can feel you, flapping your wings against this magic, but you won't get out. Come and sit.'

Anna took a seat in front of the mirror.

'I know you think me cruel.' Aunt picked up the brush and began to untangle her hair, softly. 'You and me, we've always had each other, haven't we?' Her eyes looked tired. 'I have done my best to do what's right for you and these are the thanks I get. I've only ever wanted to protect you.'

Anna could not answer.

'Your Knotting will soon be upon us – arrangements are being made. You agree now that becoming a Binder is the right decision?'

Anna's head nodded.

'Good. You see now, your magic isn't right. It must be bound.'

Anna nodded again.

'I have always been kind to you, Anna, kinder than I should, and so I will indulge you one last freedom. You can return for the last week of school, hand in all your course-work and – you may go to the ball. Peter has been calling the house almost every day to see how you are.'

Anna thought of Peter distantly.

'He tells me you're going together. You should have told me. No matter, he will come here to pick you up and I will meet him. He has promised to have you home by midnight and no later.'

Aunt held up the knot and undid it.

Anna felt as if she'd suddenly risen to the surface after being held deep underwater. Air entered her lungs in a rush of pain and bliss. She gasped and felt as if she was going to faint. Aunt pushed her forward, keeping her head low. 'Take it easy now. It can be overwhelming.'

Anna had a hundred things to say and too many thoughts to think. She rallied against the light-headedness, clenched her fists and breathed *in, out, in, out,* her body her own again.

She looked at Aunt and felt . . . hate, guilt, rage, shame and, somewhere buried deep, a decaying sort of love. She tried to find words but there was nothing left to say.

Anna waited for the next punishment to come, the finale, the pain, but Aunt simply said, 'Get some sleep. You've got school tomorrow,' and left.

In the morning Anna left her bedroom. The embroideries had been taken down from the living-room walls. Anna wondered if they were still woven into the curse mark. There was no denying it any more – she was cursed, and she was sure that her mother and aunt were cursed also. She remembered the pattern sewn into Aunt's skin: *She'd been punishing herself, just like she punishes me.*

Whatever was wrong with their magic, Anna was sure it was linked to her mother's death and had left Aunt twisted and afraid. Everything her own magic had touched had turned rotten after all, and it had certainly attracted all the wrong kinds of attention. Perhaps it would be easier to be bound. She thought of the empty, contented expression in Rosie's eyes – it couldn't be worse than the Choke Knot.

She walked to the train, enjoying the feeling of her legs moving, the wind in her hair, the riot of clouds in the sky. Selene's words came back to her. *Your mother chose to open her heart to the world, while Vivienne closed hers forever.* Anna clung to them. She would not give up yet. She knew how Aunt worked; the Choke Knot had been intended to terrify her into complying, but it had only made her see – feel – what her life would be if she complied. Whatever was wrong with their magic might have led to her mother's death, but was Aunt really alive?

At school, the flies were gone, the hallways were clean and bright and yet whispers followed her as she walked. The old sort of whisper. *What did I expect?* Between her break-up from Effie, her piano performance and her mysterious disappearance, people were interested. Anna found she didn't really care.

'Oh no, the Nobody's back and nobody cares.' She heard Darcey laugh when they passed in the corridor. Anna could have kissed her with relief. Darcey could call her every name under the sun, so long as it wasn't *witch*.

Anna went into the common room at lunchtime and saw Effie, Rowan and Manda sitting at a table. She wasn't going to avoid them any more. If she'd learnt one thing from feeling nothing for three weeks it was that feeling rejected and hurt wasn't so bad. *It's something.* Effie's eyes followed her with something like interest.

After Biology, Rowan pulled her into a long hug. 'Where have you been? Did you really have glandular fever? Mum rang your aunt but she just kept saying you were on the mend. She was threatening to go to your house and give her a piece of her mind. Were you ill?'

Anna shook her head.

'I knew it. It was your crazy aunt, wasn't it? Goddess knows, I almost told my mum, but I held back. I held back because you asked me to but I wish you hadn't. You look pale again. What did she do to you? What did you do to make her do whatever she did to you? I'm overwhelming you with questions, aren't I?'

'Overwhelm me all you want.' Anna hugged Rowan tightly and Rowan gave her a curious look.

'I tried to find out about my family's past. Aunt caught me, locked me up. That's all there is to it really.'

'You know that's like so many levels of illegal, right?'

'Yeah, but the police stand little chance against my aunt.' Anna tried to smile but it caught in her throat.

'Please let's talk to Mum. There are witch groves who will help you.'

'No. It's fine. I need to sort this on my own.'

'Anna.' It was Effie's voice. Rowan spun round, looking guilty. *She's still not meant to be talking to me.*

'Effie,' said Rowan. 'Look. Anna is here.'

'I see that.' Effie's mouth was a hard line.

'So, I'm just going to leave you two to talk.' Rowan walked awkwardly in the other direction, disappearing around the building.

Effie's mouth softened. 'You're back.'

'Looks like. Have I ruined your day?'

'You took Attis's key. He's mad at you. What did you do? What did she do to you?' Effie was always there for the gossip, the juice.

'I tried to get into the third-floor room. I failed. Aunt found out and I've been consigned to my room ever since. I'm becoming a Binder now.' Anna smiled cheerily.

'Just like that? You're going to give it all up?'

'Yes. Maybe . . .'

Effie's eyes lit up at her moment of indecision. 'Look. I'm sorry.' It came out aggressively, as if she could force Anna into forgiveness. 'I got carried away. I do that. I shouldn't have said the things I said.'

'No, you shouldn't have.'

'I wasn't thinking clearly. I was mad. I just didn't want to undo everything we'd done, to have Darcey going back to being so cruel to you. I was trying to protect you.'

Anna laughed. 'Protect me? You threw me out of the coven. I thought we were bound together forever.'

'We are.' Effie looked away and back, her eyes roiling with the storms that Anna had so long been drawn to. 'I'm not an easy person, Anna. I'm not easy to like. It's why I don't have many people in my life and I'm still adjusting, I haven't had many girlfriends before—'

'No shit.'

'Hey, I thought I was the smart mouth in this group.'

'I've learnt from the best.'

'Look. I need you. I need you to call me out on my bullshit, OK? You're one of the few people not afraid of me.'

'Oh, I'm afraid of you.'

'I'm not so sure about that. So, are we going to hang out again or what?' Effie smiled, but it had none of the menace of her usual grin – it was unsure. Anna felt her heart tug.

'Did you get rid of the video?'

'Course.'

'Then – OK.'

Effie's smile deepened. She picked a leaf from the tree beside her and placed it in Anna's hand. She put her own underneath and the leaf started to blow up into the summer breeze. Anna felt the magic at once, the pulse of Effie's hand, the life of the leaf.

'We've had some pretty good times, you have to admit.'

Anna smiled. 'Unforgettable.'

'Don't give up yet. When is this whole Binders thing going to go down?'

'At some point over the summer holidays.'

'We have time. Selene will help.'

'Will she? She didn't come when I was locked in.'

'I know. I'm still not talking to her. She was mad though, I've never seen her so mad, but she said there was no way to get to you, that Vivienne's magic was too strong.'

'Attis came . . .'

'I wanted to go with him but he said it would be less conspicuous if just one of us went. Anyway, fat lot of use he was. He didn't come back with you either.'

Anna shook her head. 'There was no breaking me out.'

'You're out now?'

'For now.'

'We'll speak to Selene.'

*Yes. Selene will help. She has to help.*

'You can come to mine before the ball and we can talk to her,' Effie continued. 'You're still going, right?'

Anna hadn't thought about it – a school ball felt entirely too normal compared to the chaos of her life, and yet she wanted to go. 'I guess. I promised Peter I would. If he still wants to, considering my absence and complete lack of communication.'

'Oh, he still wants to.' Effie smirked. 'I've been taunting him about it. So, come to mine to get ready?'

'I can ask. But Aunt may lock me back up at the thought of it.'

# THE BALL

*Ecstasy Rituals absolve the sins of the group, for sin drives out sin.*
*The sin is undertaken repeatedly until it can no longer be endured.*
*At the point of exaltation it is bound within each individual.*

Binders' Rituals, The Book of the Binders

Aunt refused to let Anna go to Effie's house before the ball
but assented to Effie coming to their house instead. Anna
was shocked at even that concession. It was truly one last
night of freedom. After the Choke Knot she wanted nothing
more than to live every moment of it – and then she would
go to Selene. She would find a way out.

Effie arrived late. 'Vivienne, so good to see you again.' She
smiled, stepping through the doorway.

Aunt smiled in return. 'A pleasure to see you too.'

If looks could kill they'd both be dead.

'Effie, let's go upstairs.' Anna wanted their interaction to
be as limited as possible.

'Wow, your room is bland,' said Effie. She began poking
through her shelves and drawers.

'Aunt wouldn't have it any other way.'

'Who's this?' Effie pulled out the picture of her parents.

Anna had been looking at it the night before and regretted

not hiding it deeper. She grabbed it off her. 'My mother – and my father.'

'She was pretty. I didn't imagine her with black hair.' Effie turned to look at Anna; her gaze became critical. 'What are you wearing?'

'This.' Anna held up an old dress. She knew it was the worst – an unflattering purple colour, long and shapeless. It was the closest she could find to something resembling an evening dress.

'We'll deal with whatever that is later, but I meant underneath.'

'What, like, underwear?'

'Don't look so shocked, you do know that's on the cards, don't you? Peter has a boarding room at the Boys' School, he's going to want to take you back there. Every guy feels obligated to try and sleep with their date at the summer ball.'

'Peter wouldn't – he's not like that.'

'You don't even know him, Anna. Anyway, I bought you something.' She took a package wrapped in tissue paper out of her bag.

'Thanks.' Anna looked at it warily. She unwrapped it and pulled out a pair of white pants and a bra, trimmed with feathery lace. 'You want me to wear these?'

Effie stood up and began to take her clothes off. Underneath she was wearing similar underwear in black. 'See? They look amazing. I figured white for you. You know: virginal and pure. Peter will love that.'

'I am not sleeping with Peter.'

'What else is there to do with him? He's a complete bore but he does have a certain intensity. Put them on just in case; besides, they make you feel sexy, trust me.'

The look on Anna's face obviously revealed she did not trust Effie, not at all.

Effie sat down on the bed. 'Look, I said I'm sorry. Can we start over? Manda and Rowan are driving me crazy, our magic is waning. I need you back. Attis told me that you missed me . . .'

'I want to come back.' Anna sat down beside her. 'But you have to promise the coven is a democracy, not a fascist state.'

'Yes. It's all free love and fairness and fairy tales, OK?' She moved some hair back from Anna's face. 'You're going to be a stunner tonight.'

'I'll wear the damn underwear, go on, give it to me. I'm still not sleeping with Peter, though.'

'Whatever. Manda said the same thing about her and Karim.'

'It's true then – they did?'

Effie nodded.

'What about her beliefs?'

'She's convinced herself it's OK because she loves him and they'll surely get married one day and yada, yada, yada.'

'Married! She's known him all of five minutes.'

Effie shrugged. Anna reflected on the fact that even fearful, control-freak Manda had slept with someone and she was terrified of even kissing a boy.

'Right, let's deal with that dress.'

Effie pulled out a crumpled red ball from her bag and shook it out. The dress unravelled like a silk waterfall, the creases falling away as if by magic. In fact, magic had almost certainly been involved. 'I think this one will look perfect.'

They got themselves ready, Effie fussing over Anna, helping her get into her dress, employing various magical concoctions, polishing and brightening her like a piece of silverware. They drank from a bottle Effie had brought and giggled, and Anna felt herself grow giddy on Effie's presence once more. To finish she twisted Anna's hair up with magic, leaving strands of it to fall about her face.

'Peter's going to drop dead,' said Effie, admiring her work.

Anna looked at herself in the mirror – her reflection was as confused as she was. The woman in it wasn't the girl she knew, her hair burnt gold, her eyes a living green, her lips red as the apple she'd bitten into many months ago.

'Wait there. You need shoes. Please tell me you're not going to ruin the outfit by putting on some sort of ballet pump or something.'

Anna had a wardrobe full of sensible ballet pumps and then she remembered. She ran to the wardrobe and pulled out the gold shoes from where she'd buried them.

'Selene bought them for me when I was young.'

'Selene buys you gifts?'

'For every birthday she's been around.'

'How nice for you,' Effie muttered resentfully. 'Put them on then!'

They were beautiful but small, sized for an eleven-year-old, which was the last time she'd tried them on. As she slipped into them they grew to fit her feet, the heels lengthening elegantly at the same time.

The doorbell rang.

Effie pretended to faint against the wall. 'That'll be your prince in perfumed armour, Peter. Attis has never been on time for anything in his life.'

They made their way down the stairs. Aunt looked as if she'd swallowed sandpaper when she saw them. Anna tried to hide the slit in the dress as best she could.

'Anna, I hardly think those heels are appropriate.'

'I'll make sure she doesn't break her neck,' said Effie, smiling sweetly.

Anna couldn't believe she was opening the door of her house to Peter. In a light grey suit with his blond hair brushed back from his face, he'd never looked more handsome. He held a red rose wrist corsage in one hand.

'You look beautiful,' he said, offering her the corsage. She slipped her hand through it.

'Thanks to me.' Effie stepped forward. Peter's eyes trailed away from Anna and took in Effie instead, her long legs revealed by the see-through skirt of her black dress.

He nodded. 'Effie.'

Anna turned around to say goodbye to Aunt, who was watching them intently, a smile taunting her mouth. 'Excuse me.' Aunt pushed her way forwards. 'Vivienne Everdell. Good to meet you.' She extended a cordial hand to Peter.

Peter gave her a winning smile. 'Vivienne, very good to meet you. Thank you for taking all my calls. I imagine I became rather a nuisance.'

'Not at all. I'm glad Anna has found a gentleman like yourself.'

'I promise to take good care of her tonight.'

'She must be home by midnight.'

'The car is already booked.'

She gave him an appraising look. 'I'm trusting you, Peter Nowell.'

'Never trust a man with perfectly polished shoes,' said a voice from behind him.

Peter and Aunt scowled at Attis in unison.

'Better late than never,' said Effie, stepping out to him.

Attis drank her in. 'You look ravishing. Now, I don't have a car booked but I have a bottle of whisky and a killer playlist.'

'Sounds perfect to me.'

Peter moved aside to let Anna out and only then did Attis look at her, his eyes widening just a little. They hadn't spoken since the garden. If he was angry, he didn't show it. Anna was staring at him too. He looked different. She'd never seen him out of tracksuit bottoms or jeans. His suit was jet black, his shirt crisp white, his hair still wet, falling into his eyes.

'You guys want a ride?' he offered, still looking at Anna.

'I think we'll be fine.' Peter took Anna's hand and pulled her towards a dark black BMW parked next to Attis's dilapidated Peugeot.

'Anna, you forgot something,' Aunt called. Anna hurried back to the doorway and Aunt yanked her close and whispered: 'Enjoy yourself tonight but remember, no matter how much of a gentleman they may look, they'll still break your heart.'

The ball was held in the Boys' School hall. Anna could only get so excited by the decorations. There were balloons and streamers and flower displays on the confetti-covered tables, but if they'd been in Equinox no doubt the stained-glass windows would have been pouring down the walls and people would be floating off in giant balloons . . .

Peter went to fetch them drinks. Anna stood lost for a moment in the crowd when Rowan pushed her way through the press of bodies, dragging Manda alongside. 'Anna!' Their dates, Karim and a skinny boy that Anna presumed was the trumpet-player, watched them go. 'Your dress is sending me into seizure it's so hot. Where did you get that?'

'Effie, obviously. You both look beautiful.' She smiled. Manda was wearing a rather formal pale blue dress and Rowan had gone eye-catching in a neon green skirt that puffed out from her waist.

'I know.' Rowan twirled. 'I'm so glad you and Effie made up. At last, the dream team Dark Mooners back together. What did I tell you, Manda? It's all sorted. Mother Holle help me, where's David going now?'

Rowan made off after her date and Manda glanced at Anna, nose in the air. 'I'm sorry, Anna. I was wrong.' The admission obviously pained her.

'It's OK. I'm sorry too, for my part in the mess.'

Manda seemed surprised by Anna's apology. 'I just – I – finally felt like I belonged. I didn't want to lose it.'

'I know.'

'I still think Darcey deserved what she got, mind you, but Headmaster Connaughty – that was wrong. Effie's sorry about it all anyway.'

Anna wasn't sure if Effie was that sorry but she nodded. Manda looked back towards Karim, as if to check he was still there.

'So, you guys are together then?'

Manda blushed 'Yes. We're in love. I'm still freaking out about everything, but I think I'm keeping my cool on the surface.' Manda turned to check Karim's whereabouts again.

Anna smiled and then noticed Peter coming towards them. 'Come on, Anna, let's get a drink.'

Manda made eyes at her and hurried off towards Karim.

Peter was the perfect date. He was attentive, bringing her drinks, introducing her to his friends. They sat and chatted over the music, tentatively getting to know each other. He held her hand tightly and told her she looked beautiful every ten minutes until Anna really started to believe it. She talked to people who had called her names and taunted her in the past and now they were smiling at her and acting as if they had always been friends. They weren't her friends.

'Peter, I'll be back in a minute, I'm just going to catch up with the others for a bit, OK?'

'Effie,' he said darkly. 'Anna, stay with me, I don't want to let you go tonight.'

'I won't be long, I promise.'

Anna pulled away and went in search of them. She located Effie and Attis leaning against the wall at the back of the hall, observing proceedings and attracting attention without trying.

'I'm surprised you've managed to separate yourself from

Peter long enough to find us,' Effie mocked. 'Did you try the punch yet? Feeling frisky?'

'I'll make sure to avoid the punch if you had anything to do with it.'

'Oh, I just threw a couple of Selene's potions in there. Here, have some of this.' Effie handed her the bottle from earlier. Anna looked around to check for teachers and then took a swig. Effie threw her head against the wall. 'This is even more boring than I'd anticipated. Shall we go to Equinox already?'

'I can't. Peter . . .'

'That's the problem with dating a cowan.'

'We're not dating.'

'Not yet,' said Attis, watching the crowd.

Rowan stumbled into them. She was with Manda.

'Oh, there you are,' said Rowan. 'I'm not so sure David really wants to hang out with me. He's spending most of his time with his friends, so sod it, I thought I'd do the same. And Karim is talking to his ex-girlfriend—'

'They're just chatting. I'm very chilled about it,' said Manda, her eye twitching. 'I don't want to seem crazy and drag him away – yet.'

'Forget them, let's dance,' said Effie.

'Finally!' Rowan cheered. 'Someone wants to dance with me.'

They took to the floor, the crowd parting for Effie as always. They formed a circle and let loose, Effie surreptitiously passing the bottle between them. Anna was sure it had a little magic in it too – she felt more and more free with every sip. Attis moved between them, picking up Rowan, spinning Manda round. When he came face to face with Anna, he took her hand and twirled her away and back again forcefully, his hand grabbing her waist, crumpling the satin of her dress.

Anna leant into his ear. She could smell the smoke and

fire of his skin. 'I'm sorry', she shouted over the music, 'for stealing your key.'

He spun her away and moved on.

They danced and grew giddy. The rest of the room melted away and Anna imagined herself outside again – under the moonlight, the fire roaring in front of them. The others must have felt it too because they all began to dance with abandon, ridiculous, imbecelic abandon. They soon found themselves doing the rain dance again: Rowan shimmying, Manda stomping, Effie jumping on Attis's back and calling forth the rain; lights spinning, crowds gathering and limbs crashing.

Lightning flashed overhead suddenly, eclipsing the lights in the room. Thunder cracked the air like a whip. Rain began to pour outside. They looked at each other and laughed hysterically. Effie grabbed Anna's hands and spun them around, revelling in the magic. *How can no one else in the room feel it?*

Anna caught sight of Peter in the crowd. Darcey was next to him, whispering in his ear.

'I've got to go,' she said to Effie, breaking away.

She walked over to them. 'Peter, want to dance?' Anna extended a hand to him.

'Why would he want to join the freak show out there?' Darcey sneered.

'Sorry, I've got to go.' Peter took Anna's hand.

Of everything that had happened that year, nothing was so satisfying as Darcey's face at that moment. They weaved into the crowd and Peter drew her close to him. 'You guys looked pretty interesting . . .'

The rain was still pouring outside.

Anna laughed. 'We got carried away.'

The music began to slow. Peter pulled her closer and time seemed to slip away as they danced.

Anna lifted her head up to look at him. 'Are you and Darcey definitely over?'

Peter nodded firmly. 'Over. She was always a lot to handle, but after everything that's happened this year, she's nothing to me now.' He tilted her chin up towards him. 'I swear you're getting more beautiful with every hour. How did a girl like you fly under the radar for so long?'

Anna laughed and looked down, choosing not to recall everything that had brought her to this moment. He moved her hair from her face and leant in. The kiss was gentle, barely there at all. She pulled away and smiled at him. *Her first kiss. It wasn't so scary.*

He pulled her tighter, his arms caressing her back. He kissed her again. She kissed back and his breathing quickened. 'Everdell, you're delicious.' He kissed harder now, his hands running up into her hair. 'You smell so good.' He kissed down her neck. 'God, I want you.' She hoped they were hidden in the dark of the room.

'Peter . . .' She pulled away.

'Anna.' He was breathing fast. 'Let's get out of here. I've got a room.'

'I'm not sure—'

'Nothing has to happen, but it could . . .'

'Let's just stay here for a bit.'

'Come on. I know you've been waiting for this moment.' He smiled, his eyes implacable. He trailed his hands down her arms and took hold of her wrists. He pulled her gently towards the door.

'No, Peter, I want to stay here.'

He kissed her again. 'We could be alone at last.' He pulled harder.

'I'm sorry.' She knew she was ruining everything, but she couldn't. *Every guy feels obligated to try and sleep with their date at the summer ball.*

His smiled dropped, the blue of his eyes turning cold. 'Anna . . .'

'She said she doesn't want to go.' Attis appeared beside them.

Peter's lips turned up, revealing teeth.

Attis towered over him. 'Why don't you do everyone a favour and leave instead?'

'Whatever.' Peter looked back at Anna and stormed off.

Attis took her hand and then they were dancing, slowly, maintaining a careful distance from one another. Anna was too ashamed to say anything.

'He's a fuckwit, Anna.'

She let out a shaky laugh.

'Do you want me to punch him? I did it once and it felt good.'

She tried to process the last few minutes. That had not been the calm, composed Peter she knew. 'He said nothing had to happen . . .' She could still feel his hand on her wrist.

'It's a good line.'

'Do you use it?'

'No. I wouldn't lie to sleep with a girl.'

Anna looked up at him. 'I'm sorry I took your key.'

'I told you not to dig, to put yourself in danger.'

'I know. I was stupid, but I was desperate. I knew you wouldn't understand.'

'Did your aunt hurt you?' He looked down at her, eyes blazing. Anna felt tears rush into hers. She'd tried to forget those three long weeks. She found she couldn't tell him.

Attis looked away, his jaw clenching. 'You should have let me in, that night, when I came.'

'I couldn't.'

He nodded. Anna realized they had grown closer – Attis's face was inches from hers. His lips exactly where Peter's had been when they kissed. She could feel his arms around her and wanted to sink deeper. To escape again.

Then she saw Effie over his shoulder – staring at them.

Anna dropped Attis's hand. 'Effie.'

'What?' said Attis.

'Effie's waiting for you. I'm going to get a drink.' She pulled away.

'Anna, don't try to find him.'

'I won't. Right now, he's a massive fuckwit.'

She went to the drinks counter, reeling from everything that had just happened. A couple were making out passionately over the punch.

There was some general kerfuffle on stage and then the music was cut. Darcey walked out into the centre, hair bouncing, one hand holding up her long, silver dress, the other holding a microphone.

'Thank you.' The microphone screeched and she glared at the flustered-looking sound guy. 'On behalf of the student council, thank you all for coming. The council has done a spectacular job of bringing my vision to life, a round of applause is in order.' Everyone clapped and cheered. 'Now, I don't want to stop the partying for too long – oh and by the way, after-party at mine tonight, guestlist only – but first, it's that time of the night that we all look forward to.' Darcey pointed at the large screen behind her. 'The council and I have put together our favourite pictures and memories from the school year. Embarrassment is compulsory.'

The screen lit up and a slideshow began, scrolling through pictures and memories that Anna hadn't been a part of. People began to cheer and laugh as their photos were shown – pulling faces, assuming stupid poses, drunk or captured kissing someone in the dark. Then a photo of Rowan.

Anna's heart stopped.

Another photo of Rowan appeared, more unflattering than the first. Laughter began to bubble up from the crowd. Another photo of Rowan – the pictures from the horrible game they had all played. Darcey had seeded them throughout.

Just enough to humiliate, not enough to raise suspicion. Darcey began to snigger on stage. Anna had presumed that, after everything, on some deeply buried level Darcey's taste of her own medicine would have changed her perspective, blunted her cruelty.

The laughter suddenly stopped.

Anna's glass dropped from her hand, lemonade fizzing over her gold shoes.

The photo montage was gone. A video was playing instead. Darcey stood, rooted to the spot, watching herself on screen with Headmaster Connaughty.

The hall was completely silent. Nothing but the horrifying sounds of the video.

Slowly, the whispers came, shocked inhalations, murmurings. Darcey did not move.

The teachers had begun to panic, trying to cut it off. The screen went blank. Anna located Headmaster Connaughty running out of the hall.

Darcey still had not moved. Her eyes were far away. *Watching her future crumble.*

The noise in the hall exploded. The sound of the rumours returning all at once, deafening. The video cut to static and within it seven circles. The Eye.

Darcey ran.

'Where is she?' Anna pulled Rowan's shoulder. She couldn't think straight for the anger pulsing through her. 'Where's Effie? Manda, where is she?'

Manda looked pale. 'I – I don't know . . .'

'Did you know she hadn't destroyed the video?'

Rowan shook her head but Manda fiddled with her hands nervously. 'She said she wasn't going to do anything with it.'

'Oh! And you believed that? How convenient.' Anna pushed through them. It was hard to get through the crowds.

Everyone was excited, feeding off the drama. The ball was over but the fun had just begun.

'I knew it. I knew they were at it . . .'

'How could she? It's disgusting!'

'How could he? Isn't it illegal?'

'My eyes are burning!'

Anna found Attis. 'Where is she?'

'I don't know. I'm looking for her too. Anna – calm down.'

'No. I don't want to be calm for this. She released that video, I know it!' She threw his hands off her. 'I trusted her, again!'

'I don't know where she's gone.'

Anna pushed past him. 'Has anyone seen Effie?' She grabbed at random people. 'Have you seen Effie?'

'I saw her like twenty minutes ago. She went that way, with Peter.'

*With Peter.*

She spotted Tom and stepped in front of him. 'Tom! What number is Peter's room?'

'Number fourteen. Why? You gonna show him a good time?' He made a stupid hooting noise.

Anna was already gone, propelled by a rage she'd never known before. She ran down the corridors, heading towards the boarding block. She could hear footsteps behind her – Attis calling – but she would not stop, she could not stop.

*Number eleven, number twelve, number thirteen . . .*

Number fourteen. Anna touched the handle and the door sprang open under the fury of her touch.

They were in the bed together.

'Anna!' Peter shouted, covering himself with the sheets.

Effie appeared behind him, hair in disarray, lips flushed red. Her eyes flickered momentarily with something like guilt. Anna had been ready to yell and scream about the video but now she didn't know what to say. The betrayal ran deeper, too deep for words to surface.

'We were just having fun.' Effie grabbed at Peter's discarded shirt. 'I told you there's really nothing else to do with him.' She laughed.

Anna stared at them.

Effie's laughter died. 'Oh, come on, you don't even like him and you're not as innocent as you pretend.' Her voice was scathing.

Peter stuttered. 'Anna, I didn't mean to—'

'Anna.' Attis took her arm. 'Come on, leave them.'

Effie sprang out of bed, throwing the shirt over her head. 'Attis Lockerby, you stop right there. It wasn't like that. He hit on me, OK? I just want to go home. Take me home.'

'Take yourself home,' Attis spat. He put an arm around Anna and flicked his hand out. The door shut in her face. 'Come on,' he said, moving her down the corridor. Anna sank into him, tears of anger running down her face.

'Attis! Come back, right now!' She heard Effie call behind them, but Attis did not turn around, did not stop.

They were on the road within moments, the school in the car mirror disappearing from sight. The sights of it stayed with Anna – the video, Darcey's face, Effie and Peter. *Effie.* How could she?

'Where am I taking you?' said Attis.

Anna knew she should go home, back to Aunt, away from Effie forever, but the words would not form. All of her carefully controlled emotions were charging through her at once – and it hurt like hell – but she couldn't give them up. She'd come too far to go back. An urgency she'd never felt was at her back like a knife, around her neck like a necklace tightening . . .

'Take me to Selene.'

Attis looked unsure. 'Effie might come back.'

'I need to see Selene.'

They didn't speak again. Attis wound through the traffic

at breakneck speed, through the noise and lights and chaos of London. Anna stared out of the window, her fingers fluttering back and forth over her Knotted Cord.

The house was quiet.

'Where is she?' said Anna.

'I'll call her,' said Attis. Anna sat down on the kitchen stool. 'Selene, can you come back to the house? I don't care if you're on a date. Anna's here. She and Effie – they've fallen out.' He emphasized the words slowly. 'She needs you. Now.'

He put down the phone. 'She's on her way.'

Anna pulled at her dress – it was too tight. 'I need to take this off. I need to get this off me.'

'OK. You can borrow some clothes upstairs. They're Effie's though.'

'I just need to get this off.' The dress was suffocating. She wanted to shred it to pieces. She pulled the red rose off her wrist and threw it in the bin.

'Let's go.' They went into Effie's dressing room and he pulled out a pair of jeans and a jumper from the wardrobe. She kicked the gold shoes off.

'Can you undo it at the top?' Anna scrabbled at her back, unable to find the zip.

'Sure.' Attis approached her hesitantly. She turned around, her back to him.

She only realized how fast she was breathing, how angry and desperate she was, as he came up behind her. He drew her hair out of the way – his hands brushing her neck. She breathed out all at once – the air around them stilling. He pulled the zip, following the shiver down her spine.

'Anna,' he said, his voice cracking, stepping closer.

She could feel his breath on her neck, the heat of him. Her legs were stuck to the floor. The dress hung on her, open.

She turned around slowly. It was like losing her free will again, only this time, instead of not being able to feel anything, she could feel it all – too much – not enough – she wanted more. His hands were painful flames on her skin; his lips were longing; his eyes were the place you go before sleep – smoke and dreams and escape.

'Attis,' she exhaled and he lowered himself towards her.

The kiss was slow and sweet and agonizing, like one of his magical symbols, turning her molten in his arms; beneath, a fire roared, a heat Anna had never known, a heat that only grew against the impossible softness of his lips. She grabbed at the collar of his shirt as his hands pressed against her back. She wanted to sink into him forever, for every last knot inside of her to come undone. She felt her dress fall off her shoulders . . .

The front door banged shut and they jumped apart.

'I'm back.' Selene's voice.

Anna picked up the clothes. Attis turned away. She put them on hastily. She didn't know what to say. There was too much to say. She had never felt so much in one single moment and she didn't know what it meant. She looked back up but Attis wasn't smiling, his brow was dark.

'Anna . . .'

'Anna!' Selene called distantly.

'Come on, let's go.' Anna took his hand and they made their way down the stairs and into the kitchen.

Selene surveyed them quietly. 'So, my little matchstick, Attis tells me you've had a falling-out with Effie. What's happened?'

Anna saw now there was no time to waste. She told Selene everything. About the video, about Peter, Effie, about Aunt and her three weeks of hell, about the fact she had to become a Binder, how twisted they truly were. About needing to escape. *Now.* 'You'll help me, won't you? You said you would. Please, Selene, I don't want to become a Binder. I have to get away.'

'Hush now, of course I'll help.' Selene pulled Anna into a hug.

Anna felt as if she were seven again, meeting Selene for the first time on her balcony, wishing she could float away with her. The tears came thick and fast. Anna tried to clear them. 'I'm – I'm sorry I ruined your date.'

Selene waved a hand, laughing at the absurdity of the situation and wiping a tear from her own eye. 'Oh, don't be silly. He was just a plaything; he doesn't even know my real name. Tonight I was femme fatale Carmenta Foy.' She threw her scarf over her shoulder.

Attis snorted. 'Who's Carmenta Foy?'

'My pseudonym. Every woman should have one.'

*Carmenta Foy. Carmenta.*

Anna felt her world sink around her.

*When can you come and see me? Can you get rid of HER tonight? Carmenta x.*

The message found on her father's phone after he had killed her mother.

The thoughts came crashing at once, impossible to comprehend. The name – it was so unique, so specific. Selene was the other woman? Selene had betrayed her mother? Had been the cause of her mother's death? Maybe she'd killed her herself. Fear poured through Anna like ice.

*I have to get out of here.*

'I just need a moment,' said Anna calmly. 'Wash my face, get a tissue . . .'

'OK, sweetie. Then we'll get you sorted – I'm formulating a plan.'

Anna left the room, walked upstairs to the bathroom and looked in the mirror. The horror of what she'd just heard was etched all over her face. She remembered Selene lying in the golden bathwater, telling her she'd once loved a man – *my father?* The exact woman Aunt had warned her against.

Anna had to tell Attis. They had to leave. Now.

She went to Selene's bedroom and took the feather from

where it floated on the mantelpiece. She crept back down-stairs and stopped at the kitchen door, but the murmur of whispers stopped her.

'Is she in love with you yet?' Selene's voice, low and bitter. 'Or have you messed that up too?'

'I don't know,' Attis replied gruffly.

'You don't know? You told me you could make any girl fall in love with you. She has to be for this to work. How am I meant to know if the curse has begun?'

'I think it has.'

'Think isn't good enough. For Goddess's sake! I created you for this one reason! You know we have to stop her from leaving when she comes back down. She can't escape.'

'I know.'

Anna reached for her Knotted Cord, but the feelings that had been surging through her had already died. She tightened the cord and felt calm for the first time since the video of Darcey had started to play. Detached. Collected. Her pathway clear. Her heart in pieces but her future sealed.

Selene had killed her mother and Attis was in on it.

*I created you . . .*

Attis wasn't a witch. He wasn't human.

*I created you . . .* a memory rose to the surface. Manda reading from Selene's spell book, from the pages that seemed to have been used: the spell for a golem, a man made from earth and kept alive with human hearts and blood.

*I created you . . .* He was no more than an illusion. She could still feel his kiss on her lips. She couldn't love what wasn't real.

She walked back into the room. They looked at her and she threw the feather in the air before they had time to react. They froze. Their movements stretched across time.

Anna grabbed Selene's handbag and ran.

\* \* \*

She hailed a taxi and gave her address. Cressey Square. *Home.* She checked Selene's purse – she had more than enough money to cover it. She could barely begin to process what had just happened – the betrayals stacked against her. It was too much. All too much.

It was just before midnight when she got back.

Aunt opened the door. 'Where's Peter?'

Anna looked up at her and fell into her arms.

'I'm sorry, Aunt. I'm sorry for everything,' she sobbed. 'You were right, love is evil. Magic is a sin.' The two were one in Anna's mind now. Rotten at their core. *Cursed.* They had ruined everything. She was at the black empty centre of the Eye now and there was only one way out. 'I want to become a Binder.'

Aunt pulled her away and wiped the hair from her face. 'Come on, let's go upstairs.' She took Anna to her room and retrieved a glass of water. 'Drink and calm down. Then tell me what's happened.'

Anna tried to collect herself but it came out in a blur. 'My magic. I know, I know something is wrong with it. The curse mark. It shows the curse mark. It's dangerous, Aunt, and everything got so out of hand and Effie, Effie was meant to be there for me, but . . . but she was with Peter. I liked him . . . I loved her . . . I hate them both. Why? I just don't know why she would do that to me.'

Aunt looked unsurprised. 'Because it is in her nature to do so.'

'Then I went back to Selene's and . . .' Anna looked at Aunt with gravity. 'I think she had an affair with my father. It's hard to explain, but I think she did.' The words made her feel sick. 'Love ruins everything, just like you said.'

She couldn't tell Aunt about Attis, that was too much, too tender to touch. 'I don't want to feel like this any more. Please take it away. I want to be a Binder.'

She had made a decision. Chosen her path. Relief flooded through her, numbing the pain. Magic had failed her; everyone she loved had betrayed her. Except Aunt. Aunt had said it all along, that she would come to see what was best and now she had. She wasn't weak to join the Binders: nothing was harder than giving it all up; she'd been weak to give in to magic in the first place. Look where it had left her: cursed, ruined, broken.

'I sometimes thought it might have been Selene who betrayed your mother,' said Aunt, her face troubled. 'She liked your father, that much I knew, and she seduces any man in her sights, but I never had any proof she was the one. I didn't want to believe it.'

'Selene betrayed my mother just as Effie betrayed me. She was Carmenta,' said Anna, ashamed. 'I'm sorry. I researched their deaths. I needed to know, but I don't want to know any more. I just want to forget. Please keep her away from me. Keep them all away from me.'

'I won't ever let Selene near you again. The Knotting ceremony will go ahead at once. Tomorrow.'

'Yes, yes,' said Anna, wanting it, desperate for it.

'I knew you would choose right because I know you, Anna. I know you better than anyone else in the world.' She held Anna's face in her fingers. 'It will still be hard though, my child. A sacrifice must be made and you have to be willing to make it. It's what your training has been for. I believe you are strong enough but you must promise me, when the time comes, you will do it. There's no choice either way – I've bound your will before and I can do it again – but it's easier, easier if you are in control of your emotions. You must trust me.'

*If we don't have trust, we don't have anything.*

Anna looked back into Aunt's eyes, as green as her own. 'I know about the bindweed. The poison.'

Aunt's grip on her tightened but she didn't look away. 'It was for your protection. Don't you see? It was to protect you from this, what's happened to you. I never wanted you to go through this. It's a hard truth but magic and love are a worse poison. Look at you, my child, you're broken.'

Anna bent forwards, the grief escaping at last in deep shuddering waves. 'I'm ready. Just make this stop.'

'I know, I know.' Aunt soothed her, holding her head against her. She had never held her like that. Anna's tears soaked into her shirt and Aunt didn't even wipe them away. 'I wish I hadn't been right, but your magic is cursed, just like your mother's. It must be bound. Everything will be better then.'

'What is the curse?'

'Love, it is love.'

# MIRROR

*Truth is but a mirror of our own sins. We do not live by truth which can be used against us, but only by silence – words unsaid; memories forgotten; emotions unmade.*

*Introduction, The Book of the Binders*

Anna lay down on the bed, exhausted. She didn't want to think. She hurt all over and yet she couldn't say what hurt. She had no control over this pain, but at least becoming a Binder was her choice. A life of pain and punishment, tests and trials, but perhaps, one day, she'd regain her independence, prove herself, become a Senior Binder and practise magic again – when she was ready. When the pain was long gone . . .

She felt Attis's kiss on her lips as she fell asleep.

In her dreams his lips were sweet and soft – but then he wasn't there any more, it was just air. Effie was in his place, laughing, crows flying out of her mouth, descending on Anna in black circles. Anna was looking in a mirror and her mother was staring back at her, saying something but Anna couldn't hear the words – Selene coming up behind her mother with a knife, only it wasn't Selene, it was Aunt and the knife was made from silk, red silk . . .

She woke with a start. She reached for her light and switched it on. The fairy-tale book was on the floor again. Its fall must have woken her. She was glad – her dreams were torture. Soon she wouldn't have to dream any more. She held it in her hands as if it could somehow fill the emptiness inside of her.

She took out the picture of her parents.

'I'm doing this for you.' She touched her mother's face. 'I won't let love kill me too.' She felt, with a cold, terrifying certainty, that it would.

Anna tried to find reassurance in her mother's eyes but they were too busy looking at her father and he back at her. Anna wanted to tear the picture apart, separate them for good, but could not. It held her captive; and then she began to feel it: the emotion at the moment it was taken, like the photographs in the vintage shop. It jolted through her, clear as the sky in the picture. Love. *Love.* She searched the picture harder, trying to find cracks in it, but could find nothing but love.

*Why then? Why would you kill her if you loved her so?* The photo was taken not long before it happened. *Is love that sick? That you can love someone completely and still do that to them?*

She remembered Effie in bed with Peter. *Yes.* Selene calling herself Carmenta. *Yes.* Attis's lips on hers. *Yes.* Her lips on Attis's . . . *Yes.*

All of the questions she'd been trying to bury inside her began to spill out. *Aunt says my magic is cursed by love, but what is the curse? Why won't she tell me still?* Anna recalled Selene's hushed words – that she had to be in love with Attis for the curse to work. *Why did she create him? For me to fall in love with him? Did she betray my mother too? How are the betrayals connected? Is Effie in on it too? Have she and Attis both been laughing behind my back while I fell for him?*

Anna shook her head, trying to block the questions out. It

didn't matter any longer. She had decided. Even if Aunt still had her secrets she was the only one who truly loved her . . .

*Then what's in the third-floor room? No! I don't care! I don't care!*

Anna banged her fist on the front of the book in frustration. Its image shimmered on the cover, catching the moonlight from her window. A tree above and a tree below. A perfect mirror.

Nana Yaganov's words returned with sudden force: *The truth is within the leaves. The mirror within the mirror. The mirror is the key.*

*Leaves . . .* what if Nana had not been referring to the leaves of a tree, but the leaves of a book? A book with a mirror on the front? The book in her hands. If the riddle was referring to the book and the truth was within its pages – was a mirror hiding inside the fairy tales? *The mirror is the key.*

Anna opened the book to the first tale: 'The Eyeless Maiden', who sought the truth and had her eyes pecked out for it. She read it again and again and again. The maiden created a lake in the forest which became a mirror. *The mirror?* There were three keys – one silver, one water, one blood. *How can that help me? Perhaps Nana wants me to end up with my eyes pecked out . . .*

She turned to the second fairy tale, 'Little Red Cap'. Despite the grandmother's grisly death, it was a happier tale, not quite so lashed with punishment. This girl wandered off the path too but managed to defeat the wolf in the end with her little bag containing twig, needle, coin and thimble . . . each becoming wind, a mountain of earth, a raging fire and a river.

A tune rose up in her mind:

Needle is the dagger, commanding smoke and fire.
Twig is the wand, stirring wind and air.
Coin is the pentacle, in tune with soil and earth.
Thimble is the chalice, containing water's breath.

It was the nursery rhyme Rowan sometimes sang.

Anna tightened her grip on the book. The fairy tale was hiding a simple truth. *Needle, twig, coin, thimble* . . . they represented the elemental tools: dagger, wand, pentacle and chalice. *What if there's more to the fairy tales than little warning stories for children? What if they contain buried knowledge? Hidden spells? Is 'Little Red Cap' really the instructions for an elemental spell?*

Anna flicked back to the first fairy tale and read it again, her mind racing. As she read it, it was as if the spell mapped itself out for her, the words arrows pointing her in one direction. Three keys: one silver, one water, one blood. The maiden throws them together and they become a lake. When the moonlight touches it – a mirror.

*One last spell can't hurt.*

Anna barely knew what she was doing but she rose from her bed. She walked to her dressing table and picked up the silver mirror from the antique set. She wrapped a jumper around her hand and smashed the glass with her fist. She pulled the shards away until there was nothing left but an empty silver shell. She took her glass of water from her bedside table and the needle from her embroidery. She went to the balcony, opened it and stepped out into the moonlight.

She placed the silver shell on the floor. *A silver key.*

She poured the water into it. *A water key.*

She pricked her finger with the needle and squeezed a drop of blood into the water. *A blood key.*

She waited for the moon to come back out from behind the clouds.

She repeated Nana's words as if they were a spell: *The truth is within the leaves. The mirror within the mirror. The mirror is the key.* She plucked at the threads of magic: silver, water, blood, moonlight, stitching them together.

The moon revealed itself above. Anna watched with fascination as the water in the silver frame froze over – turned hard

– became a mirror. A brilliant, silver, magic mirror. A mirror made of moonlight. She picked it up and looked into it.

Effie's face stared back at her.

'What is my curse?' she asked.

Effie smiled.

Anna couldn't say how, but she knew the mirror had all the answers she needed. She could feel them, beating their wings against the glass, struggling to get out. Effie continued to smile serenely. It was not a smile Anna recognized on her, it was so serene. That smile, her black hair, reminded Anna of someone. *My mother.*

Effie's face and her mother's almost seemed to interchange in the mirror as she looked at it. Anna blinked and the face was Effie's once more. She reached for the photograph of her parents and held it up against the mirror. How had she not seen it? The similarity between her mother and Effie. She turned the photo to the mirror and saw, for the first time, the true picture beneath and not the chimera. There was not one baby in her mum's arms, but two. Anna stared at the photo for several minutes and then turned to the mirror again.

'Are you my sister?'

Effie nodded, her smile all Effie's now, menacing and mesmerizing, exploding her life into shards of glass.

There was no time to pick up the pieces. 'Should I go to the room on the third floor?'

Effie nodded again and Anna nodded with her.

She looked back at the photograph, at her mother's smile. She owed her this much. Anna stood up and walked to her door, mirror in hand.

There was no one left to trust now. She had to find out what was in the third-floor room . . .

*The mirror is the key.*

*   *   *

She crept downstairs and took the ninth key from the rack. Aunt's key. The end of it began to move and shift in her hands like a puzzle that would never be solved. She made her way up silently to the room on the third floor. She looked upon the door that was the dead end of her life.

She turned around so she was facing away from it and held the mirror up so the keyhole was reflected. She took the key and inserted it into the mirrored keyhole. It passed into the glass of the mirror without resistance, only a gentle ripple, like a pebble dropped in a lake. In any other circumstance Anna would have marvelled at the magic but now she held the mirror steady and turned the key . . .

She heard the door unlock behind her. She turned back around and tried the handle.

It opened.

The room was larger than she'd expected. There was a huge four-poster bed in its centre below the window, moonlight spilling onto tangled red sheets. A dressing table stood opposite, a small rose bush perched on it alongside several picture frames. There was a cupboard against the far wall. Nothing stirred. Except for the unmade bed the room was unremarkable.

Anna picked up one of the frames on the dressing table: her father was in the photograph – not with her mother – but with Aunt. She looked at the others. All of the pictures were of Aunt and her father. They were young, Aunt's hair bright as her own.

She walked to the cupboard and opened it, releasing a cold, chilled air.

She screamed silently.

Inside it was full of hospital blood bags and jars – jars containing hearts. She picked up one of the bags and held it to the moonlight. Printed on it was 'King's College London Hospital' – Aunt's hospital. The hearts began to beat, all of them, all at once, pulsing against the glass, bulging and bleeding. Anna backed away and the roses on the dressing table opened, meeting her silent scream with their own. She heard a noise behind her. She spun around – a shadow was standing behind the door. It must have been in there with her the whole time.

It stepped forward, its face suddenly revealed in the moonlight. Anna couldn't breathe. Her world ceased to make sense. It was a man. A face she knew from a photograph: her father. The word had no meaning as she thought it. *Father. My father.*

He stared back at her, unmoving. The hair dark and curly, longer than in the photograph, the eyes slightly downturned as if they would crinkle when he smiled, the jaw square and dusted with five o'clock shadow. A handsome face. *There's something wrong with it. There's something very wrong.* The eyes – like the eyes in a painting – they followed you, but they weren't alive.

*This isn't my father. This isn't human!*

The fear came all at once, unleashed by an involuntary revulsion. Anna tried to dart past him but he moved towards her. She dropped the mirror and it shattered. She tried to duck and run out of the room, but the man pushed her back and then his hands were on her neck – strong – the face before her unchanging as he tightened his grip, eyes flashing in moonlight, but there was nothing behind them for the light to find.

She kicked against him and somehow managed to rip free of his grip. She fell on the floor, reaching for the mirror and the shards of glass. She curled her fingers around one but he was on her. She thrust it into him; he did not cry out, but pushed her down. His hands found her neck. Tightened around it. Anna struggled for breath.

'Let her go.'

Anna gasped as he released her neck.

Aunt was in the doorway. 'Take her to her bedroom.'

Aunt moved aside and the man forced Anna downstairs. He threw her into her room. Aunt followed her in and slammed the door behind them. The man stood in the corner watching.

'Are you going to make me bind your free will again? I'll do it. I don't need a cord. I could bind you right now without batting an eyelid.'

Anna could not speak. She could not think. Her horror was too great, her fear greater than any she had ever known. She would have faced a thousand dark cupboards over the creature that stood in the shadows.

'Sit down.'

Anna's legs gave way.

She'd always been surprised by how in control Aunt was when she was angry – until now. Now Aunt's silent seething erupted in a high and desperate howl, the veins of her neck pinging free. 'You've ruined everything! Why didn't you trust me? Sixteen years of meticulous work and you had to go through your teenage rebellion tonight.' She laughed, running clawed fingers through her hair.

'Effie is my sister,' said Anna, hardly believing the words.

Aunt moved towards her; she slapped her face, hard. 'How do you know that? How did you get into the room?'

'Tell me the truth.'

'The truth?' Aunt repeated and Anna knew her question was absurd. Aunt didn't deal in the truth. She believed her own lies. She laughed again and then breathed in, trying to control herself. 'Yes. The truth is all that may work now.' She sat down on the bed next to Anna. 'You will see then that I was right all along.'

'Tell me.'

'So impatient!' she snarled. 'Do you know how patient I've had to be? Oh yes, Effie is your sister. Your twin sister, in fact.

Your mother and I were twins too, of course, and all of us are cursed. The great family curse: *One womb, one breath, sisters of blood, bound by love, so bound by death.'* She laughed again, shuddering and broken. 'You know what our silly little curse is? Love. Nothing but love. That we'll fall in love with the same man and it will tear us apart. Generation after generation for hundreds of years – nothing but love and pain and death.'

Anna tried to process Aunt's words. She and Effie were twins. Were both cursed. She recalled the occasions when the curse mark had appeared. Effie had always been there too – Rowan's fall, the salt circle, the static, the blood. *The symbol wasn't just for me, it was for both of us!*

'Does Effie know? Does she know that we're twins? That we're cursed?'

'Oh no.' Aunt smiled with satisfaction. 'Effie doesn't know anything. She's as unaware of the curse and your connection as you are, but she was still drawn to you and she still ruined your life, as I knew she would. She will kill you in the end. It's how it always ends, our curse.'

*'It's how it always ends . . .'* Anna repeated Aunt's words, trying to understand them. If that was the curse then Selene wasn't the other woman – Aunt was. 'What do you mean?' But Anna knew; she knew already. 'My father never killed my mother, did he? You did.'

'Your mother betrayed *me*, Anna, tried to kill *me*! Your father loved me; we were happy together.' Aunt's expression turned to a grimace, her wrinkles contracted with pain. 'She took him away from me, seduced him with love magic and potions from Selene no doubt. Got herself pregnant like a whore. I came to rescue you but she hated that your father still loved me and she tried to kill me. She stabbed him and attacked me, but I was the stronger witch.' Anna wasn't sure if the noise Aunt was making now was laughter or sobbing. 'I had no choice . . .'

Anna couldn't help imagining what Aunt had described in her head, but she didn't believe it. Not any more. She was sure there were grains of truth in it, just enough truth to be plausible, but it would be bound together with lies.

'Your precious Selene helped me though.'

Anna looked up.

'Oh yes. We formulated a plan. Fortunately, your mother had kept you both as her dirty little secret. She hadn't wanted me to find her out and so no one knew she'd had one baby, let alone two. Selene would take Effie and I would take you. I held you in my arms and I knew even then that you and I, we were meant to be together. We would raise you apart and at sixteen bring you back together and let the curse unfold – where we could watch you, where it could be controlled, before you could hurt each other. We made it out to be a murder. Selene planted the message on your father's phone pretending to be a lover: Carmenta. We took Effie away and left you there. The police swallowed the whole story hook, line and sinker.'

Aunt, Selene, Attis . . . they'd all known. Everyone but Effie. Anna could take little solace in that – Effie was her curse.

'I'm glad your little plan worked,' said Anna, wondering if she could smash her water glass over Aunt's head. *Perhaps I'll have time – but then –* She looked at the man in the shadows.

'It was the best thing for you, for both of you,' Aunt snapped. 'If you'd grown up together, it would only be worse now. I never wanted you to feel the pain I felt when your mother betrayed me. The Binders helped with it all, of course, to protect us, to protect all witches.'

'What the hell do the Binders have to do with this? How does this help anyone?'

'You think your curse can just be left to run riot? Curses are the sin above all sins – the dirtiest, most rotten form of magic. It must be bound. You'll be free then – I'll be free.'

Aunt's eyes were desperate. 'But it's greater than that, don't you see? The Binders understand the bigger picture. They always knew the Hunters would return one day and it's happening, it's happening now as we speak—'

'I don't believe a word the Binders say.'

'Oh, but you will. Magic has lured the Hunters back out of hiding. We warned them all, but no one listened and now they are back – back and hunting out powerful magic – and there is no magic as powerful as a curse, Anna. The stench of it will bring their darkness to our door.' Aunt's face twisted with disgust. 'We are marked and we must be bound.'

Anna thought of the Eye sewn into Aunt's flesh. *Marred. Marked.* Nana had said the cursed were at risk too. She'd spoken of a prophecy . . .

Anna looked up. 'What's the prophecy?'

Aunt's disgust twisted tighter, into a smile. 'You really have been doing your research, haven't you? The Binders pay no attention to the claims of fate. We are bound only by our own desires, not some outside force. But the power of a prophecy cannot be denied. It can be used against us.'

'What is it?'

'That the Hunters will rise again when a curse is born – a curse that will bring the downfall of the whole world.'

'The whole world,' Anna repeated. It was as dramatic and apocalyptic as a prophecy ought to be.

'I don't believe a word of it, but others will and it only adds to the urgency of our cause. Curses must be silenced, they must be bound, everywhere, and you and Effie are to be the first. If it's possible, it will be a great victory. Do you see how important you are now?'

'The first? How can we be the first? You have the same curse and you were bound.'

Aunt froze, her mouth still half-open – mid-battle.

'Weren't you?'

'My magic was never officially Knotted. No.'

Anna started to laugh. Aunt snapped her mouth shut and Anna tasted blood.

'Don't think I've had it easy. I've been through endless trials and untold pains and it hurts me to practise magic just the same, but it was too late for me – I was already lost. We decided to wait until the curse was new again, until we had built enough power to bind it.'

'How convenient for you. Fresh guinea pigs for your madness. It's all for the greater good then? The punishments, the cruelty – it's all so you can protect witches from a threat that no longer exists. How very heroic.'

Aunt looked as if she would bind Anna there and then. 'The threat is already here, Anna, and everything I do, everything I have done, is to keep you safe. The Knotting will go ahead tomorrow and you will not resist.'

'I won't do it.'

'Why? Because I lied? It doesn't change the curse. It doesn't change love. I brought you and Effie back together, but I didn't make her betray you – she did that all by herself. I always knew she would, just as your mother betrayed me.'

Anna had enough anger for both of them. Aunt and Effie.

'You think I haven't known what you've been up to this year? I know how the mind of a sixteen-year-old works. If I forbid it, oh, you'll do it! And I know you. I allowed you little freedoms and rebellions – your lies and secrets – your magic. Oh yes, I was allowing that too. Reducing your amount of bindweed, giving the curse room to flourish – enough for you to grow close to Effie, enough for you to fall for Peter, enough to see your heart break tonight. It broke my heart too, all over again.'

'You don't have a heart left to break.'

'I don't have a heart?' Aunt's face contorted. 'I raised you, didn't I? I loved you! I loved your father. I still do.' She looked over at the corner of the room.

'What is it?' said Anna, unable to look directly at him.

'He looks just like him.' Aunt smiled. 'We used his blood. Selene helped me create him. It's a memory of your father, Anna. It's all I've got left after your mother took him away from me.'

*A golem.* Anna thought of the lingerie in Aunt's drawer, the crumpled sheets and she knew what Aunt did with him up there, on the bed where her parents died.

Aunt stood up and pulled her dressing gown tighter. 'I have carried this curse with me for decades, the weight of it crushing me, the sin of it dirtying my body and my mind. I've spent my life making sure you'll never have to feel the same way, that you will never have to suffer.'

It was Anna's turn to laugh then. 'Suffer? I've suffered at your hands my entire life.'

'A little suffering makes you stronger. It was enough, enough to prepare you, not enough to kill you.'

'That's not how parenting works.'

'You don't know how hard it is to be a mother.'

'You're not my mother, you never have been and you never will be.'

Aunt looked away when she said the words. She turned back, her eyes tight with pain. 'The Binders arrive tomorrow afternoon. You will be bound, and then you will forgive me.'

# LOVE

*Love is the most dangerous of all emotions. Unless tightly bound it is the undoing and ruining of us. Binders. Unbound. Cowans. All.*

*Binders' Training, The Book of the Binders*

Aunt left the room and the thing that was not her father followed her out. *For a moment, I thought . . .* Anna could not follow the trail of thought, the pathways it led to were dark and full of pain. *It's not my father. It's not my father. It's a golem. If that thing is a golem – what is Attis?* She brushed that thought aside too; whatever Attis was, he was somehow in on all this. He had lied, just as he said he didn't.

Anna lay back in bed. There was no point trying to escape. Aunt had locked all the doors and her magic would be too strong to break. She did not sleep. She waited and poured her secrets into the nanta bag, having no one left to turn to but herself.

Daylight came and outside it was a brilliant summer's day. She watched kids playing in the neighbour's garden, rested her head against the glass and felt the warmth of the sun trying to get through. Aunt came for her at midday, knocking on the door.

She'd run Anna a bath. The water was searing hot, dotted

with rose petals; they floated serenely, and yet the scents were sharp and vinegary. Aunt scrubbed Anna down and then left her to dress in a coarse shift that had been left on her bed, crisply ironed as always.

Once Anna was ready Aunt suggested lunch, speaking as if everything was normal – as if nothing had happened. Anna followed suit. She went downstairs and sat with Aunt at the table, forcing down her food. They prepared cakes for the meeting and Aunt made biscuits.

The doorbell rang at three o'clock.

'They're here. Boil the kettle.'

Anna heard them arriving, being led into the freshly spruced-up living room. When called, she appeared with a tray of cakes. The curtains were drawn. The golem stood in the corner of the room, watching. Peter was tied to a chair in the centre, unconscious, two empty chairs next to him. Anna almost dropped the tray. *Almost.*

'What's he doing here?'

'He is required,' said Aunt.

Anna turned cold. She found it hard to move.

'You aren't going to disappoint us today, are you?' Mrs Withering smiled her non-smile.

Anna turned away from Peter. 'Of course not. Tea, anyone?'

She went back into the kitchen and prepared the teas. When she returned Peter's head had lolled forwards, his fair hair shadowy in the dimly lit room. *What are they going to do to you?*

'Anna, how's school?' said Mrs Dumphreys. Her silk shirt was an unsightly salmon pink.

'Good, thank you. I'm glad it's the holidays.'

'Your ceremony is well timed,' said Mrs Bradshaw, pincering a biscuit. 'You'll have plenty of time to settle into your new life as a Binder. It does take some adjusting to.'

There was a knock on the front door.

'Ah, they've arrived,' said Aunt, leaving the room.

Anna heard voices she knew and then Selene and Attis walked in. Attis had Effie in his arms, as unconscious as Peter.

'We've brought her,' said Selene, not looking at Anna.

Anna had managed to maintain some vestige of calm until that moment, but seeing Attis and Selene – it was too much. She held her Knotted Cord and dug her nails into her hands, drawing blood. She hated them. She hated them both.

Attis walked past, not looking at her either. He placed Effie down on a chair back to back with Peter's. Mrs Withering made a gesture with her hands and cords appeared around Effie's arms behind the chair, tying her to it. Her black hair fell over her face. *I hate you too, Effie Everdell.*

'I'll stay for the ceremony,' said Selene, taking up residence against the wall.

'Selene . . .' Aunt replied threateningly.

'I am not leaving. I raised that girl.'

'Suit yourself, but you won't enjoy it.' A smile pulled at Aunt's lips.

Attis stood next to Selene, arms folded.

'Who is *he*?' said Mrs Aldershot.

'Just one of Selene's playthings. He needs to leave,' said Aunt. 'Now.'

'You'll have to make me,' Attis replied.

Aunt sighed. She raised a hand and cords wound their way around Attis's body, pinning him to the wall. She turned to Anna. 'Now, Anna, it's time for your final test. If you pass, we shall proceed with the ceremony. Take out your Knotted Cord.'

Anna did so, her hands steady.

'You have proved to me over the years that you are able to control all of your emotions, but there's one left to master: love.' Aunt looked at Peter. 'Here he is – the boy you love, the boy who Effie betrayed you with, but you still love him, don't you? I know that much about our curse. It is relentless. Feel it. I want you to feel how much you love him.'

'I feel it,' Anna replied, refusing to feel anything at all.

Aunt took out her own cords and began to cast a spell. 'Now you must show me you are in control of that love. Tie it away in your cord. Crush it.'

Anna nodded and began to tie a knot in her cord: the seventh and final knot.

'If you can't, he will die.'

Anna's heart raced. There was the catch. *There is always a catch.* She looked at Peter, slumped in his chair, but as the spell began it was not Peter who cried out.

It was Attis.

He drooped against the cords holding him to the wall. The Binders turned in unison towards him, faces twitching with confusion. Aunt looked back and forth between Anna and Peter – Attis and Effie – eyes growing wide.

Attis cried out in pain again, his entire body turning rigid, veins straining along his face and neck. Anna realized what was happening: She was doing it. *I'm killing him!* 'No!' she cried out, her carefully controlled emotions exploding. 'No!'

'Drag him to the centre,' Aunt commanded. 'He's the one she loves.'

*No. I can't love him.* The cords disappeared from around Attis. He crumpled to the floor. Two of the Binders pulled at his legs, drawing him towards them. He writhed in agony, his face racked with it . . . It was unbearable.

'He will die, Anna,' Aunt called. 'If you don't control your love.'

Anna fell to her knees, hands fluttering over Attis as if she could somehow stop the pain, but it was Aunt's spell and it was too powerful. *I love you. I love you. I can't love you.*

She remembered that she hated him too. *Yes! I hate you!* She meant it. Her hands were shaking so badly she dropped the cord. She picked it back up and continued to form the final knot. She pulled it tight with hatred. Attis cried out again, full of torment. *It's not working. Hate is not working! It's not strong enough!*

She found her love again – stripped all else away until her love for him was as naked and skeletal as his white key. *Love, who laughs at locksmiths.* Her heart beat with it. She pulled the knot in the cord tight again, breaking the bones of it.

Attis was panting, his eyes wide with fear and pain. He clutched a hand to his heart, his lips turning blue.

'Not good enough, Anna, he's dying.'

Anna remembered sitting with Aunt in this very room, listening to music but not being able to feel it, letting it wash over her, no more than a collection of notes, a pretty pattern. *Love is the same: a pattern, a collection of memories and feelings, anger, joy, grief, fear, desire, hate.* She didn't need to separate them. They were all love. She looked at Attis and let them wash over her, separating herself from them instead of them from each other. *They mean nothing.*

Attis moaned.

Anna tightened the knot. *Nothing.* A calm came over her.

She was suddenly aware of love, but she couldn't feel it. It was an interesting sensation, but not one that touched her heart. If she kissed him now she would not feel what she had felt before.

She gave the knot a final tug.

Attis gasped for air. His body relaxed from its contortion, his face slowly returned to its normal colour. He rolled over and looked at Anna – a different kind of agony on his face. She felt nothing for him. In fact, she'd never felt more clear-headed. Her heart slowed, her hands stilled; she looked around at the Binders and found she didn't hate or fear any of them. She didn't feel much of anything at all. If this was a taste of how it felt to be bound then it wasn't so bad after all.

'It is done,' Aunt declared. 'She is ready.'

'Only just,' Mrs Withering sneered. 'Besides, who is this boy, Vivienne? You told us she was in love with the other.'

Aunt's lip quivered with irritation. She turned to Selene accusingly.

'He's Effie's boyfriend,' said Selene. 'You know that.'

Aunt looked at her long and hard. 'Did you do this? Did you know Anna was in love with him? It was meant to be Peter. Effie betrayed her with Peter.'

'I didn't know, but there was as much chance of Anna falling in love with him as there was of Effie falling in love with Peter. The curse works either way and a man is a man. Does it really matter?'

Aunt turned to look at Anna strangely. 'It seems betrayal is not clear-cut.' She frowned and then barked: 'Get rid of the other one. He's not needed any more.'

Several Binders put down their cups of tea and moved towards Peter. Anna thought for a moment they might kill him but they carried him out of the room. Others picked Attis up from the floor and dragged him onto the chair with difficulty. He was still weak and did not resist as they bound him with cords. Anna wondered distantly why he was still required.

'Let us prepare,' said Aunt.

She clicked her fingers in Effie's face and she began to wake, slowly, taking in the scene around her. Her eyes widened cavernously. Anna had never seen Effie look afraid. She pulled wildly against her restraints, only stopping when she saw Attis through the corner of her eye. That was when the true fear set in. Effie had no idea what was happening.

'Ah, she wakes,' said Aunt, bending down to smile at her. 'You owe me an apology, Effie Fawkes, for how you acted at my dinner party. It was extremely rude.' Effie raged ineffectually against her bound mouth. 'I think you owe Anna an apology too.' She turned Effie's head towards Anna. 'Are you aware she is your sister?' Effie's eyes widened as she tried to comprehend Aunt's words. 'Twins, in fact. I bet it's a relief in some ways, though, to know that Selene is not your real mother. She's not fit to be anyone's mother.'

'Leave her be, Vivienne!' Selene begged.

Aunt continued calmly, taking her time. Enjoying herself. 'It seems you've already lived up to our family curse by betraying Anna with Peter, just like I said you would, just like your mother did to me. Although it appears that the one you both love is this pathetic excuse for a human being.' Aunt pointed at Attis, who was beginning to stir in his chair. 'Anna just proved her love for him in front of all of us and now she will bind the curse before you destroy her life any more than you already have.'

Effie twisted to look at Anna, her expression confused, desperate, scared, but Anna could see the hate there too – the hate that had already been forming, simmering and seething now beneath the dark moons of her eyes. Anna reviewed it distantly. *I don't hate you any more, Effie.* The last of her emotions had given themselves up to the Knotted Cord.

Mrs Withering grabbed Anna's arm and led her towards the third seat, facing Effie and Attis: Her two betrayers. *Or did I betray you, Effie?* They bound her legs to the chair but left her arms free. Anna dropped her Knotted Cord into her lap.

Selene cried out suddenly. 'What's happening? No! Stop this!' Cords wrapped around Selene's body, locking her to the wall. 'Stop!'

'You think we would let you roam freely during the ceremony?' said Aunt.

'Vivienne! You know I won't stop it – I want this to happen as much as you!'

'I'm not sure you do,' said Aunt, putting her hands on Effie's shoulders. 'You see, I haven't been entirely honest with you, Selene. One little white lie over sixteen years isn't so bad though, is it? We couldn't tell you – you'd never have agreed to it. You see, she must die too.' Aunt ran a hand through Effie's hair. 'For Anna, she must die.'

'No!' Selene struggled against her bindings desperately. 'Vivienne, no! No! You can't mean it. For Marie, for Dominic, for any love left in you – you can't!'

'I'm doing this for love.'

'The girls were not meant to be harmed – just him, just him.' She was crying now. 'He's the curse! You don't need anything else! Please. Oh please—'

Effie and Attis pulled against their restraints like puppets wiggling uselessly on their strings, their magic not strong enough to resist the nine women surrounding them. Attis turned to Anna; his eyes, which had been so resolute, were full of panic, tearing themselves apart. *You didn't expect her to die either . . .*

'Sin drives out sin, Selene. We require the power of the curse to bind the curse and perhaps his blood would be enough,' Aunt considered. 'But his blood and her blood together – now that is the true curse. The bindings will be stronger if she is sacrificed too.'

*The sacrifice: they are the sacrifice.*

Selene pulled against the knots, hair falling over her face, tears streaming. Anna had never seen her look so ugly. 'No.' She shuddered. 'You promised me – not the girls!'

Aunt made a knot in the air and Selene's mouth snapped shut.

'Perhaps if you'd raised the girl better, if she wasn't so wild, the Binders might have considered it, but no, Effie cannot be allowed to live.' Aunt grabbed Effie's chin and looked into her eyes. 'Evil like her mother. The apple never falls far from the tree.' Effie snatched her head away. She began to cry too – desperate, angry tears – Anna had never seen her look so small. Attis went wild in his chair. *He loves her*, thought Anna distantly.

'Let us begin.' Aunt handed each of the Binders a closed rose. She gave Anna a rose too. 'Hold this and hold on. Remember, when your time comes you must make the necessary sacrifice. You must trust me. I've only ever wanted what's best for you. If not, we will be forced to make it for you.' She kissed her on the head. 'Be strong, my girl. Weakness in feeling, strength in control.'

Anna felt far away, as if she were watching the whole scene from above: the Binders putting their teas down, taking their roses, and stepping forward, pushing chairs and sofas back; stripping off their cardigans, jumpers, silk shirts, trousers and floral skirts, until they were in vests and T-shirts, tights and pants – bare, wrinkled arms exposed, heavy Binders' necklaces and bruises revealed around their necks – undoing their buns and ponytails, loosening pins, shaking out their hair.

They sat in a circle around them, faces all pinched, all hideous, candles flickering over them with muted flames. Selene writhed against the wall, tears rolling down her cheeks.

'Magic is the first sin; we must bear it silently,' they said in unison.

'We call on the Goddess of the Closed Rose and the Nine-Knotted Cord, the Goddess of Silence and Secrets.' Aunt's voice was low and strong.

'Goddess of Silence and Secrets,' they repeated.

'Today we call on love, which is the curse and will bind the curse.'

Anna felt the magic rise in the air, weaving through them, scented with love. The roses began to open, excruciatingly beautiful, vines extending from them, growing long, wrapping around the Binders' exposed bodies.

'We call on love.'

Around their waists and breasts and weaving through their hair, down their arms.

'We call on love.'

Vines tightening, thorns entering their flesh – puncturing – blood welling up and running over their bodies; hallowed faces lifting to the sky.

'We call on love.'

They turned to each other and held one another, kissing each other's faces, lips, bodies – thorns deepening, blood smearing – falling onto the floor, hair growing wild, streaked with blood.

'We call on love.'

Anna could feel love in the air, a dark and curious pattern, designed to suffocate.

Mrs Bradshaw held her rose out. 'By knot of one the binding has begun.' She took the lengths of vine and knotted them, thorns cutting into her hands as she did so.

They each knotted their rose in turn:

'By knot of two it cometh true. *Yisocoritu.*'

'By knot of three, so mote it be. *Nareg.*'

'By knot of four, 'tis strengthened more. *Fireg.*'

'By knot of five, so may it thrive. *Refa.*'

'By knot of six, the spell we fix. *Iseder.*'

'By knot of seven, silence of heaven. *Yoj.*'

And then Aunt:

'By knot of eight, the hand of fate. *Velo.*'

All of them together:

'We wind, we bind with thorn and twine.

By knot of nine, the spell entwined!'

Their hands were bleeding, the thorned and knotted vines twisting in and around their fingers, growing, extending out to meet the other vines – joining – until the entire circle was holding one, single vine. The scene was horrific.

'We bind! We wind! We bind!
We bind! We wind! We bind!
We bind! We wind! We bind!'

The pressure of the magic was like a screw tightening. Circling her. Petals flying. Unbearable. Anna had never felt pain like it before. She struggled to breathe. Her head hammered with their words. The vines extended into the centre – Anna's own rose growing out to meet them, the eight knots encircling her – and, finally, wrapping around Effie and Attis, ending over their hearts.

'Anna, it's time for you to make the sacrifice!' Aunt called. 'Tie the rose vine in your hand – the final knot – and they will die! Their blood will bind you. Their death will complete your necklace.' She looked at Effie and Attis. 'Remember what they have done to you. What they all did to you. You own them now. They are yours to do as you will. One single knot.'

Anna looked down at her rose, thick with magic, petals whirling fast around her, the spell tightening. She knew how it ended, she could feel the magic forcing its way into existence, ready to complete the narrative the Binders had begun. It was crushing, urging, relentless as the chanting. Inevitable. If she pulled the vines tight Effie and Attis would die and she would be bound. Free of pain. Uncursed forever.

Attis was turned away but Effie's eyes met hers.

'You can feel how much she hates you, can't you?' said Aunt. 'You think she wouldn't kill you if she had the chance? She'd get rid of you in a moment to keep Attis for herself. She must die! She will destroy your life. But him – you don't have to give him up. You can keep him forever, like I keep your father.'

Anna looked at the golem in the dark corner of the room. The thing that was not her father.

'Do it for your mother, who would see you live. Quickly. It must be now! Do it or we will do it for you. I don't want to have to use the Choke Knot, Anna – but I will.'

*I have no choice then, either way. I never did.* Anna could feel the spell striving for its end. Attis turned to her then, one last time. She felt nothing. She looked into his eyes, not knowing who he truly was behind them – perhaps they were all smoke and mirrors, nothing really there at all. *Perhaps.* She turned to Effie, feeling nothing either, but the meaning in Effie's eyes was clear – she looked at Anna as if she would kill her. *My sister,* Anna thought curiously, *black hair. . . just like our mother's.*

*Anna looked at Aunt then, her green eyes. . . just like mine.*

Beneath the rose in her hands, Anna picked up her Knotted Cord from her lap, the movement so small no one saw her do it. The cord that had controlled her whole life had won in the end – every single feeling bound. She was thankful for it. It had made her decision easy, freed from emotions. It would be the last decision she would ever make that way.

She would not become her aunt.

Anna dropped the rose and began to undo the knots of her cord, hands a blur, moving faster than they had ever moved before, stronger than she knew. It took several moments for the women to realize what she was doing but, by then, it was too late. Anna had undone the knots.

Every single one.

Anna felt it all at once: every moment of training, every sick, sadistic task, every emotion held back and tied up, suddenly undone, streaming through her blood. She looked at Attis and Effie and felt everything there too. She hated how much she loved them, still. *My sister.* The word was no longer a curiosity but something real, something unbreakable, a power that surged through her like water bursting a dam. The magic in the room drew towards her, meeting what was within her in a chaos of emotion. *It's mine now.*

The Binders tried to get to her – all of their minds were bent on it, but she could feel their magic growing weaker. The bindweed was taking hold. She'd taken it from the kitchen cupboard and put as much as she could in each of the teapots, easily a month's worth.

She cast a circle, strong and hard: *You won't get through. I won't let you.* She twisted the vines around the Binders' hands and arms, tighter and tighter. They shrieked in pain.

Aunt fought against it. 'Anna! No! What are you doing? You must kill them! We must bind the curse! I will forever be cursed if you don't! You will be cursed! Your children will be cursed! It will go on and on forever . . .'

'No, Vivienne. I will never do what you say again.' Anna snapped Aunt's mouth shut. Vivienne's eyes went wide with rage – *terror?* The power of the binding spell was still crackling in the air, thirsting for blood, longing to complete its final knot.

'NO!' Anna forced her own magic against it. 'YOU CAN'T HAVE US!'

She thought of her mother and father and used the love that surged through her to break free from her restraints. She raised a hand to Effie and Attis and made a gesture in the air. Their cords fell to the floor. They stood up, looking at their freed hands.

Effie ran to Anna and beat her fists against her and then they were hugging, holding on for dear life. Anna felt Effie's magic join hers, fighting the power of the Binders around them – their magic was weakening but not quickly enough. *I can't hold them off for much longer . . .*

Anna turned to unbind Selene but then Effie screamed. She spun around and there he was, raising the knife to his heart – his knife of many blades: the sacrifice blade. Long and narrow and terribly sharp. Attis brought it down in one fast swipe.

He fell to the floor.

Effie made a strangled sound.

'He's made the sacrifice,' Aunt shouted. 'It's not too late, we can still seal the spell.'

They began to chant again.

'We bind! We wind! We bind!
We bind! We wind! We bind!
We bind! We wind! We bind . . .'

Anna dropped to the floor next to Attis. *Why?* The blood was pouring out of him too fast for questions. She pushed her hands against his chest, trying to stop the bleeding. She could feel the Binders' spell tightening in the air around them once more, taking hold.

Effie came at her with Attis's knife. For a moment Anna thought she meant to kill her but then she lowered the knife to Anna's hand. Anna opened her fingers and Effie drew the knife along her palm and then did the same to her own. They clasped bloody hands and lowered them onto Attis's wound, Effie's face as wild with panic as her own.

His blood welled to meet their own, but his heart was not beating beneath their palms.

Hand in hand with Effie, Anna had never felt so powerful and yet – it was too much. The Binders' spell was closing like a noose.

Anna raised a shaky hand to Selene and with a burst of energy, released her from her restraints. *Help us!*

'Selene! Do not resist us. You know he must die,' Aunt commanded. 'For the girls.'

Anna looked at Selene, pleading.

Selene looked back and forth between them.

'Please, Selene,' Anna cried. 'We need you!'

Anna felt Selene's magic join the fight – resisting the

Binders, pulling back their magic, giving Anna and Effie a moment . . .

They pressed their hands harder onto Attis's wound, looking at each other. Imperfect mirrors. Anna couldn't bear to see the hope leaking from Effie's eyes. 'Live! Oh please, live! You have to live!' Effie cried.

His heart began to beat beneath their palms – barely more than a whisper and then stronger, stronger . . .

'No,' he moaned. 'I must die.'

'No, you live, Attis Lockerby! Do as I say!' Effie screamed at him.

He opened his eyes and looked at her and then to Anna. 'LIVE!'

The wound closed beneath their hands. He reached his own hand up to meet theirs. They clasped it and then – they were joined. The force of their magic united. Together, with the Binders weakening, it was easy to force the binding spell back, to unpick its thorns, undo its knots. Suddenly, the petals began to fall to the floor, strangely silent.

The spell was gone.

'No! What have you done?' Anna heard Aunt calling.

Anna gasped for breath. The Binders were just women once more, sitting in their vests, blood smeared over their faces, vines withering in their hands.

Aunt fell forwards and grabbed at the knife, eyes blazing with an anger Anna had never seen but had always known was there. The anger that killed her mother. Aunt lunged at Effie, bringing the knife down with intent. Attis stopped her and the knife went flying but then they were on him – the other Binders – wielding the last of their magic, blocking his path. Selene joined him in the fight to push them back, but there were so many of them, too many—

Anna tried to reach out for Effie but Aunt stood up between them. The power roaring from her could not be held back by the bindweed. She had finally let go. She made knots in the air, pinning Effie to the floor. She reached for the knife. Anna knew Aunt would do it – kill Anna's sister, just like she'd killed her mother.

Anna turned to the golem. The thing with the face of her father. With all of Aunt's focus elsewhere she didn't feel it as Anna unwound Aunt's magic surrounding him and took control.

Aunt had the knife – was moving towards Effie – Effie was struggling on the floor. As Aunt raised the knife, Anna brought the golem up behind her. It grabbed the blade from Aunt's hands. The blade sliced deep into its hand but the creature did not cry out. It threw the blade away and then picked up Aunt and threw her too.

Its heart belonged to Anna now.

Aunt turned to Anna in shock. She swivelled back to the golem and directed all her magic at the creature, battling against Anna's own – Hira against Hira – Anna struggling against Aunt's unbreakable breaking will. *I will not give in to you again.*

'You think you can overpower me?' Aunt laughed, but the golem was coming towards her. Anna could feel the waves of Aunt's rage beating against her Hira. Anna cried out against it, feeling Aunt's power growing stronger, unsure how long she could last against her. She urged the golem on but Aunt was so strong, so relentless – but then Aunt made the mistake of looking into the golem's face. The face of the man she'd once loved. Anna felt it then, the small crack in Aunt's armour, a single loose thread. Aunt's magic faltered just for a moment – and a moment was all Anna needed.

*Your love has never been as strong as your hate, Aunt . . .*

As Anna's magic took hold, Aunt's grew desperate, clawing, scrabbling, fluttering, but Anna did not relent. The pain of fighting her was almost too much to bear – but she did not relent. With terrible clarity she knew what she had to do. The only escape she'd ever truly have.

The golem's hands wound around Aunt's neck.

Anna cried out with a final, desperate surge of magic, not knowing if it was love or hate that drove her. All she knew was that she was losing the only mother she'd ever had. The golem's hands tightened – Aunt choking, clawing at his hands.

*I'm sorry. I'm so sorry, Aunt . . .*

'Anna,' Aunt spluttered. 'I love . . . you . . .'

*No! No!* Anna cried out, falling to her knees, feeling herself weaken. *I can't . . . I can't . . .*

But the golem's grip did not weaken. It tightened. Through her tears Anna realized that the golem's power was no longer her own – another's had wrapped around it. She looked up from Aunt—

Mrs Withering stood above them. The Binders behind her had overpowered Selene and Attis, holding them back. They were screaming, yelling, but Anna could not hear them. All she could hear were Mrs Withering's words.

'I can't risk her living, you see.' She smiled as Aunt's green eyes began to turn red. 'We should never have listened to Vivienne in the first place. We should never have let any of you live, cursed and rotten as you all are. A war is coming – we certainly can't let you live now.' Anna tried to pull the golem back but she had already given everything, all of her magic. Mrs Withering completed the job efficiently.

Aunt went still. Her mouth twitched, but nothing came out.

Silent, at last.

'Good.' Mrs Withering rubbed her hands together, her true smile revealed at last – small and sharp, full of bloodthirsty ferocity. The golem moved towards Anna. 'Now. Your turn.'

'What's going on?' Anna heard a distant voice. Mrs Withering spun around.

Commotion. Cries. People. Magic in the air. *Aunt is dead.* Anna tried to hold onto reality but her world was breaking apart, turning black. *Aunt is dead.* Screaming. Hands on her. *Attis?* Holding her. Pulling her away.

Anna clung onto him and cried for love.

Darkness took over.

# MOTHER

*The fire never dies; beware smoke on the wind.*

*Tenet Nine, The Book of the Binders*

'We must speak to the Seven at once.' Bertie Greenfinch had one hand on a plump hip and one on a mug of tea. Not one of the china teacups – they had all been smashed. 'They can't get away with this in this day and age! Going around binding magic against young girls' wills! Making sacrifices! Sacrificial magic is not allowed. It is not within the Balance. The Binders must be stopped.'

'It's an outrage,' another witch agreed.

The house was busy with Wort-Cunning witches. It was strange to see them in Aunt's pristine kitchen. Rowan and Manda had brought them just in time. They'd gone searching for them after the ball but hadn't been able to find anyone – Selene's house had been empty. In the morning they'd tracked down Anna's house and watched as the Binders arrived one by one, knowing something wasn't right. Rowan had gone home and spilt everything to Bertie – about Anna's curse, about her aunt. Bertie had rallied the troops.

If they hadn't turned up when they did . . . Anna didn't want to think what might have happened. They could not have held the Binders off forever, and yet, if they'd shown up earlier – Aunt would not be dead. *Are you really dead? Did I kill you?* Anna reached for her Knotted Cord but it wasn't there.

She sat with a blanket on her shoulders, sipping on some warming concoction Bertie had given her, listening to their plans. Entirely numb. They had tried to make her lie down again but she wanted to know what was happening. She didn't want to be left alone with her thoughts.

The Wort-Cunnings, arriving in numbers, had fought the Binders back and they'd fled. Bertie was planning to cover up Aunt's death with magic – make it look like a heart attack or suicide or stroke. They hadn't decided yet. They'd taken her body upstairs and an unconscious Peter back to his dorm room, never to remember. The golem was to be destroyed. Anna never wanted to think of that creature again.

Manda and Rowan tried to talk to her but Anna was too exhausted to explain anything; she couldn't explain anyway. Nothing felt real. Effie hadn't looked at her or spoken either. Anna caught Attis's eye several times but she looked away. He, like Selene, had fought on their side but she still didn't understand how he was involved, who or what he was. All she could see was him raising his knife, the blood spilling out of his open wound, his perfect skin broken. *Why?* She wanted to pound her fists against him. *Why would you do that?*

'We can't speak to the Seven,' said one of the witches. 'They aren't back.'

'They are.' Bertie nodded with slow significance. The room stilled. 'I have it on good authority they've returned. But . . .' She went quiet.

Anna looked up. Attis turned to her. 'Anna, are you OK?'

'Fine,' she replied, still not meeting his eyes.

Effie spoke for the first time, directing her words at Bertie. 'What? What's happened?'

'Yeah, Mum, we need to know what's going on,' said Rowan.

'Nothing. Nothing any of you need to know right now.'

'The Seventh, the one who escaped, has come out of hiding and, though nothing has been said officially, there are rumours she has spoken of hunters – that we are being hunted!' a Wort-Cunning in a bright knitted waistcoat announced skittishly.

Gasps around the kitchen.

'Tania!' Bertie chided. 'Now was not the time.'

Tania put up her hands. 'Sorry. I just think everyone deserves to know.'

'What does that mean? *Hunted?*' another Wort-Cunning cried.

They descended into fraught discussion.

'We knew something was going—'

'Witches have often been under attack—'

'Of course she doesn't mean *the* Hunters, they're not real—'

'What else can she be referring to?'

'We don't know what her words mean yet,' Bertie quietened them. 'She may not be referring to the Hunters in *that* sense, but that we are under threat from someone, something. There's no need to panic. The Seventh has raised the others. They have returned. Whatever is happening, they will put a stop to it.'

Selene scoffed. 'Some group of fools are probably calling themselves the Hunters. This isn't the sixteen hundreds! What can they do? Send us to the stake?'

'Still,' said a woman with grey hair piled up on her head like a bird's nest. 'Considering the ongoing anti-magic suspicion in the news, we ought to keep a low profile, for now, until the Seven deal with them.'

'That's exactly what they want us to do,' said Selene dismissively.

'Iris is not saying we curtail our magic,' said Bertie, 'but that we take extra care right now to ensure it doesn't become exposed.'

Anna couldn't process what they were saying. The Binders were mad. She'd just seen it with her own eyes. *We are being hunted. Hunted? What if the Binders were right all along?*

Bertie clapped her hands together, as if to drive the fear from the room. 'Right, let's finish cleaning up this mess. Iris, will you take Rowan and Manda home? You three' – she looked at Anna, Effie and Attis – 'need to rest. Now.'

Anna wasn't sure she'd ever sleep again.

'You might want to see this.' A freckled Wort-Cunning appeared in the doorway. 'Come quickly!'

They emptied from the kitchen into the living room. The bloodstains on the carpet were gone. The rose plant in the corner was in bloom. The TV was on. It took a moment for Anna to place why she knew the image on the screen. The red-bricked building was her school – a news reporter stood outside it.

'. . . arrested for questioning after having inappropriate relationships with a female student' – a photo of Headmaster Connaughty flashed onto the screen – 'following released video footage showing the headmaster with a student during an after-hours ballet class.'

Bertie put a hand to her mouth. 'That's your headmaster.'

The rumours had finally completed their work, got their pound of flesh. Anna felt her hatred return, unfettered now by the knots that had held her emotions in place. Whether she hated Effie or herself more, she wasn't sure.

'In a bizarre twist, the student in question is claiming she was forced into the relationship by a satanic cult of witches made up of pupils from the school. The details of this are not yet known but Headmaster Connaughty had previously been in touch with police over a recent school break-in where this footage was obtained.'

Footage flashed onto the screen. Four blurred white dresses and a man with horns on his head. A fire in the centre. Faces unknown.

Anna put a hand to her mouth. Their magic was out there for all to see.

'The students in question appear to be practising some sort of fire ritual. Whether it is linked in any way to the allegations as yet remains unclear but the questions are certainly troubling.'

It was the room's turn now to look at them.

*The fire never dies; beware smoke on the wind.*

Selene tried to hug her, but Anna pulled away. She, Effie and Attis had returned to Selene's house after a tense journey – the car alert with silence, none of them knowing what to say, whom to trust. They'd left the Wort-Cunnings in a flap about the footage of them on the school grounds. Anna didn't care. If they were caught and punished, so be it. They deserved it. *I deserve it.*

'You must get some rest,' said Selene, perched on the end of the bed in the spare bedroom.

'I ruined Headmaster Connaughty's life.'

'You tried your best to stop that spell.'

'My magic was cursed and it got out of control. The rumour spell—'

'Your magic is not cursed. You have a curse. It's not the same.' Selene looked at her with intensity. 'That gossip spell was an evil spell with mean intent, pure and simple. I didn't take it seriously when you told me. It's my fault.'

'The curse mark chased me more than it chased Effie.'

'It wasn't chasing you, matchstick, it was trying to warn you. And your magic expressed it more than Effie's because it had been contained for so long by the bindweed. It was unleashing so much power at once . . . and you were falling in love,' said Selene gently. 'That was making it stronger. I didn't know it would make its presence felt quite so clearly, mind you . . .'

*Falling in love.* It sounded so gentle, but love had proved to be as destructive as Aunt had promised.

'I killed Aunt.' The words did not feel real. *Is she dead? Is she really dead?*

'You did not. That Binder woman—'

'—finished what I started,' said Anna, remembering her moment of hesitation. Would she have done it? If Mrs Withering hadn't taken over – would she still have done it? The question formed a hard knot around her heart. *I could have.*

Anna felt the world go black around her again. She leant forwards, trying to catch her breath. *Are you really dead?*

'Hey.' Selene reached for her. 'Don't blame yourself. You can't blame yourself. Vivienne was going to kill Effie and you—'

'You know what the worst part is?' Anna pulled herself back up. 'I still hate her,' she cried. 'I hate her.'

'That's OK.' Selene hushed but Anna pulled away.

'I hate you too, Selene.'

'I know.' Selene looked tired for the first time: bags under her eyes, mascara smudged. There was no golden glow about her now.

'Why did you lie to me?'

'Because I made a promise to your mother that I would protect you. Both of you.'

'But you wanted the curse to go off! You wanted the Knotting to take place! You wanted him to die!'

'Yes. Only him. Not you and Effie.'

'I don't understand . . .'

Selene sat down next to her and sighed. 'You and Effie are twins, cursed to fall in love with the same man and be torn apart by it, one of you fated to kill the other. That was written in the stars long before you were born. Your mother and Vivienne were cursed just the same, but they knew from the beginning, from when they were little girls. Their father thought that being open about it might prevent it from happening – but it happened anyway.'

'How?' Anna could barely keep herself together but had to know the truth. At last.

'Vivienne met Dominic first, at Edinburgh University where she was studying. I think they started dating properly when she was in her second year and they were together until the end of her studies but then that summer – he met Marie on a trip to London at a conference after-party. Oh, they fell in love so quickly, that night perhaps, that very night. She didn't know who he was and he didn't even know Vivienne had a sister, she'd kept Marie a secret, paranoid as she was even then. Marie had always thought if she didn't believe in the curse then, somehow, it wouldn't happen. She'd been determined to live her life in spite of it, but it found her. She was distraught when she realized what had happened, Anna, you have to believe me. She ended it and tried to find Vivienne to make it right, but she'd disappeared.'

Selene shook her head sorrowfully. 'The Binders had found her instead. Vivienne could never deal with her emotions even then. They took her in; they were only too happy to welcome a broken soul like her. They brainwashed her and – oh, they loved the story of the curse: dirty magic only they could make clean.' Selene's voice was full of vitriol.

'They couldn't find Vivienne and your mother and Dominic couldn't stay apart. I tried to warn Marie against it but she loved him. Stupid. Stupid. She fell pregnant and they went into hiding – she knew Vivienne would come for her and she feared for you. She was determined to find a way to break the curse and give you a normal life. She called me one night. She'd found a way through – an antidote to the curse – a spell . . .'

Anna thought of Nana's words: *There are only two things in this world which can break a curse. The magic of the one who cast it in the first place. Or a spell more powerful . . .*

'A living spell. A man who was not truly a man at all, whose blood would break it. She had what she needed to cast it, all except someone willing to – to give birth to him . . .'

Anna's mouth dropped open.

Selene's eyes flickered with memory, one hand touched her stomach. 'I know it sounds insane – it was insane, but she needed me. I'd done nothing good with my life; perhaps it was one thing I *could* do . . .'

'You – you gave birth to Attis?' Anna couldn't comprehend it.'Yes. We cast the spell and I fell pregnant. We had a plan – it would take time – but it was something. Marie and Dominic were going to move abroad and raise you, but then . . . Vivienne called me. It was late, I'd just been sick – the damn thing inside me was causing me hell. She told me to come to Marie's house, that I was required. I knew then she'd found them. When I got to the house, they were already dead.' Selene stilled, tears running from her eyes.

'How did it happen?' Anna asked, not wanting but needing to know the truth. 'Aunt said that my mother had attacked her.'

Selene growled. 'No! Vivienne bound Dominic's free will. Your mother was asleep when your dad strangled her and then he killed himself. Vivienne had become a powerful Binder. He had no choice.'

*The Choke Knot.* Anna knew how that felt all too well. She couldn't begin to imagine the hell her father must have gone through.

'I could have killed Vivienne there and then but she had you in her arms. What could I do? That was when she presented the Binders' plan to me. We'd raise you apart. We'd

bring you back together at sixteen. Let the curse unfold and
sacrifice the boy you'd fallen in love with to bind it. It had
all been worked out.'

'Why would you agree to that? It's madness.'

'That's the problem with a story, Anna, it doesn't capture
the complexity of it. The actions are there but the motives are
hidden in the shadows or they are the hands that form the
shadows on the wall. I feared what Vivienne would do to you
if I didn't comply. And your aunt did something for me once,
before the curse . . . another story in itself . . . and I was
scared, I was scared she'd undo it. She threatened to. She
anticipated that I was selfish and a coward and I did as she
asked, because I am both of those things.' Selene looked up
at Anna and smiled sadly. 'But I was carrying my own secret.'

'Attis.'

'Yes. Vivienne intended to bind the curse but I had the
key that could break it forever.'

'Attis is your son.' The words felt so strange to say.

'I gave birth to him but he's not my son. He's a spell.'
Selene looked away and then back fiercely. 'But Effie is my
daughter. I raised her. I wasn't a good mother but I tried, for
Marie. I tried to be there for you too. I wasn't much good
at that either . . . Vivienne hated me visiting and I hated
seeing her, hated every fibre of her being. I took Attis to a
dear friend of mine and he agreed to take him in, under one
condition of mine: that when the time came Attis would
leave with me and wouldn't return.'

'To sacrifice himself,' said Anna, realizing everything. 'Attis
knew he was a spell. He knew he had to end the curse.'

'He knew he had to try. We didn't want you to have your
magic bound, but the Binders' ceremony seemed like our
only chance. They would raise more magical power than we
ever could alone; they would make a sacrifice. We just had
to make sure Attis was it. Vivienne always said you and Effie

couldn't know, that it would be better to let the curse run its course, but now I know: she didn't want you growing up as sisters, knowing about the curse, because she always intended for you to kill Effie . . .' Selene took a shuddering breath. 'I didn't know – despite everything, I still believed there was some good left in her. That she wouldn't hurt Marie's daughters. I underestimated her.'

'She underestimated you.' And I, him. 'I can't believe Attis was prepared to die for us.'

'Anna, he's been waiting his whole life to do it. He said he would do anything for—' She stopped.

*For Effie. He loves Effie and he only needed me to love him to set off the curse. It hadn't been real. Of course it hadn't.*

'It was his purpose,' said Selene. 'It still is.'

'That's why he hated me digging into my family's past, trying to discover the truth; he needed me to commit to the Knotting – so he could die.'

'Yes.'

'It didn't work.'

'No. I don't know if that's because you stopped it and saved him or because we don't understand how it works yet. Or perhaps the curse is broken? And we just haven't realized?' Selene looked at Anna hopefully.

Anna shook her head. 'No. It isn't. I love him, Selene.' She had vowed never to fall in love but there it was. A crime of passion. *I betrayed Effie too – would I do it again?* 'I love him,' she said. 'And I love Effie and I hate her.' Anna could feel the emotions inside of her, unrestricted, conflicted, free to flex into the light and dark. 'The curse is alive. I can feel it inside of me.'

Selene closed her eyes. 'Don't say that. This can't be happening again.'

'It's not. I hate Effie, but I don't want to kill her. Aunt was wrong. Raising us apart didn't make it easier for us to kill each other – it made it harder. I never loved her like a sister and so I don't hate her like a sister either. She may well want to kill me, of course.'

'She doesn't, Anna, she doesn't. In spite of the curse, you two saved each other in there.'

Silence descended.

'Why, Selene, why are we cursed?'

'If we had the answer to that, my little matchstick, none of this would ever have had to happen. Curses are a black hole; it's impossible to know how they began and when they will end.'

Anna thought of the *Everdell* family book beneath her bed, the family history erased – someone knew the truth and had chosen to hide it. *Curses attract attention like a carcass to flies . . .*

'The Hunters,' she said. *The Ones Who Know Our Secrets – do they know hers?* 'Aunt said the curse would attract them and now we've left a breadcrumb trail leading to our door. Darcey is calling us witches!'

'There's no such thing as the Hunters, but it's true, we don't know what is going on right now and, paranoid as she was, Vivienne wasn't lying when she said curses are a powerful form of magic. We need to keep it a secret.'

'But Darcey's claims are going to attract attention.'

'That's on the news because a headmaster has had relations with a pupil and not because some teen girl is spouting rubbish about magic! Anyway, the Seven have returned and they will take care of whoever or whatever is supposedly *hunting us.*'

Anna wanted to believe her, but after everything she'd seen over the last year, she didn't believe rumours went away quite so easily.

'The Binders won't want to let us live either way.' Anna remembered Mrs Withering's words. *Your turn.* 'They know we're cursed.'

'The Binders will be dealt with,' Selene seethed. 'We have a whole army of Wort-Cunnings ready to take them on and that Withering woman will have to go through me. You are safe. You are free. It's all over.'

But how could Anna ever be safe? How could she ever be free? *I am cursed and Aunt is dead because of me.*

'I'm sorry, Anna. I'm sorry I've failed you, Effie, your mother . . . I was never the woman she was, but I will try. I will try to find a way to stop the curse.'

Selene lowered her head. Anna moved closer, took her hand and squeezed it.

'Don't give up yet. You're the only mother Effie and I have now and we're going to need you. But you need to know this.' Selene looked up into Anna's furious green eyes. 'I will not let Attis die.'

*Mail Today, 30 July*

## The Six Faceless Witches?

*Witchcraft. A term that's not been used with gravity or fear for hundreds of years, but with the mystery of the Six Faceless Women remaining unsolved and what can only be described as unnatural, inexplicable events spreading across the capital, many are now asking the question: Were the Six Faceless Women witches?*

*'We don't wish to frighten people but we think it's important that police and public alike face this potential reality,' says Halden Kramer, Head of Communications for the Witchcraft Inquisitorial and Prevention Services [formerly the Institute for Research into Organized and Ritual Violence]. 'The symbol of the Eye, discovered on the women's necks, has long been associated with curse magic and there is now mounting evidence to suggest that some darker, not yet understood force may be involved. We may be dealing with witchcraft of the direst form.*

*'Our Lead Researcher, Marcus Hopkins, is now in discussions with police and key government departments. He believes it is essential that every incident linked to witchcraft or magic across the capital is thoroughly investigated. No stone left unturned.'*

*Police are refusing to comment on these new revelations but continue to urge the public not to panic.*

*Watch our interview with Lead Researcher, Marcus Hopkins, and share your thoughts on the Six Faceless Women: witches or not?*

*The women met at midnight. The hour of their death. They each remembered vividly how it had felt to die. Even how it had felt after. And how it felt now, to be alive again; different lives, different bodies, different faces – the same languages, the same memories. There were Seven of them but together they carried a thousand lives, a thousand centuries. They had known this before and yet they had never known anything like this – the feeling of dread in their bones, the darkness on the horizon, shadows stirring, fear unfurling its hand. They pulled back their grey hoods, raised their faces to the sky and began to sing the old songs, the Moonsongs.*

*The stars stirred; the scent of smoke swirled on the wind.*

# ACKNOWLEDGEMENTS

Thank you to my parents, Elizabeth and James Thomas. Mum – for reading *Threadneedle* more than anyone, possibly more than me. For someone as magical as you to love its magic meant the world to me from the start. And dad – for taking it upon yourself, with your usual dedication, to proofread the entire book. One day, maybe, I'll be as good at grammar as you. Rowan's house is inspired by the home I grew up in – a place of warmth, kindness, silliness and laughter (and a constant supply of freshly made cakes). I am so lucky to have parents like you, who have supported all my weird and wonderful endeavours over the years; who have always believed in me and made me believe anything is possible. Without you, this book would simply not exist.

My husband, James Williams, who has been witness to every stage of madness in the creation of *Threadneedle* and its world. You have always supported my dream without question and I love that you take such joy in seeing me flourish. Thank you for always being there with your wise words of encouragement and often-needed hugs. And the Williams family who took me in when I first moved to London and have always made me feel part of the family.

My brother, Rhodri Thomas, for having such faith in me that you became *Threadneedle's* first and only investor, lending me the money I needed to make ends meet when writing it. And for being its first reader and reading it in a single day (fastest reader I know). My sister, Ffion Currie, for your creativity and strength. I know I can always turn to you for sage advice and a push in the direction I need to go. My hugely supportive brother-in-law, Cameron Currie, and your amazing children who always light up my imagination: Llio, Dylan and Eily.

Roger Couhig, the coolest uncle and best storyteller I've ever met.

My friends and personal coven members, Abigail Tryhorn, Alison Palmer-Quinn and Sanaa Ibrahim. I knew *Threadneedle* could be something when you all read it and loved it. Abi's feedback remains my favourite of all time: 'I think Attis could be topless more'. Zuzanna Reymer who always has my back. Chloe Battle and Orla Keefe, my circle of love. Bethan Walker and Jennie Herbert – our weird antics at school live inside this book.

My wonderful agent Alice Lutyens who believed in *Threadneedle* from the very start even though it wasn't a straightforward book to take on. You have remained its fierce and passionate advocate.

Natasha Bardon and the team at HarperVoyager whose creativity and hard work have brought this book to life. I remember our first meeting – the hour flew by in a whirr of discussion and laughter, and I knew I'd found my people.

The early readers of *Threadneedle* whose feedback was invaluable: Jayne Ebury and Melissa Magment – your extraordinarily detailed notes helped shape the book into what it is today – Sophie Williams, Annie Eaton, Ellie Hearsum, Neela Patel, Claudia Roberts, Julien Clin, Angus Dunsire, Matthew Rothwell, Martyna Reymer, Lorna Dixon, Jackie Harries and Heather Lazarus.

Lynne Clifton, a wonderful artist, who gave flourish to my Threadneedle letters with her magical handwriting.

And my son, Taliesin Williams, who has absolutely no awareness of *Threadneedle* but has reminded me that the real world can be just as magical as the imagined one.